D1456732

# SUPERPOWERS

SUPERP

# OWERS

A Novel

DAVID J. SCHWARTZ

Copyright © 2008 by David J. Schwartz

Published in the United States by Three Rivers Press, an imprint of the Crown Publishing Group, a division of Random House, Inc., New York.
www.crownpublishing.com

Three Rivers Press and the Tugboat design are registered trademarks of Random House, Inc.

Library of Congress Cataloging-in-Publication Data

Schwartz, David J. (David John).
   Superpowers : a novel / David J. Schwartz. — 1st ed.
   1. College students—Fiction.   2. Supernatural—Fiction.   3. Power
(Philosophy)—Fiction.   4. Self-actualization—Fiction.   I. Title.
PS3619.C4865S87 2008
   813'.6—dc22                                        2007049778

ISBN 978-0-307-39440-8

Printed in the United States of America

*Design by Maria Elias*

10   9   8   7   6   5   4   3   2   1

First Edition

For Mom and Dad, for their patience

# EDITOR'S INTRODUCTION

### by Marcus Hatch

It all started at a party, which is damn convenient if you ask me, and if this weren't a true story I wouldn't expect you to believe it. People go to parties all the time hoping something will start there— a romance, a career, the best weekend of their lives—but how often does it happen? I'll tell you: it doesn't, not unless you're in a movie or a book. Real life doesn't have clear-cut beginnings or endings. Everyone's got a backstory, even if they don't carry it on them like business cards. (But wouldn't it be nice if they did? Someone could make a mint marketing it, four-color foldout brochures with baby pictures, family history, educational background, favorite books and sexual positions, police record, that kind of thing. Save us all a lot of heartbreak. That's assuming that anyone could be reduced to a glossy two-thousand-word Kinkos job, which is an ass-you-me proposition if I've ever heard one.)

Anyway, as I was saying, this is a true story. I know some of you won't think so, and I feel sorry for you, I really do. But I was there, and I saw some of it, and what I didn't see I heard about, from someone who knows the whole story. Being as this is a true story, there's no point looking for allegory and symbolism and that sort of thing. This isn't some snooty book where people nobody likes do things nobody cares about for reasons nobody can figure out. That's what they call literature. This here is journalism, and journalism deals with facts, not muddy things like theme and such. So.

Fact #1: The party took place on Saturday, May 19, 2001, at 523 West Mifflin Street, Apt. 2, Madison, Wisconsin, 53703.

Fact #2: Five people attended the party, all of them inhabitants of 523. Charles Frost, age twenty, and Jack Robinson, age nineteen, hosted their downstairs neighbors Caroline Bloom, twenty, Harriet Bishop, twenty, and Mary Beth Layton, twenty.

Fact #3: Of the five, only Charles Frost was available to be interviewed in the aftermath of these events, and except for the events witnessed by your intrepid reporter, the following is based on his account alone. The others—well, you'll understand why I was unable to interview the others by the time the story's told, and the only way to tell it is to start it.

Read on.

Charlie Frost had the look of someone waiting for a punch line. It wasn't that he seemed about to burst out laughing, but that he had an anxious way about him—as if he were afraid the joke was on him, or worse, that he wasn't going to get it. He was pale and tall and bit his nails and habitually forgot to get his hair cut for months at a time, so that his brown locks ranged from close-cropped and neat to moppish and view-obstructing. Charlie was on day forty-one of his most recent haircut, and he looked like the scruffy fifth member of a struggling boy band. Judging by his ensemble—wrinkled green army pants, a Nike T-shirt, and red Chuck Taylor sneakers—the band's wardrobe person had either taken the day off or was hoping to be fired.

Charlie and two other young men shared a second-floor flat, if that was the word. *Flat* implied sprawl, and one thing their apartment didn't do was sprawl. It creaked, sagged, and let cold air in

3

during winter, but it did not sprawl. The building was in its early forties, and after half a dozen renovations most of its rooms were higher than they were wide. It was a terrible place for a party.

Charlie and Jack had gotten around that problem by setting up on their front deck, and by inviting only three guests. The alcohol they had brewed themselves, or Jack had. His brother Lloyd had given him a brewing kit for Christmas, and this was his third attempt at making beer. The first batch had turned green, and he had put too much yeast in the second; one night in April Charlie had woken to the sound of exploding bottles. He'd thought it was someone shooting out the windows, and he'd fumbled around in the dark for a phone to call 911 until Jack knocked on his door and told him it was the beer.

Jack was not as tall as Charlie, but he was more physically impressive, with coal black hair and broad shoulders. He had grown up on a farm an hour from Madison, and Charlie had wondered a few times if his parents had ever strapped him to the plow.

"We should have backup," Charlie said. "What if the beer doesn't turn out?"

"It'll turn out fine." Jack inspected the refrigerator, which contained the beer, five frosted glasses, and an empty bottle of ketchup. "Besides, backup is your department, Dr. Nelson."

Dr. Frank Nelson was the name on Charlie's fake ID. He was cautious about using it because the photo was of a bearded man, and Charlie had never needed to shave more than twice a week. There was also the matter of the 270 pounds the license credited Dr. Nelson with, easily twice the amount of flesh clinging to Charlie's bones.

Despite this, Charlie had managed to lay his hands on a couple of bottles of Captain Morgan, which he had hidden in his room. He was half-hoping that Jack's Madison Maibock would turn out to be undrinkable. Then he would have a chance to save the party, and score some points with Caroline.

Caroline Bloom didn't know it, but she was one of the primary reasons for the party. Charlie had wanted her from the day he had first seen her, on August 15, 2000. August 15 was the traditional and much-dreaded moving day for renters in Madison, a day of U-Hauls, abandoned furniture, and enough cardboard boxes to enclose the campus in a corrugated wall. Charlie had been carrying a crate filled with CDs from Jack's truck when he saw Caroline for the first time.

It was ninety-four degrees and humid, but while Charlie was sweaty and sunburned, Caroline's shoulders showed tanned and healthy under her yellow tank top. She sat on the front steps, drinking from a bottle of water while a pair of young men struggled to fit a couch through the front door of 523. Her brown hair was tied back from her neck, and Charlie stared as she swallowed. She saw him as she finished drinking and smiled.

"Moving in upstairs?" she asked.

He nodded.

"Maybe I'll see you around." She followed the couch inside, her cutoff jeans moving in fascinating ways.

"Downstairs neighbor?" Jack had asked, carrying a dresser up the steps.

"I hope so."

A goal had presented itself to Charlie: "Sleep with the curvaceous dark-haired girl who may or may not live downstairs." Charlie set such goals several times a day but rarely gave them much subsequent thought. "Sleep with the cashier at the convenience store" was a common one, or "Sleep with the girl who sat in front of me in history on Tuesday." But most of these random lust objects left his thoughts as quickly as they left his line of sight.

Caroline might have been no different if she hadn't been his neighbor, and if Charlie had been able to find something wrong with her. She wasn't snooty or stupid, and she didn't have an annoying laugh. She didn't flirt with every man she saw, but she wasn't shy either. In the end Charlie had decided that if anything, she was probably a little too good for him.

As if his insecurity were a summons, a knock fell upon the door.

Charlie answered it. "Good evening," he said, trying not to sound like Bela Lugosi and failing.

"We brought food," said Harriet, and she handed him a sack of blue tortilla chips. Mary Beth followed with an ice cream bucket full of salsa. Charlie waited by the door for a moment, but no one was behind them, only the narrow stairs twisting down to the first floor.

"Where's your roommate?" Mary Beth asked.

Charlie shut the door, wondering if she knew he had been about to ask her the same question. "He's in the kitchen, getting the beer."

"Not Jack," Harriet said. "The other one."

"Scott? He mostly stays with his girlfriend. I haven't seen him in days."

"We haven't seen him in months," Mary Beth said. "You'd tell us if you guys had killed him, right?"

Charlie nodded. "We like to keep the community abreast of our many crimes." He gestured toward the hall with hands encumbered with chips and salsa. "Let's head to the deck."

Again, *deck* was perhaps not the correct word. Accessible only through the window in Jack's "bedroom" (which had once been a walk-in closet), the deck was the railing-enclosed roof of the first-floor porch. Jack and Charlie had furnished it with a few lawn chairs and an old table with crooked legs.

Charlie set the food on the table. "Where's *your* roommate?" he asked.

"She had a date," Mary Beth said.

"Oh." Charlie replayed his last conversation with Caroline in his mind, trying to find the ambiguities hidden in the words "See you there."

It wasn't as though Harriet and Mary Beth weren't attractive in their own right. Harriet was five-foot-six with deep brown skin, and she wore her dark, curly hair short. In Charlie's fantasies she wore leather pants and high-heeled boots, a white see-through blouse over a black bra, and a chain belt.

(Charlie's fantasies were detailed and—except for the costuming—strictly grounded in the plausible. It was not enough to simply imagine having sex with Catherine Zeta-Jones. It was important to establish, within the context of the fantasy, the manner in which he met Catherine Zeta-Jones, became friends with her, helped her through a difficult divorce, and finally screwed her brains out in a Cannes hotel, aided by a bottle of Cristal and her acquisition of a Grand Jury acting prize.)

Charlie's fantasies about Mary Beth were no less elaborate but tended more toward the breathless and sweaty. Mary Beth was small, but he liked her red hair, and her cleavage—not that she ever showed it—was spectacular. Tonight she wore jeans and a baggy sweatshirt, while Harriet was dressed in white pants and a T-shirt reading CORPORATE RADIO SUCKS.

"Anyone thirsty?" Jack stepped through the window, balancing a tray of chilled glasses in one hand and a six-pack of bottles in the other. He eased the tray onto the table and pulled a bottle opener from his pocket.

He cracked open four bottles and poured glasses for each of them. "A toast," he said. "To another year of classes done."

Charlie took a small taste. The color was right, and the head was healthy but not too fizzy. It was a bit sweet, not enough to offend, and light, with a hint of an aftertaste. He took another sip, and then a long drink.

"You did it," he said.

"He sure did," Harriet said. "Nummy."

"I hope there's more," said Mary Beth.

"Of course." Jack grinned.

It was a warm, cloudless night, but the stars were obscured by the city lights; only the crescent moon and the bright triangle of Deneb, Vega, and Altair were clearly visible through the haze. For a Saturday night, Mifflin Street was quiet. There were only two parties on the block, music and people spilling out onto the sidewalk in an invitation to a police raid. It was the first weekend after finals, last chance to party for those who were headed home for the summer. Across the street a couple packed belongings into a van, pausing after every load to kiss and hold hands.

Charlie was drifting off on his own, as he tended to do. He rose to put on some music but realized that the Stop-and-Starts—Jack called the band next door that because they had never played a song all the way through—were playing in the attic next door.

Harriet leaned back in the plastic lawn chair and put her feet up on the railing. "They're getting better," she said.

"What makes you say that?" Jack asked.

"The drummer stopped playing fills all the time instead of keeping the beat, and the bass player is starting to understand chords. The problem is the guitar player. He can't sing and play at the same time."

"He can't sing at all," Charlie said.

"That's true," Harriet said.

"Harriet writes music reviews for *The Campus Voice*," Mary Beth said. Charlie had been watching Mary Beth for a while, he realized. He liked her smile.

"I've never seen your name in the *Voice*," Charlie said.

"I have," Jack said. "You really ripped into Creed. I like that album."

"I never told you not to," Harriet said. "It's just an opinion. I'll never understand why people get so angry about it—I get some seriously threatening letters. You wouldn't believe how much pent-up rage the average Britney Spears fan has."

Jack laughed and set his beer glass on the table, which shifted alarmingly and sent an empty beer bottle tumbling to the deck. It rolled down the shingles and fell to the sidewalk below, shattering.

"Jesus!" came a voice from below. "Who's throwing shit at me?"

"Caroline?" Mary Beth looked over the railing. "I thought you went out for the night. Where's your date?"

"I don't know and I don't care. The restaurant sucked, the movie sucked, and he sucked. Is there any beer left?"

Ten minutes later they were all on their second bottle of Madison Maibock and deep into the snacks.

"The best thing about salsa is there's no fat," said Caroline. She was wearing tight khakis and a cut-sleeved blue top, which was closer, in Charlie's mind, to appropriate fantasy attire.

"You look nice," he told her.

"Thanks," she said.

"Caroline made that top," Mary Beth said. "She's a fashion

genius." Charlie didn't know Mary Beth all that well, but he had noticed that she was quick to brag about her roommates but hardly ever said a word about herself.

He put his feet up on the rail and surrendered again to the shyness that always came upon him in groups. He followed the conversation with his eyes, laughing with the others but feeling separate.

Somewhere between the fourth and fifth beer, after they had finished off all the salsa and Caroline had moved her chair closer to Charlie's, clouds blocked out the visible stars and a humid breeze blew down the street. The breeze made Charlie wonder how long ago everyone else had gotten smart and gone inside. Mifflin Street had gone silent. He looked up and saw tree branches swaying eerily in the damp air. A plastic cup skipped down the middle of the street, flashing intermittently beneath the streetlights.

"Maybe we should head inside now," Charlie said. An instant later a flash of white cast the street in stark shadow and light. Then all the lights went out, and the music stopped.

Charlie remembered stumbling inside as the first sheets of rain cascaded onto the deck, and he remembered spilling a stack of CDs over the floor inside. He remembered saying that they might as well finish the beer while it was still cold. What he didn't remember, to his eternal regret, was having sex with Caroline Bloom. Bits and pieces came back to him later—fumbled groping in the hall, banging his shin on the bed, someone closing the door on them after they were both naked. But as to who had instigated the encounter, what had been said, or even how it had felt, he was only ever able to reconstruct a blurry and incomplete picture, one he was never sure was the truth.

# SUNDAY

**M**ary Beth dreamed that a springer spaniel in a lime green jumpsuit chased her with a machete until her mother—her real mother—took the machete from the dog's four-fingered cartoon paw and replaced it with a tommy gun. She woke as the springer took aim, its long tongue lolling out the side of its mouth.

She tried to read the clock, but it didn't make any sense. 12:00? But it was light out. And it couldn't be noon, because she'd set the alarm for 8:00 so she could get to the library early. Finals might be over, but she wanted to get a jump on the summer session.

She couldn't stop blinking. No, the numbers were flashing. 12:00 . . . 12:00 . . . 12:00 . . . 12:00 . . .

"Shit!" The power had gone out, she remembered now; how she'd gotten back downstairs and into her own bed, wearing only a T-shirt that she wasn't sure she owned, was a mystery. She looked

11

for her watch, but it was nowhere in the tangle of clothes on the floor. She pulled on sweatpants and stumbled to the door. She squeezed the knob, and it came off in her hand.

Mary Beth tried to fit it back into the door, but the shaft was bent. She dropped the doorknob and tugged at the gap above the door. With a metallic groan the hinges gave way, and the door collapsed in on her. She reflexively caught it in one hand and leaned it against the wall.

Mary Beth took a deep breath and stepped into the hall as if amazing feats of strength were part of her morning ritual, which they were not. She had long ago resigned herself to being small and, if not helpless, at least better off walking away from trouble and making sarcastic comments from a safe distance. She had been the tallest girl in her class in sixth grade, and had for a few short months enjoyed the feeling of towering over the boys. She had imagined herself to be intimidating, though truthfully she was a gawky girl with a mouthful of braces and a wardrobe consisting primarily of sweater sets in pastel colors. Her reign as the tall girl was short-lived. She stalled out at five-foot-two, and one by one the other girls in her class outgrew her.

She was used to it, now. Mary Beth had found her identity in being the good student. They called her Bookworm and Teacher's Pet and other things that ought not to have stung as much as they did. But no one had ever labeled her athletic, or strong.

Her heart beating hard, she gently pushed on the half-opened door to Harriet's room and peered in at the battery-operated clock. 2:08, it said. Half the day was gone.

How much beer had she drunk? It hadn't seemed like so much, and it hadn't seemed to affect her in the beginning. But sometime after the lights went out she had lost track of what was happening. She remembered stumbling down a hallway looking for a bathroom. She remembered Caroline and Charlie entwined and naked on the floor of his bedroom. The thought made her vaguely nauseated.

She went to the kitchen, thirst refusing to be ignored. Her eyeballs felt scratchy and sunken, her muscles stiff and dry. She reached for the refrigerator handle and pulled it right off the door.

She broke into a sweat and set the handle on the kitchen table. She eased the refrigerator door open from the side. Carefully, as if she were handling a thousand-year-old ceramic baby, she lifted a pitcher of Kool-Aid from inside and set it on the table. Then she slowly shut the door and crossed to the cabinet, which she opened with her fingertips alone. She reached for a glass and held it gingerly as she lifted the pitcher to pour.

The phone rang, and Mary Beth tensed. The glass shattered in her hand, and the pitcher handle crumbled in her grip, leaving the body to fall to the floor and shatter, spattering her toes in Kool-Aid and splinters of broken glass.

Mary Beth crossed to the phone on sticky feet and picked it up on the third ring. She said "Hello?" five times before realizing she'd snapped the cord in two. She slammed the receiver down and the entire apparatus fell from the wall, fused into one useless heap of plastic.

When Harriet came home an hour later Mary Beth was sitting on the couch. On the coffee table in front of her lay her doorknob, the refrigerator handle, the destroyed phone, the toilet handle, a TV remote bent at a right angle, the splintered remains of a broomstick, and a cardboard box filled with shattered glasses, plates, bowls, and one pitcher.

"Don't ask me to shake hands," said Mary Beth.

"What's going on?" Harriet stood in the doorway, as if afraid to enter. The trepidation on her face made Mary Beth want to cry.

Instead she picked up a shard of broken glass and jabbed at her wrist with it.

"Jesus, girl!" Harriet moved to stop her but stopped short. There was no blood.

"I can hardly feel it," said Mary Beth. She pressed the glass harder into her skin, and it snapped into three smaller pieces. She held her arm up for Harriet to inspect. There wasn't even a mark on it.

Harriet leaned back against the wall. "I am having the weirdest day," she said.

"You?" Mary Beth waved a hand at the wreckage on the coffee table. "Are you saying you've got something to compare with this?"

"Yes. I was invisible for an hour and fifteen minutes today."

"Invisible?"

"Yeah. As in, not visible. Unseen. Gone."

"But you're here."

"For now I am." Harriet shrugged off her backpack and tossed it into her bedroom. "I went into the *Voice* to finish up an article that has to be in tomorrow. The only people in there were Jake and Darren, the editors. They were sitting on the couch in the news-room, bullshitting. I came in, we said hi, I went to my desk. I wasn't feeling great after last night, and I was having trouble concentrating on what I was doing. And my eyes were bugging out on me."

"Bugging out how?" Mary Beth asked.

"Everything looked sort of flat. Two-dimensional. And the colors were really bright, brighter than normal. I thought I was passing out, but I could still hear Jake and Darren talking. Then I realized they were talking about me."

"What were they saying?" Mary Beth asked.

"The usual crap. I'm a snob who treats the rest of the staff like no-talent hacks. I don't care about that—they *are* no-talent hacks, especially Jake and Darren—but the point is that nobody would talk like that in front of me. I started to say something, but then I realized I wasn't there. No reflection in the monitor, no lap or legs in my chair, nothing except bright colors spread across my vision. I nearly puked."

"No one noticed?"

"What's to notice?"

"I don't know. Disembodied tapping on the keyboard. The chair moving around."

"Jake and Darren only notice the rest of us when we're making them look bad. They were still talking about me when I dragged my invisible ass out of the office and hit the ladies' room. It was bad. My depth perception was screwed up, and I banged my knee into the doorway because I couldn't see myself. I thought I was going to pass out, but I couldn't even throw up. I couldn't even close my eyes, because my eyelids were invisible. And then, all of a sudden, I was back."

"Your *eyelids* were invisible?"

"Yeah. Gross, huh?" Harriet moved to the bathroom but halted in the doorway. "You broke the toilet?"

"Sorry. You can still flush, but you have to take the cover off."

"What the hell is happening?"

"If I knew that, maybe I'd know how to stop breaking everything."

Harriet shook her head. "I mean, how is it we both start exhibiting weirdness on the same day? Did you put something in the salsa?"

Mary Beth thought about it. "Some of the tomatoes *were* a little green."

"It doesn't make sense." Harriet picked up the refrigerator door handle and tapped it against her other hand. "I can't think about it right now. Let's go to the SERF."

"I was thinking maybe I should see a doctor," Mary Beth said.

"What's a doctor going to do? Once he breaks half a dozen needles on your skin he's going to be calling Freaks-R-Us."

"Maybe that's not a bad idea," Mary Beth said. "I can't touch anything without breaking it. I'm going home to visit next weekend. What if I go to hug my mom and shatter her rib cage?"

"Exactly why you should get a handle on this now, so you won't hurt anyone." Harriet stepped into her room and started changing clothes. "We'll hit the weight room and see how strong you actually are."

It was a beautiful afternoon, and most of Madison seemed to be out walking dogs, riding bicycles, playing volleyball on the commons outside Witte Hall. Mary Beth kept her eyes lowered, convinced that everyone could see her freakish new abilities. She had searched her image in the mirror for larger muscles, for some increase in mass that could explain what was happening, but she couldn't see it, and Harriet said she hadn't noticed anything either.

"How can you be so calm?" Mary Beth asked her.

"I already had my freak-out session, remember? I spent an hour spent huddled in a stall wondering if I was dissipating into nothing. But whatever's going on with me . . . don't take this the wrong way, but I don't think I'm dangerous. We can worry about me once we get a handle on what's happening with you."

"Dangerous." As frightened as she was, Mary Beth had to smile.

"You can feel sexy about it later," Harriet said. "For right now just don't touch anything."

Across from the Southeast Recreational Facility a crowd of boys were playing basketball on the concrete courts. Mary Beth wondered if she could jump now, or shoot a basket. When she reached the steps to the SERF she bent her knees, and with a little hop she sailed up and over all the stairs, to land and fall on her face outside the doors.

Harriet crouched at her side, looking around to see if anyone had noticed. "Don't do that again, either," she said. "Are you OK?"

Mary Beth bounded to her feet. "Not a scrape," she said. "What do you think that was, about twelve feet vertical? I wasn't even trying."

Harriet clicked her teeth and stepped past her. "I'll get the door."

Mary Beth didn't like the gym. She liked working out, liked pushing herself, sweating, even enjoyed being mildly sore afterward, but she hated the gym. She didn't know if it was a lingering aversion that she'd acquired in high school phys ed—she had vivid and unpleasant memories of boys leering at her in her sweats—or if it was simply a fear of being embarrassed by her own clumsiness and ineptitude. Either way, her dislike kept her from visiting the SERF more than a couple of times a month.

Today, though, she was looking forward to showing off a little. She and Harriet skipped the locker room and headed directly for the circuit.

There were only a few guys on the machines, but just inside, Harriet stopped and swore.

"What's wrong?" Mary Beth asked.

"Hatch."

"Huh?"

"Marcus Hatch," Harriet said. "On the leg press. Used to write for the *Voice* until he went over the edge. Conspiracy theorist. Couldn't write an objective piece about a bake sale."

"The Asian guy over there?"

Marcus Hatch looked as though he spent every day in the gym. He was lean, but his olive skin was taut over well-defined muscles. His hair was cut military short.

"He self-publishes a little rag called *What They're Not Telling You*," Harriet said. "After Jake and Darren fired him, he tried to convince me to work on it with him. Told me it was my duty as a black woman to agitate against the muzzling of the individual voice."

"Is that a quote?"

"Pretty close. Let's go over here. Hopefully he won't see us."

Harriet guided Mary Beth to a biceps press. "You ever used this one before?"

"No." Mary Beth usually stuck to the treadmills or the stationary bikes.

Harriet made some quick adjustments to the seat, then looked Mary Beth over. "How much do you weigh?"

"Very funny," Mary Beth said.

"Seriously. Ballpark figure."

Mary Beth felt the blood in her ears. "One fifteen, maybe." If it wasn't in the ballpark, it wasn't further than the parking lot.

Harriet raised an eyebrow but set the pin at 120 pounds and stepped back. "Let's see if you can lift your weight," she said.

Mary Beth settled into the seat and gripped the bar. She had a moment of doubt—what if the last few hours had been some sort of hormonal fluke? She'd heard of mothers lifting cars off trapped children, adrenaline giving them strength they didn't really have. She took a breath and pushed forward gently.

The bar swung forward and up so effortlessly that Mary Beth glanced over to be sure the pin was still in.

"How did that feel?" Harriet asked, keeping her voice low.

"How did what feel?" Mary Beth lowered the weight back into place without a sound. She was grinning again, and she wondered if she was still a little drunk from the night before.

"Put it up to two-forty, then."

Two-forty felt even easier than one-twenty, maybe because she wasn't tense this time. The machine only went up to four hundred, and she handled that without breathing hard.

"I could probably lift the whole machine," she said.

"Keep your voice down," Harriet said.

"Ms. Bishop!" Marcus Hatch smiled at Mary Beth but addressed Harriet. "I don't think I've ever seen you here before. Are you working on a story? Or are you still wasting your talents on hip-today, gone-tomorrow bands?"

"Oh, Marcus, you flatterer." Harriet, too, looked at Mary Beth when she spoke.

"Aren't you going to introduce me?" Marcus asked.

"Mary Beth, this is Marcus Hatch, the most egotistical man on campus. Marcus, this is Mary Beth Layton, my roommate."

"Nice to meet you." He looked past her. "What are you two doing? I don't usually see spotters in the circuit room."

"Mary Beth's just learning the machines," Harriet said. "I'm helping her find a good level to start with."

"It looked like she was doing all right." Marcus's eyes were narrowed, and Mary Beth realized he was trying to find the pin. Panic hit, and she started talking before she had any time to think.

"I was just about to try lifting four hundred," she said, and forced a laugh that came out as a mindless giggle.

"Really? Well, no harm in trying, is there?"

"I was just joking," Mary Beth said quickly.

"She could hurt herself," Harriet said.

"I doubt it," Marcus said. "You'll know pretty quickly whether it's going to happen. Why not try it? Just for laughs."

"Sure," Mary Beth said, ignoring the message Harriet was trying to send with her eyes. "No harm in trying!"

She took a deep breath and gripped the bar. Then she flexed the muscles in her arms and put on her best impersonation of a weak little girl. She made her arms tremble and held her breath until her face was red. Then she relaxed and let her arms fall to her sides.

"Not happening," she said, breathing heavily.

"I guess not," Marcus said. "Well, I've got to go run some laps. Nice to meet you, Mary Beth."

"Nice to meet you," she said, and watched him leave.

She stood up. "Pretty good, huh?"

"There's a problem," Harriet said slowly.

"What? He probably just thinks I'm dramatic." Mary Beth felt good, maybe better than ever in her life. She wondered if she was more powerful than a locomotive, or able to leap tall buildings in a single bound. She wondered if she could fly.

"It's not your acting ability I'm worried about." Harriet pointed to the bar. There was a subtle but noticeable bend near its center.

It didn't work over the phone, and Charlie was sure that was all that was keeping him from losing his mind. He had to be near someone for it to work. Anything closer than ten or fifteen feet was too close, as he'd learned that morning.

It had started before he'd woken up. He'd been having someone else's dream. He couldn't have put into words how it differed from his usual dreams, because he rarely remembered them. But this jumble of images didn't belong to him.

When he had opened his eyes, feeling bleary and thirsty and

sore, he had wished to be someone else; someone who hadn't gotten so drunk and slept with someone he barely knew. *I have to get out of here*, he'd thought.

"Where are my pants?"

Charlie had to do some mental connect-the-dots to make sense of the voice. It was a woman's voice. She sounded like she had just woken up. He was just waking up. He had slept with someone. Caroline.

"I found them, never mind." He blinked away sleep and rolled over to look at her. She stood beside the bed, pulling her khakis up over her lovely and quite naked ass. Her dark hair fell tangled down her bare back. She sat and started to pull on her socks.

*Panties*, he heard her thinking. *Where are my panties? Forget about them. God, I have to get out of here before he says something.*

"What do you think I'm going to say?" Charlie asked.

"What?" She turned to look at him, pulling her top on as she did so. "How did—what are you talking about?"

But that wasn't what she was thinking. *This is creepy. He's creepy. No, it's not his fault. What was I thinking?* He could hear her need to escape, to be away from him.

"I have to go to work," she said, and although he knew what she was thinking, that she didn't have to be at work for five hours yet, he let her go without protest. It wasn't until later that he had time to be hurt.

He lay in bed after she had gone, trying to make sense of what had happened. He was remarkably calm, he thought. "I'm remarkably calm," he said out loud. He imagined narration by Stone Phillips: "Charles Frost is remarkably calm for a young man who's begun to hear other people's voices in his head. He lives life as he always has, with one small difference."

He stayed calm while he brushed his teeth and got dressed. There was no one around, and his thoughts were his own. It was when he went out to get some lunch that it hit him, like a slap in the face with an industrial dishwasher. Just scattered thoughts at first, but once he was among the Sunday crowds, he was overwhelmed.

*Going to fail shouldn't have eaten those college kids think they can't be pregnant after I got the high score on one quarter to last me the fucking suits broke a nail I need to work out damn she's hot need sleep coffee food sex money wonder would he have sex with god don't let Grandpa die what's wrong with that guy?*

Charlie slumped against the side of a building, clutching at the cool brick and sweating in the shade. He tried to focus beyond the cravings and revulsions flowing through him and figure out where he was. He managed to turn himself back toward home, too preoccupied with the foreign thoughts to be conscious of his own fear.

Some of the thoughts were not words, though he was able to turn some of them into language. Many were images and emotions that yanked at Charlie's under-brain and set his heart racing like a chipmunk on PCP. He could stay with one mind, but it didn't help; he found himself inside the thoughts of a homeless man at a bus stop who was convinced that the three girls across the street were assassins sent by his enemies. He jumped into one of the girls and found her cocooned in an elaborate fantasy involving a horse whip, a Great Dane, and a man who seemed to be her stepfather. He reeled away from her and into a bicyclist weaving down State Street between the buses and taxicabs, mulling over a mathematical proof that Charlie wasn't even capable of articulating. And yet in the seconds before the bicyclist passed out of range Charlie found that he understood what the symbols represented and saw the complex beauty of the problem. He thought he might weep for the elegant machinery of the cosmos; it was as if a door had opened in the fabric of the universe and he had been invited through—

"Watch where you're going!"

Charlie was sprawled on the sidewalk, and his hands were scraped. A sunburned man led his family around him, thinking that Charlie was high. An unforgiving corner of the man's mind wished the drugs would kill off all the junkies and leave the world to decent people. His daughter took her father's hand and thought that someone should call a doctor, that when they got to the movie theater she'd ask her mom for money to call a doctor, except money for a phone call might buy gummy bears too. . . .

Charlie got to his feet and focused on placing his feet. He found that he could block out some of the sharper thoughts and coast instead through the emotions, letting rage and doubt and lust and happiness flow through him like a stream. Disconnected and directionless, the emotions themselves were less overwhelming than the dark and irreconcilable ideas beneath them.

The crowds thinned closer to his block, only single pedestrians or small groups. Some people stared at him, and he realized that he was running. He was no longer swept up in the mindstream that threatened to pull him under and drown his thoughts in the press of so many others. Even so, he didn't slow down until he reached the last intersection before his block.

There was traffic, and after a few speeding thoughts sprayed over him he stepped back from the curb. Instantly he was inside someone else's thoughts.

*Fucking bitch kill her talk to me like that she knows I love her kill her she had her chance teach her how much I kill her always treated her right ungrateful—*

Charlie turned, nearly lost his footing, and came face-to-face with a nondescript sandy-haired young man. He'd seen him before; he lived on the block somewhere. He looked perfectly calm.

"You all right?" he asked Charlie.

"I'm fine." Charlie backed away. "Thanks. See you later."

The other man stared after him for a moment, then crossed the street. Charlie followed at a safe distance, remembering at the last second to check for cars. When he made it across, the other man was gone.

Back inside his apartment, Charlie thought about crying. He wasn't sure it was the appropriate response. It wasn't as if he'd suffered a great tragedy. It had been stressful—he was still trembling—and people cried from stress, sometimes. But it had been brief, and there didn't seem to be any lasting damage. He decided not to cry.

He lay on the couch and thought about telepathy. Telepathy was one of a large set of things that took so much energy not to believe in, like Bigfoot and UFOs and compassionate conservatism, that Charlie had always reserved judgment on their plausibility. He couldn't disprove their existence, but neither had they seemed very likely, until now.

Of course, there was always the chance that he wasn't reading minds but rather losing his. Charlie picked up the phone. He didn't need to call 911—if it wasn't worth crying over, it wasn't an emergency. Could the police trace incoming calls? There was a way to disable caller ID, but would it work on the police? It must. They couldn't trace every incoming call, he hoped. He didn't want them backing up the fruit truck yet. If he was going to go crazy, he wanted to do it on his own schedule.

He dialed *67 and the number for the nearest precinct.

"This is Detective Bishop, how can I help you?"

"Hi. I'm— I have a problem. I'm hearing voices. In my head."

"What are they saying?"

"Nothing right now. It's only when people are around."

"I see. Do people make you nervous?"

"A little, I guess. But that's not what's causing this. It's like I can hear them inside my head. I can hear what they're thinking." *I sound like a lunatic*, Charlie thought. *He's sending a squad over right now.*

"You hear what they're thinking? What are they thinking about?"

"Sex, mostly."

"Huh. That sounds about right. How long has this been going on?"

"Since I woke up this morning."

"Have you been using any drugs, Mr. . . . ?"

"No." He was crying. Did that make this an emergency after all? "I don't use drugs. I just— I thought you might know what to do."

"Here's an idea. You own a hat? Ball cap, anything?"

"Yeah."

"You have some tinfoil?"

"I'm not sure."

"Take some tinfoil and line the inside of the hat with it. If you can find some pipe cleaners, tape some of them to the tinfoil, with the wires touching the foil. That should ground the mind energies and keep the foreign thoughts out of your head."

Charlie let out a breath. "Are you making fun of me? I saw this routine on *NYPD Blue*. I called you for help."

"Just try it, Mr. . . . what did you say your name was?"

*He thinks I'm a loon.* "OK," Charlie said.

"And listen, if the voices don't go away, and if they start telling you to do things you don't want to do, like if they tell you to hurt people, or hurt yourself, call us first, OK?"

"It's not . . . OK. I will." Charlie hung up.

He turned on the TV and flipped through the channels for a while. The people there were flat and distant, for which he was grateful; if he had started hearing Opie's and Andy's thoughts he would have known he was crazy.

He walked to the front window and watched the people out on the street for a while. Then he went to his room, dragged his futon into the farthest corner from the door. Even if someone knocked, he shouldn't be able to hear their thoughts.

He locked the door and curled up in a ball in the dark.

**P**rofessor Mason peered up at Jack, his eyes ridiculously enlarged by his thick lenses. Jack was never comfortable being the focus of Mason's attention. He was used to stares—he was a big guy, and people always gave him a good look, as if to make certain he wasn't dangerous. But Mason looked at him the other way, the way that Jack dreaded, as if he questioned the plausibility of someone so solid and muscular having a working brain.

"You must be careful to do good work, Mr. Robinson. Dirty slides and a dirty lab mean bad data, and my data is very important to me. Your work is not something to be rushed through simply because you want to lay around in the sun today."

It was raining sheets outside, but then Mason had probably slept in the lab again. Most of the time he wasn't sure what day it was.

"I understand, Professor," Jack said. "I'm doing good work, I promise you. I just finished a little early today."

"Go, then." Professor Mason waved his hands at Jack, as if shooing an animal.

"I'll be in early tomorrow," Jack said, but Mason was already back at his bench. Jack grabbed his jacket and left. There were people around, so he strode casually up the hall and down the stairs to the front entrance.

It was ten in the morning and yet almost pitch-black. Rain cascaded off the roofs and dripped through the maple leaves. There were only a few people on the street, and they were all hunched beneath umbrellas, struggling against the wind.

Jack looked behind him—there was no one in the entrance hall. No cars on the street, and no pedestrians nearby. No witnesses. He looked at his watch. 10:04:38.

He took off running, dodging raindrops as he went.

He couldn't evade them all, of course, not in this downpour. He had to be careful where he put his feet, and watch for obstacles— mailboxes, pedestrians, cars. They were all the same to him, at this speed—a bicyclist hydroplaning alongside the curb was as stationary as a lamppost. But if he ran into something or someone, he didn't know what might happen, and he didn't want to find out. He wanted to *know*, sure, but this wasn't like Mason's experiments. There were no controls, and no safe conditions to test it under.

He knew he was moving fast; he felt the exertion, and the exhilaration. But he saw his surroundings clearly, even more clearly than before. He was alert to everything around him, except sounds, which he left behind him. He heard only the sound of his own breathing, and that in a hollow, truncated way. It was more as though the world had slowed around him than that he had speeded up, but that was a relativity problem, and not one he wanted to think about.

He cut through Library Mall, where water stood immobile above the fountain like an ice sculpture. A thrown football hung over a knot of mud-soaked players poised on the grass, arms out-stretched and legs planted in impossible postures. Raindrops hung like molten gemstones. Jack picked his way among them, down the alley between the University Bookstore and the Lutheran church, across University Avenue and down Lake Street.

How had this happened? Yesterday he hadn't cared; he'd been having too much fun testing himself. He didn't care that much today, if he was honest with himself. But these were definitely strange phenomena. At some point he should try to find out what was going on.

Not today, though. He reached Mifflin Street, climbed the steps of 523, opened the left-side door as gently as he could manage, and let it fall shut behind him. He stopped at the base of the stairs and looked at his watch. 10:04:45.

Door to door in seven seconds. He could run to England in about—well, a few hours, anyway. He'd have to cross an ocean, but maybe he could run over the water at that speed, like a water skate. He'd have to test it out on the lake later.

*I'm a superhero*, he thought. *I'm faster than a speeding bullet. I can walk on water, or at least run very fast on water. Maybe.*

He slogged up the stairs to the apartment. He didn't want the girls downstairs to hear a staccato of footfalls and come up to find out what was happening.

The steps creaked. Dust motes revolved through the air. It took longer to walk up the stairs than to run three miles! This was going to be tough to adjust to.

He finally made it to the apartment. No one seemed to be home. He walked—slowly, ever so slowly—back to Charlie's bedroom, and knocked. Silence. He tried the door, but it was locked. He knocked again. "Charlie?"

"What."

"Are you sick or something? I didn't see you at all yesterday."

"Yeah. I'm sick."

"Too much beer, or too much Caroline?"

"What do you want?"

"Just checking on you. I'm going home for the afternoon. You need anything?"

"No."

"All right. Later."

Jack shoved a few books into his backpack, locked the door, moved slowly down the stairs and outside, and looked up and down the street to make sure no one was around. He looked at his watch. 10:10:33.

He hitched up his backpack and took off running.

He went northeast on Mifflin, turned right onto Bassett and took it to Wilson, then Wilson to Broom to John Nolen. He passed among speeding cars and leapt over the spray kicked up by them. It was like running through a freeze-frame.

He took John Nolen to the Beltline, the Beltline east to Highway 18. The speed limit here was sixty; the cars around him might as well be in a showroom. His heart was pounding; he was getting an erection.

Maybe he didn't need the job at the lab. He could do the work of an eight-hour shift in a few minutes—but he couldn't do it in a workplace, not without drawing a lot of attention. Discovery meant doctors and needles and those suction-cup wired sensor thingies you always saw in the movies. He'd be sedated and locked up and probed and pinched and shaved, and he wasn't going to let that happen. He had to be careful.

He turned off Highway 18 and onto Highway 26. Maybe he could work from home. Stuff envelopes or something. Of course, stuffing envelopes was still stuffing envelopes, no matter how fast he could do it. There had to be something more exciting.

Home was a farm off the highway, all but the top of the silo screened by trees. He slowed as he moved up the driveway, not wanting to kick up a cloud of dust. Grace was at school, but Mom's cherry red Blazer stood in the parking space out front, next to a silver Taurus Jack had never seen before. Dad's Chevy was tucked up next to the house, the same spot it had been in for months.

Jack ducked inside the machine shed and straightened his hair as best he could in the mirror inside the combine. He looked a bit ragged, but he didn't look as though he'd just run forty miles in—he checked his watch—under four minutes. He wasn't even winded.

He crossed the courtyard formed by the lee of the barn, silo, machine shed, and the garage that had been slumping toward collapse for almost a year now. It was a long walk, but now that Jack was here he was in no hurry to be inside. He paused before the screen door, knowing that its creaking would make retreat impossible. Then he took a deep breath and went inside.

"Morty!" His mother came into the living room while he was wiping his shoes on the mat. "I wondered if you'd be coming today." She squinted out the windows. "I didn't see you pull up. Where's your truck?"

"Parked behind the shed." He hugged her, looking past her to the bare spot on the wall where the TV used to be. "Whose car is that outside?"

"The new nurse. Sylvia moved to Milwaukee, you know." She followed his gaze to the bare spot on the wall. "We moved it into his room." She looked as though she would say more but smiled and squeezed his arm instead. "Are you hungry? I could make you some lunch."

He was starving. "That'd be great, Mom."

"I'll make some soup and sandwiches," she said. "Why don't you go say hi?"

She left him in the living room. He heard voices at the end of the hall—"his room," she had called it, though all Jack's life his mother and father had shared that bedroom. His father's voice was deep but rough, phleghmy. The new nurse's voice was cheerful, grating. Jack forced a smile—tentative and friendly, but not cheerful. It was important not to look cheerful, at least, not right away. He knocked at the open door.

The new nurse was small and plump and looked to be in her forties. She was taking his father's blood pressure, and only glanced up at Jack. "You must be one of the sons," she said around her stethoscope.

Jack's father was sitting in his old recliner, the one he wouldn't let them get rid of since it smelled of cigarettes. "If I have to quit smoking 'em, maybe I can still get a buzz off the chair," he'd said when they tried to buy him a new La-Z-Boy for Christmas. Jack wondered if his father could actually smell anything anymore. He'd told Jack a few weeks ago that everything he ate tasted like cardboard.

He looked better today, relative to how terrible he had looked last week. His hair was all but gone, and what was left looked like gray thread. An IV drip was hooked into his arm, and a breathing tube in his nose. He looked like a deflated version of the man Jack had to look at pictures to remember. He wondered if he had ever really looked at his father before the diagnosis. Not in a long time, he decided.

"Hi, Dad." He crouched in front of the chair, and put his hand over his father's. He squeezed it gently.

"Morty." His father's eyes were still alert, most of the time, but they looked at him slantwise from a head that rested at an odd angle against the back of the chair. "Morty, this . . . this is Alice. Alice, this is Morty. The rest of the world . . . calls him Jack, but here he's still . . . Morty."

"Nice to meet you, Morty."

"Nice to meet you."

Alice tore the Velcro of the blood pressure sleeve and unwrapped it. "You're doing well, Zeke. Ready to eat something?"

"I suppose."

Alice put away the blood pressure kit. "I'll let you two chat, then, while I get you some lunch."

"So, Morty . . . ," his father said, pausing to catch his breath, "you get your . . . grades yet?"

"Not yet, Dad. Probably be a couple of weeks."

"Ah. Still raining out there?"

"Yeah."

"Traffic bad?"

Jack almost smiled. "Not too bad, no."

"I was hoping you'd . . . you'd come down today."

His father's breathing was so slow and labored that Jack felt guilty for the speed he had awoken with on Sunday. He wondered if the cells in his body were living faster, too. If his father had been given this instead of him, would his body be able to outpace the cancer, to kill it and heal? Or would the cancer be killing him even faster?

"We need to . . . discuss some things. I spoke to your brother." Jack's brother Lloyd was an actuary in Chicago, though he visited a couple of times a month.

"What about?"

"The land. Mom told you we hired . . . the Carlson twins for the summer?"

"Yeah."

"They'll do good work . . . they'll need help during the harvest, but . . . they'll do good work."

"I'll be able to help a lot," Jack said. "Weekends, and sometimes during the week, too."

"That's good," said his father. "What I'm worried about . . . is after this year. I'm worried about who's . . . who's going to take on the farm. After."

A chill ran from between Jack's shoulder blades to the base of his spine. "Is that really something we need to talk about now? We don't know what's going to happen."

"Mortimer." Zeke Robinson's voice was firm. "Don't . . . don't bullshit yourself. Listen. Your mom can't do it alone. Lloyd doesn't want to . . . take it on. He's got a life . . . down there. He's engaged, did Mom tell . . . tell you?"

"No." Jack didn't even know Lloyd had a girlfriend.

"Yup. Ask Mom . . . about it. Now Lloyd don't want it . . . and maybe I'm old-fashioned, but . . . I wanted to ask you . . . before I talk to your sisters. I know you got school . . . and I know it's a lot to take on. But maybe you wanted to, once. All I'm asking . . . is you think about it."

Jack thought he would start crying if he answered, but he managed to contain himself. "I'll think about it, Dad."

"That's all I ask."

Jack's mother brought in a card table. "Soup'll be ready in a minute," she said as she set it up.

Alice followed with a plate heaped with roast beef sandwiches.

"Would you like a sandwich, Zeke?" Jack's father made an expression of distaste. "All right. I'll get you something to drink, then, so you can take your medication. That's not optional."

Jack turned on the TV, and they watched *Judge Judy* while Alice fed pills to his father. Zeke sipped cranberry juice through a straw to wash them down, and forced down half a bowl of the vegetable soup his wife brought in, but the effort seemed to exhaust him. Jack ate half a dozen sandwiches and three bowls of soup, and he was still hungry. Neither of them said much of anything, just sat and watched the TV while Mom brought and cleared dishes and Alice made scattered, unanswerable comments.

Judge Judy was lecturing the plaintiff when Jack realized his father was asleep. He looked less drawn, less in pain while sleeping, and Jack hoped it was so.

He found his mother in the kitchen, slumped behind a cup of coffee.

"Still raining," he said.

"Well, we need it." She sipped her coffee. "It's good you came. You headed back now?"

"Yeah. Still looking for another job for the summer."

"Don't take on too much, Morty."

"I'll be fine, Mom." She looked like a little girl, hunched over the white tablecloth, a long strand of hair hanging loose from her ponytail to frame the left side of her face. He wanted to comfort her, to take her hand and let her cry if she needed to. If she dared to. It was Dad who was dying, but there were no doctors for what she was feeling.

"I'll come by on Friday," he said.

"Drive carefully," she said.

As soon as he was out of sight he ran so fast that the fields blurred past him, that his calves burned and his lungs ached. He ran to Madison and then he ran on, west and north until things looked unfamiliar and he knew he would have to stop to find out where he was. But not yet.

Detective Ray Bishop flipped through a mail-order catalog with one hand and none of his attention. He was on hold again. He spent half of his time at the station on the phone. He thought about taking up smoking again, not very seriously. He'd given it up six years before, after his divorce, and Ray didn't believe in backsliding.

Self-improvement was Ray's quiet obsession. Since his divorce, he'd given up a bad habit every time a woman left him—smoking, drinking, caffeine, biting his nails, cracking his knuckles, snapping his gum. He'd even tried giving up masturbating, but he had feared for his mental health after two weeks and relented.

It wasn't that his habits broke up relationships. There had been plenty of problems between Olivia and himself that his smoking had nothing to do with, and Barbara hadn't slept around because Ray snapped his gum. But Ray had a picture of his ideal self in his head, a guy who always knew the right thing to say and do, a guy who always looked good and smelled good, never had gas and never had food caught in his teeth. He would never be that guy, of course, but there was no reason not to aim high—what was the point of the concept of perfection, if not as a goal?

Not that it seemed to help much. The last woman he had gone out with had nixed a second date, telling him over the phone that he was "too perfect" for her. Try as he might, he hadn't been able to turn it into a compliment.

He set the catalog aside and leaned his elbow on the desk. He wished the coroner's office would get some hold music; at least then he'd know for sure that he hadn't been hung up on.

A nasal voice came on the line. "Bishop?"

"Cutler. How many bodies have you got over there, anyway? I've been waiting fifteen minutes."

"Answering the phone isn't my job, Bishop. If you guys didn't call here every hour on the hour, I'd have more time to get your answers."

"I've called twice." It was three times, but then he hadn't been on hold for fifteen minutes, either. "Do you have anything on the Tanner girl yet?"

"I was just about to call you."

"What were you going to tell me?"

"Nothing you didn't already know. Strangulation. She fought. Plenty of skin under the nails, I sent it over to the lab. No recent intercourse. Toxicology report will be a couple of days, but from the look of the tissue I'd say she was clean."

"She wasn't raped?"

"No. The report—your report, in fact—indicates she was fully clothed when found."

"She was found by her roommate. I thought she might have covered up the body."

Someone rapped on Ray's desk, and he looked up to see his daughter Harriet in front of him. She smiled and set a bulging duffel bag on the floor. Then she wandered off to read the notices on the office bulletin board.

"I'll have this faxed over," Cutler said. "Any suspects?"

"Not yet. No witnesses, and the roommate who found her was the only close friend that hadn't left town for the summer. She was shook up, I'm going to try to get a statement from her in the morning."

"Taking the night off? Another date?"

"Dinner and laundry with my daughter. You got anything else for me, Bill?"

"No. I'll call you when those lab reports come through."

"Sure you will."

Ray hung up and gathered his case papers into a manila folder before sliding the whole mess into a drawer.

Harriet read the bulletin board with a look of concentration. She looked very like her mother—thin and long legged, with a high, broad forehead. They even had the same smile, an unexpected brightening of a normally stern face.

"I hope you lock your doors when you're at home," he said, stepping up beside her.

She sighed. "Dad, don't give me the speech. I work at a newspaper, remember? I heard all about it."

"Everyone hears about it, all the time. They just think it can't happen to them. I want to make sure you're being careful."

"You taught me that, Dad. Have a little faith in your parenting skills."

"Did you know her?"

"Now I do. Marsha Tanner, twenty-one years old, brown hair and eyes, lived at 414 West Johnson—"

"Two blocks from your house."

"I know. But it happened in the middle of the day, and from the report we got, there was no forced entry."

"So?"

"So it was someone she knew, and someone who doesn't care about getting caught." She kissed him on the cheek. "Let's forget about it for a while. I thought I'd make lasagna, but we'll need to pick up some stuff on the way home."

"Lasagna's not going to make me stop worrying about you," Ray said.

"No, but you won't be able to nag me while you're eating it."

An hour and a half later—after Harriet had made him spend almost two hundred dollars on groceries he needed but never would have bought on his own, and after spending a half hour at the video place looking for a drama before settling on the Jackie Chan movie they both wanted to see anyway—Ray watched helplessly while his daughter took over his kitchen. The ideal man in his mind's eye was an accomplished cook, but apart from channel-surfing through a cooking show on cable now and then, Ray had never learned to do much more than grill steak. Harriet was putting away groceries, pulling out a pan and utensils, and assembling ingredients simultaneously.

Ray had bought his house on the East Side of Madison about four years before. He rented out the upper floor to a trio of grad students and kept a laundry room in the basement. The apartment was meticulously clean, because he was hardly ever home.

After a few minutes Harriet noticed him standing there. "Go ahead and sit down, Daddy."

"I could put some of these clothes in the wash," he said, reaching for the bulging duffel she'd left inside the door.

"No." She watched him warily until he set the bag down. "Just relax. I don't mind cooking, and I can do my own laundry."

Harriet did this about once a month. It was nice of her, but it left him with nothing to do. Ray preferred their twice-weekly lunch dates, where he felt like the two of them were on an equal footing. When she cooked for him he felt like a helpless bachelor being babied by his twenty-year-old daughter, which was exactly what he was.

He sat in the kitchen for a while and tried to make conversation, but she was too busy to give more than one-word responses to his questions. Finally he gave up and moved into the living room.

The Tanner girl was all over the news, so he put on *SportsCenter* and immediately fell asleep.

"Daddy." He forced his eyes open but didn't see anyone. "Daddy, wake up." He blinked, but he still didn't see her.

"Harry?"

"Dinner's ready." Her voice came from the kitchen now. "Are you awake?"

"I'm awake." He sat up on the couch, rubbing his face.

"Can you dish up your own lasagna? I need to use the bathroom."

"All right." The lasagna was still steaming, and there was garlic bread and spinach salad besides. He shoveled it all onto a plate and grabbed a Diet Coke from the fridge. "Do you want me to make you a plate?"

"That's OK," came her voice from the bathroom. "I'll be a minute."

"Are you sick?"

"No, Dad. I'm fine . . . I just, it's my period, if you need to know."

"Oh." Nothing made him feel so inadequate as a parent as when Harriet was having her period. "Do you need anything?"

"No, I've got stuff here. Go ahead and eat."

Ten minutes later she was still in the bathroom, and he'd flipped through seventy-some channels without finding anything to watch. The lasagna was criminally good, but he forced himself to sit with the illusion that he wasn't going to have another piece.

The bathroom door opened. "I'm going to check on my laundry," Harriet yelled. The back door slammed, and footsteps tromped down the back stairs. Ray shook his head and went to get more lasagna.

He was pouring himself a glass of water when the back door

opened again. "You'd better get some of this before it gets cold," he said. But there was no one at the door. He crossed to it and looked out. He thought he heard breathing, but there was no one there. "Harriet?"

Silence. He hurried down the stairs, his heart wanting him to move quicker yet. The washer was washing, the dryer drying, but no one was there. No one in the utility area, either, and the rest of the basement rooms were locked. "Who's here?"

No answer.

Then he heard someone walking around upstairs, and he ran, not caring if Harriet teased him, hoping it was her and he was just getting old—going deaf and hearing things at the same time.

She was at the counter, dishing up lasagna. He didn't say anything, just breathed his relief and locked the back door behind him.

"Where were you?" she asked.

"I thought you were downstairs."

"I was. I came back up. Are you OK?"

"I called, and you didn't answer. I got worried."

"I didn't hear you." Sweat stood in beaded rows on her forehead, and her breath came quick and shallow.

"Are you feeling all right?"

"Better." She swept past him into the living room.

They watched most of the movie in silence. Eventually Harriet relaxed a bit and started to giggle at some of the stunts, but she was still bothered by something. Ray knew his daughter well enough not to press her. If she thought he could help her, she would ask. Part of him was indignant that she wouldn't ask his help with all her problems, but realistically he didn't want that. He just wanted her to trust him and to feel that she could come to him whenever she wished. That, and he didn't want to drop out of her life. He wanted her around, and not just a voice on the phone. She was fun, and she was smart, and she constantly amazed him.

She woke him when the movie was over. "Must be a record," she said. "You only slept through the last twenty minutes."

"I don't always sleep through movies, you know."

"No," she said. "Some of them you walk out on."

He let her tease him for a while. She must be feeling better.

"Can I stay here tonight?" she asked when they both realized how late it was.

"Sure. Take the bed. I usually sleep on the couch anyway."

"Old habits die hard, huh?"

He forced a laugh.

"I'm sorry, Daddy." She kissed him and moved into the bedroom. "You have to be the only single guy alive who makes his bed every morning, Dad."

"And you know this how?"

"Dad!"

It was another hour before she fell asleep. Ray turned on *SportsCenter* and curled up in the TV's cool glow. *Make her keep her door locked, Lord,* he prayed as he drifted off. *Keep an eye on her for me. Please.*

There were no entries for "Super Strength" in the electronic card catalog. None for "Superpowers," either, which surprised Mary Beth, because she had expected to at least find a bunch of entries on the United States and the old Soviet Union. "Superheroes" pointed her to "Heroes," which took her nowhere. There was a subheading for "Heroes—Comic Books," but there were only two texts there, one of which was in German and the other was a comic book about Lewis and Clark kept in the Historical Society archives.

Mary Beth leaned back in her chair at the Memorial Library and looked up at the ceiling. She'd already tried the Internet. She'd Googled "Superheroes" and ended up with a quarter of a million results, but after clicking blindly through several fan Web sites, an exercise site, and a couple pages of "Superheroines in Bondage," she'd given up and decided to try the library. Now she was trying not to let her frustration get the better of her.

Over the last few days she and Harriet had scrambled to replace all the broken things in the apartment without Caroline noticing. At first she had wanted to tell Caroline everything. Since she and Harriet had spontaneously developed strange new abilities it seemed likely that their roommate might have as well. But Caroline had given no indication of any change. She still worked long hours and went out nearly every night she didn't work. Caroline went out on more dates in a month than Mary Beth had in her two years of college. Mary Beth resented this, partly out of jealousy, but mainly because she knew that if she had been working thirty hours and going out three nights a week she couldn't have kept up Caroline's 3.5 GPA.

Mary Beth was managing a 3.8, but she worked for it. When school was in session she spent nearly every night at the library, and not the social halls of College Library but the solitary stacks of Memorial, where few undergraduates ventured and silence prevailed. Her classes were hard, and she was a slow reader; sometimes she felt like she was working three times as hard as the people around her, just to keep up.

Thankfully she didn't have to work—her parents gave her more than enough money to cover tuition, food, rent, and what little entertainment she took the time for. They didn't need to do so much, but they'd been wallowing in guilt ever since her little brother had been born unexpectedly six years after they adopted her. They had tried for years to get pregnant before making her the center of their lives, and despite all she did to convince them otherwise, they were certain she bore deep psychic scars stemming from the sudden invasion of another child.

Whatever psychic scars she bore, Mary Beth was certain they hadn't originated with her brother's birth. She loved her brother, and she loved her parents; but their generosity had created a feed-back loop of guilt. Mary Beth was determined to get through school as quickly as possible so they wouldn't have to keep supporting her. She took the maximum number of credits each semester, plus summer school, and her plan was to finish in three years and then apply to medical school. Her parents, in turn, gave her still more money, and when she didn't spend it they tried to send her on vacations to Italy and Australia and Costa Rica—this past spring break they had sent her, Harriet, and Caroline to Jamaica, which had made her roommates into big fans of her parents. But while Mary Beth appreciated everything they did for her, she wished sometimes that they were a little less rich and a lot less solicitous.

Mary Beth had wanted to be a doctor since junior high, or maybe earlier. No single incident had decided her; she was simply fascinated with how bodies moved and grew and fit together. She took disease and injury personally, although she herself had rarely suffered either, and never seriously. It had something to do with her mother—her real mother, the one who had died giving birth to her, leaving her without a family for the four days until the Laytons learned of her and decided to make her their daughter.

That lonely, friendless girl, whom Mary Beth had already outlived by four years, was still a presence in her life. She had two forms: one was the resentful denizen of her dreams, who called upon a rogues' gallery of nightmare assassins to take back the life Mary Beth had stolen from her; the other was her mother as a small child, an almost-sister Mary Beth had conjured out of a child's flawed understanding of the story of her own birth. She used to spend hours talking to Wanda Benson, imagining her in pigtails and a flowered dress, a gentle girl who told good jokes and held her hand when she was frightened. Even now Mary Beth sometimes pictured her like this, though she was less proper and smiled less easily. The mother in her nightmares had become more vivid over the years than the friend in her imagination.

Mary Beth didn't blame the doctors for letting Wanda Benson die. She had no illusions that if, once having become a doctor, she were somehow able to step back in time to that delivery room, she would be able to save her mother's life. From what she had learned, it was a miracle that both of them hadn't died months before her birth. Maybe the real reason she wanted to become a doctor was as repayment for her own survival.

As much as she was enjoying being the strongest woman on the face of the earth, it was a distraction from her plans. The one-week summer session started in five days, and she was signed up for an intense lab class. She couldn't afford to be breaking things. She had to figure out how to control this power before Tuesday. With a bit of finesse she could become a trauma surgeon, freeing people trapped in crushed cars by tearing the vehicles out from around them like paper, then performing delicate operations on-site with her superior control. She could rescue miners from cave-ins and then treat their wounds. She could respond to police calls and deflect bullets that would otherwise kill or incapacitate.

She was pretty sure she could deflect a bullet. Nothing, not razors nor broken glass nor knives, could cut into her skin, despite her constant and—as Harriet finally called them—morbid attempts to draw blood. She didn't even bruise. Nor was she ever sore, even after lifting a Ford Escort over her head late Monday night when she and Harriet had walked up to Capital Centre Foods for some late-night grocery shopping. She had been walking down the middle of the silent street, giddy from junk food and the late hour, when she'd set down her bags and swept the little car up into the air, being careful to lift with her knees. For the first time she had felt a bit of strain, a tightness across her shoulders when she went to set it down, and she wondered if she was near her limit. She would have tried to lift a Toyota 4Runner next if Harriet hadn't hissed at her to get inside before she drew attention to herself.

Yet she was able to type on the library computer without shattering the keys; and although the effort was more than that of, say, lifting the table upon which said computer and five others sat, she had hope. She had never had to think about being gentle before, but she was determined to learn her own strength, to blend in. She pictured calling up her parents and telling them she was dropping out of school to become a superhero. It would be worse than joining a band.

She had to know what was happening, and ever since she was five years old Mary Beth had relied on libraries for answers. With a few exceptions, which were not failures precisely but rather cases of questions leading to more questions (such as Who is God? and What is death? and Why are boys so stupid?), she had never been let down.

Possibly she wasn't looking in the right places, but she didn't feel as if she could explain her situation to a research librarian without being referred for psychiatric counseling. So after an hour of fruitless searching she found herself standing outside, looking out over Library Mall, completely at a loss.

"You look like you're at a loss." Marcus Hatch was beside her, smiling.

Mary Beth grimaced. "Where did you come from?"

He looked sheepish, if it was possible to look sheepish in a calculated way. "I followed you," he said.

"How charming," Mary Beth said.

"It wasn't a creepy follow. It was a hey-there's-that-intriguing-young-lady-I-met-the-other-day-but-didn't-get-a-chance-to-talk-to follow."

"They look almost identical."

"Hey, I'm sorry." Marcus put up his hands. "If being interested in you is such a turnoff, I'll go away."

Mary Beth started across the Mall toward State Street. "You're interested in me? Why would that be?"

Marcus matched her pace. "What can I say? You made quite an impression."

Mary Beth managed not to break stride. He might just be using a figure of speech. She had done her best to bend the bar back into shape, but it was still visible, at least to her. She didn't know if someone would investigate, or if they could trace her if they did. There must be hundreds of fingerprints on the equipment in there.

If she told Marcus to get lost he might get more suspicious than he already was. Of course, if she suddenly became sweetness and light he'd be suspicious, too. Assuming that he was suspicious in the first place, which she couldn't be sure was the case. She mentally chased her tail like this for a few seconds, finally coming out with, "Huh."

"Huh? What do you mean by that?" Marcus asked.

"I was just wondering if this approach usually works for you. Following and flattering. Seems a bit nineteenth century to me."

"I've been slapped once or twice. In your case, I hope it doesn't come to that."

Was he implying that he knew she could slap him through a brick wall? Or was he just being smarmy? "You aren't afraid of me, are you?"

"Should I be?"

Mary Beth wished he'd ask his questions and stop hinting around, if that was what he was doing. His insinuations made her feel as though she had a dirty secret, and she didn't like that. It was a secret, but there was nothing dirty about it.

"Are you going to follow me home?" Mary Beth asked, picking up the pace.

"Did you finish your research?" Marcus asked in return. "I didn't think there were any classes going on yet."

"I'm done talking to you," she said.

"For now you are. You'll change your mind eventually."

"Good-bye," she said, and left him behind.

She didn't go home. She was on her way when she passed a video store with a large poster advertising the *X-Men* movie out on DVD. She remembered the X-Men from her search of the World Wide Web as well, and she started to wonder if she wasn't overlooking an important resource.

After consulting a phone book, she took a downtown bus out to Monroe Street. She saw it immediately. She'd probably been by here twenty or thirty times and never noticed it before, but it was hard to imagine how; the sign was a large, bold, red and white. ARTEMIS'S COMICS.

She entered, blinking at the shadowed contrast to the sunlight outside. Shelves lined the walls, stacked with comics. Garish titles blared from glossy paper; *Flash*, *Spider-Man*, *Fantastic Four*. Beside the new comics were rows of graphic novels shelved tightly together, and in the center of the room, a cluttered display table with action figures and other collectibles.

"Can I help you?" A small Asian woman stood behind the counter.

"I hope so," Mary Beth said. "I need to do some research on

superheroes. For a paper." She flushed at the lie, certain she wouldn't be believed.

"OK. What aspect of superheroes? Vigilantism, supergroups, superhuman powers, secret identities, costume fetishes—"

"Secret identities," Mary Beth interrupted. "How they fit into normal society, that sort of thing. Controlling their powers so as to handle everyday activities."

"OK. You know, the secret identity isn't usually that much of a focus. Most superheroes deal with it to some extent, but it's largely background. And some superheroes don't have secret identities. The Fantastic Four, for example. Everybody knows that Reed Richards is Mr. Fantastic and his wife, Sue, is the Invisible Woman."

Mary Beth made a mental note to tell Harriet that the name "Invisible Woman" was already taken.

"Or someone like the Hulk, who is widely known to be the alter ego of Bruce Banner. He can't keep his identity a secret because the Hulk is something he can't control."

"I'm more interested in examples of maintaining a secret identity."

"Right. Lots of characters maintain secret identities, but some are more realistic than others. Batman is Bruce Wayne, but Wayne isn't someone you or I can necessarily relate to. He's an obsessive and a scientific genius in perfect physical condition with an ungodly amount of money. Someone like Spider-Man is a bit more down-to-earth. Peter Parker goes to school, struggles to make money, worries about his Aunt May. The fact is his life becomes more difficult as a result of his powers. But then that's nearly universal."

"It is?"

"Sure. That has to happen, because otherwise you don't have much of a story. But besides that, there are two opposing axioms that govern much of what happens in the realm of superheroes. One is Spider-Man's motto, 'With great power comes great responsibility.' The other was said by Lord Acton, the British historian: 'Power tends to corrupt; absolute power corrupts absolutely.' Superheroes and supervillains exist in the gray area between those two statements. When you make yourself responsible for maintaining order, are you allowing your power to corrupt you?"

Mary Beth shook her head. "I don't understand. Are you saying that just by having power, you become dangerous?"

"Some people would say so, and then some people think of power as the only way to make things better. It's like the difference between the Arthurian Sword in the Stone and Tolkien's One Ring. Have you ever read *Watchmen*?"

"No. Is that a comic?"

"Yeah. We have the trade paperback. If you're not that familiar with comics it might take you some time to absorb it, but it'll help. That, and some *Spider-Man*, and maybe some *Daredevil*—"

Mary Beth spent almost a hundred dollars at the store, then took the bus back to State Street and walked to Mifflin. From two blocks away she saw that there was a commotion near her house. There were three police cars on the street, their lights flashing, and a small crowd had gathered. She quickened her steps.

The police had pulled up in front of a house just a few doors down from hers and across the street. One uniformed officer stood near the cars, talking to a plainclothes detective. The crowd stood watching, some whispering, most silent. She saw Charlie Frost standing in the street alone, and she walked over to him.

"What's happening?" she asked.

"Nothing right now." Charlie was wearing a baseball cap, something Mary Beth had never seen him do before. Among the greasy strands of hair sticking out from under the cap was what seemed to be tinfoil.

"What *did* happen, then?"

"They arrested him." Charlie motioned at the cars, and Mary Beth realized that there was a young man with sandy hair in the backseat of the nearest patrol car. He looked as though he'd been crying.

"Who is it?"

"I don't know his name." There was a defensive note in Charlie's words. "He killed her, though. Marsha Tanner."

He shut his eyes and whispered something. It sounded to Mary Beth like he was saying, "I can't hear him now."

"That girl over on Johnson? Why did he kill her?"

"Because she broke up with him."

"The cops said that?"

"No." Charlie adjusted his cap. "I have to go. This isn't working." He all but ran into the house.

ixteen was trying to get her attention. He lifted his arm and waved his fingers instead of his hand, like an amateur beauty queen in a parade. Caroline smiled at him from across the room and nodded as politely as she could manage. She had six salads in her hands, and the food for Twenty was finally up. She delivered the salads to Eighteen, fetched the food and brought the sauces to Twenty, took a drink order that Seventeen shouted at her on her way past, and finally reached Sixteen, who didn't stop waving until she was standing next to him.

"Is everything all right?" she asked.

He sat back heavily, as if waving her down had taken his last ounce of strength. "My wife's steak isn't done." He was perhaps fifty, with a graying beard and a paunch that cradled his tie like a pillow. He was indignant, whether because of the food or her delay in getting to him she couldn't tell.

"I'm sorry." Caroline turned to his wife, a narrow-faced woman with rectangular spectacles and her hair pulled back into a tight bun. "You ordered it medium, didn't you?"

"Yes." The woman sat far back in her chair, eyeing her steak as though it were a rabid weasel. It was rather pink—definitely not medium—but Caroline didn't think it was likely to attack.

"I'll replace it right away." Caroline reached for the plate, but the man shook his head.

"We're in a hurry," he said. "We have to be at the Civic Center by seven-thirty."

It was ten after six, and the Civic Center was two blocks away. "It's no problem," Caroline said. "I'll have them put a rush on it."

"I'll eat it," said the woman, looking as though she would have to plug her nose to do so.

"I can bring you another one, cooked the way you want it. Or I can bring you something else, if you like." Caroline considered snatching the plate away and running with it.

"No," said the man. "I just wanted to call it to your attention."

"What can I do to make you happy?" Caroline asked.

They looked at her as if the question was ludicrous, and it probably was. Caroline guessed that the only thing that might make them happy was seeing the manager flagellate her with the bleeding steak.

She offered again—between apologies—to take the steak back, but by now they were ignoring her, so Caroline retreated to the bar.

"Two Tanqueray tonics, a Jack and Coke, and a Sapphire rocks," she told the bartender, Ken. "And a shot of Cuervo for me."

Ken smiled, but he put up only four glasses. At times he could be convinced to slip her a drink, but rarely this early in the night. "Freaking out already?" he asked. "It's only Thursday."

"The lady at Sixteen doesn't like her steak, but she won't let me take it back."

"Did you tell Vincent?"

Caroline shook her head. Vincent was the owner and very possibly insane. A week ago he had dropped to his knees and wept to a family of four after the eight-year-old boy found a dead ant in his dinner salad. He had paid for their dinner, given them each a cake and enough gift certificates for two weeks' worth of dinners. Then he had stormed into the back room and put the busboys to work scouring the salad bar with bleach in the middle of the dinner rush.

"What about table Nineteen?" Ken asked.

Caroline had been trying to ignore Nineteen. They had been her first dinner customers, a couple in their mid-thirties, very into each other. She wore leather pants and high-heeled boots and a white T-shirt that strained against breasts that Caroline and the other waitresses all agreed weren't real. He wore a Harley-Davidson T-shirt, several gold chains, and jeans so tight Caroline could read the serial numbers on his keys. Before dinner they had spent more time sucking on each other's earlobes than on their drinks. There was no inappropriate touching, exactly, but it wouldn't have surprised Caroline if they had found a way to have sex through their clothes and from separate chairs.

Things had cooled by the time she took their dinner order. They had eaten in an icy silence, and now they were arguing in low tones. When she cleared their plates she had heard her calling him a dickless wonder and him calling her a fucking whore.

"I don't think anyone else can hear them," Caroline said. "I'm afraid if I say anything they'll get loud."

"You shouldn't have to say anything," Ken said. "That's Vincent's job."

He was right, and after she delivered the drinks to Seventeen and made sure there were no unhappy diners at Twenty, she went to find Vincent.

He was in his office doing paperwork. He didn't look up when she entered, but she knew he was aware of her presence. Announcing herself would only make him grumpy.

Vincent was the only child of Feodor Christos, the man who had opened the restaurant more than fifty years before. There was a picture of Feodor on the wall, taken when he was in his forties, and at forty-two Vincent resembled the man in that picture very much. He had the same thick, wavy brown hair, the same deep-set eyes, the same sharp chin and cheekbones. The primary difference in their appearances was that Feodor was smiling, which was something Vincent rarely did.

He looked at Caroline over his glasses, still leaning over his desk, his pen poised.

"Two things," she said. "I have a woman at Sixteen whose steak is underdone, but she won't let me replace it. And I have a couple at Nineteen that I'm afraid is going to make a scene. They've been arguing for about fifteen minutes. Quietly," she added quickly. "But I'm afraid they might get loud."

"Did Sixteen ask to have the steak taken off the check?"

"No, but I wanted to warn you in case they do."

He stood, and she followed him out of the office and down the hall lined with his father's memorabilia: pictures of Feodor with mayors and legislators and governors, autographed photos of Anthony Quinn and Tony Curtis and Raquel Welch, clippings from the local newspapers about Feodor and reviews of the restaurant. At the Christmas party Vincent had, after several martinis, told Ken that his father was haunting the restaurant.

"I suppose that's true," Ken had said. "After all that time the place absorbed a lot of his character."

"I'm not talking about his character," Vincent had yelled. "I'm talking about the bastard's ghost." He had gone on to describe several late-night visitations before his wife dragged him away and took him home.

When Caroline told stories about her job to Harriet and Mary Beth, they always told her that she should quit, that it was unhealthy to work for a lunatic. If the money hadn't been so good, she probably would have. She had made a deal with herself that if Vincent ever flipped out on her, she would walk out and never come back. But so far she had dodged his tirades, though she had witnessed several.

She might be in for one tonight. Once he had dealt with the diners, he might scream at her until he went hoarse. Caroline had rehearsed quitting countless times in her mind; she would pull off her apron, throw it in his face, and tell him he had turned into his father. It was a bit of a cheat, since the elder Christos had died a few years before Caroline had started working there. But it was well established, through the stories of the longtime employees, that: (1) Vincent had hated his father while he was alive, and (2) Feodor, like Vincent, was prone to emotional outbursts and verbal abuse. In fact, the only major difference between the two seemed to be that while Feodor had been renowned for his ability to make his customers feel welcome, Vincent could be awkward to the point of being rude.

He was on his best behavior tonight, however. He spoke to Nineteen, and soon they were smiling at him, if not at each other. They talked to him for a couple of minutes and then left, surprising Caroline with a 20 percent tip. Then Vincent apologized to Sixteen, told them he would take the steak off their bill, and gave them a gift certificate besides. He sat with them for nearly half an hour before they left for their show, and managed to charm them so thoroughly that the woman even thanked Caroline as they left. The tip sucked, but she had expected that.

Vincent waved her over after they had left. She tensed, wondering if he would scream at her. Had they told him she had said something rude? Had there been something about her body language that offended them?

It was neither of those things. "Who cooked that steak?" he asked.

"Don." She was sorry to have to tell him. Don was a nice guy, but he wasn't a very good cook. Now Vincent would probably fire him.

He didn't, though. He pulled Don aside and talked to him in low tones for several minutes, Don paying close attention, nodding almost continuously. Then Vincent stood for a while by the bar, exchanging occasional sentences with Ken. Caroline kept one eye on him while she handled her tables. The rush was over, and they would probably close early, unless Vincent decided to keep them all out of spite.

She didn't see him go over to the waitress's station and start inspecting it. The first hint she had that there was something wrong was when she heard something clattering across the floor. Vincent was dropping coffeepots.

The three businessmen who had just sat down at Seventeen looked stunned. She took their drink order and went to the waitress station to find out what was going on.

Kendra and Sharon were standing there, listening to him rant. "Decaf coffee lids go on the decaf coffee*pots*," he said, not loudly. "Look at this! Where is the lid for this one? Where are you putting the lids?"

Caroline moved slowly toward the bar. The worst thing to do when he was on a roll was to respond. She started ordering her drinks from Ken.

"You don't care? You're going to fucking care!" Now he was loud. The restaurant had gotten quiet, but Vincent didn't seem to notice. "Decaf lids on the fucking decaf pots! Regular lids on the regular goddamned pots! When are you going to learn that I'm in charge here? I'm the man!" He seized a bus tub, piled all the coffeepots and lids into it, and stalked with it back into his office.

They didn't see Vincent again that night. The hostess went into the office to get permission to close at ten o'clock. There were only two tables left. Vincent told her to wait until ten-thirty.

"I hate being here this late," Sharon said to Caroline as they punched out at twenty to eleven. "He likes to keep us here. It makes him feel important."

Caroline followed her out the back door and into the parking lot. "If he wants our respect, why does he act like that?"

"He learned from his dad," Sharon said. "I could tell you stories."

"I think I've heard them," Caroline said.

"Not all of them. Not by a long shot. See you later, honey." Sharon got into her old Plymouth and drove off in a cloud of exhaust.

Caroline looked around. No cars. No one on the street. All the businesses around Christos were long closed.

She took a deep breath and flew up into the air.

It was a warm night, and only a few wispy clouds veiled the moon and stars. The city spread out below her as she rose, the capitol and the lakes and the campus. She looked down over it and breathed in the clear air.

She had bought a compass earlier in the day. She pulled it from her pocket now and took a reading as she rose straight up into the sky. Then she turned and flew south, slipping the compass back into her pocket.

It took little thought, and less effort. All she had to do was think a direction and she was moving, warm air rushing around her, the ground speeding away below. Except it was her that was shooting through the air like a rocket over the farm country south of Madison, with only the stars to keep her company.

She hadn't said anything to anyone. She never would. She didn't know why this was happening, and she didn't care. All she knew was that on Sunday night, after spending the day hungover and angry at herself for sleeping with Charlie, on top of which work was insanely busy and Vincent fired one of the waitresses for being ten minutes late and she spent most of her shift waiting for a scream that never escaped, she had started to walk home and found herself soaring over the rooftops instead.

She'd been out flying every night since, except for Monday night, when there were thunderstorms and she'd been terrified of being struck by lightning. How did planes handle that? She had to remember to look that up, when she had some time.

No lightning tonight. She was afraid of colliding with a bat, but she had convinced herself that a bat would notice her before she noticed it and steer clear. Most of the birds flew far above her, and planes were higher still, although they sounded terrifyingly close. She had panicked last night when a jet passed overhead; she'd been sure it was about to ram her, and she'd set down in a pasture, where the smell of cow pies got into her clothes.

She tried a few stunts, spinning like a corkscrew, somersaulting through the air, flying on her back. She laughed. It was impossible not to laugh, impossible not to feel good while she was flying.

She didn't care about Vincent or snotty customers or busboys staring at her ass all the time. None of it could touch her; it was all down there, and she was up here, out of reach.

After a while it started to get cool, and Caroline looked at the compass again and turned back north. She felt good, cleansed, but by the time she reached the lights of Madison she was tired as well. She passed high over Lake Monona and wended her way to the 500 block of Mifflin. No one was on the street. She saw a few windows lit, but no one framed in them. Safe.

She landed on the other side of Bernard and crossed to her block. Music played from the house next to the Laundromat, but otherwise the street was quiet. She walked swiftly to 523 and opened the front door with her key.

Once inside she saw by the VCR—someone had broken the microwave, which she usually used as her clock—that it was nearly 3:30. She groaned. She had to work a double shift tomorrow, ten to ten, and she was going to be doing it on less than six hours sleep. She was back on earth again. She couldn't wait to leave.

t was so late it was early, and Harriet hadn't slept yet. She'd covered the Difficult Love show at the Barrymore, and she was trying to type up her review and the interview she'd done before the show. The show had been disappointing, and she was trying to say as much without trashing the guys in the band, who had been funny and charming without trying to get into her pants.

Harriet didn't mind doing interviews, but doing reviews and interviews both felt like a conflict of interest. There was always a tinge of guilt any time she had to trash someone she'd met and liked, and when she interviewed jerks it was even harder to be objective about their music.

In a perfect world she could either write the reviews or do the interviews, but during the summer the *Voice* was always understaffed, and as the arts editor she had to shoulder most of the burden for her section. She didn't mind the work. Music was all she'd ever been interested in—she'd learned the violin, the guitar, and the piano as a child, and been terrible at them all. She couldn't play, but she got good at listening. She found that the further into a good song she went, the more the music expanded. It enveloped her, cradled her, shook her up. It changed, depending on how she listened. That was what she wanted to do with her life, listen to music.

From her bedroom she heard the apartment door creak open, and she looked at the clock: 4:47 A.M. Mary Beth was in Milwaukee visiting her parents, so that left Caroline.

There was no reason for Harriet to spy on Caroline. She told herself she was just bored and restless, that it was insomnia and procrastination. Her own privacy was important to her, and she would never, under normal circumstances, invade someone else's.

She shut her eyes as she went invisible. As soon as it was done she saw through her eyelids anyway, but the shift in her vision that accompanied the change—from soft color to bold two-dimensional splashes—tended to make her nauseated.

After the night at her dad's place, she'd been determined to control what was happening to her, and after a few tries she had discovered that it wasn't difficult at all. Ever since that first time she had been putting so much effort into not changing that she'd created a mental block for herself. It was a terrific relief to find that when she wanted to disappear from sight she could do it with a thought.

She hesitated before opening the door, remembering that she was in her underwear. But it was warm, and no one would see her anyway. It made no sense that her clothes should go invisible with her—she hadn't even thought about it until Mary Beth had mentioned it the other day. Mary Beth had said something about the woman in the Fantastic Four, how she had an invisible force field that surrounded her. Harriet didn't have a force field as far as she could tell, but she'd tried dressing and undressing while she was invisible; clothes she put on disappeared with the rest of her, and clothes she took off suddenly appeared.

Maybe it didn't make sense. Harriet was no science expert. But she didn't see how an invisible naked person was easier to explain than an invisible person with clothes on. Mary Beth could research the question all she liked, but it wouldn't change anything.

Harriet opened her bedroom door, careful not to make any sound. She slipped out of her room and shut the door behind her. Light came from the open bathroom, shining a flat bright yellow against the deep sky blue of the hallway. Humming came down the hall.

Harriet groped forward, trailing her hands along the wall, until she stepped on something sharp with her bare feet. She hissed involuntarily and froze.

The humming stopped, and Caroline popped her head out of the bathroom, hair blue-black against the yellow light, hot pink toothbrush held between her enamel-red lips. She looked around and then disappeared into the bathroom, humming again.

Harriet crept up to the bathroom and peeked around the corner. She had to stifle a gasp at what she saw.

Caroline was floating in midair, brushing her teeth. She rested one hand on the sea green Formica of the sink, her fingertips spread, as if she were steadying herself. She looked into her own eyes in the mirror, smiling around the toothbrush. Her bare feet hovered over the ground, purple polish glittering from the nails of her wiggling toes.

Harriet took a step back and leaned against the wall.

Caroline spit into the sink, rinsed her toothbrush, and poured water into an orange plastic cup that she kept by the sink. Then she spun in midair, her red pajama bottoms a blur of color, and laughed softly.

She started to floss, and Harriet retreated down the hall. Super strength, invisibility, flying. She tried to decide if she'd been cheated.

The party. This had all started on Sunday, the day after the party. Could Charlie or Jack have put something in the beer? That sounded crazy, but all things considered, Harriet wasn't willing to dismiss it. Maybe the party was a dead end, but she had to check into it.

She got into bed and lay awake, wondering if this was all somehow deliberate. Jack worked in a chem lab, she knew that. But how likely was it that he'd developed a formula that gave people superpowers? Then again, likelihood and probability had gone out the window the moment she looked in the mirror and saw nothing there.

She tried to sleep for an hour or so, then got dressed. She was going to be invisible again, but there was a difference between wandering around half-naked and invisible in her own apartment and running around half-naked and invisible in someone else's. She left the apartment and climbed the stairs to the second floor.

Unfortunately, being invisible couldn't get her through a locked door. She sat down on the landing and looked at her watch, but there was nothing there, of course. It must be six o'clock by now. On a Saturday. What was she doing here so early? She should go back and finish typing up her review. She should get some sleep.

There should be a hotline for things like this. Some nonprofit group. "Objects burst into flame at your touch? Can't urinate without shattering the toilet? If you've found yourself gifted with superpowers that you don't know how to use, call the Super Freaks Hotline, and we'll get you back on your way to becoming a productive member of society. Meet others like yourself. Get help with costumes and code name selection. All in a discreet environment safe from prying government agents."

She woke herself up with her snoring, and blinked at the cracked white wall of the stairwell. She was too tired to keep this up. Maybe she'd just call the boys later and ask them if they'd been going through any changes lately. Or possibly something that sounded a little less like the sort of thing a child molester might say to a sixth-grader.

She stood up just as the door opened. Jack stepped out wearing a scarlet backpack, a bright yellow T-shirt, and a pair of mercifully sober khakis. He locked the door, turned around, and vanished in a rush of air.

Harriet's breath was sucked out of her, and she struggled to breathe while the front door fell quietly shut.

Superspeed. Why did everyone else get the cool powers?

There was no point in going after Jack, but she didn't want to wait here all morning either. She squared herself in front of the door, her fist poised somewhere in front of her. She wondered if she'd left normal life far behind her already. Maybe she should simply go back to bed, pull the covers up around her head, and pretend that she was just like everyone else. Other people had mood swings, asthma attacks. She could just be the girl who disappeared every once in a while.

She knocked. When Charlie opened the door she would slip past him into the apartment while he was still trying to figure out who'd been knocking. She'd watch him for a while and see if he did anything strange. She didn't think that would be breaking and entering. It was something her father would arrest her for if he ever found out about it, she was sure of that. But she wasn't going to get caught.

She knocked again. Her heart pounded. She wasn't a sneaky person. She minded her own business. She knocked again.

She began pounding on the door in a rumba beat. The sound reassured her that her hands were still there.

When Charlie finally opened the door she reacted too late to slip past him. He crowded the doorway, squinting through her. He had grown a patchy beard since she had seen him last. He wore a tattered blue bathrobe and held a Twins cap in his hand. The inside of the cap was lined with something that looked like tinfoil.

"It's six-thirty in the morning, Harriet."

She glanced down at herself, wondering if she had become visible. She hadn't, but he wasn't looking at her—his eyes wandered, looking through her.

"It doesn't matter. I was up anyway." He sighed. "I guess I'm not the only one."

Harriet swallowed to clear her throat. "Are you reading my mind?"

"Yes." Charlie put the Twins cap on. "This helps muffle it some." He stepped back from the door. "Maybe you should come inside, so we can talk."

O n the bus back to Madison Mary Beth finally relaxed. All weekend she'd sat on her hands to remind herself not to touch anything. When she couldn't avoid using her hands she had been tentative and clumsy. Her mother asked if she was sick, and Mary Beth had let her believe it. It was a good excuse to avoid a potentially disastrous trip to the mall; Mary Beth hated to think what might happen if she tried too hard to fit into a pair of designer jeans. As it was, she had put a dent in the roof of the Jeep when she bumped her head on it. Her mother had been too relieved that she was OK to think about it much. "You always did have a hard head," she had said, after checking for blood.

She had played the sick card with her younger brother as well. They wrestled all the time, and until recently, when Peter had hit his growth spurt and started to get big, they'd been evenly matched. But Mary Beth didn't trust herself to keep her strength under control, so every time he punched her playfully in the shoulder she had to tell him she wasn't up to it. Besides, Peter was getting to the age when grappling with his older and not-blood-related sister might not be the healthiest thing.

She was tired of keeping secrets. She had read all the comics she'd bought, and she was overflowing with ideas that she couldn't wait to tell Harriet about. She had taken voluminous notes, even made some sketches. They were bad sketches—stick- and balloon-figured superheroines in unflattering costumes. Caroline was a better artist, but she wasn't in on the secret.

The secret was starting to feel like a box that she was trapped in. A box she could move around in but couldn't leave. A box on wheels, maybe. On Saturday her dad had struggled to drag his new grill around the house and onto the back patio. Three years before, at the age of fifty, he'd had a heart attack. Mary Beth wanted badly to go out and carry the 180-pound grill around for him, but she had read enough *X-Men* in the past five days to be afraid of how they would look at her afterward.

Despite that, Mary Beth was so excited about her new plans that she almost resented the fact that she had to be in class tomorrow. Almost. She still wanted to be a doctor. This other thing wouldn't be a distraction from that. She wouldn't let it be one.

"Bet you can't help it." Her birth mother sat in the aisle seat beside her. Wanda Benson was about ten, had pigtails, and wore a dirty T-shirt and jeans. "Doctor or superhero? That's pretty easy."

"I can do both." Mary Beth had learned back in elementary school to say the words silently to herself. Maybe her mother wasn't really there, but sometimes it was easier to talk to her than to think things through on her own.

"Bet you don't want to," said Wanda. "You didn't study for your lab at all. You read those comics all weekend."

"Nora must have thought I was losing my mind." When Mary

Beth was speaking to Wanda she always referred to her adoptive mother by her first name.

"You know those people in the comics? Like Daredevil? That's not real."

"I know that."

"I'm not talking about powers," Wanda said. "I'm talking about being a lawyer and a superhero at the same time. That's totally unrealistic."

"Well, it won't be easy. Managing the time will be a definite challenge."

"Yeah. 'Specially when you become a resident and start working fourteen-hour shifts and being on call all the time. You can't just run off and leave all the sick people every time the world needs to be saved."

"Maybe."

"If I was superstrong I wouldn't be a stupid doctor. I'd make money lifting heavy stuff for people, and I'd have a secret base nobody knew about, and I'd put the bad people in a big jail in space so they wouldn't hurt any kids."

"How am I supposed to get into space?" asked Mary Beth.

"What?" The boy in the seat ahead of her turned.

Mary Beth acted like she had just woken up and told him she must have been talking in her sleep. She closed her eyes and pretended to doze off.

"I can be whatever I want," she told Wanda without saying a word. And then she did doze off, to dream of a hospital filled with balloon-figure doctors and stick-figure patients.

# EDITOR'S NOTE

## by Marcus Hatch

Some people need everything explained to them. You can't just dump some girls, because they have to know *why*: what they did wrong, can't it be fixed, how could you whisper all that sweet stuff and then say you never want to see them again. And if you take the time to give an honest answer, there's no way you're going to get any bittersweet breakup sex, so you're better off just cutting them loose and not returning their calls.

So don't think I don't realize that some of you are expecting me to explain how five ordinary college students acquired these extraordinary powers. Well, you're going to have to get used to disappointment. There are two reasons you'd want to know that: first, because you want to know if you can duplicate the results and get some superpowers of your own, which you will then use to carry out your no doubt nefarious plans; second, because you want to see me explain it and then send me smug letters telling me that's impossible, my science is all wrong, I am a moron and should be digging ditches instead of calling myself a journalist.

So even if I knew how this all happened, I wouldn't tell you. I'm not in favor of having a bunch of superhumans running around, and although you might not believe it, I'm thinking of you when I say that. That's the plural *you*, all of you, not just the ones wishing they could sneak into the girls' locker room or break into Fort Knox or cut the morning commute by a factor of ten. You'll see what I mean. For the rest, I haven't got time to read a lot of letters from people whose greatest talent is making their impressive knowledge pale in comparison to their overwhelming arrogance.

So let me say this right now, and anyone who can't handle it can put the book down and go read a nice murder mystery: I'm not going to try to explain how this happened. At no point in this narrative will you find a scientific reason for what is scientifically impossible anyway. Bruce Lee said that an intelligent mind is nourished by the search for answers, and not by conclusions. Maybe you won't be nourished, but you'll have to be satisfied.

I n Cleveland Caroline had worked at a German-themed restaurant where she'd had to wear a dirndl that pushed her breasts up nearly to her chin and men three tables away stared every time she leaned forward to set down a drink. Once a week there was an employee meeting, almost always on days Caroline didn't work. She had to take the bus there after school to sit and listen to the owner say the same things he'd said the week before—push the wurst, spilled beer is lost profits, and his favorite couplet, "If there's time to lean, there's time to clean." Then she took the bus home, by which time it was six o'clock and she had to start dinner.

Meetings were a waste of time. She would have told Mary Beth as much, but there had been only the note: "Meeting 5:30 Friday, the Attic." Caroline wasn't even getting paid for this meeting, and it didn't look like anyone else was going to show up. No one besides Charlie, who sat at the opposite end of the attic, wearing a stupid baseball cap. He'd been there when she'd come in. She'd nodded at him and looked away before she saw whether he nodded back.

The attic of 523 had always been a dusty place, low-ceilinged and with a floor that seemed to be made of thick cardboard. It had three windows, two of which were covered with plywood. Grayness seemed to flake off the walls and into the air, making it difficult to breathe.

Caroline hardly recognized the attic now. Mary Beth had pulled the plywood off of the windows, leaving an open breezeway through which cool air was blowing. She had placed lamps on the bar, set an easel in front of it, and five chairs around that—the kitchen chairs from their apartment, Caroline noticed. A pitcher of ice water sweated on the bar with a tray of glasses and a plate of crackers and cheese.

Caroline cleared her throat, which was—either from the lingering dust or from the thick silence between her and Charlie— clogged with phlegm. "Has your roommate been around?" she asked.

Charlie played with the brim of his cap before answering. Looking at him now it was easy to be angry at herself for sleeping with him. His hair stuck out from beneath the cap in brittle tufts, and his thin beard made him look unwashed, which Caroline was almost certain he was. He wore stained red sweatpants and a T-shirt torn in several places.

He had looked good enough that night, despite his lack of fashion sense; it was actually sort of endearing, how utterly oblivious he was to his appearance. That, and the beer, had gotten her into trouble. It was too bad, because she liked Charlie. But in her experience, sex and friendship didn't mix. It was simpler, and safer, to sleep with guys she didn't particularly like and to dump them when they became insufferable—or, in rare cases, when she actually started to like them.

He was answering her question, and she had to think for a second to remember what she had asked.

"I haven't seen Scott," he said. "Actually, I heard someone moving around in his room last week, so maybe he was here. I didn't go out to look."

"You couldn't tell?" Caroline asked. "I mean, with the, the mind thing?"

"No. I have to be pretty close to someone for it to work."

"So that morning after we . . ."

Before she could go on she heard someone tromping up the stairs behind her. Mary Beth climbed into view, followed by Harriet and Jack.

"Sorry I'm late." Mary Beth handed Caroline a stapled stack of paper. "Took me longer at Kinkos than I thought it would."

"Kinkos?" Caroline looked down at the document she was holding. OPTIONS FOR SUPERPOWERED INDIVIDUALS, it read.

Mary Beth handed copies to Harriet and Jack, who blinked at the changed appearance of the attic before taking their seats. Charlie held up a hand as Mary Beth started to approach him.

"Could you just toss it to me?" he said.

Mary Beth flung a handout in his direction. It spun, and the pages flared out to fall in a heap a few feet short of Charlie's chair. He sighed and stood to retrieve it, retreating again quickly to his seat.

Mary Beth took her place in front of the easel. "The handout is just a survey of the different routes I think are open to us, based on my research. Maybe we should take a few minutes right now to look through it."

"Let's just get started," Caroline said.

"All right," Mary Beth said. "The first issue is that of going public or not." She wrote IDENTITIES: PUBLIC OR SECRET? on the easel pad. "I see a lot of problems with revealing our identities, but it's worth discussing."

"No it's not," Jack said.

"It might not be a bad idea," Harriet said. "We could control our own destinies that way. No shady government outfit would be able to kidnap us and do tests on us, because they'd be toasted by the public."

"You're assuming the public will love us," Jack said. "They might be terrified."

"It's all in the spin," Harriet said. "I could handle press releases and interviews, minimize the negative publicity."

"You can't control it all," Jack said. "And I don't want the press all over me and my family."

"They'll be all over us anyway, and if we're confidential we'll have no way to answer back," Harriet said. "The police will be after us, too."

"Why the police?" Jack said.

"Vigilantism is against the law."

"It's against the law to help people?"

"No. But if we're going to be anonymous, we can't claim a citizen's arrest. We can't testify in court. We're not going to be enforcing the law, and we might as well face that right now."

Mary Beth wrote USE PRESS TO ADVANTAGE? PRESS HARRASSING FAMILIES? and VIGILANTISM = ILLEGAL. Her handwriting was smooth, clean, and legible.

"I have a question," Caroline said. "What the hell are you guys talking about?"

They all looked at her. "We're trying to decide how to approach this," Mary Beth said.

"Approach what?"

"The group."

"What group?"

"The superhero group."

"I didn't join any superhero group. Was there a meeting before this one?"

"I guess we all just assumed—"

"I didn't," Caroline said. "My first thought upon finding out you all had developed strange abilities was not, 'Oh goody, now we can all fight crime together.'"

"What was it?" Charlie asked.

Caroline wasn't going to get into that. Her first thought had been disappointment. She had been looking forward to a lifetime of quiet nighttime flights, the solitude and the quiet and the sensation of passing effortlessly through the air. Being found out was like being dragged back down to earth.

"Who are we going to fight?" she asked. "Muggers? Young Republicans?"

"Hey, I'm a Republican," Jack said.

Caroline squinted at him. "You are?"

"Let's put politics aside," Mary Beth said. "What are your objections to the superhero group?"

"Do you want a list?"

"Sure." Mary Beth turned to a clean page.

"Fine. First, Madison doesn't need a superhero group due to its tragic shortage of supervillains. Second, if we dug up some supervillains we'd have to fight them, which I don't know how to do, and getting killed isn't on my list of summer plans. Third, Harriet just said it's illegal. Fourth, I already have a job, and school, and a social life. Fifth, I don't look good in spandex. Should I go on?"

"Let's address those first," Mary Beth said. Numbered 1

through 5, she had written NEED, FIGHTING SKILLS, LEGALITY, SCHEDULING, and COSTUMING.

"Are we going to be wearing spandex?" Charlie asked.

"God, I hope not," said Harriet.

"First," said Mary Beth. "Does Madison need a superhero group?" She underlined NEED twice. "Who'd like to start?"

"There isn't much crime here," Harriet said. "There were maybe five murders last year."

"How many mad scientists and giant monsters were there?" Caroline asked. "This isn't exactly a city under siege. What are we going to do, break up rings of bicycle thieves?"

Mary Beth wrote down STOP BIKE THIEVES.

"My dad's a cop," Harriet said, "and even as quiet as Madison generally is, there are still too many crimes for them to solve."

"I don't think we're ready to start *solving* crimes," Jack said. "We're not detectives. We don't even know how all this started."

"Did you do something to the beer?" Harriet asked.

"What?" Jack looked genuinely shocked. "No. What could I have done?"

"Why do you think this is happening?" Mary Beth asked.

"I just told you, I don't know."

"You're the scientist," Caroline said.

"Yeah, well, I'm not sure science can explain this." Jack spread his hands. "What do you think happened?"

"I don't care," Caroline said. "Don't you understand? I can *fly*. *Why* doesn't matter to me in the least. So I'm not convinced that the universe is telling us to put on costumes and start making fools of ourselves."

"My only point was that I'm sure the police would appreciate any kind of help we could offer," Harriet said.

"What does that mean?" Caroline asked. "They're going to give us honorary badges after they slap the cuffs on us for breaking the vigilante laws?"

"I think we should help any way we can," Charlie said. "I know I wish I had."

"What do you mean?" Mary Beth asked.

"I mean Marsha Tanner," Charlie said. "The guy who killed her—the first day I went outside, I got inside his head. He was thinking about killing her then, and I didn't do anything about it. He looked normal, you know? Sometimes when I'm angry, I might think about hurting someone. But he meant it."

"You didn't know," Harriet said.

"I was the only one who *did* know," Charlie said. "That's my point. We *can* do this, and to me that's reason enough that we should. It's not about whether there's enough demand. It's about what's right."

Mary Beth wrote MARSHA TANNER next to NEED.

Caroline held back a sigh. They must all think she was horribly selfish, and possibly she was. If Harriet hadn't caught her floating in the bathroom she would have kept right on being selfish, without anyone making her feel guilty about it.

"All right," Caroline said. "It's the right thing to do. But do we know how to do it? Just because I can fly doesn't mean I can take down a guy with a gun."

Mary Beth underlined FIGHTING SKILLS.

"I know a little," Harriet said. "I've taken tae kwon do, karate, and wing chun."

"I've seen all of Bruce Lee's movies at least six times," Charlie said.

"Are you making fun of me?" Harriet asked.

"I took the free self-defense class the UW Police teach," Caroline said. "But they didn't teach me anything about fighting while flying."

"Can you teach the rest of us what you know?" Mary Beth asked Harriet. She had written H: TKD, KARATE, WIN CHUNG (SP?) on the board.

"Maybe," Harriet said. "But we can't do it at the SERF or anything."

"We could do it on my parents' land," Jack said. "There's enough acreage that we could work without being noticed or interrupted."

"My dad might pay for me to start classes again," Harriet said. "He'll worry less if he thinks I can kick ass."

Mary Beth wrote JACK'S PARENTS' LAND—TRAINING.

"I don't know if I can fight, or even train," Charlie said. "When I get that close to somebody, I just sort of fall into their head."

"Can't you control it at all?" Harriet asked. "I couldn't control the invisibility at first, but now I'm doing fine."

"I can't turn it off," Charlie said. "It's like Mary Beth's strength—I just have to deal with it. The hat helps some."

"Maybe we can see about getting you some more effective headgear," Mary Beth said.

"I don't think we've addressed the fact," Caroline said, "that the moment we use our powers on someone, we'll be breaking the law, whether they're bad guys or not."

"I've thought about that." Mary Beth underlined LEGALITY. "But I think ethical considerations outweigh the legal ones. If we see someone being assaulted or robbed, we have a moral obligation to do anything we can. In other cases, that might mean calling the police. We're able to intervene more directly, but we have to stay anonymous in order to protect ourselves."

"Maybe we shouldn't be anonymous," Charlie said. "Maybe someone could help us."

"I agree with Jack on that," Mary Beth said. "There are too many unknowns. We might not be safe, or our families."

"It's different for me," Charlie said. "I was supposed to go home this weekend, but I had to tell my parents I was sick. Then I had to talk them out of coming down here."

He hunched forward in his chair. "I'm not saying I'd turn you guys in. If I decide to tell someone, I'll leave you out of it. But I keep thinking maybe there's someone who could help me out. I mean, now that it's happened, I can't believe it's never happened before. There might be some medicine or special training or something to make this a little easier."

Caroline shifted in her seat. She hadn't really thought about Charlie's situation. Everyone else was energized by their new abilities, while he seemed drained, almost shrunken. "Maybe we can figure out some kind of headgear, like Mary Beth said. We should at least try that before you give yourself up to be poked and prodded."

Charlie nodded. "We can try it. But I really hope it works."

Mary Beth turned back to her easel. "Next item is SCHEDULING, as in, do any of us have the time to add crime fighting to their life?"

"I do," Jack said. "I could have stopped a dozen muggings in the time we've been in this meeting."

"Settle down, Flash," Harriet said. "You don't need to show off."

"I don't think I can call myself Flash," Jack said. "DC Comics might sue."

"We'll talk about code names later," Mary Beth said. "Right now we're talking about time considerations. We may have to plan on working in groups of two or three, for the most part. It would be best if we could manage nightly patrols." Mary Beth wrote SMALL GROUPS and PATROLS under SCHEDULING.

"We should invest in a police scanner," Jack said. "That way we can know when something's going on, and maybe help."

"Yeah," Caroline said. "That way we can always be sure to have cops around to arrest us afterward."

Mary Beth wrote down POLICE SCANNER. "OK. I think we've all got things to work on. Jack and Harriet will look into training, and I'll check out police scanners. Charlie, can you figure out a time for another meeting in about a week? And there was one other thing . . ."

"Costuming," Jack said.

"Oh, yes," Mary Beth said. "I was hoping Caroline would take charge of that. Could you design costumes for us? Something non-spandex?"

Caroline glared at Mary Beth, knowing she'd been played. She'd been making her own clothes since she was ten, but she'd never dressed superheroes before.

"I'll work on it," she said finally. She wondered if she hadn't known that this was going to happen all along—the team, everything. Maybe she'd been so angry because she felt guilty for not pursuing it on her own.

"Are we done?" Jack said. "I'm starving."

"You ate a sack of hamburgers and most of a watermelon before the meeting," Harriet said.

"We can wrap up," Mary Beth said. "I hope you'll all take a look at the handouts. And do think about code names for next time." She took down her easel pad, and Harriet helped her carry the water pitcher and glasses. Jack was already gone.

Caroline was left with Charlie.

"You should probably go first," he said.

"Because if I don't, you'll get a headful of me when you walk past?"

"Right."

"Did that happen after we . . ."

"Rocked the casbah? Shook the pillars of heaven?"

"I don't know that we did either of those things."

"Are you kidding? Herds of buffalo thundered across the prairies. Eagles wept."

"I don't remember much, to be honest."

"I don't either," Charlie said. "But it's you and me, so it must have been something spectacular. Who's to say it wasn't?"

"I see." Caroline laughed. "So, the earth tilted on its axis."

"Now you've got the idea. It was the best sex ever known to man. We could never top it."

"We shouldn't even try."

"Nope." Charlie still looked like the living dead, but his tone was light. "We might knock the moon out of orbit."

Caroline's shoulders had relaxed far enough for her to realize how tense she had been. "So, what did you hear?" she asked.

"Nothing incriminating."

"Good. Well. I have to go design some superhero costumes." She stood. "You know, if you ever . . . if we can get your power under control, maybe I could take you flying. It's pretty incredible."

"Sure. If I can get this under control."

Caroline looked out the window—it was gray outside, the streetlights just coming on. It was going to be a nice night for flying.

She started to say more, but the Stop-and-Starts began buzzing and pounding from the attic next door.

**T**he baby didn't like jelly, Prudence Palmeiro decided. Prudence could eat an entire jar of salsa with chips for lunch, a black bean enchilada with extra chili peppers for dinner, drink three cans of Diet Coke, and sleep soundly all night. But a little grape jelly on her toast in the morning, and she spent the rest of the day gnawing on Tums.

She should start taking notes on foods that made her sick. She had four and a half months to figure out the kid's food preferences, without ever having to deal with turned-up noses or watching him push his food around the plate. She was already thinking of the baby as a he, although she didn't know for certain and didn't want to know. She wanted there to be a surprise at the end of all this.

She peeled more paper off the roll and popped another antacid into her mouth. "So that covers the stories for the rest of this week, right?"

"Just about," said Bill Boxer, her producer. "They want a reedit on the campus sexual assault story."

Prudence bit into the Tums. "Again?"

"The dean's office is revising their statement."

"God." Prudence shook her head. "Tell me something good."

Bill looked at Tommy Tang, Prudence's cameraman. "Do you want to tell her?" he asked.

"Kindersley Construction is under investigation," Tommy said. "Someone in the governor's office saw the report and decided they couldn't ignore it."

"That *is* good," she said.

"The station is very pleased," Bill said.

"Pleased enough to let me out of some of these mommy stories? Car seat safety, kids' summer reading clubs, the feature on the school superintendent—"

"We've been over this."

"Have we? Remind me."

Bill looked at Tommy for help, but Tommy just shrugged. "The station wants to exploit your image."

"That would be the image of a successful woman of color, right?"

"That would be the image of a successful young woman of color pregnant with her first child. The station wants to soften your image a little. You come across a little cold to some people."

"Because I do tough investigations? Because I practice journalism?" Prudence leaned back and shut her eyes. "God, I hate this business."

"No, you don't," Tommy said.

"No, I don't. Bill, I'll do that crap, but I won't go soft. And I want something serious."

"Car seat safety is serious."

"You know what I'm talking about. The sexual assault story?"

"I'll fight for it at the rundown," Bill said. "I promise. But it would help if you would agree to do the pregnancy updates."

The station wanted her to do periodic reports on her pregnancy, to highlight health issues for expectant mothers and their newborns. They thought it would be a great ratings coup. Prudence thought it sounded like a desperate plot twist on a stale sitcom.

"Tell them we'll do a feature on my OB/GYN visit next week if they run the sexual assault story tonight."

Bill's eyebrows went straight up. "You sure you want to do that?"

"It seems to be the only way I can get any leverage. Tell them I'll give them two reports a month if they let me do two stories *I* want."

"I'll tell them."

He would, Prudence knew; he would make it clear that it was an ultimatum while still being diplomatic. That was why she worked with him, and not with Tamara, who was a perfectly competent producer. Bill was far better than competent, and Prudence hoped she would be able to take him with her when the network came calling.

"What else have you got for me?"

"There is one thing, but there's not enough there to go with yet."

"What is it?"

"A lot of strange police reports over the weekend. Tommy talked to the watch commander."

"Yeah," Tommy said. "People claim that some invisible guy was running around town. Stopped a purse snatcher and saved a kid on a tricycle from being hit by a car. A few other things, but they were sort of confused."

"An invisible man? Come on, guys."

"There are thirty-four different reports," Tommy said, "ranging from runaway dogs being returned to bicycles being righted as they were about to fall. And for every incident reported, the watch commander said there are probably four that go unreported."

"Every report mentioned someone invisible?"

"Every report said the benefactor was never seen. He must have been getting around pretty fast, too. There were reports from everywhere between Sun Prairie and Middleton, sometimes only ten minutes or so apart."

"That would have to be an entire team of invisible people." Prudence fished another Tums out of the roll. She wondered if the baby was going to come out of the womb with a craving for antacids. "Stay on that one. And get me a copy of the police reports."

It was an old UW football helmet, a remarkably ugly design from the early 1970s: white, with a red oval into which an anemic white *W* had been squashed. The upper arms of the *W* had been truncated by the oval, making it look droopy and tired. Charlie imagined Badger football circa 1972, players drowsing in the huddle, linemen falling forward on the grass before the ball was snapped.

"Found it at an antiques store," Caroline said. "If it works, I'll paint it up and make it pretty." She sat across the living room, far enough away that all Charlie got from her was a dim sense of discomfort. The tinfoil-and-pipe-cleaner contraption under his cap wasn't blocking everything anymore. He hadn't told anybody. He was tired of them feeling sorry for him.

Caroline had drilled several holes in the helmet and threaded bits of stereo wire through. The interior was lined with aluminum foil, and she had grounded the stereo wire to the foil. Then she had connected the other ends to numerous silicate gel packs of the DO-NOT-EAT variety and taped them to the outside of the helmet.

"Thanks," Charlie said, because it would be rude to say what he was thinking.

"Go ahead and try it out," Caroline said.

"OK," Charlie said. "It might be better . . ." He shrugged, but she didn't get the hint.

"What?"

"Nothing." He wasn't going to ask her to leave if she was willing to stay. "Here goes." He reached for the helmet with one hand and pulled off his cap with the other.

He never managed to put it on. His skull felt as though it were imploding under the barrage of thoughts. Caroline's came first: her confused feelings for him, her directionless anger and deep sense of betrayal. But other thoughts piled on top of hers, rage and sorrow and ecstasy tackling him and then flowing to some inaccessible place inside, like water down a drain. He tried to fight, to swim up and away from it all. The minds would drown him if he didn't escape.

"Go," he called to Caroline over the rush of voices inside. He didn't know if she heard him or if she obeyed. He had the sense that he was lying on the floor, but in truth he was underwater, fighting the undertow and losing. His lungs were stripped away by the jagged edges of foreign minds. They cut him to ribbons, shredded the ribbons into bits, and sheared the bits to cells, molecules, atoms.

He woke on a bare concrete floor facing a bare concrete wall. He rolled onto his back and saw a bare concrete ceiling far above. Two men were looking down at him.

"About time you got here," said the first man. He had clean-cut brown hair and wore a cream-colored turtleneck with gray Dockers and burgundy loafers. His socks were argyle.

Charlie sat up, facing another bare concrete wall.

"About time you got here," said the second man. He had a brown ponytail and beard and wore a wrinkled flannel shirt over a torn T-shirt and cutoff jeans. His feet were bare.

Charlie didn't remember standing, but he was on his feet. "Where am I?"

"Exactly," said the first man, and raised a martini glass to him.

"Dude," said the second man, and toasted him with a joint.

"Who are you?" Charlie asked.

"Mental matrix Madroxes," answered the second man.

He looked familiar. They both did. "You're—"

"Charles," said the first man.

"Chuck," said the second man.

"You mean, this is—"

"Home," said the first man.

"It's so quiet here," Charlie said.

"Can't you hear it?" asked Chuck.

Charles waved a hand, and a choir of Charlies emerged from the darkness. They sang his lusts, his longings, his loneliness; his preferences, his peeves, his prejudices. They washed over him so swiftly that he hardly recognized them as his own.

Charles waved his hand again, and the choir went silent. "That's merely the overture," he said, lighting a cigar.

Chuck nodded, and took a hit off his joint. "You gotta learn the score."

*I'm reading my own thoughts*, Charlie thought.

*I would have thought that was patently obvious*, thought Charles.

Their thoughts played projection-style over the walls, like in a bad Oliver Stone movie. Fish swam through the air, their scales glittering with thoughts.

" 'First, know thyself,' said Aurelius," Charles said.

"No, man," said Chuck. "It was Seneca."

"How do I do this?" Charlie asked.

"Learn to swim," said Charles.

Chuck motioned at a worn but comfortable-looking chair that hadn't been there a moment before. "This could take a while," he said. Charlie sat.

Chuck reclined on a mushroom cap, wearing a multicolored terry cloth robe and sucking on a hookah. His beard was stained with resin and spit.

"You got to let go of the world a bit," he said. "You don't know what you think you know, you know?"

"No," Charlie said.

"He's speaking of introspection," said Charles from a throne upon a raised dais. He wore a smoking jacket and an ascot and dark pants with a sharp crease. "Not introspection as most people experience it, however. You have to be comfortable in your own head before you can swim in the mindstream."

"You have to find yourself, is what he's saying." Chuck blew pot smoke at a passing school of fish.

"I'm not looking for me," Charlie said. The smoke tasted like something he used to know.

"You live an unexamined life," said Charles. "One life, many facets."

"One dude, many faces." Chuck leaned back on the mushroom cap. "Stalker, slacker, masturbator."

Charles spoke from the upside-down throne. "Lover, worker, intellectual."

"Pervert," said Chuck.

"Gentleman," said Charles.

The fine print on the inside of Charlie's head was a case study of himself, a *mappamundi*. The evidence was all there. The fish giggled and changed colors and swam through him.

"Get it?" asked Chuck.

He was starting to.

# THURSDAY

Harriet still couldn't stand whiskey. Sometimes she woke with the smell in her nostrils, and when that happened it was a sure bet she wasn't going to fall asleep again; memory tied her stomach up in knots and set a dark weight on her forehead.

The boys' locker room at the SERF wasn't much different from the girls'. There was no tampon dispenser, and she was fairly certain there weren't as many mirrors, but otherwise it was much the same. Except that to her new eyes it looked completely different. She was growing accustomed to walking in two dimensions, although she still had to move slowly when she was invisible. But she didn't think she would ever be used to the way that colors jumped out at her: the powdery blue of the lockers, the tobacco-stain yellow of the wall tiles, the honey blond of the benches. Not to mention the pinks, browns, and yellows of naked male skin—but that wasn't why she was here.

The benches at Madison South High School had been white

wood-grained plastic. These benches were real wood, smooth, varnished. They looked comfortable.

Xavier had his back to her. He was knotted with muscle; there was no fat on him that she could see. She wondered if he was using steroids. Maybe he had been using them then. He had a tattoo now, a tiger on his left bicep. It hadn't been there four years ago.

She decided he wasn't using steroids. He was smart, she knew that. They hadn't been strangers in high school, not like they were now. They had been in debate together. Xavier was a good speaker; he had a musical voice, not too deep, but smooth, precise. He made you forget you were in a debate, forget to rebut his points, forget to do anything but listen. Mrs. Molina had loved him. But it wasn't his debating skills that had got him a full-ride scholarship. Universities didn't recruit debaters like they did football players.

It didn't smell like a locker room in here, not really. There was sweat, but no lingering, stale odor of young bodies. It wasn't right. She knew it was four years later and a different place, but it wasn't right.

Whiskey, and a smooth, musical voice, and maybe a little bit of attraction, those were the things that had gotten her into trouble. She remembered the feel of the bench against her back, cool at first and then warm from her heat, damp with her sweat; it was the most vivid sensation she could recapture. She didn't remember penetration, not really. She hadn't felt the pain until the next morning, along with the hangover.

X, they called him. His real name was Xavier Tyler, but everyone called him X. He encouraged it. It was a street name for a boy who'd grown up far from the streets. His father was a vice president at Rayovac, and his mother worked at University Hospital. Whatever he wanted, he got.

She wondered how tall he was now. Six-foot-four? He looked bigger to her, but maybe that was her new eyes, or maybe it was the shadow he had cast these four years.

He had waved the bottle at her after taking a swig, mischief but not menace in his eyes. When she had declined, he made her an offer. If she drank, he would answer her questions. It was an important story, the last game before the playoffs, and she needed a quote from the star senior running back. She was the first junior to be editor of the Madison South newspaper, and she didn't feel like she'd proved herself yet. She took the drink.

He was almost dressed now. His clothes fit like a second skin. Sometimes in class she heard girls talking about him, wondering who he was dating. Girls who talked about total yards and the NFL draft as if they were ESPN commentators. He was big news. His name had appeared in nearly every edition of *The Campus Voice* since she had joined the staff. He was handsome, articulate. His grades were good.

It had turned into a game. One drink, one question. Sometimes she thought back on the Harriet Bishop of four years ago and hated her for her naïveté. Her questions had been good ones, at first. She was determined to do a good job. Of course he would answer her questions. Why didn't she have a seat? He was just going to celebrate a little—he put his finger to his lips and pulled the bottle of Jack Daniel's from his bag.

She had made up his quotes later. She even felt guilty about it. She didn't make him sound stupid, or write about what had happened, and he never said a word to her about putting words in his mouth. They hadn't spoken since that night.

Four years ago he'd had a slightly wild reddish brown Afro, but now he kept it shaved close to the scalp. Clean-cut and well behaved. Team captain and spokesman. Insistent upon graduating before submitting to the draft. Model citizen.

She knew she had given him an opening when, near the end of her list of questions, she had veered off the script. Instead of asking him about potential playoff rivals she had asked him if he had a girlfriend. She took a drink to cover her discomfort; he had smiled and accepted the bottle from her. She didn't even remember his answer. She remembered him unzipping his pants and realizing that they were alone in the locker room. She remembered him sticking his crotch in her face, and she remembered shaking her head, telling him no. Somehow, he had made the alternative seem like a bargain, like it was an either/or situation and not one she could opt out of entirely. He had let her take off her own pants, and she remembered thinking, ludicrously, that it was nice of him.

Now he shut his locker, then swore and started to twirl the dial of the combination lock. Almost every day in the last two weeks he had done this. He always forgot something, usually his sunglasses, or one of the books he carried under his arm. *The Souls of Black Folk*, or *The Autobiography of Malcolm X*, or *Go Tell It on the Mountain*. She was sure he had read them, and that he would happily share his opinions of each. He wasn't stupid, not at all.

She had never told her father; she had never told anyone. It wasn't that she blamed herself. It was that she didn't want it to define her. People she had never met would think of her as That Girl Who Was Raped. The victim. Some of them would think she was a liar. Her father—her father might kill Xavier. He was not a violent man, but it would have cut him deeply, and she did not know what he might be capable of doing.

Xavier—she would not call him X, because she would not let him pretend he was someone else—Xavier opened his locker and pulled out a Ralph Ellison book. He shut the locker and grabbed his bag.

She spat and struck him just on the neck. Then she walked out, hearing him swear behind her. She looked in the mirrors as she passed, but she didn't see her reflection. It was like she wasn't even there.

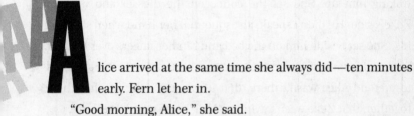

**A**lice arrived at the same time she always did—ten minutes early. Fern let her in.

"Good morning, Alice," she said.

"Good morning, Mrs. Robinson." Fern had tried to get Alice to call her by her first name, but Alice seemed determined to keep some distance. She wasn't cold with Zeke, but with the rest of them she was always businesslike, almost formal. Fern thought she understood. It had to be hard to lose a patient every few months. Growing close to the family would only make it harder.

"He's still asleep." Fern held the door while Alice brought her bag in. "Would you like a cup of coffee?"

"Oh, that's not necessary," Alice said.

"It's no problem," Fern said.

"Black, then. And thank you." Alice hung her jacket on one of the hooks near the door. It was a cool, overcast morning, but Fern could tell that the sun would burn the clouds off in an hour or so and the day would be a hot one.

"I'll bring it in to you." Fern went to the kitchen before Alice could parry her offer with another polite protestation. Offered a drink, dessert, or a second helping, most midwesterners would respond "Oh, I shouldn't" or "No, really, I'm fine." Fern's mother, a transplanted Brit, had once brought a dinner party to a halt by taking the ritual protestations at face value and refusing to serve any more food or drinks. After twenty minutes Fern's father had taken mercy upon the squirming guests and asked them if they cared for another helping.

Fern brought the coffee to Zeke's room, where Alice was just waking him up. She set the coffee on the dresser and went to Zeke's side. He didn't speak, just squeezed her hand when she took his. She sat beside him on the bed and ran her fingers over his hair while Alice took his blood pressure and his temperature. Fern tried to pretend Alice wasn't there, that it was just Zeke and her there together, that Zeke wasn't dying and her heart wasn't breaking.

When it was time for Zeke's sponge bath Fern kissed him on the forehead and told him she loved him and smiled to show him he didn't need to exert himself to answer her.

She made an early lunch for the Carlson twins. They'd been out spraying the corn all morning, and they came back hungry. Fern watched them eat the beef stew, remembering days when Zeke came in with an appetite for more than just lunch. More than once he'd left the house just moments before the bus dropped off one of the kids, tucking in his shirt and stealing a last kiss as he ran out the door.

After the Carlson boys went back to the fields, Fern started on the bathroom. At first she was just going to clean the tiles in the shower, but she found herself washing the rugs and scouring the sink and scrubbing between the floor tiles with an old toothbrush. Morty found her there a little before noon.

"Ma?" He stood in the doorway, frowning down at her.

"Hi, Morty." Fern would never get used to calling him Jack. "I'm cleaning the bathroom."

"I see that. How is he?"

She waved toward the room at the end of the hall. "Alice is with him."

"She said he's asleep."

"Well, then he's all right, I guess." It was an ugly thought, but sleep seemed to be the only time Zeke was all right. When he was asleep he wasn't in pain and he didn't know he was dying.

"My roommates and I were going to have a picnic over by the old tree house," Morty said. "Is that OK?"

"As long as you don't go up in it," Fern said. "The wood's rotted through. Which reminds me, are you ever going to take down that garage?"

"Yes," he said. He seemed jittery, like he'd been drinking a lot of coffee. "But not today, OK?"

"Seems to me I've heard that quite a few times."

"I'll do it, don't worry. Next week. I'll see you in a few hours."

"OK. Have fun."

After she polished the mirror and the doorknobs and put out fresh towels and hung the rugs out to dry, she started on the kitchen. She had finished the oven when Quinn called.

"How is he?" she asked.

"He's fine. Alice is here," Fern said, not because it was unusual—Alice came every weekday—but because there wasn't much else to say. "How are you?"

"Tired. Becky's still got the flu. None of us have slept in three nights."

"Do you want me to ask Grace if she'll drive up for the weekend and watch her?"

"Oh, Mom, I'd love that, but I can't leave her when she's sick. Grace can stay the weekend if she wants, though. We could rent some movies." There was a pause, and Fern could almost hear Quinn thinking. *I should invite Mom. But who would watch Dad then? Change the subject.* "Is it hot there? It's scorching here."

Fern hadn't looked out a window in hours. Thank God for central air—the thermometer on the back porch read 93, and she knew it was humid. She hoped Morty and his friends were staying out of the sun. She didn't even want to go out to take the bathroom rugs off the line. She was like her mother in that respect; the midwestern summers made her wilt, while she drew strength from the winters. Her father, on the other hand, had never stopped moving, in warm weather or cold.

She half-listened to Quinn while she readied a roast beef for dinner. Maybe Morty and his friends would stay. If they didn't, she'd have sandwiches for the Carlson twins' lunches through the next week.

Quinn talked about preschool and Randy's boss and some movie they'd rented last weekend. Fern let her talk. It did her good—that was Quinn, always had been, chatting to fill the silence, talking when she was nervous, when she was angry, when she was happy. Fern had never been one for talking much. The funny thing was that once she and Zeke were together she had become the talkative one, because Zeke never spoke at all unless he had something to say. Probably it was their fault that Quinn was such a talker, she supposed. She just couldn't stand the quiet around the house when she was growing up.

After a while Quinn ran out of steam, and Fern said good-bye, telling her she'd talk to Grace. She went to check on Zeke.

He and Alice were watching *Leave It to Beaver*. "How are you two doing?" she asked.

"We're doing well," Alice said. "I was just about to come and make up something for Zeke's lunch."

"Oh, I can do that," Fern said. "You know, it's after two. If you wanted to leave a little bit early today, that would be fine with me."

Alice looked at her watch. "Hm. I wouldn't mind, actually. I could stay late on Monday if you like."

"I don't think that's necessary," Fern said. "Do you, honey?"

Zeke took a slow breath and raised his head to shake it side to side.

Alice hesitated, and for the second time that day Fern was sure she knew what someone was thinking. *He's not well. But he'll be no better if I stay.*

Alice stood. "I'll need to check your blood pressure and temperature again, Zeke. Then I'll leave the two of you alone."

Grace arrived as Alice was leaving. She beeped her horn at Alice as she left and parked her rusting Honda in the spot Alice's Taurus had just vacated.

"Hey, Mom," Grace said, bouncing up the steps to where Fern stood in the doorway. Sweat trickled down Fern's back, but the heat seemed to have no effect on Grace. It wasn't until she was inside that she seemed to lose all her energy. She sprawled out on the couch and groaned.

"I hate work," she said.

"You only work three days a week." Fern moved to the kitchen, where the potatoes she was planning to mash were just beginning to boil. "It's not going to get any easier," she said.

"It will after I'm a famous singer," Grace said. "Where's Jack? I saw his truck out there."

"He and his roommates are having a picnic down by the old tree house."

"Was Charlie with him?"

"I suppose." Grace had a crush on Charlie Frost, but Fern didn't worry about it. Charlie was a nice boy, nice enough that she was sure he wouldn't take advantage of a seventeen-year-old girl.

"Quinn called," Fern said, to change the subject. "She was wondering if you wanted to go up for the weekend."

"Oh, Mom. I don't want to drive all the way to Appleton."

"Not even to see your niece?"

"I don't know. I'm going to go say hi to Jack."

"And Charlie? Don't you want to shower and change first? Maybe get your hair done?"

"Very funny, Mom." Grace came into the kitchen and stood with arms folded in the doorway. "How is he?"

Fern shrugged. "He's no better and no worse."

"Should I go say hi to him?"

"That's up to you, honey."

"But I don't want to tire him out."

Fern knew that Grace knew that there was very little that didn't tire Zeke out. Grace wanted to be let off the hook for a little while, to not think about her father dying for an hour or so.

"Go see Morty," Fern said. "You can say hi to your father when you get back."

"I can do it now, if you think I should."

"Let him rest now. We'll watch a little TV together later."

"OK, Mom. I love you, Mom."

"I love you too, Grace."

Grace had been Fern's grandmother's name, a woman she had never met who looked very severe and humorless in photographs, except for one in which she was hiking the hem of her dress up above her knee and laughing open-mouthed. "That picture was taken before the Blitz," Fern's mother had told her, and as a little girl Fern had always wondered if the bombs over London had changed everyone that way, if the city had been a place filled with laughing and dancing people one day, and become somber and dark the next. She wondered the same thing about her own Grace. When Zeke was finally too tired to keep fighting, would Grace lose the light that she seemed to carry with her, her stubborn fantasies of stardom?

Not long after Grace was gone the Carlsons came in. "We should have the spraying finished Monday," said Quentin, pulling his John Deere cap off to reveal hair soaked with sweat.

"It looks good," said Yale, "but we could use some more rain."

"I know," Fern said. They hadn't had a drop for two weeks.

"Oh, say," said Yale, "I think you might have an eagle on the property, or a big hawk. I saw something big flying around by that stand of trees on the south end. I didn't get a good look at it before it set down in the trees, but it was quite a sight."

"He says he saw it," said Quentin. "I didn't see a damn thing."

"It was there." Yale shoved his brother, and Fern scooted the two of them out before they started wrestling in the house.

Fern checked the roast and left the potatoes to cool. It was a lot of food, she realized, looking at it. She had never gotten accustomed to cooking for three instead of seven. In the back of her head she was still tailoring meals to the whole family, to Lloyd's dislike of gravy and Ursula's milk allergy. If it weren't for Morty's appetite she'd be throwing leftovers away by the pound.

She washed her hands, went to Zeke's room, and stood in the doorway. His head was turned away from her, looking out the window at the afternoon shadows. He turned and saw her and smiled.

She crossed to the bed and lay down beside him, taking his hand in hers. He put his other hand to her cheek and then ran it over her hair.

"How are you?" he asked, and she had to fight back tears.

Jack would have been more nervous, he thought, than Harriet seemed to be. She and Mary Beth stood facing each other, left feet touching at the insoles, right feet behind. "Just push," Harriet told Mary Beth, "but not quite hard enough to snap me in half. First one to move her feet loses."

Mary Beth placed her hands against Harriet's side and leaned into her. Harriet bent back slightly, twisted her torso, and put pressure on Mary Beth's right. Mary Beth pushed back, and Harriet leaned to her own right. Mary Beth's back foot came up off the ground, and she stumbled forward, yelping.

Harriet put a hand to her side. "I think that's going to bruise," she said.

"Sorry," Mary Beth said.

"It's OK. I was just trying to illustrate a point. Being strong isn't enough to win every time. A lot of martial arts is learning to use your opponent's strength and movement against them. Brawling is one thing, but the point of learning this stuff is realizing that *anyone* is vulnerable."

"Except me," Mary Beth said.

"We don't know how invulnerable you are," Caroline called down. She sat high up in one of the aging maples overhead. "A car crusher or an incinerator might hurt you plenty. Don't think you shouldn't be careful just because you're strong."

Mary Beth shrugged but didn't say anything more. Harriet rubbed her side again and nodded at Jack. "Why don't you and Charlie try it?"

Charlie had stood close by throughout the lesson so far, imitating the moves Harriet taught them but otherwise seeming to be lost in his own head. Now he moved over to Jack and flashed him a grin as they positioned themselves. Something about Charlie had changed since the incident with the helmet; he was more confident, less jumpy. He hadn't said much about what had happened, but here he was with no hat, no helmet, exuding the same wary contentment that Jack's brother Lloyd had once carried around after he'd finally managed to seal the chicken coop against an infestation of rats.

Jack started slow for Charlie's benefit, but every time he moved, Charlie countered easily. Jack sped up gradually, shifting suddenly from side to side, trying to pull Charlie off balance. But Charlie seemed to know when Jack was faking. He pushed back at just the right moments and otherwise just moved unerringly with Jack. Finally, Jack made a series of moves too quickly for Charlie to react, and Charlie stumbled back, laughing.

"You cheated," Jack said.

"A little, yeah. And you didn't?"

"That's different."

"I didn't read anything that didn't have to do with the fight. Besides, you won. And in about four seconds flat."

"Seemed longer." Jack grinned, but when he met Charlie's eyes they weren't focused on anything.

"Your sister is watching us."

"What?" Jack snapped around, looking for Grace. It had to be Grace—Ursula and Quinn wouldn't be around, Ma would have said something. He didn't think, just dashed to the perimeter of the copse of trees and found her crouched behind a Norway pine. "What are you doing, spying on us?"

Grace screamed and fell back on her ass. Jack realized that he'd given himself away completely, so he was surprised when Grace's first question after recovering was "How did that girl get so far up in that tree?"

Jack said the first thing that came into his head. "We're making a movie."

"You're making a movie?" Grace asked.

"Sure. Didn't you tell her, Jack?" Charlie came around the tree and shook his head just slightly at Jack.

*I panicked*, Jack thought.

"Where's the camera?" Grace asked.

"Caroline's got it up there." Jack forced himself to speak slowly. "We're doing some overhead shots."

"Really?" Grace tumbled to her feet and put a hand on Charlie's shoulder. "Can I be in the movie?"

"No," Jack said.

"I was asking Charlie." Grace whispered something in Charlie's ear, but instead of blushing and stammering like he usually did when Grace flirted, Charlie smiled and nodded without looking at her. Grace stared at him for a moment, then walked into the clearing to where Harriet and Mary Beth stood. "Are you all in the movie?" she asked.

"No," said Mary Beth at the same moment Harriet said, "Yes."

"Grace, we've got to finish a scene," Jack said. "Please go away."

"That's not going to work," Charlie whispered.

"What's the scene?" Grace looked up at Caroline. "You never did tell me how she got up so high. Even Ursula never climbed that high."

"What are you guys talking about?" Caroline shouted down. "I can't hear you!"

"What's she using for a camera, a tree branch? The light's not very good here. Is this some kind of a Dogme thing?" She kicked at a water bottle Harriet had left lying in the grass. "What's this movie about, anyway?"

Mary Beth and Harriet looked at each other, then at Jack.

"What did she say?" Caroline yelled.

"We're not making a movie," Charlie said. "She figured that out already," he told Jack.

"Will somebody tell me what's going on?" Caroline screamed.

Grace folded her arms and stared at Jack.

"Come on down, Caroline." Jack said it loud enough that everyone but Charlie jumped, and Caroline slid off the bough and drifted down to the ground like a spider descending from a web.

Grace's arms and jaw dropped, and she didn't speak for a few seconds. Then she took three quick steps and punched Jack in the shoulder.

"You're a superhero and you didn't tell me?"

"Ow. It just happened!"

"Come on, Mr. Strong Man. That didn't hurt."

"I'm not the strong one," Jack said. Grace looked at Charlie, who pointed at Mary Beth.

"I'm bigger than her," Grace said.

"Grace, you can't tell anyone about this."

"You have to let me come with you, then. Hey, do you have costumes?"

"So much for secret identities," Caroline said.

"Grace, you're not coming with us, and you can't tell anyone."

"I will. I'll tell Mom."

"How old *are* you?" Harriet asked.

"Grace, come here." Jack walked out of the clearing to within sight of the house, and after a moment Grace followed. In the sunlight the full heat of the day struck Jack. Sweat broke out on his forehead, and he felt dizzy.

"Listen." His own voice sounded distant. "I'll talk to the others about letting you come to a meeting or something later on, but right now I need you to please leave us alone."

"What's your power?" Grace asked.

"Didn't you see before?"

"I'm not sure what I saw."

"All right." Jack took a deep breath, then took off for the house. He slowed down enough to slip the door open, then ran to the kitchen, made himself a sandwich, and streaked back to where Grace stood. He was halfway finished with the sandwich by the time he got there.

"Where'd you go? Where'd you get that?"

"The house." He'd been starving; he hadn't realized.

"You were—you were standing there, and then you were gone. Then I blinked—"

"Yeah, I'm really fast, OK?"

"Oh, man. I wish I had some homework for you to do."

"Grace, I wouldn't do your homework."

"Yeah, but it would be cool."

He finished the sandwich. "Will you leave now? Please?"

"Do you promise to let me come with you guys later?"

"Do you promise not to tell anyone?"

Grace held out her hand, and Jack shook it. "I promise," she said.

"Me, too. Now please, Gracie. I love you, but get lost."

'm not coming out," Mary Beth said through the door of her bedroom.

"Very funny," Caroline said. "Come on, let's see you."

"No."

Caroline looked at the couch, where Harriet and Charlie sat in their costumes, eating popcorn and watching the news. Caroline had been most worried about the two of them—she had been afraid that being given the black costume would offend Harriet in some way, and she had been sure that Charlie would object to wearing yellow—but they had given her the least trouble so far. Harriet loved the monochromatic look, and Charlie seemed charmed by Caroline's insistence on referring to his costume as gold-colored.

Caroline was amazed by the change in Charlie. He'd tried to send her away that day with the helmet, but she had stayed with him, debating whether or not to call an ambulance. For nearly an hour he had lain there mumbling, the helmet forgotten on the floor. When she'd tried to put it on him he'd opened his eyes and shoved it away. "We're figuring it out," he'd said. And it seemed that he and whoever else he was talking about had done so. He'd cleaned himself up since—even if his hair was getting a bit shaggy—and he seemed a lot more together.

"You've got two minutes," Caroline called to Mary Beth. "Then I'm coming in."

Someone knocked at the door, and Charlie and Harriet froze in mid-munch. Caroline put her eye to the peephole. "Relax," she said. "It's Jack."

She let him in and handed him a bundle of red and white. "Go in the bathroom and try it on," she said.

"OK." There was a rush of air, and he swept past her into the bathroom. The door opened again almost as soon as it had shut, and Jack stepped out in the red bodysuit, looking down at the white star on his chest.

"Why a star?" he asked.

"It's a unifying symbol," Caroline said. "Five points on the star, five of us. How does it feel?"

"OK," Jack said. "A little exposed." He turned away from her and adjusted himself at the crotch.

"The Lycra should breathe pretty well. You can accessorize, though. Add a belt or a jacket, if you want."

"What about these gloves?"

"They button to the sleeve." Caroline showed him how to attach the white gloves to the rest of the costume, and then helped him put on the mask.

"I'm not sure this mask is going to work," Jack said. "It only hides my eyes. Anyone who sees us is going to have height, build, hair color, skin color—"

"It's the Clark Kent effect," Harriet said. "Nobody's going to recognize you."

"Clark Kent? That was a comic book. This is real."

"And denial ain't just a river in Egypt. No one's going to believe that plain old Jack Robinson is quicker than . . . well, you know."

"I'll get you a helmet if you like," Caroline said. "But I don't think you need to worry. There have to be a few hundred guys who look like you in Madison."

"Yeah. It'll take the cops at least a week to figure out which one is the superhero. I want a helmet."

"Fine." Caroline walked back to Mary Beth's door. "You ready now?"

"I'm not coming out," Mary Beth said.

Caroline opened the door, and Mary Beth stepped back, throwing her arms around herself, hiding the costume from view.

"Let me see." Caroline stepped in and shut the door behind her. "What's wrong with it?"

Mary Beth shook her head. "There's nothing wrong with it."

"Then what's the problem? Mary Beth, put your hands down. Jesus."

Mary Beth straightened and let her arms fall to her sides.

"Wow." Caroline had made Mary Beth's costume a deep green color, not even realizing that it matched her eyes perfectly. The fabric clung to Mary Beth's curves, and the built-in bra lifted her breasts, preventing the material from flattening them. In addition, the costume slimmed her waist and her thighs and gave her smooth lines. Mary Beth usually wore sweatshirts or shapeless T-shirts that hid her figure entirely. Caroline had never seen Mary Beth wear anything nearly so revealing.

"You look good, Mary Beth."

"It isn't me."

"Well, it's not me wearing that. It's you."

"I know, but . . ."

"I know but. If I were your mother I might think this little anxiety attack was adorable, but I'm not and I don't. So come on out."

"When are you going to put your costume on?"

"As soon as—"

"Hey! You guys!" Charlie pounded on the door.

"Girls, you mean?" Caroline asked.

"You have to see this," Charlie said. "Come on."

"They just teased a story about an invisible man," Harriet said.

A female reporter sat at a desk with a graphic reading LOCAL BRIEFING beneath her. "And finally, the last couple of weeks have seen a multitude of strange reports of an invisible man helping people out around the Madison area. Reports have come in from as far afield as Sauk Prairie, and almost all credit everything from the return of lost dogs to the foiling of half a dozen purse snatchings to an invisible man who is accompanied by a gust of wind. Now, police don't know what to make of this so far, but a police spokesman told me that with this many reports—and there have been nearly three hundred so far—something must be going on, although the spokesman also said that the department does not believe in invisibility. Rest assured, we'll be following this story as it develops. This is Prudence Palmeiro in the WMAD newsroom. Back to you, Jim."

Mary Beth no longer seemed self-conscious. She was across the living room, shaking her finger in Jack's face. "What the hell have you been doing?"

"Helping people," Jack said. "We're taking too long. Training, costumes, scheduling—I'm surprised we haven't written a statement of purpose. We're talking too much, and not doing anything."

"I agree," Charlie said. "I think it's time to get started."

"I think so, too," Harriet said. "I'm ready."

Caroline shrugged. "What do you think, Mary Beth?"

Mary Beth started to cross her arms over her chest, then dropped them to her sides. "All right," she said. "But how do we begin?"

Death's real name was Benjamin Thatcher, but he planned to have it legally changed after the job, after things had cooled down. He wanted a tattoo to match, but he'd get this one done professionally. He hated Alicia's name on his forearm, especially since it was crooked and fading, like she hadn't used enough ink. He'd get that removed first, then have DEATH tattooed between his shoulder blades, in big Gothic letters. He'd buy some weights to build up his arms and shoulders. Then instead of telling people his name he'd take off his shirt and let them read it off his back. He'd have to figure out something else for the winter, though; maybe a stocking cap with a skull and crossbones, if they made things like that.

He wasn't stupid, not like Alicia's dad used to say, so often that Alicia started believing it and threw him over for that geek at the community college. That guy was going to be sitting in front of a computer getting fat and losing his hair and needing thicker glasses than he already had. That wasn't smart. Smart was doing one job and then sitting pretty for a year. Maybe more, if he was careful and didn't spend it all on cars.

The smartest thing was the wardrobe. They couldn't stand out among the daytime crowd on the Capitol Square, so Death insisted on suits. He hadn't worn his since his aunt's funeral, and it smelled a bit. Reed's didn't fit quite right, and Johnny's was a light blue pastel number from back when Crockett and Tubbs were the thing. But if everything went right, no one would notice them until too late.

It was simple. The security guard would escort the armored car drivers out of the bank just like always. Then Johnny's sister would let herself get knocked over on the sidewalk, distracting the guard. Johnny and Reed would step up to the drivers, show them their guns, and tell them to set the bags on the pavement. Then Death would move in and sweep the bags into his duffel while Reed locked the drivers in the back of the truck and Johnny got the car, parked two spaces behind the loading area. Johnny would pick up Reed and drive away while Death and Johnny's sister just blended into the crowd.

It had to be done fast, and a lot depended on Johnny's sister, which was why Death was watching her from across the street when the guy in red caught her in mid-fall, set her upright, and whispered something in her ear. He was gone a second later; but Johnny's sister went pale and started walking away.

Death wasn't the only one who'd noticed the guy. He'd had a helmet and a big white star on his chest, and a lot of people were staring at the spot where he had been, including the security guard. Johnny and Reed must have thought this was distraction enough, because they moved in on the armored car drivers as planned. But as they drew their guns, a girl in a green bodysuit stepped in front of them. She also had a white star on her chest, Death noticed, in the moment before she grabbed the guns. One went off, but the girl didn't even flinch. She took both guns and crumbled one of them into dust.

People screamed and dropped to the sidewalk, as if there had been not one gunshot but a hundred simultaneous ones. Death started to sweat.

Johnny ran for the car, but Reed took off down the middle of the street. He hadn't gone half a block before a girl in blue swooped down out of the sky and lifted him from his feet and up over the capitol building.

Johnny started the car and screeched into the street. The girl in green stepped in front of the car, and Death thought Johnny was about to go from attempted robbery to vehicular manslaughter until the car crumpled around the girl like she was a solid steel girder anchored in the blacktop.

Death heard sirens. No one was looking at him—they were watching the girl step around the wrecked front of the car and drag Johnny out the window. Death picked up the empty duffel and started walking.

"Stop right there, Mr. Thatcher."

The voice had come from right next to him, but there was no one there. He walked on.

Something hit him across the stomach, then kicked his legs out from under him. He dropped the duffel and sprawled over the sidewalk.

"I said stop." A woman's voice. What the hell was going on?

Hands dragged him to his feet. He tried to squirm out of their grasp, but all he got for his efforts were stares from the people around him.

"Give it up," said the voice.

"Who are you?"

"We're your friendly neighborhood superheroes," said the girl in blue, who had flown in low near Death to drop Reed on the grass. Reed must have passed out while in the air, because he didn't move.

"Is this all of them?" asked the girl in green, holding the struggling Johnny in her arms. Her costume was shredded from the thighs down, but her legs weren't even scratched.

"What a mess," said the girl in blue.

"Sorry. I didn't *plan* to get hit by a car."

"Here's Jack with the last one," said the woman Death couldn't see. The guy in red ran up carrying Johnny's sister.

"Red Star, you mean?" the woman in blue said deliberately.

"Shit."

"This is it," said Red Star.

The woman Death couldn't see sat him on the bench alongside the others, and Red Star pulled out a rope. A half-second later they were tied to the bench in a row, Reed's head lying on Death's shoulder.

The girl in blue took off into the sky, and Red Star picked up the girl in the tattered green and disappeared with her.

It wasn't fair. How was he supposed to plan for superheroes?

f there had just been something to bail with. A pail, a cup, an empty beer can. Then he could have rowed while Dinah bailed. Then he wouldn't have panicked like he had, and they wouldn't have flipped the canoe.

"I'm sorry, Dinah." There were a lot of things to be sorry for; sorry for having drunk so much tequila, sorry for convincing her to come out on the lake with him, sorry for not checking the canoe for leaks first. "I'm sorry," he said again.

"How far out do you think we are?" she asked. Her hair was plastered to her head, and her teeth were chattering. She clung fiercely to the sinking canoe, looking wildly about. "Help!" she called. "Please help us!"

Oliver didn't tell her to save her breath. What would she be saving it for? They were both exhausted. Neither of them could swim all the way to shore.

Oliver didn't think of himself as a quitter. That guy in the movies, the guy who never ran out of ideas, the one who always saved the day in desperate situations—that was the guy he wanted to be. But he had nothing to work with, no tools, no materials. Just a sinking canoe, a pair of Dockers shorts, a blood alcohol level above .10, and a girl whose last thought would probably be hate for him.

He didn't hear the angel at first. It wasn't until Dinah slapped him on the shoulder that he looked up and saw the angel floating above the canoe, her hair blowing around her face, the moon casting a halo around her head.

"It's sinking," Dinah said, and Oliver realized the angel had asked about the canoe.

"I guess you'll have to ride with me, then," said the angel.

Oliver had heard that drowning was the most peaceful way to die, and now he believed it. He wasn't afraid. He would go with the angel wherever she wanted to take him.

"I'll come back for you," the angel told him. Then she swept down and lifted Dinah out of the water by her arms. "Just a little longer," said the angel as the two of them flew out of sight.

Oliver didn't go to church. He thought God was probably out there somewhere, but he'd always figured there would be time later to clean up his act. Not that he'd ever done anything really bad. Minor vandalism, the occasional cow tipping, a little too much beer now and then. The angel, though, that must mean God forgave him. There was nothing to worry about anymore.

The canoe was almost completely submerged. He let go, treading water at first. Then he just spread his arms and lay his head back to let the water wash over him. He looked up at the stars. Maybe once they were in heaven Dinah would forgive him. She had to, didn't she?

He swallowed water, then took it into his lungs, and for a moment he panicked. He coughed, but there was no air to replace the water. He reached up, touched air, slipped down again. He breathed the water, calmer this time. Even if the angel wasn't real, there was nothing he could do. He just wanted to rest.

The water was agitated suddenly, and he told himself not to struggle, then realized he wasn't. The water was rejecting him, spitting him out. No. It was the angel, pulling him up and out of the water. She was swearing.

"Fifteen fucking seconds, you can't hold on? Jesus Christ Almighty."

She had her arms wrapped around his chest, and he coughed continuously as they sped over the water. He had never heard of an angel talking like this.

"It's all right. You're going to be fine," said the angel. "I'm sorry for yelling. I thought I'd lost you."

Oliver looked up at her. She wore white gloves. Why did angels need gloves? Would they be soiled by the touch of mortal flesh?

She set him on the shore in James Madison Park. Dinah sat a few feet away, hunched beneath a blanket.

"Nearly lost this guy," said the angel. "He's got some water in his lungs." She sat him up with his head between his legs and massaged his back. He renewed his coughing with vigor.

"The ambulance is on its way," said a voice in front of him. Oliver looked up but saw nothing. Was God talking to the angel? Had God called an ambulance for him?

"It was just the two of you, right?" the angel asked. "There's no one else out there?"

Oliver shook his head and heard Dinah tell the angel it was just the two of them. So the angel hadn't come to take them to heaven. She had come to save their lives.

"You'd better get out of sight," God said. God had a woman's voice. Oliver wondered if he should tell his dad about that. Oliver's dad was always complaining about Hillary Clinton and Tammy Baldwin and Oprah. He hated feminists. He hated church, too, come to think of it. Maybe he wouldn't tell him after all.

"See you at home," said the angel, and took off into the sky. For the first time Oliver noticed she didn't have any wings.

"You're going to be fine," God said. "They're on their way." Oliver didn't hear the sirens until the ambulances had driven all the way across the grassy park to the beach.

"Tell the angel thanks," he said, but God didn't answer.

# SUNDAY

It was one thing to make the decision. It wasn't as though he hadn't weighed the alternatives over the past months. Every other path led to misery and humiliation, and he'd had enough of that, his entire life long. For a while it seemed like he was getting used to it, like he had accepted that his role was always to be the loser, the butt of the joke. But he had just been swallowing all the shame and anger. Now it was all going to come out in one blast.

He hadn't bought the gun intending to do this. Two apartments in his building had been burglarized in the same month, and he had just wanted to feel safe. That was what he'd told himself. He had no roommates to ask him about it, no children to find it and get into trouble. It had collected dust in the drawer of his bedside table until tonight.

He had means and motive, but he wasn't sure he had the balls to pull the trigger.

He sat on a bench looking over Lake Mendota. It was a warm night, and he was sweating. The gun sat in his lap. At first the cold of it had seeped through his shorts, but by now the metal had absorbed his body heat. It lay hot against his legs, lumpish and angry. He put his hand over it, squeezed the handle.

It wasn't just that she didn't love him. Low as he was, he couldn't have justified dying for that. It was that she didn't care one way or the other. No one did. Even being hated would have given him incentive to keep going a little while longer.

It wasn't even about her, really. It was about the things that loving her did to him. He made a fool out of himself over her. She made him stupid. Maybe he hated her a little bit, for making him feel so out of control, so impotent. He could admit that. But the flaw was in him somewhere, and he couldn't fix it. He lifted the gun, cradled it in his arms. Caressed the trigger with his middle finger, looked out over the lake, up at the stars. A good night for it.

A man in a yellow bodysuit sat down beside him, and he flinched. He hadn't heard anyone approach. He clutched the gun to his chest.

"Bruce, don't do this," said the man in the yellow bodysuit. He had a white star on his chest, like the superheroes he'd read about in the newspaper. "You think things are never going to get better, but you're just depressed. You need to see a doctor."

He'd seen a doctor. He'd given him pills that made him sleep all the time and nearly lost him his job. There wasn't a pill to stop him from loving her.

"You don't love her, Bruce," said the man in the yellow bodysuit. A boy, really. He was thin and his voice was too smooth for him to be more than twenty-five. Bruce considered pointing the gun at the boy, but he didn't want to kill him, as stupid and rude as he was. He just wanted to stop hurting.

He did love her. He loved her and he hated her. She wouldn't understand how right they could have been. She never gave him a chance. It wasn't anything new. He'd get so nervous when he had to speak in class or talk to a girl. He stuttered and blushed and made an ass out of himself. They called him Babbling Bruce.

"That was years ago that they called you that," the boy said. "You should let it go."

But he couldn't. He still stuttered sometimes. He managed to give presentations, provided he snuck a drink or two before, but he couldn't talk to her at all. He couldn't talk to any women. He brought the gun up under his chin, quickly so the boy in yellow couldn't stop him.

"Bruce, don't do this," said the boy. "You're upset because you think she has all this control over you. But killing yourself means giving her all the control you have left."

But it wasn't about her now, if it ever had been. Now that he looked at it clearly, it was about him. It was him that wasn't fit to live, him that wasn't worth it. He slid the gun off his chin and put the barrel into his mouth.

"Bruce, no—"

He pulled the trigger. He shut his eyes and thought of every person he'd ever known, trying to find one who would tell him he was worth something, but he knew already that he wasn't. He didn't feel anything, and he didn't hear anything. He opened his eyes.

The gun hadn't fired. A man in red stood, holding the gun, his finger caught in the hammer. Red, with a white star. More superheroes. Goddamn them.

"I thought I could talk to him," said the man in yellow to the man in red. Not men, boys. They were just boys. They had no idea.

"You tried," said the boy in red. He took off a glove and sucked on his finger. "Man, that hurt. What do you want to do now? We can't leave him here."

Bruce pulled his legs up toward his chest and lay down on the bench. He still hurt. He was still here.

She'd left her mother bleeding at the crossroads, and she was going on to Thebes to marry her father. Except that one of her mother's springer spaniel guards was chasing her with a tommy gun and a physics textbook. She could hear the dog several miles back, explaining in barked Morse code how Newton and Einstein and her high school gym teacher didn't believe she could lift a bowling ball, let alone a city bus.

She was drooling on her arm. Mary Beth sat up and blinked around the classroom, hoping no one had noticed her sleeping. She wiped her mouth with her hand and looked down at her notes. She had written "Disintegration of the Self-Fulfilling Croissant" under the heading "Paper Topics?" Her stomach growled loudly, and Professor Smith looked up at her.

Professor Smith taught graduate seminars in English during the regular school year, he had told them all on the first day of class. He had also told them that the reason he lowered himself to teach an introductory course in English literature over the summer was to give himself an annual lesson in humility. If that was the case, he didn't seem to be learning anything. He dressed like an Oxford don, or at least he dressed as Mary Beth imagined an Oxford don would dress, unless Oxford dons still wore black robes or some such thing, in which case the comparison meant nothing and she needed a long nap. He wore bow ties and white shirts with suspenders holding up dark pants that were either wool or tweed and in either case were totally inappropriate for a Madison summer. And yet Professor Smith never seemed to sweat. His glasses never slid down his nose, his bow tie never needed to be straightened, and the cuffs of his pants legs never rose above the tops of his socks.

He was utterly bald, whether from genetics or grooming she couldn't tell, although the gray of his eyebrows suggested that at least some of his hair had fallen out on its own. His eyebrows stood straight out from his face in a manner that made Mary Beth think of porn stars and drag queens, although Professor Smith's eyebrows were possibly longer than any woman or wannabe woman's eye*lashes*, natural or enhanced.

And he was pompous. He never failed to ask questions that he obviously did not expect them to know, and he assigned extra work for those who gave particularly bad answers. Occasionally someone would have the translation to an obscure Latin phrase or know the date on which some minor European poet died of consumption, and on those occasions a little bit of joy faded from Professor Smith's eyes. He obviously knew much more about English literature than any of them could ever hope to know, but he lectured as if he didn't expect anyone to learn.

Now he was looking at Mary Beth. "Now that Sleeping Beauty has awakened, perhaps she could identify a quote for us."

*Damn*.

"Who said this: '*Oedipus Rex* is a so-called tragedy of fate; its tragic effect is supposed to reside in the opposition between the overpowering will of the gods and the vain striving of men who are threatened by disaster. Acquiescence in the will of the godhead, insight into one's own powerlessness, is what the deeply gripped spectator is supposed to learn from the sad spectacle.'"

Mary Beth cleared her throat. "Aristotle?"

"Quite wrong. Aristotle held very much the opposite view. The quote is from Freud, as you might know had you slept in your bed last night rather than here in my classroom. Do you agree with him?"

Mary Beth wondered what he would say if she told him she had been up late last night pulling people out of the bottom floor of a collapsed two-story motel off the Beltline. He'd probably tell her that physical exertion killed as many brain cells as alcohol.

"I do agree," she said.

"Please, expound upon your answer."

"The play is all about fate, and the impossibility of escaping from it. The prophecy the oracle gives Laius is self-fulfilling—if he hadn't sent Oedipus away, he wouldn't have taken him for a stranger and been killed by him. The same thing happens with the prophecy it gives to Oedipus—it sends him out from his foster home and toward Thebes, to kill his father and marry his mother. The oracle is the hand of fate, setting events into motion."

"What of the third prophecy, Tiresias's pronouncement? Does it set any events into motion?"

"Yes. It causes Oedipus to look for the murderer, whom he discovers to be himself."

"So we are all pawns of fate?"

"No."

"Is that not what you just said? That the play tells us we are helpless against the machinations of fate and the gods?"

"The play tells us Oedipus is the pawn of fate. But he's only a character in a play. His life has to suck in order for the play to work."

Professor Smith sneered. "Oedipus's life does indeed 'suck,' as you put it. So what you are saying is that although you agree that Sophocles was *saying* that fate rules our lives, you do not agree that this is the case."

"Right."

"Interesting, Miss—"

"Layton."

"Miss Layton. Write me a ten-page paper on the problem of fate versus free will in *Oedipus Rex* for Monday. This will be in addition to your previously assigned paper. Call it penance for your little nap."

Ten pages, on top of the thirty pages for a week from Monday, and her lab for biochem due next week. On top of fighting crime and saving lives and trying to make quick getaways in a green Lycra bodysuit.

"Nice work." Wanda Benson slouched in the seat next to her, twirling gum around one finger. "Wonder how they'll punish you when you fall asleep during surgery."

"Shut up," Mary Beth said.

Marcus Hatch was outside in the hall after class.

"Miss Layton!" He matched step with her down the hall. "I haven't seen you in a while. I knew there was something missing from my life."

"Don't bother me, Marcus. I'm not in the mood."

"Bother you? I certainly hope I'm not doing that."

Mary Beth stopped in the middle of the hall. "What do you want?"

Marcus stopped with her. "I want to take you to dinner."

"I'm not hungry."

"But you do eat, don't you? You'll be hungry later—say, seven-thirty?"

"Marcus, I don't want to go out with you."

He raised an eyebrow. "You're direct. I appreciate that. Let me be direct in turn. I think you know something."

"I know a lot of things, Marcus. One is that you are very annoying."

"That's my job. Let me clarify. I think you know something about these All-Stars."

"All-Stars?"

"Yes. You do read the papers, don't you? Even passed through the filter of corporate sponsorship, the local media has given them ample coverage in their mediocre way. The superheroes."

"I didn't know they were called the All-Stars."

"That's what the press is calling them now. They wear stars on their chests, that's why. But you know that already, don't you?"

"Yes."

"You admit it?"

"I saw it on the news, Marcus. Do you have a point?"

"I think you know my point. Let me make something clear. I don't want to turn you in. I just want to talk to you."

"Marcus, if you have some kind of spandex fetish, that's your business. I'm not interested."

"Then you deny it?"

"Deny what?" Mary Beth asked, and walked away before Marcus could answer.

Our top story again tonight is the group of costumed heroes who have become known as the Madison All-Stars. Today the governor announced plans to assemble a special team of investigators to investigate the All-Stars' identities and the motivation for their actions. Local reaction was swift, as residents who have benefited from the All-Stars' actions spoke out at a rally this afternoon:

"They're helping people. I guess it's weird that you don't see their faces, but that's not a crime. They haven't hurt anybody, and they always turn the bad guys over to the cops. I say the governor should have better things to do with his time. He should spend money chasing criminals, not heroes."

"They'll never find them anyhow. They're superheroes, man. They probably got a secret satellite orbiting Earth, with a cloaking device and all that."

"Agents of the lord's mercy have descended upon us, and we should be grateful, not suspicious."

While the governor initiates his investigation, Madison police have their hands full with a windfall of new information on old cases. Prudence Palmeiro has more on that story. Prudence?

"Dick, police in Madison and the surrounding area have received several mysterious mailings in the past few days. Police sources tell me these envelopes contain information on unsolved cases, what police refer to as cold cases, some of them apparently as much as thirty years old. Now in some cases this information, mailed anonymously in computer-printed envelopes, has been too vague to be very helpful. But in several cases the information has led to arrests, and about a dozen cold cases in Madison alone are now considered closed. Now some police have speculated that this information may have come from the All-Stars themselves, the argument being that since the costumed group appears to have some way of anticipating crimes before they occur, they may also have some way of uncovering information on past crimes. In any case, the deluge of information has effectively brought any investigation into the identities of the All-Stars to a halt, since police are working overtime investigating these new leads in the hopes of closing more unsolved cases.

"All-Star sightings are being reported constantly, but many have been difficult to confirm. It appears that they helped clear a six-car accident on Highway Twelve near Black Earth last night, rescuing two people from a car that had caught on fire and then putting the fire out. Other unsubstantiated reports range from Blue Star flying an eleven-year-old to Meriter Hospital for a liver transplant after her ambulance suffered a blowout on the Beltline, to Red Star calming some angry parents at a Little League game in

Verona, to the previously unheard of Purple Star being seen in audience with the pope in the sky over the Arboretum. As has been the case since the beginning with this group, lots of rumor and conjecture, very little concrete evidence, and still no pictures. Dick?"

I think we can safely say that last sighting is a hoax, can't we, Prudence?

"Considering that the pope has been traveling in the Ukraine, I suspect so, Dick."

Thank you, Prudence. Prudence will have more on the All-Stars at ten o'clock. Also at ten, we'll have a feature on Prudence's search for the right crib for her forthcoming child. Crib safety is a big concern for new parents, and we'll have expert opinions on how to keep your baby sleeping safely and comfortably.

Right now, we've got Holly Henson with the weather. Holly?

*he's having a heart attack*, Charlie had said. *Her pills— nitroglycerin pills—they're in the bathroom upstairs. She's fallen in the kitchen. You have to hurry.*

Jack hadn't bothered with the costume. He just pulled on the gloves and ran. Charlie was calling the paramedics, but Jack would be there before Charlie picked up the phone. He knew it was up to him. Traffic and stoplights meant nothing. He cut through the warehouse apartments at the end of Mifflin, over the railroad tracks and through a shopping center parking lot.

*I call it the mindstream*, Charlie had told him. *It's like every mind on the planet is connected, even though they don't know it. I can skim along the surface and look for someone who's thinking about hurting someone or is in trouble or has a guilty secret.*

*So nobody has secrets from you*, Jack had said. He didn't think Charlie would take advantage of that kind of power, but it was still spooky. All the thoughts that had gone through his head, the stuff he would never tell anyone about—it was all open for Charlie to read. The things he could barely admit to himself, Charlie could know them all inside of a moment. Maybe he already did.

He said it didn't matter. *I have as bad or worse inside of me. I had to wade through all of that, come to terms with it, before I could feel comfortable in my own skin again.*

Jack didn't think he could have done that. He didn't want to know that much about himself. It was hard enough to deal with the stray thoughts spinning out of him, the ones he didn't ask for, the ones that just bubbled up from some dark place inside him. He wished his father would die, so they could all start healing. He wanted to use his power to rob banks so he could stop worrying about money. He thought things that he was sure would get him blacklisted from dating for life if women ever started keeping a list of depraved men.

He wove between the cars on Regent Street and down Lake. Exhaust fumes plumed motionless from tailpipes, solid cobwebby clouds. A running boy hung in midair, a geosynchronous sidewalk satellite.

Jack ran.

He was a superhero, but it wasn't quite what he had thought it would be. It felt good, helping people, but it never stopped. He couldn't stay awake more than eight or nine hours in a row, and he was eating eight big meals a day, and he couldn't afford it. He went to All-You-Can-Eat buffets and gorged himself, and two hours later he was ravenous. He was losing weight.

What bothered him most was that he didn't feel like he was doing enough. He ran all day, between classes and shifts at the lab and the job he'd taken at a sandwich shop on State Street for the summer. (The manager loved having him there during the lunch rush—he could make a cold sandwich in thirty seconds flat. He could have done it faster, sure, but not without drawing lots of attention.) He'd helped hundreds of people, maybe thousands. But he felt like he was always letting someone down.

He took Drake Street past the zoo and turned off into a little neighborhood surrounding a park. The house was brick, very nice, well-kept garden. Too big for one person. The doors were all locked. He shoved a rock through a pane of glass in the back door and waited an eternity for the shards to fall. Then he reached through and opened the door. If there was an alarm, so much the better. He'd be gone before the security guards were in their car.

She lay next to the refrigerator. She didn't look that old. Her hair was faded brown, and she didn't have a lot of wrinkles. Maybe she'd had work done. The house was nice enough, she probably could afford it. She wore a steel gray skirt and jacket. The skirt had hitched up nearly to her hips when she fell. Jack looked away and ran upstairs.

Fine woodwork on the banisters and rails. Depression glass in cabinets on the landing, flanking a bay window crowned with stained glass. Silk wallpaper.

The pills were in an opaque white bottle. He read the directions as he went downstairs. *Place under tongue and let dissolve. Do not take with water.* He sat the woman up and opened her mouth, slid the pill under her tongue. Her eyes were closed. She was breathing, but only barely.

It wasn't that his family was broke. His father was smart, and he'd been lucky. In the forty years he'd worked that land he'd made a profit in all but a handful. He had insurance, and it was paying for his medical expenses, even more than what they had expected. They had to pay out some, but not more than they could handle.

But after . . . Jack had no idea what would happen then. He

didn't know if his mom would want to stay on the land. If she didn't, what would happen to it? He'd already told his dad he couldn't do it. He just wasn't ready to take that on. His older sisters and their husbands were settled in Racine and Appleton; he didn't think they would move back. Lloyd was anchored in Chicago. Grace had two more years of high school—what if she didn't want to move?

He should talk to them about it, but he couldn't. When he called he asked his mom how Daddy was doing and promised he'd tear down the old garage next week. Always next week. Then the two of them fumbled for a topic for ten minutes before hanging up.

The woman wasn't waking up. He took off his glove and looked under her tongue—the pill was half dissolved. He felt for her pulse. It was very faint.

He couldn't do CPR on someone who was still breathing, could he? He sat down and held her hand. It was cold.

"Come on," he said. "Come on back."

She made a high-pitched noise in her throat and stopped breathing. He lay her down and lifted her neck. He wondered if he should take what was left of the nitroglycerin pill out, but decided to leave it in. He held her nose closed and took a deep breath.

Blow. His heart was racing, he wondered if he could have a heart attack. He was different now, his heart was stronger, worked faster. What was normal for him was fast for anyone else. He willed some of his strength to the woman.

Blow. He was starving. He smelled meat—there was a package of salami on the counter, maybe she'd been making a sandwich. He tried not to drool, swallowed the saliva that flooded his mouth.

Blow. No sirens. No security company, no 911. His CPR certification was lapsed. He wasn't sure he remembered everything. He hoped her heart kept working.

Blow. He had to check the heart. He unbuttoned the suit coat, listened through her shirt. He didn't hear it. He checked her wrist, her neck. Nothing.

Don't break her solar plexus. Elbows locked. How many compressions? He couldn't remember. He tried not to rush, tried to remember the old rhythm of his heart, before everything changed. She couldn't keep up with his heart. He had to bring her back at the right pace.

He stopped after ten, checked her pulse again. Nothing. He breathed for her, twice, again. Nothing. He started the chest compressions again.

He wished her eyes were open. At least he would have some idea. Please, cough, sit up, ask me who the hell I am and what I'm doing here. Please.

He wondered if he would know. He wondered if his sped-up eyes and ears would sense it if she died, if the instant she gave out he would see something, a flicker of movement, a change in the light. Maybe a whisper as she left, a good-bye.

*Please don't die*, he thought.

More compressions, more breathing. He lost count, lost track of time, fell into a trance of compression, exhalation, interrogation. *Do you see anything?* he thought at her. *Is it safe there? Did you believe in God, and is he there with you?*

Her heart didn't beat and she didn't breathe and she didn't answer. When he heard sirens and voices he put a hand on her forehead to say good-bye and ran away.

**H**ello?"

"Why, Caroline Bloom, as I live and breathe! You do know how to answer the phone. Now if they could just teach you to dial it."

"Hi, Mom."

"Hi yourself. Why haven't you called?"

"I did call, Mom, but you moved."

"I didn't give you the new number?"

"You didn't tell me you were moving."

"Yes, I did."

"I think I'd remember, Mom. Where are you now? Butte, Montana?"

"I'm still in New York, honey."

"Eight months. Has to be a new record."

"I have a cell phone now. I'll give you that number."

"A cell phone?"

"For my new job. Didn't I tell you?"

"Mom, you never tell me anything until after the fact."

"Well, it's more exciting that way, isn't it? Are you still in Wisconsin?"

"Yes, Mom. They won't let me take my classes in Tuscaloosa."

"Did you get your check?"

"You sent me a check dated July 1999. The bank wouldn't take it. I don't think the account was open anymore."

"Uh-oh. I found it when I was moving; I thought I'd forgotten to send it to you."

"You did. Two years ago."

"Don't be snide, Caroline. I'll send you another check. A big one. I got a great new job, honey. Lots of money, great benefits, offices in the World Trade Center! Can you believe it?"

"No, I can't. What'd they hire you for?"

"To keep the books. I told you I got my CPA certification."

"No, you didn't."

"I really think I did. Anyway, I start on Monday, but I wanted to know if you'll come out for the Fourth."

"Mom, that's Wednesday. I can't get a ticket now. Not one I can afford."

"I'll pay for it, honey."

"You mean you'll pay me back. Last time it took you six months to send me the money, and it wasn't enough."

"I'm really sorry about that, honey. But that won't happen this time. I haven't been paid yet, but I'll send you the money as soon as I get my first paycheck."

"Don't you have to pay rent?"

"What are you talking about?"

"Rent, phone, heat—"

"Heat's included, honey."

"—groceries, clothes for your new job that you absolutely can't live without—"

"Stop it."

"You won't have the money right away, Mom. It's OK. I'll come for Thanksgiving."

"That's in November!"

"Mom, summer is when I make my money. And school starts in two months. I don't have money for a plane ticket right now, anyway."

"Use a credit card."

"Oh, here we go. Someone is trusting you to handle their books? Tell me the company's name, so I can tell all my stockbroker friends to divest themselves."

"Caroline, you're pissing me off."

"Mom, credit cards are how you got into trouble. I don't have money for a plane ticket now, I won't have it in a month, and I won't have money for a plane ticket plus interest every month after that. I'm not going to start with that. I'm sorry. I'd like to visit, but it can't be now."

"Fine. How's school?"

"It starts in two months."

"How's work?"

"My boss is a psycho who sees dead people."

"How's your social life?"

"Remember our deal? I don't tell you about mine, you don't tell me about yours."

"That's not much of a deal for me, is it? You'll meet someone, honey. There have to be lots of hunky farm boys there in Wisconsin."

"Most of them are working on farms. And please don't say 'hunky.'"

"This is not the conversation I was envisioning. You haven't even congratulated me on my new job."

"Congratulations, Mom. Don't screw this one up."

"Honey, I love you, but you're such a bitch sometimes."

"Right back at you, Mom."

"I have to go. Be good."

"All right. Can I—"

"Shit, there's someone at the door. I have to go, honey. We have tickets for Shakespeare in the Park."

"Who's we?"

"Oh, you'll meet him at Thanksgiving."

"Mom, you haven't—"

"Love you, honey. Bye-bye."

"—given me your new phone number."

# EDITOR'S NOTE

by Marcus Hatch

By now you're all thinking one of two things: (1) it's about time for the bad guy to show up, or (2) he should have shown up about fifty pages back.

A superhero story needs a supervillain, that's what you're thinking. Well, there aren't any supervillains in this story. This isn't some pulp novel you pulled off the rack when you thought no one was looking. This is a true story. Journalism. Facts.

The thing about real life is the bad guys are people, too, and by that I don't mean anything touchy-feely about how they have feelings and they love their parents and they stop to pet little dogs on the street. Some people don't have feelings and don't love their parents and go out of their way to shoot little dogs on the street. But most of the bad guys aren't so easy to spot.

All right, I'll grant one point. You can see the dates we're dealing with, and you know what's going to happen eventually. Maybe there is one supervillain here, but he doesn't know that our heroes—and I'm not even going to go into how exactly I justify calling them that, after everything that happened—he doesn't even know that they exist. If he did, then I guess they'd be the villains, as far as he was concerned.

This is the thing about power, I think. To some people—those of us who have none—anyone who has it and uses it is a villain. To those who have it, anyone who tries to stop them from using it is a villain. Because we're all the heroes of our own story, no matter what horrible things we might be doing.

Sometimes people do terrible things with the best of intentions. I don't think that makes them less guilty. But if you understand their reasons, you might find it more difficult to condemn them out of hand. You might find it more difficult to call them villains.

On the other hand, sometimes people do terrible things with the absolute worst of intentions. But even there, I don't think they're supervillains. I think they're just people.

Ray Bishop slapped the table in front of Benjamin Thatcher. Thatcher's lip quivered under his mustache.

"I'll ask the questions as many times as I want, until I'm satisfied. You don't have any say in the matter."

"You can't hold me." Thatcher stuck out his chin and blinked his watery eyes. "I didn't do nothing."

"I've got you on conspiracy, Benjy," Ray said. "Or would you rather I called you Death?"

Thatcher blushed. "Reed shouldn't ought to have told you about that."

"Why not? You wanted to wait until you were a badass to unveil your badass name? Never happen, Benjy. You're not cut out for it. You're pudgy."

"I'm not pudgy! I'm just big-boned."

"You're soft. Do you really want to see the inside of a prison?

Those boys in there, they're hard. They didn't plan things—they did them. Things you'd shit yourself just hearing about."

Thatcher's face went stony pale, but he stayed silent.

"Just answer my questions, Benjy, and I'll make it known you cooperated. You'll get a year of parole and you'll be planning another robbery in broad daylight in no time."

Thatcher shook his head. "I ain't never doing that again. It was like those star people knew what I was going to do before I did it."

Ray started the tape recorder in front of Thatcher. "So tell me about them."

"What do you want to know?"

"You said you saw two women and one man, but you heard a third woman. You're sure you didn't see her?"

"I looked. She wasn't there."

"Can you describe the voice?"

"How do you describe somebody's voice?"

"Start with how you knew it was a woman's voice."

"I just know. It wasn't gravelly, like a guy. It was kind of smooth, not too high-pitched. A nice voice. Called me Mr. Thatcher."

"Was that before or after you were punched in the gut?"

"Before, I think."

"What was the first thing she said?"

"She told me not to move."

"She said 'Don't move'?"

"She said 'Don't move, Mr. Thatcher.' She knew my name, dude. I still say it was Alicia."

"Alicia Williams, your ex-girlfriend? Did she know about the robbery?"

"She could have. Maybe I said something when I was drunk sometime."

"Did it sound like her?"

"Not really."

"What else did she say?"

"After she hit me, she told me not to move again. Then she asked the one in blue, the flying girl, she asked her if that was all of us."

"All of what?"

"All of us. You know. Me and Reed and Johnny and Johnny's sister."

"Can you describe the woman in blue?"

"I done that already."

"Do it again."

"She was pretty hot. Not as hot as the chick in the green, but pretty hot."

"That doesn't help me much. What color was her hair?"

"She had dark hair. Short. No, with a ponytail. I mean, a braid."

"Which is it, Benjy?"

"See, it looked short at first, because it was all pulled back, you know? Then I saw her from the side, and she had a braid maybe halfway down her back."

"You're sure."

"Yeah, I'm sure."

"How tall was she?"

"I don't know. She was flying around. And I was sitting on the bench, except after the invisible one kicked me."

"Was she taller than the woman in green?"

"The invisible one?"

"The one in blue, Benjy. Use your head."

"She was about as tall as the red guy. What'd she call him—Red Star. Hey, wait a minute—she called him something else before that."

"What was it?"

"I don't remember. Started with an *L*, I think."

"Think, Benjy."

"I don't know. La, la, la, la—Jack! That's what it was, Jack."

"Jack starts with a *J*."

"I know. I'm not stupid. I just got confused. *L*, *J*—they look alike, kind of. His name was Jack, I know it."

"You're sure?"

"Positive."

"Did you hear any other names?"

"No. Just that Red Star, Green Star shit."

"OK, the woman in blue. Was she white, black, Asian, Hispanic?"

"White, I think. She was pretty tan. Could have been a Mex."

"Any distinguishing features?"

"Well, she had a nice body, but I'm not sure I could identify it in a lineup. I'd be willing to try, though."

Ray kept going, but Thatcher didn't have anything more to say. He had given the same descriptions every witness had given, but he had also given him one thing he hadn't had before—a name. Jack.

**H**alfway through the door Jack realized there was someone in the living room with Charlie: Scott. It took Jack a second to run to his bedroom, change out of his costume, put on jeans and a T-shirt, and run back to the door.

"Did you just say 'whoosh'?" Scott asked. His face looked ashen.

Jack wasn't sure how long it had been since he'd seen Scott. A few weeks, or a few months? Jack himself wasn't at the apartment that much, and Scott hardly came by except to get his mail and drop off his rent check. He rarely stayed for longer than a hello. Jack wasn't sure if that was because Scott felt awkward there, or because he just couldn't bear to be away from Cecilia for long.

Scott had met Cecilia when they were both freshmen. Scott thought it was love at first sight; Jack was pretty sure it was just two kids away from home for the first time looking for someone to have safe and frequent sex with. He and Scott were roommates that first year—randomly assigned by the university—but Cecilia was in their room more often than Jack. Three or four times a week he came home to find Scott's Star of David hanging on the doorknob. That was the signal Jack had agreed to respect, and although more than once he thought about telling Scott to find another place to do his mattress dancing, he never did.

He found other places to spend his afternoons. He went to the library or to dinner. If he needed a nap he curled up in the lounge, and if he needed to relax he visited Charlie in the room next door. They played cribbage and listened to the Who loud enough to drown out any stray moans from the room next door.

Cecilia was prone to dark moods and jealous hysterics, and Scott worked desperately to make her happy. She went home to Kansas City the summer after freshman year, slept with an old boyfriend, and convinced Scott that he was to blame. When the guys had gone out last summer for Jack's birthday, Cecilia called Scott's cell phone, claiming to be sick, and convinced him to head home to take care of her. It was difficult for Jack to be tactful about Cecilia. He thought she needed psychoanalysis more than she needed a boyfriend. Obviously Scott had issues of his own, though, because he wouldn't hear a bad word about her. Scott thought Cecilia needed him to protect her; Jack and Charlie thought Scott needed to be protected from Cecilia. They just didn't know how to do it.

"I didn't say anything." Jack shut the door. Charlie was trying to give him some sort of signal, but Jack couldn't figure out what he meant. Was something wrong with his hair? Was Cecilia behind him with a knife? He resisted the urge to look over his shoulder.

"She dumped me," Scott said.

Jack almost said, Not again. The first time Cecilia had dumped Scott he'd been relieved, even though the breakup seemed to have turned Scott into a zombie. In the long run it would be a good thing, Jack was convinced. But three hours later Cecilia had called up in tears, and they hadn't seen Scott again for nearly three months. They'd broken up eight times since, never for more than twelve hours, and by now Jack dared not let himself hope it was really over.

"That's harsh," Jack said. "I'm sorry."

Scott put his head between his legs as though he were going to faint. "What am I going to do?" he wailed.

Charlie was still doing the shimmy with his eyes, and Jack finally looked behind him, to Scott's bedroom. The bed was hidden by suitcases and boxes. Some of them looked like they had been kicked by a mule.

"She threw his stuff out the window," Charlie said.

"I think I'm going to throw up," Scott said.

"You're hyperventilating," Jack said. He grabbed a paper bag from the pyramid of Scott's belongings and dumped the textbooks within on the bed. "Breathe into this."

As soon as Scott's breathing slowed down he ran into the bathroom.

"Is this for real?" Jack whispered to Charlie.

"He believes it is," Charlie said. "I'll try and get a read on her to be certain. But apparently she's been sleeping with a basketball player for a couple of months."

"Unless he's as much of a doormat as Scott, that's not going to last," Jack said.

Charlie nodded. "She'll come back to Scott when it's over."

"And if something doesn't change, he'll take her back."

"This is going to get complicated, with him back in the apartment. He's going to have questions."

"I know."

"But you'd rather take the risk of him finding out than let him get back together with her."

"Quit reading my mind."

"I'm not. We just happen to be thinking the same thing."

Jack looked at the boxes and bags in Scott's bedroom. "We have to get him out of here tonight, get his mind off her. Is there any trouble brewing?"

"Kids playing with fireworks. Couple of teenagers thinking about robbing a pizza shop. The girls can probably handle it on their own."

"It's supposed to be Caroline's night off. I think she has a date."

"We'd better talk to her, then."

"I'll talk to Caroline," Jack said. "You get him out of the bathroom."

When Jack opened the door to go downstairs his sister Grace was just climbing the last step.

"What are you doing here?" Jack asked.

"I'm going to the fireworks with Nathan. I came up early."

"Nathan Carswell? Does Mom know you're seeing that loser?"

"Mom likes him," Grace said. "Speaking of Mom, you owe me for not telling her about your superpowers."

Jack stepped into the hall and shut the door. "I told you to keep it quiet."

"I am. Charlie knows. Is he around?"

"Scott doesn't know."

"You mean your other roommate? What's he look like?"

"He looks like hell. His girlfriend dumped him. Which means

he'll probably be around a lot more, which means we can't have you shooting your mouth off here. It'd be best if you just forgot all about it."

Grace crossed her arms. "Not happening. You promised me you'd let me come with you sometime."

"I shouldn't have said that. It's too dangerous."

"I just want to watch. I can stay with Charlie."

"Charlie doesn't need the distraction. This isn't a game, Grace."

"I'll tell Mom."

"No you won't. You've never been a squealer, Gracie, and you're not going to start now. I'll make it up to you some other way. I'll get you something great for your birthday."

"That's not what I want, Mortimer."

"Gracie, I can't do it. What if you get hurt?"

"I won't."

"If you do, Mom and Dad will never speak to me again. I'll never forgive myself."

"It's my life! I can take responsibility for myself."

"That's good. But I'm not doing it."

Grace spun and tromped down the stairs. "I'll tell Mom," she called back.

"I doubt it," Jack said.

Harriet knew she shouldn't have told them she could handle it on her own. Jack could have stopped them, or Mary Beth, but the only advantage she had was that of surprise. The fact that no one could see her wasn't an advantage. It had nearly gotten her killed tonight. If only Dad hadn't been working, she'd have been watching fireworks in Sun Prairie, far away. If only.

An hour and a half, she'd waited. Charlie had said there would be two, maybe three of them, depending on how many friends the kid talked into the robbery. There would be one gun. That's what Charlie had said.

If she'd waited outside, it might have worked. But it was a cool night for July, and despite Caroline's claims that Lycra was insulating, Harriet had been shivering out on the street. After waiting nearly an hour she'd slipped in the door behind a customer, certain that there would be a chance to slip out again. But there hadn't been any customers since, just phone orders, and the delivery guy used the back door. She didn't think she could get into the kitchen and out the back without being noticed, so she stayed where she was, crouched in the corner, waiting.

There were three cooks on duty, and they were listening to Stevie Wonder and Sly and the Family Stone and making fun of one another and generally having a good time until the door opened and two kids stepped in with masks, one of a gorilla and the other of Richard Nixon.

"What'll it be, boys?" asked a balding black man whom Harriet had decided was the owner, or at least the manager.

The kids in masks didn't answer. They fidgeted in the pockets of their light jackets, and Harriet tried to figure out which one had the gun.

"You need some time? Take your time." The manager wiped his hands on a towel and cracked open a can of root beer. "You going to a costume party or something?"

The gorilla whispered something to Nixon, and Nixon turned, shaking his head to indicate he hadn't heard. Harriet moved between them and the counter. She still couldn't tell which one had the gun. Both had large bulges in their jacket pockets.

The manager had noticed them, too. "If you boys aren't going to order something, you'd better move along. I don't want trouble. Logan, maybe we better call the sheriff's office, tell them their pies are ready."

"Don't." Nixon pulled a gun on the manager. Harriet grabbed his hand and twisted the weapon out of his grasp. It fell to the floor, and she picked it up. To Nixon it must have looked as though it simply fell to the ground and disappeared.

When she straightened, though, the gorilla had a gun of his own, and it was pointed at her. "What's happening?" he said, his voice cracking. "Who's there?"

"I don't want trouble," said the manager.

"How'd you do that?" asked Nixon.

Harriet tucked Nixon's gun into her belt and lunged for the gorilla. She couldn't break his hold—he had both hands on the gun. She shoved his arm up, but before it was pointed harmlessly at the ceiling, it went off, the muzzle flash catching the edge of her vision. She kicked the gorilla's legs out from behind him and went down on top of him. He let go of the gun, and Harriet rolled away with it, blinking her eyes to clear away the powder.

Somebody was shouting. Nixon ran out the front door, and the gorilla struggled to his feet and followed. Logan was on the phone, but she couldn't see the manager or the other cook.

"They shot him," Logan was saying.

*No*, Harriet thought. She ran around the counter. The manager lay on the floor, his shoulder oozing bright red. The other cook was putting clean rags over the wound.

She left the guns on the floor and ran out, ignoring the bells and Logan's panicked glance at the door. She looked up and down the street, but Nixon and the gorilla were gone.

**C**harlie liked barbershops. He liked the smell of clippings and the blue sterilizing fluid in which the combs and scissors were kept. He liked the feel of the chair, and the warmth of lather against the back of his neck. He liked to close his eyes and just listen to the snip of the scissors and the hum of the electric clippers.

Charlie's favorite barbershop in Madison was four blocks from his house and just a block from the capitol. On weekdays it was always filled with men in suits whom Charlie imagined to be legislators or aides to the governor. They joked with the barbers as they nestled under their smocks, watching the news or dozing while they received shaves or haircuts they never seemed to need. When Charlie came in on weekdays he felt out of place; the barbers looked him over and told him they weren't sure they'd be able to take him. When their chairs were empty they looked calmly around the shop and out onto the street, then motioned Charlie over, as if there would be just enough time to finish his cut before the lieutenant governor arrived.

Today being a Saturday, there was no crowd, just two barbers and a jowly old man sitting at a table under the wall-mounted television. The barbers sat in their chairs, one reading the paper, the other watching CNN. The TV viewer stood as Charlie entered and wiped at the seat of the chair.

"Haircut, son?" he asked. His look said Charlie was long overdue.

"Please." Charlie settled into the chair as the barber swept a smock around him and tied it at the neck. "Short."

The barber nodded, as if that much were obvious. He pumped the chair higher and moved around to the back, reclining it and gently lowering Charlie's head to the sink. Charlie shut his eyes before he had to be told, and relaxed as the warm water washed over his hair, his eyes shielded by the barber's rough hand.

"You in school?" asked the barber.

"Yeah."

This was the ritual of the barbershop. The barber would ask what Charlie was studying, make some comments about sports or the weather, and fall silent. Charlie didn't say much. He preferred to listen to the old men talk.

The barber behind the newspaper turned the page and cleared his throat. "Hal, you still got that septic tank up at your lake place?"

"Yup," said Charlie's barber as he toweled Charlie's hair.

"Says here they passed more stringent laws regarding septic systems due to concerns over contaminations in the groundwater."

"Up, now," Hal said to Charlie, and sat him up straight.

"Seems to me you'd better have someone check to see you're

up to the new codes, Hal. Before the state inspectors come around, that is."

"I'll do that, Guy." Charlie caught the annoyance from Hal. Guy was fishing for an invitation to the lake place for next weekend, but Hal had told him two years ago he was never inviting him again, after Guy had gotten hammered on Jim Beam and pissed on the carpet.

Hal took up the scissors and comb and circled Charlie like a boxer sizing up an opponent. After a few circuits he sidled up beside Charlie and started cutting.

"Lot of hair you got here, son," said Hal.

"Sure is," said the old man under the television. He was staring at a checkerboard in front of him, but he made no move. He wore a beige jacket and a gray herringbone cap, although it was already eighty degrees outside.

"What's on the TV, John?" Hal asked.

"Babies having babies." Charlie saw that there were teen pregnancy statistics on the screen.

"Like those two kids out in Jersey a few years back," said Hal. "Damn shame, that. Baby in the Dumpster."

"Delaware," said Guy. "Happened in Delaware."

"Stupid," said John. "No excuse. Wear a goddamned condom."

"Got that right," said Hal.

"Ain't that hard," said John. "Just put the fucker on. You can't figure it out, you damn sure ain't ready to have a baby."

"These girls," said Hal. "They have to lay down the law, these girls. Don't sleep with him if he won't wear a rubber."

"What do you think about abortion, Hal?" John asked.

Charlie caught a flash from John, a memory from forty years ago or more. A girlfriend, a doctor, a cash transaction. John and the girl broke up, graduated high school. She became a nurse, married a doctor, never had children.

Hal took a step back, inspecting Charlie's head. "I can't say I like it much," he said as he resumed his work. "But I'll tell you, I never had to carry a child before—"

"Thank God for that," said Guy.

"—and I can't say I'd want to if I wasn't planning on it. Not to say someone shouldn't be more responsible than that. But in the real world people make mistakes, and in the real world there are a lot of kids out there nobody wants."

John nodded. Guy turned the page in his newspaper. "You boys see that Brewers game last night?"

"Hell, no," said John.

"Says here we'll be paying for that stadium into the next decade."

"Used to be a good team," said Hal.

"Not since '87," said John. "They had a shot then, until they lost twelve straight."

Neither Guy nor Hal responded to that, but they were both thinking about a Saturday back in May 1987, the day after the Royals had knocked the Brewers out of first place in the AL East. Hal hadn't shown up for work that Saturday, because he was in jail for beating up his wife. He had never lifted a hand to her before that or since, and they had never divorced. But she lived in Eau Claire now, near her sister. Since 1987, Hal hadn't paid much attention to baseball.

"Put your head down for me," Hal said, and Charlie complied. He looked down at the white floor, littered with locks of hair that might or might not be his, lying damp and disconnected on the vinyl. His hair, his blood, his bones, all just like everyone else's at the basic level. Everyone with secrets. Everyone making mistakes.

A tall black man in a blue dress shirt and green pants entered, and Guy put his paper down. "Ray," he said. "I wondered if you'd be coming by today."

"I had to," said Ray, easing himself into Guy's chair. "I'm getting a bit shaggy."

"Working today?" Guy spread the smock over Ray's lap.

"In about an hour," said Ray.

"Keeping you busy?" John asked.

"Oh, yeah. Lots of cold cases getting hot. More work than we can handle."

"I read about that," Guy said, leaning Ray back toward the sink. "Anonymous information, the paper said."

"Anonymous, yeah," said Ray. "I'd sure like to know who it's coming from."

"You still looking for those All-Stars?" Hal asked.

"I am," said Ray.

Hal shook his head. "You ought to leave them be. You never saw the police harassing Superman."

"Vigilantism is illegal," Ray said. "These people aren't trained. Someone's going to get hurt."

"I thought you had too much to do already," John said.

"I'm just working on this here and there," Ray said. "But I'll find them eventually."

"You can't catch them if they don't want to be caught," Hal said. "They're something better than you and me. Keep your head forward," he said to Charlie.

"One thing at a time," Ray said. "First I need to find out who they are."

Hal combed Charlie's hair back and looked him straight on to make sure the sides were even. Then he had him put his head forward again and shaved the back of his neck.

A phone rang, and Ray fumbled beneath his smock. Guy stood at ease with his scissors while Ray talked.

"I have to go," Ray said when he hung up. "We'll have to finish this up later."

"What's happening?" Guy asked, pulling the smock from around Ray's neck.

"We just arrested one of the All-Stars."

t appears that reports that a member of the All-Stars was arrested yesterday may have been premature. We go to Prudence Palmeiro for details.

"Thanks, Dick. As we reported yesterday, police sources indicated that they had apprehended a man whom they believed to be a member of the All-Stars. However, it now appears that the man was either an impostor or a copycat. Witnesses tell us that one Bernard Reiss entered a Laundromat on East Washington Avenue wearing a green jumpsuit with a cardboard star pinned to his chest at about ten A.M. yesterday morning. From what we understand, Mr. Reiss then accused a female customer of attempting to rob a change machine and pursued her around the Laundromat until she and another customer managed to subdue him and notify police. According to the witnesses I spoke to, Mr. Reiss does not appear to be a member of the All-Stars. First of all, the All-Star known as

Green Star is, by all accounts, female, and in addition Mr. Reiss has been described as being in his sixties and noticeably overweight."

Prudence, I understand that the police chief made a statement a short time ago?

"That's correct, Dick. Police Chief Monica Miller stated that Mr. Reiss was exhibiting delusional behavior and would likely be remanded to the custody of his family after being assessed by police psychiatrists. She also had some harsh words for her own officers, saying that some of them needed to think before speaking. She told us there had never been an official presumption that Mr. Reiss was a member of the All-Stars. I asked the chief why the police would wish to arrest the All-Stars, and she indicated that there was no active investigation targeting the All-Stars. At this point police would simply like for them to come forward to answer some questions."

Did the chief indicate whether she expected any more copycat behavior like this?

"She did express concern that others might consider taking part in vigilante behavior, and she reiterated what she has said ever since the department first acknowledged this situation, that this sort of activity is dangerous and shouldn't be undertaken by members of the general public."

Thank you, Prudence. Coming up in sports, could the Brewers lose a hundred games this year?

Professor Smith's office was a windowless hole in an inner hall of the Helen C. White Building. Mary Beth wondered why a tenured professor with his standing couldn't get a better office, but perhaps he preferred dark and cramped to bright and spacious.

"Miss Layton." He glanced up from his gray desk. "Please have a seat. I'll be just a moment."

Two gray chairs faced the desk. Mary Beth sat in the one that wasn't stacked with books. Books hid the walls of the room, packed into ceiling-high shelves, shoved into boxes, piled on the floor. Mary Beth guessed that there were more than a thousand books, maybe more than two thousand. She wondered how many books Professor Smith had at home.

Professor Smith set his pen down and shut his book. "Miss Layton, do you think people tell the truth?"

Mary Beth hadn't known what to expect from this conference. Everyone was supposed to meet with the professor to discuss their midterm paper before they started their final paper, but when she'd asked classmates what their meeting had been like, none of them had seemed to want to talk about it.

Mary Beth had thought he might ask her to defend her paper, then rip apart her proposal for the final. Or possibly he would sprout wings and drop heavy books of literary criticism on her head. Instead he seemed almost casual, as if he were actually interested in her answer. It had to be a trap.

"I think people tell the truth as they see it."

Professor Smith leaned back in his chair and still managed to look stiff and formal. "Explain."

"I think some people only see what they want to see, what fits with the things they believe. Anything that contradicts it, they ignore. So they may think they're telling the truth, but it's the truth according to them."

"So truth is subjective, because people are not objective. No matter what we do, we all operate from a set of prejudices, don't you think?"

"I suppose so."

"Certainly so. I myself have prejudices against illiterates, drunks, and believers of any sort."

Mary Beth caught herself staring, so she coughed and looked around the room. Her paper had been a comparison study of *Moby Dick* and *Catch-22*. She wasn't sure there was any connection between that and the professor's line of questioning.

"What are we talking about?" she asked finally.

"What are you studying, Miss Layton?"

"I'm premed. I'm a biology major."

"Very noble. I think you should drop it and study English." He set her midterm paper on the desk. "Your insights are fresh and interesting, and your arguments are well founded and persuasive. They need work, of course, but the raw talent is there."

"I'm going to graduate this year. I have two semesters left."

Professor Smith nodded. "Do you enjoy biology?"

"It's required."

"Do you enjoy it?"

"Not really, but I need it."

"What kind of doctor are you going to be, Miss Layton?"

"Probably a pediatrician."

"Ah. You like kids."

Mary Beth didn't like the professor's tone of voice. "Yes. I've always wanted to be a doctor."

"Always?"

"OK, not always. I wanted to be a rodeo clown when I was five."

"What changed your mind?"

Mary Beth laughed. "I didn't think it seemed like a career with a lot of potential."

Professor Smith nodded. "So now we come to your prejudices. You think that being a rodeo clown is a dead-end job."

"I didn't say that. It probably doesn't pay a lot."

"I would imagine that most rodeo clowns have other full-time careers in addition to their part-time work behind the barrels."

"I guess."

"You could be a full-time doctor and a part-time rodeo clown."

"I doubt I'd have time for that," she said. "I'll have four years of medical school, another four years of residency, and I'll probably be working sixty-hour weeks after that."

"It doesn't sound like you'll have time for much, will you?"

"Probably not."

"Time to read?"

"Probably not."

"Do you like to read?"

"Yes."

"Why do you want to be a doctor?"

"I told you."

"I'm not sure you have."

"To help people."

"That's it? Forgive my cynicism, Miss Layton. While I believe you are a caring soul, I doubt you are free of self-interest."

"Well, I'd like to make money, too."

"The kind of money rodeo clowns don't make."

"I guess not."

"Or English professors."

Professor Smith was almost smiling. Mary Beth sighed.

"I don't know what you're getting at, Professor. I'm not looking down on you because you don't make as much money as a doctor might. I don't know how much money you make."

"But money is important to you."

"It's nice to have. Better than not having any."

"How much do you suppose an English teacher might make, to start with? Enough to live on?"

"I would hope so."

"Do you know why I teach the summer introductory course, Miss Layton?"

"To give yourself an annual lesson in humility."

Professor Smith waved a hand. "I mean the real reason."

"I have absolutely no idea."

"I teach the summer course because there is always, among

the illiterates, drunks, and believers—the great majority of whom are merely fulfilling course requirements—at least one engineering, business, or premed student who is in the wrong field of study. I like to catch those students and steer them in the right direction."

"You're telling me that I'm in the wrong field of study."

"Yes."

"Are you saying I'll be a bad doctor?"

"I suspect you would be an excellent doctor. But it would be a mistake. You are free to make your own mistakes, of course. But I will do everything in my power to convince you to change your course." Professor Smith opened a drawer and pulled out a sheet of paper. "I'm teaching a seminar in the fall on the lost generation. It's an intensive course. We will read two novels or the equivalent every week, and each student will do a presentation in addition to weekly papers. Undergraduates need my approval to register. You have it."

Mary Beth took the paper. "My fall course schedule is set."

"It is? No elective courses you could change? You must have some open credits to fill."

"Professor, I—"

"Tell me you'll think about it."

"I'll think about it."

"Good. Now, let's talk about your paper."

Caroline woke with the side of her face pressed against a cold window. It was raining, and the world pitched and yawed around her. She was in Jack's truck, but where was Jack? She yelped as she realized no one was driving, then realized the truck was parked. In the rain, on the street. It was dark. She looked for a clock.

Beer. That was why she was here. She'd drunk a lot of beer. They all had. Harriet had passed out already—she'd drunk even more than a lot, because she was still upset about the man who'd been shot at the pizza shop. They'd drunk so much beer that there wasn't any left.

Charlie had offered to drive, and she'd offered to come along— why? She didn't know. That was good, because if she didn't know, then Charlie wouldn't know. Although she must know, because if she didn't know she wouldn't know that it was something she didn't want Charlie to know, in which case maybe Charlie knew already but didn't want her to know that he knew.

Why were they drinking so much beer? Not even good beer. Cheap beer. Why not drink Jack's beer? Not ready for a few weeks yet, that was why. Not in time for Jack's birthday. Jack's birthday! That was why the beer. Charlie was buying it. She'd come along because beer made her horny, and she wanted to be horny with Charlie. Oops. Now she knew why she was here, and Charlie would know, too. Charlie could look at her and know what she was thinking. He could close his eyes and know. It was scary, but it was exciting, too.

There was no clock in the truck. She fought with the door for a while before she noticed it was locked. She unlocked it and lurched out onto the sidewalk.

She stood carefully still, but the pavement moved under her feet while she looked for someone with a watch. An umbrella bobbed toward her, and she asked it for the time. It looked at its watch and told her and she thanked it and turned around and threw up on the curb. Her puke looked like wet cookie dough. The rain broke it apart and swept it toward the storm drain.

She had forgotten the time already, but the umbrella was gone. She crept back into the truck and shut the door. She wasn't sure where Charlie was, but he better get to the liquor store before nine, or he wouldn't be able to buy any more beer and the party would be . . . well, it would be sober. Jack seemed sober already, actually. He said his metabolism burned alcohol as fast as he could drink it.

"How did I get so wet?" she asked out loud. She hugged her arms around her soaked T-shirt. The cold was sobering her up, and she could see the rest of the night ahead of her already. It was just a matter of following her current situation to its logical conclusion. Drunk and cold with wet clothes would become hungover and parched with no clothes, lying next to Charlie and wishing she could know his mind as easily as he knew hers.

Caroline knew some people thought she was a slut, because

she dated a lot. But she rarely slept with the guys she dated. She never even drank on dates. Dates were for clear thinking, for getting a real look at someone. If he was rude to the waitress or he wasn't funny or he was too into money or himself or her tits, that was it. It was better not to waste time, to put a stop to things before one of them might get hurt.

The problem was that she *wanted* sex. Sometimes she wanted to make speeches to her dates, describing in detail what she might have done with him if he hadn't farted and giggled about it, or made subtly racist jokes, or slurped his spaghetti and tapped on the table with his class ring all night. Sometimes she saw boys on the street whom she wanted to take by the hand, bring home, and send away a six-pack of condoms later. Instead, every month or two she got drunk and attacked the nearest penis.

The driver-side door opened, and Charlie entered behind a case of Milwaukee's Best and a brown bag with a bottle inside. His short hair was plastered to his head, and his shirt was plastered to his chest. Caroline wanted him to kiss her.

Charlie reached for her, and she closed her eyes. He pulled something out of her hair. "You've got leaves in your hair," he said. "What were you doing out there? You're all wet."

Caroline ran her hands through her hair and faced the windshield as Charlie pulled into traffic. "I was trying to find out what time it was," she said. "You didn't have any trouble?"

"No. The clerk had a fight with his girlfriend earlier. She threatened to set his apartment on fire. He didn't even ask to see my ID."

By the time Charlie was done talking Caroline couldn't remember what she'd asked him, so she just grunted and leaned back into the headrest. The truck bounced hard over cracks in the asphalt and sent up sheets of water from puddles along the curbs. Caroline closed her eyes and told herself to fall asleep.

Charlie gasped and pulled over. His voice was tight. "Wait here."

"What?" She sat up straight. "You've got something, haven't you?"

"Yes. But I think you should stay here."

Caroline stared at him. "I'm a little drunk," she said.

"It's all right," he said.

"You're just going to talk to them?"

"Yes."

"OK."

She watched him run across the street and up the steps toward a big house. She squinted up the street but couldn't see a street sign. She had no idea where they were. What if Charlie needed help? What if she had to get the others? She was way too drunk to be flying. She didn't even have her costume. Neither did Charlie.

At least it was dark. She opened the door and flew toward the house Charlie had entered.

She was still trying to decide whether she should knock when she rammed into the door. She hardly felt it as it splintered and collapsed. She was invulnerable.

There was a boy sitting on some steps. He ran, and Caroline followed him to another door. He closed it behind him, and she had to break that one down, too. There were stairs behind it, stairs going down to a basement. A basement with a couch and a TV and candles and a refrigerator and several boys and a girl. One of the boys was Charlie, and he wasn't talking. They were hitting him. The girl was half-naked and crying.

Caroline started hitting boys. She moved fast, not as fast as Jack, but fast enough that she had to be careful not to hit Charlie or the girl. She hit hard. The boys were yelling and the girl was crying and then Charlie was telling her to stop, it was over.

Charlie said something to the girl, but she picked up some

clothes and ran away and Charlie didn't go after her because he had to help Caroline up and she didn't realize her head hurt until he helped her up. She asked him what had hit her.

"The wall," he said.

"Better call the police," she said.

"Let's get home first," he said.

"The girl—"

"She's safe, or she will be. She lives down the block. I don't know if she'll want to press charges."

Caroline couldn't talk anymore. She didn't think this night was going to end naked after all. She wanted dry towels and a warm bed and sleep.

"You shouldn't sleep," Charlie said. "You might have a concussion."

Caroline didn't answer him. He knew what she was thinking already. It wasn't fair.

Mary Beth had hands like Cecilia's. Not exactly like Cecilia's—Cecilia had long fingers, and she bit her nails. Mary Beth had short, stubby fingers, and her nails were pink. She moved her hands a lot while she talked, which was something Cecilia did, except Cecilia sometimes threw things.

Maybe it wasn't Mary Beth's hands that reminded Scott of Cecilia. Maybe it was just that everything reminded him of Cecilia. Waking up reminded him of Cecilia, and eating, and watching TV, and masturbating. Especially masturbating. Masturbating reminded him of sex with Cecilia, which was wild and uninhibited and sometimes put him in fear of his life. He was making a habit of checking the scratches on his back and sides every morning. Once they were all healed, he told himself, it would really be over.

Mary Beth was very nice, but he doubted that she was like

Cecilia in bed. He wondered if he would look back on Cecilia in twenty years, when he was married with kids and dogs and minivans, and remember her as the best sex he had ever had. His fantasies couldn't even equal it. Masturbation was something he did for survival now, like eating and breathing and defecating. There was no joy in it, just a temporary release. Back in high school he used to sit in class and look forward to masturbating, once when he got home, once after going to bed. Mornings, too, sometimes. Now he waited until it was late at night, too late for Cecilia to call and ask him to come back, and then he jerked himself off roughly, angry at himself and at Cecilia and at basketball players everywhere.

Mary Beth had stopped talking. She was a little drunk, but not drunk enough not to notice that he was hardly paying any attention to her. "I'm sorry," he said, and drank from the same empty beer bottle he'd been drinking from for forty-five minutes. Where was Charlie with the beer?

They were alone in the living room. Mary Beth and Caroline had put Harriet to bed a couple of hours ago. Harriet had been crying about some guy getting shot, but Jack had told Scott that it was something that happened a long time ago, in the 1980s. He thought Jack was in the attic now—he'd heard someone walking around up there before. He hoped it was Jack.

"Have you heard a word I've been saying?" Mary Beth asked. Something in her tone reminded Scott of Cecilia.

"Um. You were talking about . . . magazines." He remembered saying something about perfume ads a while ago, just to keep up his end of the conversation.

"Yeah, well. I don't understand it. I mean, I'd like to think that all those women know what they're getting into. But even if I thought that, and I don't, it's one thing for a magazine that's about sex, you know? *Playboy* is about sex. A woman posing for *Playboy* is going to be naked. But this *Maxim* garbage Charlie gets. These are, like, successful women, and here they are almost naked in this magazine. I mean, what is it with guys? Do you have to look at naked women every twenty-four hours or your heart stops?"

Scott laughed politely. He wondered if Charlie had any of those magazines in his room. He wondered if Alyssa Milano was in any of them. He liked Alyssa Milano; she reminded him of Cecilia.

The door flew open, and Charlie entered, half-leading, half-carrying Caroline. Caroline looked around the room with an expression somewhere between a grin and a grimace.

"What happened?" Mary Beth helped Charlie sit Caroline down on the couch.

"She hit her head," Charlie said, glancing at Scott.

"Rainy," Caroline said. "Rainy brainy. Bet you didn't know I was thinking that, Charlie barly."

Charlie put a hand on her forehead. "I was worried about a concussion, but I don't know much about them."

"Was she unconscious?" Mary Beth asked.

"I don't think so. But she wants to go to sleep."

Mary Beth took Caroline's face between her hands. "Honey, listen to me. You can't go to sleep right now, OK? Stay awake for a while and talk to me."

"Mary Beth," Caroline said in the tones of a schoolteacher reprimanding a foolish student. "Don't fall for this boy. He knows what you're thinking."

Mary Beth looked at Charlie, who was blushing. "Anything else you want to tell me?"

"I got sick," Caroline said. "Tossed my cookie dough." She laughed.

"Did you get the beer?" Scott asked.

Mary Beth looked at him incredulously.

Charlie stared at him for a moment before tossing him the keys. "It's in the truck."

"That was a stupid thing to say," Scott told himself as he walked downstairs. It was still raining hard, water changing shape as it trickled over eaves, off the deck, and struck asphalt below. Scott pictured himself on the deck in the summer sun, tan and happy, flirting with girls in bikinis below. He wondered if anyone would ever have sex with him again.

The truck was parked in the driveway beside the house. He kicked up mud and puddles running to it. He struggled with the passenger-side door, the rain soaking him through, draining down his back and his pant legs to the ground. By the time he got the door open and lifted the beer and the brown bag into his arms he was shivering.

He turned around and found Jack right behind him. He didn't even look wet.

"They're back?" Jack asked.

"Where did you come from?"

"Let me take something."

Scott handed him the brown bag, then followed him back to the porch. Jack held his hand out for the keys as they mounted the stairs, and Scott handed them over.

"You don't seem drunk," he said.

"I don't feel drunk," Jack said.

"Why didn't you drive, then? To get the beer?"

"Because Charlie isn't drunk either. Also, I had some things to check on."

Scott wanted to ask what kind of things Jack could be checking on in the attic during a rainstorm, but when Jack opened the door he remembered that there were other things going on.

"Oh, I forgot to tell you—"

"What happened?" Jack asked.

"She hit her head," Mary Beth said.

"Boom!" Caroline said. "Up, up, and bam! Bang! Pow!"

"I'm going to take her downstairs," Mary Beth said. "Charlie, will you help me?"

"Why would you need—oh. Sure." Charlie whispered something to Jack as they helped Caroline through the doorway and started down the stairs.

"Is she going to be OK?" Scott asked.

"Of course," Jack said. "Mary Beth's practically a doctor. She'll be fine."

"I hope so." Scott twisted open a bottle of beer, but the taste only made him realize how drunk he already was. "Seems like the party's kind of done," he said.

"Yeah," said Jack.

"Happy birthday, man." Scott remembered that he hadn't even given Jack a card. "You want this beer?"

"No thanks. I think I might walk up to Cap Centre and get a snack."

"OK. I guess I'm going to bed."

Scott waited until Jack was gone to check Charlie's room for magazines.

ay knew the doorbell was working—he could hear it ring-
ing through the door. He fingered the button again.

Ed gave up on his cigarette and ground it out on the doorstep.
"Maybe he's out," he said. "Maybe he's flying patrol."

Ed was grinning, which was something Ray often wished he
wouldn't do. Ed was compact and kept his head shaved, which
along with his blond eyebrows made him look sort of alien. He
dressed better than he should be able to afford, in silk shirts and
ties and Italian shoes and a leather jacket for every day of the week.
He and Ray weren't partners, exactly. They worked their own cases
but helped each other out when necessary.

"It's early," Ray said. "Let's give him a couple of minutes."

He rang the bell again and heard someone swearing inside the
house. It was a nice split-level house, with a deck and a pool out
back. Recently painted, with two cars—a Mercedes and a Toyota
4Runner—in the attached garage.

The man who answered the door was exactly what Ray had expected. Six-foot-three, about 270 pounds, forty-one years old, heavily bearded. "Jesus, Mary and Joseph," he yelled, launching spittle from his lips. "I became a goddamned atheist so I could sleep in on Sunday mornings. You'd better have a . . ."

He stopped talking when he saw their badges. "Sorry to disturb you so early, sir," Ray said, "but we have a few questions. Are you Dr. Frank Nelson?"

"What's this about?"

"Can we come in?"

"Is it necessary?"

"No. We can stand here on your doorstep while your neighbors come out their front doors to get their newspapers, and you can spend the next month trying to convince them that we weren't the police."

"I don't care what they think," Nelson said, but he stepped back to let them enter. "Is this going to take long?"

"We'll see." Ray pulled a plastic bag from his jacket. "Is this your driver's license?"

Nelson took the bag and squinted at the card inside. "Yes. I lost that three months ago. Where did you find it?"

"At the scene of a crime."

"Hey, I wasn't— When did this thing happen?"

"Last night."

"I was at a birthday party last night. My wife's aunt turned seventy." He handed the bag back to Ray. "I don't think I can help you."

"You've had your license replaced?"

"Yes."

"Can we see it?"

Nelson sighed. "Hold on. It's in the bedroom."

He left the room, which seemed empty in the absence of his

bulk. Ed looked over the pictures on the mantel. "No capes here," he said.

"They don't wear capes," Ray said.

"Ray. You don't think this guy has anything to do with the All-Stars."

"I'm just following evidence."

"Why?"

"Ed, I don't want to have this conversation again."

"I think you're jealous because these All-Stars are doing our job better than we can. You want to be the supercop in town. You resent that they can do things you can't, and you want to put a stop to it."

"Spare me the psych evaluation, Ed. You're just lazy."

"OK. I'm lazy and I like the fact that I've got some superheroes helping me out with my job. They stop the bad guys, they catch the bad guys, they give us the leads we need to find the bad guys, and lock them up. Ray, nobody tries to lock up Spider-Man."

"Yes, they do."

"Well, Superman then. I say we let it lie. They're not hurting anyone who doesn't deserve it."

"Who decides who deserves it?" Ray asked, and was grateful that Dr. Nelson's reappearance stopped Ed from rattling off some pat answer. Ray knew that Ed wanted to find the All-Stars, too, but only because he was curious. The thing Ed loved about the job was finding out secrets, going through other people's dirty laundry. It wasn't a particularly admirable trait, but it made him a pretty good detective.

"Here," said Dr. Nelson. The license had been renewed on April 24. Ray didn't bother to call it in.

"You say you lost the other ID?"

"Yes. I was using an ATM downtown, I think it must have fallen out of my wallet."

"You're sure it wasn't stolen?"

"All my credit cards and cash were still there."

"This was in April?"

"Yes. My wife and I went to a concert at the Civic Center."

"Did your son go?" Ed asked.

Nelson turned to Ed as if he'd forgotten he was there. "No. He doesn't care for Bach."

Ed picked up a picture from the mantel. "How old is he?"

"Seventeen."

"Looks older. Looks a lot like you, actually."

"Yeah, a lot of people say that."

"So you don't suppose he might have slipped that license out of your wallet one night back in April? Maybe to buy some beer for his buddies?"

Nelson's jaw clenched. "No. Steven wouldn't do that."

"Here's the thing." Ed set the picture back up on the mantel. "Who'd carry around a driver's license that isn't their own? Unless you've got some security clearance that we don't know about, it would probably be in order to buy alcohol. That means a college student, maybe, or a high school kid."

"So that leaves you with, what, forty thousand suspects in the area?"

"Maybe. Except that I don't think many kids could pass for six-three, two-seventy. Which makes me wonder where Steven was last night."

"At the same birthday party with my wife and I."

"And he stayed there all night? He didn't leave a little early to hook up with his friends?"

"He left at about nine-thirty," said Nelson.

"You're sure of the time?" Ray asked.

"I'm sure." He looked from Ed to Ray and back again. "Any more questions?"

"Yes," Ray said. "I wonder if you know the date of the concert, the night you think you lost the license."

"Not offhand, I don't. I suppose I could find out."

"That would be very helpful," said Ray.

Nelson frowned and lumbered out of the room again.

Fifteen minutes later Ed was driving them back to the station. "This is a dead end," he said. "We're never going to know exactly what happened at that place last night. Those kids aren't going to tell us the truth, and the girl will never come forward."

"We don't even know if there was a girl," Ray said.

"You're just proving my point. Look at the evidence, Ray. Two shattered doors, five bruised engineering students and some underwear that may or may not have come from a rape victim who's nowhere to be found."

"And a driver's license."

"Which might belong to any number of possible accomplices, victims, or vigilantes. Which may have been lying in that basement for three months. Did you ask our victims about it?"

"Don't call them victims," Ray said.

"All right. Our righteously beaten possible rapists. Did you ask any of them about the ID?"

"Not yet. I wanted to have something to brace them with."

"Well, my friend, you've got nothing."

"I've got an eyewitness who claims he saw a girl fly through both those doors before nearly putting him and his housemates into a coma."

"The same eyewitness claims that the panties we found had been there for months, and that he and his well-behaved friends were just watching TV. Let's see if his story changes when the lab comes back with a positive for semen on that couch."

"It probably will."

"You're damn right it will. And you'll have nothing. Ray, if Blue Star was there, she was doing some good."

"She put those kids in the hospital," Ray said.

"Fuck, Ray, they're rapists! We may never prove it, but we both know it. If I was the one with superpowers and a mask, those kids wouldn't be breathing."

"Would that make you a hero, or just a murderer?"

"Tell me that if some little prick raped Harriet, you wouldn't want him dead. Don't give me the Dukakis answer, either. I know you."

"Fine. I might kill him, yes. But then I'd expect you to arrest me."

Ed laughed so hard that Ray thought he was going to drive off the road. Ray shook his head, and then laughed, too.

"You're a hell of a guy, Ray." Ed turned into the station parking lot. "A hell of a guy."

There was too much to do at the station for them to be out chasing phantom leads, but they both had needed to get out for a while. Ray made some notes in his All-Stars file, then spent the rest of the shift writing reports and taking a confession from a grandmother who'd just been nailed for murdering a transient in the early 1960s. The mysterious know-it-all that all the detectives were calling Sherlock (whom Ray was convinced was somehow connected to the All-Stars) had fingered her in the latest mailing. Sherlock had provided a detailed account of the incident. Ray had to use every word to convince her that she was caught.

When she started talking it was in a monotone, not looking up from the purse in her lap. The transient had stayed with her one night while her husband was away on business. They'd had consensual sex, but in the morning she'd panicked, certain one of the neighbors would see him leaving. She'd drowned him in the tub, wrapped the body in old bedclothes, and dumped it in Lake Monona. The body had been recovered six weeks later, but was on record as an accidental drowning, possibly alcohol-related.

She asked if she would be out for her grandson's birthday on Thursday. Ray told her he didn't think so. She nodded calmly and put up no resistance as she was cuffed and led from the room.

Ray looked at his watch. It was four-thirty. He was supposed to have picked up Harriet at four.

He turned the old woman's file over to the desk sergeant and signed out.

"You have a phone message from your daughter," the desk sergeant said.

"I'm sure I do," Ray said. "I'm on my way right now."

He made the drive from the station to Harriet's place in ten minutes. Harriet was talking on the phone as she answered the door. "It sounds serious," she said, "but are you sure you need me? My dad's here. We're supposed to do a movie night."

Her editor, Ray decided. Some kind of story emergency? That seemed unlikely. The paper was publishing once a week for the summer. He sat down at the kitchen table and immediately wished he hadn't. Getting up again would be a chore.

"Can't Jack? . . . I know, but this is supposed to be my night off."

Ray closed his eyes. This was karma, he supposed. Plenty of times he'd had to cancel on her, when a case was eating him up inside.

"Don't lay that guilt trip on me. I've been doing my part and— yes. *Fine.* I'll be out in a couple of minutes." Harriet lowered the phone and looked for someplace to slam it down, but it was a cordless, and the best she could do was to emphatically punch the button.

"You're canceling?" Ray said.

"I'm sorry, Daddy. It's . . ."

"The paper," he finished for her. "I know. Should we try for later in the week?"

"Wednesday," Harriet said.

"Wednesday's good," said Ray and hauled himself out of the chair. "I'll let you go."

Harriet kissed him on the cheek. "I love you, Daddy."

"I love you too, honey."

Ray walked back to his car. Something about work was bobbing up from his subconscious. He knew from long practice not to think about it, to just let it emerge on its own.

He turned up the police radio as he started the car. "—peat, all vehicles in the vicinity of—"

A truck pulled out of the driveway next to Harriet's house and honked its horn.

"—hostage situation. Officers under fire, gunman believed to have three hostages. All vehicles proceed to corner of Harper and Grove."

Ray heard something slam and looked up to see the truck driving off, with Harriet in the passenger seat. A blond boy with a crew cut was driving.

Ray pulled into the street going the opposite way, half-listening to the radio. The hostage mess was on the other side of town, and the area would be swarming with police and sheriff's deputies in about thirty seconds. If he was needed, it would be somewhere else, while half the force was dealing with the gunman.

He stopped for gas. It wasn't the ID. Ed was right, that was a dead end. No fingerprints, a campus full of suspects. He'd have better luck finding the girl who'd been assaulted than he would finding the kid who'd been using Dr. Nelson's ID for the last three months.

He paid and pulled into the drive-thru line at the Taco Bell next door. It was fatty and it gave him gas, but he was too lazy to cook tonight and too hungry to even wait for microwave food.

"Stand by," said the dispatcher. "Stand by . . . the gunman is in custody. The hostages are unharmed. Gunman's accomplice also in custody. Green Star has been sighted in the area, other All-Stars may be nearby. The All-Stars are considered very dangerous. Do not attempt to engage the All-Stars. Report any sightings—"

Jack. Harriet had mentioned a Jack on the phone. Red Star's name was Jack. Green Star was a small woman with reddish brown hair. So was Harriet's roommate Mary Beth. Blue Star had dark hair and tanned skin, like Harriet's other roommate, Caroline.

The blond boy in the truck—a couple of witnesses had mentioned a Yellow Star, a skinny kid with moppish blond hair. And Ray realized now that he'd seen the kid before, in the barbershop.

None of which pointed to Harriet. Except that she had gone with the blond boy. Was she Sherlock? No. Ray had read enough of Harriet's writing over the years to know her style, and none of the accounts he'd seen over the past month matched it. Maybe she wasn't involved. None of the witnesses had mentioned an African-American female.

Then he knew. The invisible girl that Ben Thatcher had talked about, the one that had popped up in a few witness reports. No one had said anything about an African-American female because none of them had seen her.

Horns were honking at him, and he realized that it was his turn at the drive-thru. He eased off the brake.

*Jesus*, he thought as he pulled forward. *My daughter's a superhero.*

Jack drove with the windows open and no radio. He liked to listen to the morning sounds. The residential streets were nearly silent; lazy wind chimes and early-risen birds made soft, musical sounds, but most of the alarm clocks and automatic coffee machines would make no sound for three hours yet.

He left the truck running at the end of the block. He retied his shoes and loaded a few dozen newspapers into his bag. A dog barked in its sleep.

Jack shut the door of the truck, strapped his watch to the rearview mirror, pressed the button to start the stopwatch, and took off running.

Now the silence was complete, except for the sound of his breathing and his heart. Five blocks, down and back. Thirty-five newspapers. When he got back to the truck the stopwatch was just turning over to one-hundredth of a second.

He climbed in the truck and pulled up to the next block. There were two apartment buildings on this street, and he had a key for the outer doors. Forty-six papers. It took him fourteen seconds, most of which he spent unlocking the doors without destroying the keys. The next street was a short one, and he didn't even set the stopwatch. He drove to the last route.

The distribution manager had started him out with four routes. He said that was all anyone had ever been able to finish in time. The first night Jack had done the routes, gassed up the truck, eaten a big meal at Perkins, and taken a nap in his truck before going back to the warehouse. He stayed there with the manager until eight in the morning just to show him that he had plenty of time left over for more routes. When there were no complaints, the manager gave Jack two more routes, saying that was all he thought was humanly possible. Jack didn't argue. He didn't want to arouse any suspicion.

Today he was taking his time between routes, breathing the morning air and pretending that there was nothing to think about. When he started to think he thought about food: rare, juicy steaks, peppery mashed potatoes, warm apple pie. Sometimes he dreamed about food now. He was losing weight; his mom had noticed. He had told her he was worried about summer finals, which wasn't true. He had more time to study than he knew what to do with; he'd read his texts three times or more, and the only thing tricky about the tests was writing slowly enough not to attract any attention.

The last paper route was all apartment buildings. The tricky thing was carrying all the papers—seventy-two in one building alone—but he just stacked them near the inside door and went back when he ran out. The route took him twelve minutes, most of which was driving between buildings. Altogether, the six routes had taken him forty-seven minutes. He drove to Perkins, picked out one of the extra papers, and brought it inside.

The waitress's smile faded as he ordered three omelettes and eight pancakes, with all the bacon, toast, and hash browns that came with them. Jack had to repeat himself twice because he was talking too fast. He ignored her sigh and started on the sports page, stretching his legs out in the booth.

"Is it not bad enough that you must deliver it? You read it as well?"

Jack peered over the top of the paper and saw a tall Asian man smiling at him. The man's face was familiar, but Jack didn't think he'd ever spoken to him before.

"We have not met," said the man, with only the barest hint of an accent. "Yet I feel that we must have much in common. We have many of the same classes, you recall? They herd engineering students here, have you not noticed? First this course, then that one, single file, do not push. And then I see you have begun to deliver the papers as well. This is strange coincidence, don't you think?"

Jack folded the paper shut. "Strange, yes. I— My name is Jack."

"I am Solahuddin Sutadi," said the man, and he sat down opposite Jack as if invited. "It is more than most Americans can recall or pronounce, so you may call me Sol."

"Sol," Jack said. "It's nice to meet you, Sol."

"Of course." Sol glanced at the paper. "You are missing nothing. By the time we deliver it, it is old news. The world will not suffer to be put down in black and white. And in this country, you are not allowed the truth in any case."

Jack tried to think of a response, but Sol shook his head and waved a hand, as if to say he could handle the conversation on his own.

"Not that you are unique in this respect. And there are other considerations in favor of this country. Amenities, one might say. Such as education. There are perfectly serviceable engineering schools in my country as well, but it is important to broaden one's horizons, as they say."

The waitress set a large orange juice in front of Jack. "Would you like to order as well, sir?" she asked Sol, offering him a menu.

Sol didn't reach for the menu. "Please, yes. I would like two eggs sunny-side up with two wheat toast, hash browns, and a blueberry muffin."

"It comes with bacon," said the waitress.

"I do not eat of the pig," said Sol. "I would like to substitute the muffin for the bacon, if that is possible. I will have coffee, however, if it is very hot."

"OK." The waitress swept away from their table in a rush.

"This is a terrible place, you realize," Sol said. "But at this time of morning one has few choices. Are you aware of an establishment near the confluence of Lake Street and Washington Avenue where men gather early in the morning to eat breakfast and watch pornography?"

Jack shook his head. "I hadn't heard of that, no."

"I was once forcibly ejected from those premises," said Sol, "due, I believe, to the fact that I am neither bearded nor a member of a labor union. I am at a loss to understand it otherwise. Do you enjoy pornography?"

Jack coughed and looked around for the waitress. "I suppose," he said. "If it's tasteful."

"My friend, what point is there in tasteful pornography? I have some videotapes I could show you. They are not only not tasteful, in some cases they may be illegal. But I see that this subject of pornography makes you uncomfortable. The legacy of the Puritans will never die, it seems. What would you rather we discuss?"

"I don't know," Jack said.

"Do I offend you?"

"No," Jack said. "I just don't know you very well, that's all."

"May I ask you, how do you come to know someone, in your country, generally?"

Jack laughed, shrugged. "By talking to them, I guess. So you're from where, exactly?"

"I am from Indonesia. Jakarta, or close enough that it's not worth mentioning the actual village, because you won't have heard of it anyway, any more than I had ever heard of Madison, Wisconsin, before I applied to the university here. Our family was the only family in the village with money, for which fact I assure you I am properly ashamed and in atonement for which I will someday build a mosque."

"So your family has money?"

"Yes. Enough to send the eldest son to America and pay his tuition, but not enough to pay for books. One semester, eight hundred dollars' worth of books! This, and my desire for a car, necessitated the taking of a job at Taco Bell. After I had earned enough to purchase a sporty yet dependable Toyota Camry, I took on a couple of motor routes as well. Is your story similar in its tragic scope?"

Jack shrugged. "Financial aid covers tuition and some rent. I do work study at a lab on campus, I work at a restaurant on State Street, and I deliver the paper."

"So we are both oppressed workers under the thumb of the American Man, do you agree?"

Jack laughed. "I don't feel that oppressed."

Sol's smile disappeared. "Then it is more serious than I feared.

You are so far gone that you are numbed to the indignities you are suffering. There is only one cure."

"What's that?"

"You must come with me tomorrow morning to watch pornography and eat eggs. We will demand our right to watch acts of sexual perversion with skilled workmen both active and retired."

"You've got porn on the brain."

"I am twenty years old, my friend. I would not be healthy if I did not think about sex constantly. Would you prefer to think about the problems of the world? There is poverty, war and hate, oppression, persecution and discrimination. But you and I are but students. We can do nothing to combat these things. Only study. And when we can study no longer, we must release the tensions heaped upon us by our mad professors. We must fornicate in defiance of the madness of the world. It is our divine animal right to watch acts of perversion on videotape, and to participate in them whenever possible!"

The waitress arrived at the table as Sol was speaking and set Jack's omelets and pancakes in front of him. "I'll bring your syrup right out," she said.

"Maybe you could keep it down a little," Jack said. "You'll offend the waitress."

"I was not speaking of her. But come to speak of her, do you think she does not think of fornication? Do you think that the fact of her ovaries forces her to think only motherly thoughts, that she sees herself as a virginal Madonna? You give her too much power when you think of her in that way. She is as much a slave to her biology as you and I. She desires the sexual act as well."

"Your syrup," said the waitress faintly and ran from the table.

"I am doing it again," said Sol. "We will discuss something else. Do you know these All-Stars?"

Jack chewed with deliberate care. If he'd been alone he'd have finished the plate already, but he was being careful around Sol. He wondered if he could have given himself away somehow.

"The superheroes?" he asked, once he had swallowed.

"What is happening there, do you think? Is this more of your government's smoke and mirrors?"

"I don't think so," Jack said.

"No? Why not?"

"They had some pictures the other night."

"They were not good pictures. One blurry glimpse of a woman in blue does not constitute evidence. You are familiar with the X-Men?"

"I've heard of them."

"In the Fall of the Mutants, after they sacrificed themselves to defeat the Trickster, and then were brought back to restore the balance of the cosmos, they could no longer be detected by electronics. They did not show up on cameras."

"That sounds pretty out there," Jack said.

"By which you mean what?"

"It sounds pretty hard to believe."

"Perhaps. But it is the type of thing that superheroes are known to experience. I am not convinced that these All-Stars are true superheroes. There have been no lights in the sky, no rifts in the fabric of the dimensions. There are no supervillains. And what is a superhero without a supervillain?"

Jack shook his head. "I don't know," he said around a mouthful of eggs and toast.

"A fool in tights."

arriet stood in front of the house and looked at the note again.

"Exclusive Story on All-Stars Developing—Need Your EXPERT ASSISTANCE—See Me at Office ASAP."

The note wasn't signed, and the envelope had no return address—it had been slipped under the door at *The Campus Voice* offices with just her name on it. But she knew who it was from.

She strode up the short path and mounted the concrete steps to the small, cluttered porch. The house had recently been repainted a light, inoffensive green, and the hedges that dominated the tiny lawn were freshly trimmed.

She stabbed at the doorbell.

Was "EXPERT ASSISTANCE" meant to imply that she had some special insight into the All-Stars? Could he actually know that much? Or was he just trying to appeal to her ego?

She rang the doorbell again just as Marcus opened the door. "I hear you, Miss Bishop. You must have received my message."

He looked good and managed to dispel the effect entirely by knowing it. Harriet wondered if he had ever owned a T-shirt that wasn't a size too small.

"I got your note. I don't know why you sent it to me, but I got it."

"I can see you're not interested," Marcus opened the door wider. "Why don't you come in?"

Harriet pocketed the note and stepped inside. The place hadn't changed, as far as she could tell. The front hall was still empty and needed vacuuming. The two rooms to the left of the entrance, divided by a wide arch, were still cluttered with books, file cabinets, computers, and a couch littered with blankets and pillows.

"Still sleeping on the couch?"

Marcus shut the door behind her. "It's been a while since you worried about my sleeping arrangements."

She avoided his eyes. "What's this about, Marcus?"

He sat down at a computer and started clicking through folders.

"Are you going to answer me?" she asked.

"I'm showing you," he said. "Look."

What she saw was a blurry image of a brown-haired woman wearing green. The background was even more indistinct, and she seemed to be surrounded by flowers.

"Is she on a parade float?" Harriet asked.

"What?"

"It looks like she's on a parade float."

"That's Green Star."

"Is she a parade marshal? Is that what you wanted to show me?"

"Let go of the parade thing. Let's not play games."

"It's a bad picture, Marcus."

"She was running past the capitol gardens. Let me show you the next one."

The next was not quite as blurry but showed only the masked head of the woman in green, in shadow.

"Look familiar?" Marcus asked.

"She looks like Green Star is supposed to look, I guess. But it could be anybody."

"Could it be your roommate, Miss Layton?" Marcus clicked to the next picture.

The next picture was clearly Mary Beth, without her mask. Although the photo appeared to have been taken through the half-closed blinds of her window, her face and costume were clearly visible.

"You see now why I called you in to consult on this."

"To remind me that you're a pervert?"

"I didn't take any nudes. And if you insist on bringing up our sex life, you were the one with the problem, not me. But you're just trying to change the subject." He smiled. "Not much fun being on the other side of the interview, is it? Tell me what you think of this one."

The next image was of Harriet's house, from across the street, after dark. The silhouette of a person was clearly visible in midair, emerging from the attic window.

"You've been spying on my house?" Harriet asked.

"I notice you don't seem surprised by the content of these photographs."

"Marcus, you don't seriously think Mary Beth is strong enough to do the things Green Star is supposed to have done."

"All I have are facts. I personally saw Green Star lift two men with one arm, and credible witnesses say they saw her lift an SUV over her head to prevent some convenience store robbers from escaping. And I know now that Mary Beth is Green Star."

"That's ridiculous."

"What's ridiculous is you pretending you don't know what's going on. You're in on this somehow, or you wouldn't even be here, the way you avoid me."

"To avoid you I'd have to think about you."

"You think about me. You're still in love with me."

"I was never in love with you."

"You were. You never said it, but you were."

"You're so goddamn conceited."

"And you're so afraid of losing control that you can't relax. But this really isn't taking us anywhere. I'm curious about your reaction to these photographs."

"They're obviously fake. You pasted Mary Beth's face in there with Photoshop and drew in that silhouette above the house."

"That's possible," Marcus said. "But you know me pretty well. Do you really think I'd do that?"

"If you thought I knew something you might doctor up some fake evidence and show it to me, hoping I'd give something away. It might even work, if I knew something."

"I think you do. I think you know everything that's going on with the All-Stars. But I don't need to get answers from you. The police are investigating this, you know."

Harriet knew. Charlie had told her that her dad was on the case, and he scared her more than Marcus did.

"If I were to publish these pictures I bet I'd get a lot of attention. The police would probably want to ask your roommate some questions. Probably both your roommates, and yourself as well. They'd start keeping an eye on your neighborhood to catch any costumed crusaders slipping through backyards to their secret base in your attic, or wherever you have it. I have to say, it's sort of sexy. What's your connection to it all?"

*He doesn't know I'm one of them.* Harriet was surprised by her reaction to that. Of course, no one had ever mentioned a young black woman at any of the All-Star appearances, because no one had ever seen her. But she had an urge to tell him about Black Star and the costumes and how it felt when things went right and they caught the bad guys and saved lives and how it felt when things didn't go right, like at the pizza parlor which she still had nightmares about and how she had gone to the hospital five nights in a row to check on the manager and sent flowers to him anonymously when he'd gone back to work but she still didn't feel any better. She wanted to tell Marcus how the colors went flat and bright and elementary when she went invisible and how sometimes she deliberately ran into things to be sure her legs were still there. She even wanted to tell him about how sometimes she watched people when they thought they were alone, listening to their conversations in restaurants and a few times even following a couple home and slipping inside with them and watching them talk and get ready for bed and pretending she was one of them, a normal person in a normal relationship instead of a fucked-up person pretending to be normal. She wanted to tell him all those things, and she remembered then that she had been in love with him, damn him, but it could never have worked because she couldn't have a normal, healthy relationship.

What she finally said was, "What is it you want, Marcus?"

"Is that some sort of admission?"

Harriet wanted Charlie here so he could tell her exactly what Marcus knew. She should have talked to the others before coming here, but she'd thought she could handle Marcus the way she used to when they were together. It wasn't like that now.

"What is it you want?"

"I want an interview with Mary Beth. I won't print any pictures. But I want to ask her some questions. In return I'll keep her identity secret."

"And stop the surveillance?"

Marcus hesitated. "For a while."

"For good."

"I won't lie to you, Harriet. This is too big for me to sit on indefinitely. I have to keep investigating. But I'll promise to protect Mary Beth's identity and that of any other All-Stars I discover. It's not important to me to unmask them."

"You're going to make it political, aren't you?"

"How would I do that?"

"You're going to make Green Star into a poster child for your causes. I know you. You're going to twist this."

"I'm going to report facts."

"Marcus, you pick and choose your facts. You know what you're going to say before you do your research. Look at this!" She waved at the bookshelves around her. "All you read are crackpot conspiracy theorists who think there's a secret cabal behind the assassinations of everyone from FDR to Buddy Holly to Tupac. I don't want you painting my roommate as a revolutionary. She doesn't need a high profile."

"She's already got it."

"Not as an enemy of the state!"

Marcus stood and moved toward the front door. "Why don't

you go talk to her. I'm running something about the All-Stars in next week's issue. It's up to you and her whether I run her story or my pictures."

He was hurt, Harriet realized. She'd just said all the things that other people said about him, taken all the doubts she'd ever had about him and thrown them in his face.

"I'll call you," she said.

"One more thing," Marcus said. "In case anyone thinks they can come in here and wipe those pictures off the hard drive, they might want to know that I've installed cameras here. I've also got backups on disk and printed copies in a safety-deposit box. Just in case anyone was to think they could get rid of all the evidence."

Marcus wasn't even gloating. He wouldn't look at her.

"I'll be in touch," Harriet said, and left.

**C**harlie knocked and concentrated on not picking up anything from the other side of the door while he waited. The
temptation was always there, and he had succumbed to it a couple
of times. But it was one thing to sift through the minds of strangers,
and another to violate his friends.

"Come in," said Mary Beth.

She was sitting on her bed. She was so small—somehow the
costume made her seem bigger, made it seem less unbelievable that
a woman her size could lift two tons without strain. Now the books
strewn on the bed and the floor seemed more solid than she.

"Reading?" Charlie asked.

"Not really," she said. "What did you find out about Marcus?"

It sounded abrupt to her ears as well—he felt the ripple of
regret she sent out. But she said nothing more.

"He knows," Charlie said. "He followed you last week after we busted up that chop shop. He took the pictures Harriet saw and a couple of others."

"God. What's he going to do?"

"He'll publish the photos unless you let him interview you."

Mary Beth laughed. "I'm so stupid. I knew he was suspicious, ever since that day at the SERF. But I kind of thought he was hitting on me, too."

"He was, a little." He didn't see the point in telling her what he'd found out about Marcus and Harriet. Harriet must have her reasons for keeping it secret.

"But I thought that was his whole point. I thought he was trying to blackmail me into dating him. And I thought— Well, I guess you know what I thought."

Charlie kicked at the floor. "I didn't . . . I'm trying not to do that too much. What you think is your business."

"How can that be true?" she asked. "I mean, I'm not trying to accuse you. But how can you not be poking around in everyone's heads? Don't you want to know?"

"Know what?"

"Sit down," she said, and patted the bed next to her. When he did she shifted closer, just a half inch or so. Charlie smelled her shampoo and some kind of fruity body wash. Peach, he thought.

She turned to face him. "What's he going to ask me?"

"I don't think he knows yet. He thinks we're in danger. He thinks the government will see us as a threat, sooner or later, and try to arrest us."

"Why would the government think we're a threat?"

"Because we're free agents. He thinks they'll want us to work for them, and he thinks that's a bad idea. He thinks the government is afraid of losing control. Either he's paranoid or I'm naive. It's hard to say."

"Charlie?" Mary Beth's voice was soft. It was hard to imagine her carrying a bus out of a lake, as she'd done last week. "What's it like? Knowing what people are thinking, getting into their heads. What's it feel like?"

Charlie thought about Chuck and Charles, about swimming through his own subconscious. He wasn't going to tell her about any of that.

"I could ask you the same thing. What it feels like to be more powerful than a locomotive."

"I asked you first."

"It's hard to describe," he said. "It's like being in a car, in the driver's seat, but not having any control. You see the road signs, and the other cars, and dogs running into the street, but you can't make the car obey the road signs or stop it from hitting the dogs or the other cars. The car speeds up when you want it to slow down and makes a U-turn when you want it to keep going straight, and all you can do is watch."

"So everyone else's life is out of control?"

"I'm not saying that. A lot of things I do might not make sense to other people. It's just—emotions play hell with logic. I never really understood how true it was. I see people drive away people they really care about, and get involved with people that are no good for them at all."

"Why do people do that?"

"I don't know. I think it has to do with being afraid. People are afraid almost all the time. I think maybe if we weren't afraid, we wouldn't do anything at all."

Mary Beth pulled her legs onto the bed and turned toward him. "Do you know what I'm afraid of?"

Charlie's heart was pounding.

"Tell me right now if you want to leave," she said.

Charlie couldn't look at her. If he looked at her, there would be no more talking.

"I think what turns me on is that you already know what I'm thinking," Mary Beth said. "It's like it's all out in the open. Of course, it's not. I have no idea what *you're* thinking. And you won't even look at me."

"I want to," Charlie said. "But not yet."

"Then tell me what you're thinking," Mary Beth said.

Charlie looked at a poster of the Dixie Chicks on the wall. "I have this fantasy," he said. "I have ever since I met you."

He heard her close her mouth and swallow. "Go on."

Charlie closed his eyes. "It's a hot day, early in fall semester. I'm walking across Library Mall, heading home for lunch, when it starts to rain hard. I let the rain soak me—it's a warm rain, but it's cooler than the day. I stand out in the open until I feel the water trickling between my back and my backpack, and then I duck beneath the covered walk in front of Memorial Library.

"I'm standing there wondering if I've ruined my shoes when you come running out of the rain. Your hair is plastered to your head, and you're laughing. You see me and you stop laughing, but you're still smiling. There's no one else around.

"You put up a hand to wipe the hair from my eyes, and I put a hand to your face. Your skin is warm and slick with rain. You lower your head like you're going to draw away, but instead you kiss my palm. Then you run out into the rain again, smiling back at me over your shoulder, daring me to chase you.

"I chase you. The rain is not as hard now, but the sidewalks are carpeted with water, and the puddles kick up after your feet, fat warm drops splashing over my pants.

"At a stoplight I stand behind you, both of us breathing hard. I put out a hand toward your arm, but I don't touch you. I hold my hand close to your skin and feel your heat. I see the outlines of your bra through your T-shirt. I feel my blood pumping.

"We race to the house. My hands open and close on the rain and the warm air. I imagine they are on you, undressing you, squeezing you, opening you. I'm out of breath. My calves burn. I keep running.

"On the porch I catch you and we kiss. I taste the rain and your sweat and my tongue licks the water from your neck. We gasp for breath, still panting from the run. My hands wring water from the seat of your jeans, and you reach yours between my legs.

"You push me away long enough to unlock the door, and we stumble inside, hands fumbling at each other and at soaked-through shoes. I follow you into your bedroom—here—and you push me against the closed door, shoving your tongue in my mouth. Our clothes are wet, and they stick. I peel your shirt off, and you rip mine. Your skin is smooth and hot and I want to taste it all.

"On the bed I'm still wearing my socks, and your jeans are down around your ankles. It happens fast. We're both excited, and when it's over we're still out of breath from the run."

Mary Beth's voice was hoarse. "What happens next?"

Charlie looked at her. "The second time we take it slow, in the dark."

She raised her hands, then put them back down on the bed. "I'm afraid of hurting you," she said.

Charlie kissed her instead of answering. Her lips were soft and her skin was soft and he was very hard.

"Is this one of those things that wouldn't make sense to other people?" she asked when their lips parted.

"Probably," Charlie said and rose to shut the door.

*What They're Not Telling You*

Volume 2, Issue 31

### Green Days: The WTNTY Interview

It is not usual for this paper to give precedence to local events, but for this week's issue we found ourselves on top of a big story. Our out-of-state readers may not have heard of the Madison All-Stars and their vigilante activities, but even if you have heard of them the mainstream media is not telling you the whole story.

It is not a good summer to be a criminal in Madison. One police official estimated that the All-Stars may have foiled as many as two hundred crimes, ranging from purse snatching to murder. They appear to have foreknowledge of these crimes, as they often ambush criminals in the act. In addition to their visible exploits, they are believed to be connected with the reams of anonymous tips that have been arriving at police headquarters for six weeks. These tips come in the form of detailed descriptions of unsolved crimes. The same police official tells WTNTY that the department expects to clear over a hundred unsolved cases based on information received so far.

The All-Stars themselves could hardly be more mysterious. They wear tight-fitting, solid-color costumes with white stars on their chests, which identifying mark sparked their nickname. Red Star appears to be male but rarely stands still long enough for anyone to be certain; he is apparently capable of moving so quickly that he cannot be seen. Blue Star is a young woman who flies gracefully without any visible means of support. Green Star is also a young woman, gifted with unbelievable strength and apparently impervious to pain or injury.

There are rumors of other All-Stars, most notably of a male Yellow Star. Other rumored teammates run the rainbow from Purple to Gray to Fuchsia. But Red, Blue, and Green Stars appear to be the core of the team, and this week we have an exclusive interview with Green Star.

**WHAT THEY'RE NOT TELLING YOU:** How strong are you?

**GREEN STAR:** I don't know, exactly. I've lifted a bus—that was probably twelve or fifteen tons. It was pretty heavy. I don't know that I could lift much more than that.

**WTNTY:** Fifteen tons? That's a lot.

**GS:** Yes. It was hard work. Smaller things, like pickup trucks, they're not very difficult.

**WTNTY:** What's your mission statement, as a group?

**GS:** We don't have one. I guess it would be to help people, any way we can.

**WTNTY:** Does that bring you into conflict with the law?

**GS:** You mean the police?

**WTNTY:** I mean the law. The law doesn't always help people. Sometimes it puts them in jail.

**GS:** Criminals, yes. We work with the police in that respect, although technically what we do is against the law.

**WTNTY:** You mean vigilantism.

**GS:** Yes.

**WTNTY:** How do you reconcile breaking the law in order to put criminals in jail? Isn't that the sort of thing that we get up in arms about when the police do it?

**GS:** Which question do you want me to answer?

**WTNTY:** Take your pick.

**GS:** I suppose it's a question of faith. We believe we're doing the right thing. We cross a line, but we believe it's for the greater good. I think most people in Madison would probably agree.

**WTNTY:** What you're saying, really, is that the law doesn't apply to you.

**GS:** I wouldn't say that. I would say that the law didn't anticipate us. We can do things no one else can do, and we decided, once we realized what was happening, that we wanted to do something positive.

**WTNTY:** You wanted to try to help.

**GS:** Of course.

**WTNTY:** What if you make a mistake, and someone gets hurt?

**GS:** We try not to let that happen.

**WTNTY:** Of course, but that's not what I asked. Say that with your incredible strength you shatter someone's rib cage or break their neck. Say that you kill someone.

**GS:** I wouldn't do that.

**WTNTY:** I'm not saying you would do it on purpose. I'm saying that your strength is far beyond that of us mere mortals. If some foolish person decides to try and fight you, who's to say you won't accidentally kill him?

**GS:** I think you're trying to make people afraid of us. Is that the purpose of this interview?

**WTNTY:** The purpose of this interview is to ask you some hard questions. Would you like to answer?

**GS:** I don't know what's going to happen. I've handled myself well, I think, and I'm very careful. But there's always a possibility of something going wrong.

**WTNTY:** What would you do if you killed someone like that? Would the law apply to you then? Would you turn yourself in to the police, or would they take you by force? Do bullets even hurt you?

**GS:** I've only been shot at once. I'm not sure if the bullet actually hit me.

**WTNTY:** You haven't answered the rest of my questions.

**GS:** I think I'm ready for this interview to be over.

**WTNTY:** I have more questions.

**GS:** There may be contradictions in what we're doing, but I think that people understand that we're the good guys. I think they trust us.

**WTNTY:** But isn't that why we have laws? Because we can't trust people? If we could just take everyone's word for it, we wouldn't need insurance or police or locks on our doors. What you're really saying is that because you're stronger than us, you don't have to live by the same rules.

**GS:** That's not true.

**WTNTY:** It's true that you're stronger than us. And it's true that you don't live by the same rules. Are you saying that one has nothing to do with the other?

**GS:** It goes back to the unanticipated. I didn't expect this to happen to me. None of us did. We have the choice of sitting back and letting bad things happen, things that we could prevent. We choose not to. It's not our fault that the rules don't work for us.

**WTNTY:** So you want the world to adjust to you?

**GS:** I think it has to. We're here. We're not going away.

**WTNTY:** What do you think has to change?

**GS:** I'm not qualified to answer that.

**WTNTY:** I don't see how anyone could be more qualified.

**GS:** If I tried to make rules for myself, I would be what you're trying to make us out to be. I'm just saying that something has to change. Something already *has* changed. I don't see how we can be the only ones.

**WTNTY:** Perhaps you're not. How did you acquire your power?

**GS:** I don't know how it happened. I just woke up one morning and I was stronger. I can't explain it.

**WTNTY:** Was it the same for your teammates?

**GS:** I think so. You'd have to ask them.

**WTNTY:** How many are there of you?

**GS:** How many do you think there are?

**WTNTY:** So there are more than three?

**GS:** I'm not here to play games.

**WTNTY:** All right. So there are at least three of you, and none of you knows how you acquired these powers. Have any of you made an effort to find out?

**GS:** I'm not sure how we would go about doing that. I'm not sure what it would accomplish, either. The powers are a fact of life for us now.

**WTNTY:** Don't you owe it to those around you to understand where your strength comes from? You can't even quantify it—you don't know your limits. Don't you think that's dangerous?

**GS:** I know my limits pretty well by now. We've covered this. I think we should move on to a new question.

**WTNTY:** Will you reveal your identity to the public?

**GS:** No. I'm not prepared for that. None of us are.

**WTNTY:** Do you mean the other All-Stars?

**GS:** Yes.

**WTNTY:** Are you afraid of something?

**GS:** I'm afraid of losing my privacy. I'm afraid that the public and the press might not give me room to breathe.

**WTNTY:** Not to mention the police.

**GS:** Yes, the police as well. We don't know what the official reaction might be if we revealed ourselves. For now, we've decided that it's in our best interests to keep our identities a secret.

**WTNTY:** Are you concerned about other law enforcement agencies, or the military? Some of them may already be watching you.

**GS:** That's true. We have thought of things like that, although I don't know what sort of interest we can realistically expect from them. This has never happened before, to my knowledge.

**WTNTY:** Perhaps that's because it's been hushed up.

**GS:** Perhaps. It might be naive of me, but I prefer to think the best of our government. I think their intentions are good.

**WTNTY:** Always?

**GS:** Well, yes. I don't think anyone sets out to do the wrong thing. I just think that sometimes a situation gets out of hand.

**WTNTY:** But doesn't the fact that you could potentially be one of those situations make you nervous? Say that the president decides that you need to be brought in for an interview. Maybe all he wants is to find out more about your group, maybe give you an award. But the NSA or the FBI or whichever organization gets the assignment starts working up threat analyses and has to figure out how to handle you if you're not cooperative, and before long Madison is crawling with secret agents poking into everyone's lives, and when they do find you they may bring heavy weaponry, and one wrong word from you or one sweaty finger on the trigger of some high-powered gun and you've got a mess on your hands.

**GS:** Is there a question in that, or are you just displaying your paranoia?

**WTNTY:** The question is, don't you see a potential for disaster? How will you handle it if something like that happens?

**GS:** There are a lot of things that *could* happen. That was true before I had this power. It's one thing to be prepared. It's another to let the fear of what *could* happen paralyze you.

**WTNTY:** Are you prepared?

**GS:** As prepared as one can be without knowing what one is preparing for.

**WTNTY:** Thank you for speaking with us.

# TUESDAY

ack ran.

He wondered about time, and how it changed while he ran. He knew about relativity, but he wasn't sure he understood it. When he ran, only seconds passed, but it seemed so much longer—he could see the things around him and react to them, and he had lots of time for thinking. He was thinking now that maybe if he ran as fast as he was capable, then maybe he could go back in time and arrive before it happened. Maybe he could make it not true.

He was remembering things he hadn't thought about in years. He remembered a football game in junior high, when he'd started a fight with his own quarterback because he wouldn't throw to him. He remembered his dad watching him, and he remembered thinking that he should stop fighting, that he should walk away and count to ten or something. But instead he had kicked the other boy in the leg and knocked him down. He looked at his father then, and saw disappointment etched into his tanned and furrowed brow. When his father turned away from him, Jack started to cry.

He remembered another football game, one he hadn't played in. He had been a high school freshman at the time, and his brother Lloyd was a senior. Lloyd wouldn't drive him to the game, because he was taking a girl. Jack's father drove him to the game and parked his truck next to Lloyd's Nova. His father had asked him if he could find a ride home, and when Jack said he could, his father stabbed Lloyd's tires with his hunting knife. Lloyd had to buy new tires, and it wasn't until weeks later that he found out what had happened to the old ones.

Jack was crying now. Tears slid down his face and fell from his cheekbones, swept away by the wind of his passage. He wondered if the tears fell quickly as he left them behind, or if they became motionless with the world around him, ticking forward millisecond by millisecond. He wondered if there would be some spark of his father left when he got home. But there was no point. Even if there was a way for him to drag his father back into life and pain, he would not do so.

He ran until he reached the farm, and then he ran into the machine shed and pulled out a crowbar and a hammer. He ran to the old, leaning garage that had never recovered from the fall of the old maple's bough.

"Listen," his father had said all those months ago. "We've got to take down that garage. Your mother is threatening to do it herself."

"Uh-oh," Jack said. It was an old joke between them that his mother was incompetent with tools, although it wasn't true, and she got so angry about it that they never joked about it in front of her anymore. "I could come down tomorrow."

"I've got a doctor's appointment tomorrow. How about Saturday?"

Jack hadn't asked what the doctor's appointment was for. He wondered sometimes if he should have, if asking would have been a countersign by which God would have known to clear the cancer up overnight. He wondered if his dad had been scared, if he had suspected what the doctor would find.

"Saturday's fine," Jack said.

The next day they'd found a tumor on his father's lung; on Saturday he was in the hospital having a biopsy done. By the following Thursday his parents were in negotiations with four doctors for a few extra weeks of life, and the garage was still standing. Leaning.

Jack carried a ladder over and tore the roof apart, shingle by shingle, board by board. The doors were already gone, so he tore out the framing and pried loose the siding, working carefully even though he was moving faster than the eye could see, trying to keep the structure balanced as he dismantled it.

When time ran out on him and the skeleton of the garage collapsed he stood looking at it for a long time. A long time was thirty seconds for him now. A long time was eight months of pain and helplessness. A long time was the rest of his life without a father.

"Morty?" his mother called from the doorway. "Morty, honey. Come inside."

He threw down the tools and ran to her, but slowly.

# EDITOR'S NOTE

by Marcus Hatch

You've probably noticed by now that a man named Marcus Hatch appears in this book, and if you're an astute reader you may have noticed that Marcus Hatch is my name as well. I'm part of this story—this *true* story, as I feel I need to keep reminding you all. At the same time, it's not *my* story. I'm at best a minor character, and I've made an effort to keep that Marcus Hatch from obstructing the story of the principals.

Despite this, some of you may think I've sacrificed my objectivity by writing about myself, and in the third person, no less. Not to mention that this minor character used to sleep with one of the main characters. Might still have feelings for her, even. Might have been struck by self-doubt when she questioned my objectivity back on July 23. Might wonder if she'll read this, wherever she is.

It's complicated, sure. But do you think that the corporate news giants, *The Wall Street Journal* and *The New York Times* and Gannett and AOL/Time Warner and Reuters have self-doubt, or even self-awareness? They're corporate entities. Hive minds. Juggernauts don't search their souls. They just keep on rolling, and woe betide the truth if it gets in their way.

I'm as susceptible as any journalist to accusations of not being objective. What Harriet had to say bothered me, and then I decided she was right. Not only was I not objective, I *shouldn't* be objective. Objective, in this world, means detached credulity. It means using the word *alleged* a lot when it's not legally necessary. It means forfeiting your right to be outraged.

I refuse to become that kind of a filter for what I see happening around me. I refuse to bleach the facts of all implication. When this story looks done I'll be tamping down the grounds to get those last bracing drops of outrage. Or maybe I'm a French press. The coffee metaphor is breaking down. The point is, *I was there*, and I'm not after ratings, I'm not trying to scoop the competition. I write in the service of truth, not objectivity. Witness the fact that the Marcus Hatch in this book is kind of an ass. The whole truth, ladies and gentlemen. Nothing but.

For those of you still clamoring for objectivity, I'll tell you in exactly what respects I am not impartial. One, I believe that your government—wherever and whenever you're reading this—is lying to you, often for what it believes is your own good. Two, I believe that corporations—all of them—are lying to you, for *their* own good. Three, I think that everyone else is pretty much just trying to get by.

So now you know where I'm coming from. Add hot water to this story and dilute it by the above and by a factor of Charlie Frost and United States foreign policy in the twentieth century and the English language and all of western civilization, and you'll have a cup of dark, steamy truth.

Simple.

**S**he landed on Christos's roof next to the man. He was holding a cigarette and staring at the capitol building, which stood out white-gray against the night, illuminated by spotlights.

"You aren't planning to jump, are you?" she asked.

She'd flown over downtown three times before she saw him. Mary Beth called it patrol, but to herself Caroline called it needling, because of the haystack quality created by the sheer number of streets and houses and cars. Caroline needled three or four nights a week and rarely found anything that required her attention. She'd been about to quit for the night when she spotted the man on the roof of Christos.

He must have climbed up the fire escape somehow; there were no doors on the roof. What she couldn't figure out was how he'd brought the chair behind him four stories up.

He glanced at her. He wore black pants and a brown jacket, and dark facial hair clung to his puffy face. He was young, but heavy.

"I know you," he said in an accented voice, and looked back at the capitol.

"Yes . . . they call me Blue Star. I was wondering if—"

"Shut up for a minute, will you? I'm enjoying the view."

Caroline had seen the capitol plenty of times, enough that it didn't impress her anymore. She wondered what the man was seeing.

"One of the guys I work with thought that was the Statue of Liberty," said the man. "He had heard of it, but never seen a picture." The accent was Mexican, but very faint. He had yet to give her a second glance.

"He thought the capitol was the Statue of Liberty?" she asked.

"Not the building," he said. "The statue. Up there, see?"

Caroline saw. It was a gilded statue of a woman with an eagle in her hand and a badger on her head. She wondered how stupid this man's co-workers were.

"I hope you're not planning to jump. I was at a wake earlier tonight—a good friend of mine's father died. His family is really hurting. I'm sure you wouldn't wish that on your family."

"My family?" He finished his cigarette and flicked it over the edge. "Those people are not my family. They are my family's family. I barely know them."

"What?"

He sat on the chair and pulled out another cigarette. "You don't know who I am, do you?" he asked once it was lit. "I told you, I know who you are."

Caroline wanted out of this conversation, but there was no

choice, no one else around to hand this guy off to. "I guess you've heard about me on the news," she said. "I'm afraid I don't—"

"I saw you, the other night. You came out the back after we were closed. You thought everyone had left. You looked around like you were sneaking. Then you took off into the sky, like a little rocket." The man mimed a rocket taking off with his hand and blew smoke after it. "Super white girl."

*He saw me.* Caroline stared, trying to place him. "Are you . . . do you work here? At Christos?"

He opened his jacket to show a white work shirt. "This is my secret identity, Joseph. But by day I am that master of spray-arm and garbage disposal, José the dishwasher. My power is invisibility." He held out the pack of cigarettes. "Smoke?"

"Thanks." Was he going to blackmail her? She needed Charlie here, to tell her what this guy was thinking. She took his lighter and looked for a place to sit. "How did you get the chair up here?"

"Twine. I tied one end to the chair and the other to my belt. When I got up here I dragged the chair up." Caroline remembered Vincent accusing some of the cooks of putting chairs on the roof as a prank a couple of weeks ago.

"I— Is it José or Joseph?"

"I can't decide. Call me Joe."

"It's nice to meet you."

He nodded. He was still staring at the statue on the capitol. "Your friend's father, was he a good man?"

"I didn't know him," Caroline said. "But his son—my friend— he's very upset."

"Of course he is. I think I am jealous, actually. I never knew my father."

"Me neither."

"How long have you been flying?"

"About a month now. A little more."

"How did that happen?"

Caroline shrugged. "I have no idea."

"Well. That seems about right."

"What do you mean?"

"I mean, you made it to college, right? And you're white. So obviously you also need the added advantage of a superpower."

Caroline considered telling him about Harriet but decided that would just make her sound stupid. Besides, he already knew more than he should.

"So what's it like?"

Caroline squatted on the roof to rest her legs. "What's what like?"

"Flying. What'd you think?"

"I don't know," she said.

"Who does, then? You're the only one who knows."

Caroline hoped that wasn't true. Lately she had been thinking that there must be someone else somewhere who could do what she could. In the beginning she had liked the idea of being unique, but in the last few days the thought had become frightening.

"It's like freedom," she said. "It's like—I didn't realize it until I could fly, but before that I was chained to the ground. I was stuck there. Now it feels like I can do anything."

"You can fly," said Joe.

"Yes. It feels good."

She was starting to feel uncomfortable. She was too close to him, and the costume was too revealing. He knew who she was.

"Are you going to tell anyone what you saw?"

"Who would I tell?"

"I don't know. The people you work with."

Joe shook his head. "We speak the same language, but they are not my friends. You know what their greatest ambition is? To own a BMW. They don't know how they would pay for it or what they would do with it once they have it, they just want it. It is the highest achievement they can imagine."

"What about you? What's your ambition?"

"I aspire to become a busboy."

Caroline laughed. "Not really."

"It is the best I can hope for." He flicked the last half-inch of cigarette at the roof's edge. "My mother wanted me to come to America, you see. To go to school here. I was only allowed to watch American TV, so I could learn English."

"Your English is very good."

"Thank you. As you can see, it has been a great aid to me in my career. My mother died, you see, and I decided to come here because she wanted that. It was a mistake."

"I'm sorry. I . . . I was at that wake tonight, watching my friend and his family, and I tried to imagine what it would be like to lose someone that important to you. It's never happened to me."

"Never?"

"I've never even been to a funeral before. Tomorrow will be the first."

"Amazing. I have been to at least fifty. What about grandparents?"

"My mom's parents died before I was born."

"So your mother is all you have."

"I'm not even sure I've got her sometimes. I mean, my family is just different. I love my mom." She was afraid he would say something sarcastic about her being a poor little white girl again, but he was quiet.

"Are you going to go to school here?" she asked.

"I am an illegal alien with very little money. As well as that worked out for Superman, I lack even the power of the GRE."

She put out her cigarette on the roof and stood. "Is that why you're up here? Are you going to jump?"

"I am not going to jump," he said very slowly, as if she might not understand. "I come up here at night to smoke and think, and to avoid my cousins. You may be excused to find someone else to save."

"OK. Thanks for the cigarette. I guess I'll see you at work."

"I guess."

"You won't tell anyone?"

"*Ai yi*. I won't tell anyone. Go away now. Go call your mother."

He stared out over downtown, at the banks around the capitol, at the Convention Center to the south, at the faint shimmering of the lake beyond.

Caroline took off into the night. She was tired, and the funeral was tomorrow at eleven. She was going for Jack's sake, but she didn't think she was ready.

**S**cott hadn't worn the suit since his cousin Rachel's wedding in April, and he seemed to have gained weight since then. That, along with everyone staring at his yarmulke, was making him sweat profusely.

It didn't help that Charlie had been sobbing quietly since they'd come into the church. This morning he had told Scott he wasn't sure he could come. He wanted to be here for Jack, he said, but he didn't know if he could handle it. Scott thought Charlie was being melodramatic, but the girls were all treating him like it was his father that had died. Mary Beth sat next to him, her hand on his shoulder, whispering in his ear. Scott didn't understand. It was sad, but they barely knew Jack's father. Charlie was being disrespectful of those with genuine grief.

A woman in the pew in front of him turned to look at Charlie, and her eyes fell on Scott, who forced a smile. The woman looked like someone who crocheted and made preserves when she wasn't out milking cows. She made a face and turned to say something to her husband, who after a look back dug a handkerchief from his pocket and handed it to Scott. Scott started to hand the handkerchief to Charlie, but the man grabbed his hand. He was not rough, but the skin of his hand was, and Scott was aware of his own smooth hands. He had never held a shovel or a hatchet and he had never worked on an engine. At home he raked leaves a couple of times a year, and afterward there were always blisters on the webbing between his thumbs and forefingers.

The man pointed to Scott's forehead and released his hand. Scott wiped sweat from his eyes, his lips, his neck. When he was finished—he wanted to wipe his armpits, but he didn't think it was appropriate—he would have offered the handkerchief back, but the man and his wife had turned to face the front again.

When the casket arrived everyone in the church turned toward the back. Jack was there with the family. Scott hadn't seen him since it happened; he looked terrible. He was thin and there were lines on his face and his hair had gone gray in spots. He and his brother walked on either side of his mother and followed the casket in. Jack's mother wore a black dress and a black hat, and she looked as though she'd decided that there'd been enough crying for now and she wasn't going to start up again. Jack looked as though he had been unplugged from everything, as if he were operating on battery power and might run down at any second.

The funeral was long enough that by the end of it Scott would have had to wring out the handkerchief in order to keep using it. In the parking lot afterward Charlie sat on the bumper of Jack's truck while the girls made concerned noises.

"Are you up to going to the cemetery?" Harriet asked him.

"I don't think so." Charlie looked at Scott. "I don't think it's a good idea."

Scott had been seeing a lot of looks like that in the month since Cecilia had thrown him out of a moving car and driven over him repeatedly while throwing Molotov cocktails at his head. That was how it had felt, at first, so he hadn't really thought about the weird vibe that Jack and Charlie shared with the girls downstairs. Lately, though, he had wondered what was going on that they didn't want him to know about. Had his return put a stop to some orgiastic club? Were they afraid he might find the bodies they'd buried in the backyard?

Charlie made an explosive sound with his nose, and it took Scott a moment to realize that he was laughing. "I'm sorry," he said when he caught his breath. "He— I was just thinking of something funny."

"Are you feeling better?" It came out grumpier than Scott had intended, but he *was* grumpy, so he didn't feel too bad about it.

"A little bit. But I'm not going to the cemetery."

"Jack will understand," Caroline said.

"Just take care of yourself," Harriet said. "We'll see you back at the house."

"You can drive the rest of us, can't you, Scott?" Mary Beth asked.

"I can drive," Scott said. "But I don't think it's all right for Charlie to stay behind. Jack's our friend. Whatever your problem is, you should get over it and come along."

"It's not something I can just get over," Charlie said. "I know you think I'm being dramatic, Scott. But other people's grief is hard for me to deal with."

"Yeah? I'll bet Jack's grief is tough for him to deal with. We're supposed to be there to support him when things like this happen."

"Charlie *is* here," Mary Beth said.

"This is the easy part. The cemetery is hard. That's where it hits you. That's where it becomes real. When Jack looks around, I don't think he should have to wonder where you are."

"Scott," Charlie said, "I know what you're saying. But it's precisely because the cemetery is harder that I can't go. Maybe I'm a little unhinged today, I don't know. But I can't deal with it."

"Jack knows how Charlie can get," Caroline said.

The girls flanked Charlie, as if protecting him from Scott. Scott was so angry he felt sick. It wasn't the cemetery anymore—it was the weird solidarity between Charlie and the girls. The exclusion he'd felt since coming back to the house. It was his own fault, he knew. He'd moved into his own world, just him and Cecilia, and then that world had ended.

"Scott," Charlie said. "Please. Will you drive the girls out there?"

"Fine," Scott said and turned to walk back to his Saturn. Moving day was August 14. Scott, Charlie, and Jack were supposed to move to a new place on West Washington Avenue. He wondered if it was too late to get out of the lease and get a place of his own.

Mary Beth walked into her room wearing nothing but a towel, but Charlie didn't even sit up to notice. He lay on her bed wearing the khakis and T-shirt he'd thrown on after showering, a pillow over his head. Mary Beth knew he was tired, and she wondered if he was asleep.

"I'm not asleep." Charlie lifted the pillow and sat up to tuck it under his head. "I think I'm too tired to sleep. There was so much . . . I've gotten used to keeping it all under control. I didn't like that."

Mary Beth sat on the bed next to him. "Is Scott still angry?"

"He was when he left," Charlie said. "He's driving around somewhere. I think we should tell him."

"I don't think we should tell anybody," Mary Beth said.

"We already have," Charlie said. "Jack's sister knows."

"The one with the crush on you?" Mary Beth poked him in the stomach.

"Grace, yeah. Although I think she's over me now. She was doing it as much to annoy Jack as anything else." He sighed. "Poor kid."

Mary Beth said nothing, but she was thinking about Wanda. Charlie must know about Wanda by now, but he had never said anything. Maybe he thought she was crazy.

"No, I don't," Charlie said, and set a hand on her thigh. "Listen: Scott's my friend. I don't want him to feel shut out. He's in bad enough shape already. He knows something's going on, he just has no idea what. Can't we at least discuss it with everyone?"

"All right."

"He could help you with your research, even. He's a smart guy when he's not distracted."

"I said we could talk about it." Mary Beth lay back across Charlie's stomach.

"Your hair is wet," Charlie said.

"Do you want me to move?"

"No." He touched her cheek with the back of his hand, and Mary Beth shut her eyes.

"Poor Jack," Charlie said.

"How is he?" Mary Beth asked.

"I think he's in shock, still. He expected it, but it was too hard for him to think about his dad really being gone, so he never considered what it might be like."

"How could he know what it would be like?"

"I'm just saying this is tough for him," Charlie said. "Which I guess is obvious."

Mary Beth couldn't think of anything to say, so she kept silent. One of the nice things about being with Charlie was that he wouldn't misinterpret her silences.

"Speaking of the research," she said a while later, "I found something interesting."

"Tell me."

"I'm not sure it's anything. But over the last six years or so there have been a few reports of a flying man in the Milwaukee area. Just one-paragraph pieces in the local dailies, so not very much to go on. Except that a couple of the supposed witnesses said that he looked really old, so I started thinking about someone older who might have moved to the area recently, someone who might have a military record."

"Why military?"

"Because when I imagine the government finding us, that's what I worry about, that they'd turn us over to the military."

"Oh." He squeezed her shoulder. "I guess that makes sense."

"Anyway, I started looking through the *Stars and Stripes* archives, and I found a mention of Allied superheroes during World War II. They treated it like a joke, but then I looked through other papers around that time, and they were mentioned in a couple of interviews with returning soldiers. Saying stuff about how the 'Yankee Doodle Dandies' were a big help."

"'Yankee Doodle Dandies'?"

"Well, we didn't pick our name, remember?"

"So you think this was real?"

"I don't know. Right now I'm trying to track down World War II vets in the Milwaukee area, see if I can figure out who our flying man is."

"Maybe Caroline will have someone to fly with."

"Yeah." Mary Beth rolled to look up at Charlie. "Do you think—is she upset about us? I mean, I know you guys . . ."

"She's not upset," Charlie said. "She seems a little relieved, actually. Now that I'm no longer on the market, she doesn't have to work so hard to fight my irresistible attractiveness."

"God," Mary Beth said. "You really are full of yourself."

"You think so?"

Mary Beth sat up and leaned down to kiss Charlie. "You're hopeless."

He folded his lips into hers, and she put her hands on the back of his head. The towel slid away from her breasts. He took the invitation and kissed her chin, her neck, and worked his way down.

"Charlie," she said, "do you ever think about her?"

"Who—Caroline? Why are you asking me that now?"

"Because now is when I always think you might be thinking about her."

"I'm not," he said.

"You can tell me if you are."

"I'm not."

"The thing is, you know what I'm thinking. You know that sometimes, just for a second, I think about other guys."

"I didn't know that," Charlie said.

"You didn't?" Mary Beth tugged the towel upward. "What do you mean? You know everything I'm thinking."

"Not everything," Charlie said. "That would take a lot of time and would be kind of rude. I pick up on a lot of surface things, and sometimes something deeper. But when we're doing this, I don't get a lot, except for what feels good and what doesn't. It's like a feedback loop. I feel what you feel. It's weird. I wish you could feel it."

"So you're not thinking about Caroline."

"It's not that I never think about her. I'm not a saint. But while we're having sex I think about you. I don't even *have* to think. I can feel you everywhere."

"Promise?"

"I promise," Charlie said. "So who have you been thinking about?"

"Oh, no," Mary Beth said. "We're not going there."

"Brad Pitt? Josh Hartnett? Charlton Heston?"

"Shut up," Mary Beth said.

"Make me."

She kissed him hard, and put one hand under his shirt, running it over his stomach, tickling his ribs, squeezing his nipples.

"Ow," he said.

"Sorry." She lifted his shirt off and kissed the bruised nipple. She unzipped his pants and flung away the towel that had fallen down around her waist. She pulled off his pants and boxers together and threw them into the corner. There was the awkward moment while she dug a condom from under the mattress and tore the wrapper, but when she put it on him he closed his eyes and groaned.

She lowered herself onto him, and he sat up, holding her as she slowly moved up and down. He gasped with her, and she tried to catch her breath. Her hair was in her eyes, in her mouth, in his mouth. She was going to need another shower.

The feeling was rising, the tease of ecstasy just out of reach. She moved faster, holding on to his shoulders, hearing him talking, not hearing what he was saying. When the orgasm came she threw her arms around him and squeezed.

When she let go of him he fell back, panting, groaning. His hands went to his chest, but he seemed afraid to touch it.

"Oh, god, Charlie, what happened?" She started to touch him, but hugged herself instead. He was still inside her, and selfishly she didn't want to move, didn't want to end the feeling yet.

"I think you broke my ribs," he whispered.

his is 555-3558. Leave a message, please."

*Beeeeeep.*

"Mom? This is Caroline, are you there?

"I guess not. I'm not sure this is the right number. I tried that cell phone number you gave me, but it was out of service. Mary Beth took down this number when you called last month, but the pen broke while she was writing it down, and she wasn't sure she got it right. I don't recognize the voice on the machine. Is he your new boyfriend? If so, hello, I'm Jenna Bloom's daughter, Caroline. If not, I apologize for taking up all the space on your answering machine.

"Mom, I wish you were there. I really wanted to talk to you. I don't . . . I don't mean that as me criticizing you. I know you think I do that a lot. I don't mean to be a bitch.

"I'm having a really weird summer, Mom. I can't really get into it on an answering machine. The tape's probably going to run out on me here. I just wanted to tell you, I know I get mad at you a lot. I mean, you *are* sort of . . . you forget things sometimes, and sometimes you don't really think things through, it seems like. But I don't hate you or anything, if that's what you think. I just sometimes feel like all these people around me have parents who are close, who help them out. And we've always been different like that, I know. You taught me to take care of myself, and I'm glad you did. I'm sorry. I think I'm not making very much sense. I just miss you. I wish you weren't so far away.

"Oh, god, I'm sorry. I'm crying. I think I'm just tired. Look, I hope you get this message, and if you do, I'll be home pretty much all night tonight and all day tomorrow, so please give me a call. I—I love you, Mom."

*Click.*

**S**omeone knocked on the window, and Jack sat up behind the wheel. He blinked and saw Solahuddin standing beside his truck. He rolled the window down.

"Jack," Sol said. "Were you asleep?"

"No," Jack said.

"Have you eaten yet?"

Jack glanced in the rearview mirror and saw the Perkins sign. He had driven here without even thinking about it.

"No," he said. "I'm not hungry, actually. I don't know why I came here."

"My friend, you have just finished six routes, if I remember correctly. I hope you will forgive my saying so, but you look terrible. Come inside and eat some of this bland food."

Jack shook his head. "I can't, Sol. Thanks."

Sol put a hand on Jack's shoulder. "I heard of your father, my friend. You grieve for him, of course. Was he ill?"

"He had cancer," Jack said.

Sol said something Jack didn't understand. "It is not right," he went on then, and seemed truly angry. "My heart is clouded. I wish that you did not need to bear this burden, Jack."

"Thank you," Jack said.

"Will you come inside and eat with me?"

Jack shook his head. "Not today, Sol."

"Very well," said Sol. "I understand that it is very soon. But do not let your grief stop you from living. I am sure your father would not want that."

Jack nodded. After a moment Sol removed his hand and waved. "Rest well, my friend. I will see you soon, I hope."

"Yeah." Jack forced himself to look up at Sol. "I'll see you. Good night, Sol," he said as the sun began to rise.

**P**rudence wasn't sure whether what Marcus Hatch was doing with his face was a sneer or a leer. It wasn't a look of respect, that much was certain, but she hadn't expected that from him. She'd read a few issues of *What They're Not Telling You* since he'd printed the interview with Green Star, and what was clear on every page was Hatch's contempt for mainstream journalism.

"Ms. Palmeiro," he said. "How nice to meet you. The answer is no." He started to shut the door.

Prudence moved forward, putting her belly in the path of the closing door. "You haven't even heard my offer."

"I've spoken to your producer several times," Hatch said. "The conversations have been getting shorter, he may have told you. I'm considering filing harassment charges."

"Mr. Hatch, what if everyone you interviewed played the

harassment card? It's not very sporting of you to make a threat like that."

"Mrs. Palmeiro, there is nothing you and your station can offer me that would entice me into revealing any more than what I've already printed."

"You can't be bought. That's admirable, if unrealistic. I very much doubt that your little rag pays for itself."

"It doesn't have to. Fifteen years ago my adoptive mother sold an improved design for childproof caps to a pharmaceutical company for an amount of money so obscene that I'm not comfortable uttering it in polite company. My parents have more money than the Pentagon, and they like my little rag very much."

"So you're a hypocrite. You are the big money that you rail against."

"On the contrary. I'm an entirely independent entity, beholden to no corporate interests, which is something that must be entirely alien to you. Your station is owned by a holding company that controls forty-seven stations across the country, isn't that correct? Do you know what corporation controls that holding company?"

"As a matter of fact, I do."

"Of course you do. Because you're not allowed to attack that corporation in any way. Even if it's never been made explicit, you know that any story you do that reflects negatively on the parent company might result in your dismissal. Then there are your station's advertisers, many of them local, whose legal troubles and fraudulent sales practices you ignore because their money keeps the station solvent. Not to mention the network, which is part of a conglomerate with more power than any government in the world. You've really got to watch your step in the workplace, don't you?"

The baby was kicking, and Prudence wondered if that meant

he wanted to slap Marcus Hatch as much as she did. "What does any of this have to do with the All-Stars? It might be the biggest story of the year. Real superheroes, Marcus."

"Real people, Prudence. It's about them, not about the public's fetishistic fixation on celebrities. The point is that you and the people pulling your strings can't be trusted."

"Marcus, just listen to me for a second, all right? This story is out there, and we can't do anything with it. All we can do is speculate. The only pictures we get are grainy captures off the occasional security camera. The All-Stars don't talk to us. We don't know anything about them."

"That's really not my problem."

"Not your problem, no. But it could be your big break."

"Ah, the devil sweetens the deal for my soul."

"What is it you don't have, Marcus? What is it that your little desktop-published paper will never have?"

"The blood of the proletariat for ink?"

"Visibility, Marcus. You may be number one with a magic bullet in every basement bunker and conspiracist's compound in the country, but it'll never be in the living room of anyone who doesn't already believe what you're telling them. You're preaching to the choir, while the masses are out there just waiting to hear your truth.

"We'll give you airtime, Marcus. We'll give you a half hour, maybe an hour if we can swing it. It'll be late enough to keep the advertisers from getting too nervous, but not so late that nobody's watching. You tell them what you think they need to hear, and we won't say word one about what you can and can't talk about. We'll give it slick production values and a good crew and a commitment of a year, and whether it sinks or swims will depend on you."

"Wow," Marcus said. "I could be like Matt Drudge, only local and Vietnamese and even less respected. I think I'll run right out and buy a fedora and some suspenders.

"Mrs. Palmeiro, I'm going to shut the door now. Please take a step back. I'd hate to have to call the police on a pregnant woman."

Prudence stepped back. "You know, I talked to some people in the police department. They're considering subpoenaing your records in order to find out the identities of the All-Stars."

"I knew you weren't much of a journalist, Prudence, but I'm surprised you haven't heard of the First Amendment."

"That may not protect you, Mr. Hatch."

"I'll get a good lawyer. I'm pretty sure I can afford it."

He shut the door, and Prudence sighed and turned away.

The hug always came first. Olivia Bishop—now Parker again, and soon to be Morgan—seemed to believe that a hug beforehand made it clear that her criticisms came from a place of love. Instead, over the years, her hugs had become a warning sign for Harriet to bring up her defenses in preparation for a barrage of criticism.

Her mother released her and surveyed the apartment. Her golden silk-detailed dress and pearls clashed with Caroline's Ewan McGregor poster and the empty wine bottles on the shelf behind the couch. Olivia Bishop wrinkled her nose and rummaged through her purse for a handkerchief to cough into. Her coughs were theatrical in their resonance, and her slender frame trembled with each one.

"Harriet, baby," she said when she had ostentatiously caught her breath, "this place is a mess. Don't you girls clean up after yourselves?"

Cardboard boxes were stacked all around the living room and the halls, filled with clothes and books and dishes and things no one had bothered to categorize.

"Mama, we're moving. I told you that on the phone."

"I can see why. When's the last time you vacuumed this carpet?"

The phone rang, and Harriet ran to answer it, grateful for the interruption. But it stopped after one ring, and she had to face her mother again.

"Where's Arthur?" Harriet asked. Arthur Morgan was her mother's fiancé of eight months. One reason Arthur and Olivia were here was to get Harriet's help picking out the bridesmaids' dresses. At least, that was how her mother had put it. Harriet knew what it really meant—that she would be forced to try on thirty dresses while Olivia rattled off the ways in which Harriet failed to make them look good. Eventually she would probably settle on a lace-trimmed taffeta number with a pinafore that would make Harriet look like an eight-year old.

"Arthur is looking for a place to park the car. This neighborhood is not safe, you know. They have riots here."

"Mama, that was in the 1970s."

"They had one just five years ago, child. Don't talk to me like I don't know what happens around here."

"I'm not."

"Hmph." Her mother waved a hand in front of her. "Oh, it's so warm. Isn't there someplace to sit down?"

Harriet indicated the couch right next to her mother. "Right here, Mama."

Olivia looked at the couch and then at her daughter. "This is a very expensive dress, Harriet. That couch is stained."

"It's not like they're going to rub off—they're dry," Harriet said.

"I'll stand. So, where are you moving to?"

"Over near the zoo, on Vilas."

"That's a *much* nicer neighborhood. I hope you'll take better care of the new apartment."

Harriet sat down on the couch. Olivia narrowed her eyes but made no move to sit down herself.

"It's been a lovely summer, hasn't it? Have you met any nice young men?"

"Nice segue, Mama."

"I'm sorry, what was that?"

"I said, nice in what way, Mama?"

"Now that's a stupid question, Harriet. A nice boy is a nice boy."

Harriet loved her mother, but she was glad she lived in Chicago. Any guilt she felt about getting along better with her father evaporated in her mother's presence.

Happily, at that moment a door opened and Caroline came running out of her room, holding the cordless phone at arm's length. She was in sweatpants, a tank top and bare feet, and she hadn't showered yet. Her mouth was open and her face was pale.

"That was my mother. On the phone," she said.

Olivia gave Harriet a look that said a myriad of uncomplimentary things about Caroline.

Harriet ignored her. "What did she want?"

"Directions." Caroline dropped the phone to her side. "She wanted directions to the house. She's in town. They went too far on University Avenue. She'll be here any minute."

Harriet had never met Caroline's mother. "That's great! You said a few days ago that you tried to call her. Didn't you know she was coming?"

"No idea," Caroline said. "I'm supposed to work tonight. Oh, god, I have to change." She ran to her room.

"You're living with this girl again next year?" Olivia asked.

"Stop right there, Mama. Don't you start talking about my friends."

The bathroom door slammed, and the shower started running. Olivia looked at Harriet, sighed, and sat on the extreme forward edge of the couch. She looked poised for a quick exit.

"How's your father?"

Olivia always asked after Ray, because it was the polite thing to do.

"Dad's fine."

"Say hello to him for me, dear. And where's your other room-mate? The one who came down to shop last Christmas?"

"Mary Beth? She's at the hospital. Her boyfriend broke some ribs last week, he had to see the doctor again today."

"He broke some ribs? Fighting, I suppose. This place really isn't safe."

"Mama, it's safe. We've got our own superheroes now, haven't you heard?"

Olivia made a dismissive gesture, but before Harriet could ask her what she meant by it, the front door opened and a trio of people spilled in.

One was Arthur Morgan, Olivia's wealthy fiancé. Harriet didn't like Arthur very much, but he was dependable in his stuck-up way, and the fact that he put up with her mother made him a candidate for sainthood. Olivia, in her less guarded moments, called Arthur "Adonis in a three-piece suit," but in truth Arthur was short and chubby and cultivated a patchy beard that made him look like he had a skin disease.

Something was different about Arthur today, however. He was laughing, something that Harriet couldn't recall ever seeing him do except at British sitcoms, and even then he laughed at the parts that weren't funny. Harriet had decided that Arthur had a synesthesia of the funny, so she immediately concluded that Caroline's mother wasn't funny.

Caroline's mother was the second of the three who pushed into the room. Harriet had no doubt of that, because the resemblance was unmistakable. Tall without heels, with hair darker than Caroline's, she was stunningly attractive. She wore gray pants and a blazer over a white blouse. Harriet felt bad for Caroline having to compare herself to her mother while she was growing up.

Caroline's mother was in the midst of a story which she found, if possible, funnier than Arthur did. Between gasps of laughter she forced out sentence fragments that sent them both into ever more violent fits of laughter.

The third person was tall, dark, and handsome, not, as Harriet told herself, in the clichéd sense but in the archetypal. His hair was curly and black, his eyes were deep and brown, his jaw was solid and square. He wore a tight long-sleeve T-shirt that revealed his upper body in a way that would have looked deliberate and egotistical on any other man—say, for example, Marcus—but on him looked casual and incidental.

He shut the door behind the three of them and smiled across at Harriet, who realized that she was standing. She felt no less self-conscious about it when she saw that her mother had risen with her.

"Just a minute, Arty," said Caroline's mother. "I'll tell you the rest of it at lunch. You must be Olivia," she said and offered a hand to Harriet's mother. "I'm Jenna Bloom."

"How— It's very nice to meet you," Olivia said, and took Jenna's hand.

"And you must be Harriet!" Jenna pounced on Harriet and swept her into an enthusiastic hug. "Caroline's told me all about you. Where the hell is she?"

"She's in the shower—"

"Caroline!" Jenna Bloom looked around for the bathroom, then walked in without knocking. "Caroline, honey, I'm here!"

Caroline shrieked. "Mom, I'll be out in a minute!"

"I'm not leaving this room until I get a hug. I'll get in that shower with you if I have to."

"She's something," Arthur said.

"It appears so," Olivia said in an unfriendly tone.

"Now, Olivia, don't be like that."

Harriet wasn't sure what her mother would have said to Arthur, because at that moment the dark man stepped forward and took Olivia's hand. He said something none of them understood and raised her hand to his lips, his eyes never leaving hers.

"Oh, dear," Olivia said.

"That's Arturo," said Jenna Bloom, coming out of the bathroom with wet spots all over her blazer. "He's gorgeous, but he hardly speaks a word of English. Isn't that right, *mio caro*?" She slapped Arturo on the seat of his pants. "Now, where should we go to lunch?"

"That's a good question." Olivia was smiling. Harriet stared.

"We'll decide in the car," Jenna Bloom declared. "Caroline, get your ass out here!"

"I have to get dressed!" Caroline called from the bathroom.

"Oh, you're beautiful, just throw something on. No, wait, I'll find something for you. Harriet, where's her bedroom?"

"No!" Caroline, wrapped in a towel, stepped out of the bathroom. "Mom, I can pick out my own clothes. Oh, god," she said as she realized there were five people in the living room staring at her. She lowered her head and ran to her bedroom, followed closely by her mother, who shut the door behind her and started chattering.

Suddenly Harriet felt grateful to have the mother she did.

Caroline couldn't remember the last time she'd spent an entire day with her mother. Probably sometime in high school, on a holiday. No wonder the holidays always exhausted her.

The six of them—Harriet, Olivia, Arthur, Caroline, her mother, and her mother's boy toy—had lunch at the Great Dane, where her mother charmed the maître d' into moving them to the top of a very long list of waiting people, and where she was so busy entertaining Olivia and Arthur that she never touched her food. Caroline had never seen Harriet's mother laugh so much; she had always seemed very serious and reserved.

Caroline was still too stunned to really listen to her mother's stories. She spent the meal picking at her fish and chips, exchanging bewildered looks with Harriet, and becoming increasingly annoyed by her mother's silent but gorgeous companion.

"What happened to Lars?" she asked her mother.

"Lars? You hated Lars," her mother answered.

"I never met Lars."

"You said he sounded like a—what word was it?"

"A poseur. And he did, but at least he spoke English."

"Oh, now, Arturo and I don't need to communicate through the spoken word."

"If you start talking about the international language I'm going to have to leave the table."

"Caroline. Don't be such a prude."

Caroline had certainly never thought of herself as a prude, and the comment shut her up long enough for her mother to launch into another long and highly unlikely story of her life. Caroline knew that most of the stories were exaggerated because she had been there for some of them. She didn't complain about them because her mother invariably expanded Caroline's role and made her seem much more witty and clever than Caroline had ever been in fact. In the stories Caroline and her mother were a team, a dynamic duo, two against the world. That was how Caroline used to see their lives, so she took comfort in the stories.

At one point Harriet's mother elbowed her daughter and between gasps of laughter asked her why she couldn't be more like Caroline, which made Caroline blush and wish that she were the one who could turn invisible.

After lunch—which Arthur paid for, over Jenna Bloom's loud but insincere objections—the six of them walked around the Capitol Square, and Caroline made the mistake of pointing out where she worked. Before she could object her mother had swept into Christos and was charming a smile out of Vincent, who bought them all drinks and gave Caroline the night off.

They went to a movie at the Majestic and ate dinner at a Thai place off Williamson Street and would have driven out to the Ho Chunk Casino if her mother had gotten her way, but Olivia and Arthur were exhausted, and Caroline seized the opportunity to claim she had a headache. Once they were back at the apartment, Jenna Bloom pulled Caroline into the bathroom for a conference.

"How many weeks?" she asked.

"What?"

"Don't play dumb with me, Caroline. You call me like that, all upset. I know you're pregnant."

Caroline's mouth fell open. "Mom, I'm not pregnant. What made you think that?"

"Are you lying to me?" Jenna Bloom's jaw was set. She looked ready to uncoil.

"I'm not pregnant, Mom, and I don't know what made you think I was."

"A hysterical phone message, you've put on weight, even though you hardly ate a thing today—"

"Mom! I have not put on weight."

"You certainly have, pregnant or not."

"Compared to what? God, Mom. Thanks for coming and all, sorry I'm not having a baby. I suppose you'll be on the first plane back. It's not like there'd be any other reason to come and see me." Caroline snatched a tissue and blew her nose to hide her tears.

"You see? You're hysterical. Can you blame me for thinking something was wrong?"

"Something is wrong!" Caroline surprised herself by shouting, but instead of telling herself to calm down she got angrier. "You spend all your time wandering around the country, finding new and younger boyfriends, and you hardly ever call and I never see you and I don't even know if you care about me and if you die I don't know what I'll do—"

"Caroline. I'm not going to die."

"You don't know that." Caroline tried to catch her breath, but the words tumbled out continually. "My friend, Jack, his dad died, and it's horrible, and I don't know what to say to him because all I can think about is I only have you, and I just feel like you're so far away, Mom."

Her mother put a hand to Caroline's cheek. "You should come to New York. You'll be done in what, a year?"

Caroline shook her head. "Two years, Mom. I'm going to be a junior."

"Well, I can't keep track of all this." Jenna crossed her arms. "I don't know how to talk to you. You don't like the way I live, but I do. I'm not some slut, you know. I just like men."

"I didn't say you were a slut."

"Well, sometimes it seems like you think it. And I don't need that from you. Look, I know I'm not a great mom. I didn't plan any of this." She sighed. "But I came out here because I thought you were in trouble. I wanted to be here. If you want me to leave, I will."

"I don't want you to leave, Mom."

"Good, because I don't want to." Jenna gripped her daughter's shoulders. "I do care about you, sweetie. But I didn't choose for you to come here. I wanted you to go to school in Cleveland, remember?"

"You left Cleveland, Mom."

"Because you came here. And that's fine, that's your choice. But I thought, since you were gone, I'd do some of the things I didn't have time to do while you were at home. So I moved to Boston."

"And Manchester. And Albany. And Philadelphia."

"And now New York. I'm happy there, Caroline. I'm sorry if I haven't been very dependable. I've been wrapped up in myself, I know. But it's going to get better."

"Starting when?"

"Right now. I'm here. I'm going to stay the weekend. I'm going to take you shopping, and we'll ditch Arturo and you can yell at me some more if you need to. But I won't promise not to yell back."

Caroline looked down. "What happens when you go back?"

"I'll try and be better. You have to understand, I have a new job and I had to use all my assets to convince my boss to give me an advance to fly out here, not to mention the time off. I like my job, and I want to keep it, so I'm going to be working hard. And I like Arturo. I'm not sure I'll be keeping him, but he's fun for now. And you're more important than either of those things, believe me. But I'm not a very organized woman. Sometimes things slip by me."

"Promise me you'll try to do better."

"That's what I'm telling you."

"Promise me."

"I promise, honey." Jenna plucked another tissue from the box and offered it to Caroline. "You're sure you're not pregnant?"

"Well, Dr. Bloom, I realize that diagnoses based on telephone messages are usually conclusive, but you blew this one."

"Well, I'm glad. I can barely keep track of you, let alone a grandkid. I mean, do I look old enough to be a grandmother?"

"Yes."

"Oh, you're going to pay for that."

ack couldn't look around his parents' kitchen without thinking of his father. One day about ten years ago his mother had announced at the dinner table that she would stop cooking unless her husband remodeled the kitchen as he had promised he would when they had bought the house.

"Start tomorrow," she said, "or plan on picking up something from town for dinner. I'm tired of plaster in the saucepans and rusted hinges on the cabinets and having to fiddle with the knobs to turn the gas off all the way. One of these days this house is going to explode while we sleep."

Zeke Robinson had looked a little stunned, but the next day he started building new cabinets. He enlisted all the children in the remodeling, and in Jack's memory all the work was like play, the tiling and the staining of the cabinets and installing the new stove. He remembered the ribbons they had put all over the finished kitchen, six-year-old Grace attaching them to everything she could reach, and his father guiding his mother into the room with his hands over her eyes. He'd sat her down at the new table to watch while he and the children cooked dinner for her in the new kitchen.

Now Jack sat at the kitchen table which Lloyd and his father had bought at a flea market in Stoughton. Jack remembered his father sanding the table by hand, using steel wool to scuff up the legs so they would hold stain and paint.

Grief was exhausting. Sleep alternated with brief bouts of directionless energy. He rarely bothered to put on the costume when he went out now. He wasn't feeling much like a hero these past couple of weeks.

His mother set coffee on the table and sat across from him. He remembered the chairs, legs coming loose, his father fixing them.

"Grace tells me you're one of those superheroes," his mother said.

Jack stopped the coffee cup halfway to his lips, then set it down.

"She shouldn't have told you," he said.

"I would have figured it out myself . . . there were plenty of clues."

"I can't believe she told you."

"It's good that she did."

Jack spun the coffee cup in front of him. "You know, I've wanted to ask you if you had some kind of power."

His mother laughed. For a second Jack was angry—she shouldn't be laughing at him, shouldn't be laughing at all when her husband had just died. But as she laughed, the tightness in his chest that he had forgotten was there loosened, and he laughed too. As soon as he started he wanted to cry, but he had done so much of that already that he just breathed deep and calmed himself. That was harder, lately—his lungs seemed tight, much like the rest of him.

"No," she said. "I used to wish I did, when I was little. I was going to grow up to be Wonder Woman. I'd lie awake planning the things I would do. I'd fly over the Grand Canyon or become a bodyguard for the Beatles, and marry George. He was always my favorite. Later I didn't believe in those things, but I still wished. I thought that having power would make life easier, make it obvious what I could and should do."

"It doesn't," Jack said.

"Are you careful?" his mother asked.

"Yes." The truth was that he didn't think there was anything that could hurt him. Nothing could catch him, or even see him. He'd probably have to deliberately run into a wall to get hurt.

"It's good that you're helping people, Morty."

"You're not mad?"

"No. I won't tell you I'm not going to worry, but then I do that anyway. Just don't do anything stupid, all right?"

"I won't," Jack said. He followed his mother's gaze to the cabinets. His father used to oil the hinges once a month, to keep them from getting rusty. Jack wondered how long it had been since his father had been able to do any maintenance around the house.

He rose. "Ma?"

"Yes, Morty?"

"Do you think Dad . . . do you think he felt lonely?" Jack blinked at his tears and looked through the living room, through the front window, to the machine sheds and the heap of scrap from the garage that no one had hauled away. Beyond that was the two-lane highway that had been there all his life, and beyond that, the

Olsens' fields. The corn was waist high, a dry, brittle green that looked likely to crumble into brown at any moment. It was still so dry.

"Why do you think he would be lonely, Morty?"

"Because. Not that you weren't here, you know. But I should have come down more. I just— Sometimes it was like it wasn't even Dad. The cancer took so much, even before he died. Sometimes I think maybe I stayed away on purpose, even when I could have come. I feel like I wasn't there when he needed me."

He couldn't blink fast enough to make the tears go away. He heard his mother stand, and he turned and seized her in his arms, squeezing hard, needing something solid to keep him from falling away.

"Morty. He knew, honey. You didn't do wrong. Zeke knew how hard it was for you kids. Sometimes he asked me to tell you he was sleeping and you shouldn't come. It was hard for him, too, to have you see him like that.

"But you all came, even as scary as it was. You came and you spent time, and he was grateful for that, even when it wore him out."

"I never told him I loved him. I never said it."

"Oh, Morty. That's just something men aren't good at. He knew it. And you know he loved you, don't you?"

Jack nodded. "Yeah." He loosened his hold on her, and she pulled back to look at him.

"It won't always hurt like this," she said.

"What about you?" he asked. "You seem so calm."

"I'm not, honey. But I did a lot of my crying along the way. There'll be more, but I'll let it happen in its time."

"What are you going to do?"

"I'm going to stay right here in this house, at least until Grace finishes high school. And after that . . . I really don't know."

"OK." He wiped his face with his hands. "I love you," he said, and kissed her on the cheek.

"I love you too, Morty. Be careful."

"I will." Jack walked outside and took off running.

ere's the thing," said Charlie. "We're the All-Stars."

He sat on the recliner, the only space left in the living room that wasn't stacked with boxes. He sat straight; his ribs were still healing, and the pain forced him to maintain good posture.

"If you don't want to tell me what's going on," said Scott, "that's your choice. But don't bullshit me."

"We thought you might say that," said Jack.

"Whatever. Do you think you could pack something? I can't believe you haven't even started. It's seven-thirty, and we need to have all this stuff out by noon."

"I guess I should get started, then," said Jack, and disappeared.

One moment he was standing there, grinning, and the next he was gone. Noise came from Jack's bedroom, and then a box appeared, and another, and another, stacked neatly in front of Scott. He blinked, and the mattress was leaning against the wall in the hallway, then the box spring, and the frame leaning against the boxes. A garment bag and a suitcase appeared, and then Jack was standing in front of him holding another box.

"Could you hold this for me?" he asked.

The box was much heavier than it looked. Scott caught it against his legs and strained to lift it. As he was looking for some-place to put it Mary Beth entered the apartment.

"I'll take that," she said.

"It's heavy," he said.

She plucked it from his grasp and held it up with one hand. "Why don't you hand me a couple more, I'll start loading up the truck."

Jack stacked two more boxes on top of the first. "Use both hands," he said. "You'll attract attention."

"OK." Mary Beth bounded down the stairs, no strain evident in her breathing. Scott wondered if there was some trick going on, something with magnets or mirrors.

"Do you honestly think it's more likely that we'd develop some elaborate hoax than that we're telling the truth?" Charlie asked.

"I guess not, but . . ." Sweat prickled on the back of Scott's neck. "I didn't say anything."

"I'm sorry, I really am. I can't help it."

"Did you just read my mind?"

Charlie shifted in his seat, grimacing with discomfort. "Ouch. Yeah, I did. I would have told you before, but we didn't know how you'd react."

"We decided to show you all of it at once," said a girl's voice. "That way you can't pretend it's not happening."

"Who said that?"

"I did." Harriet appeared. One moment she wasn't there, the

next she was. "We're taking a big risk telling you all this, Scott. But Jack and Charlie think we can trust you. Are they right?"

Scott's mouth was dry. "I need some air," he said, and left before anything else could happen.

He ran down the stairs and out onto the porch, where he stood sweating. Moving day was traditionally hot, except when it was rainy. Today was both: the temperature was supposed to get into the high nineties, with humidity enough to drown insects and small birds, and thunderstorms were supposed to show up in the afternoon.

Scott leaned on the porch rail and looked up and down the street. Pickups, U-Hauls, and Ryders dwarfed the few compacts still parked along the curbs. Students who hadn't been up before ten all semester had been up since dawn loading stereos, beer signs, computers, bookshelves, file cabinets, desks, stuffed animals, beer bongs, CDs, and even a few books. Detritus lined the curb, broken tables and soiled couches and discarded clothing, anything too large or too old or simply too much trouble to take to the next apartment. Vans with shifty, bearded men inside rolled up and down the street, scanning the garbage for treasures. A fiftyish couple in overalls was salvaging a couch without cushions.

Mary Beth climbed onto the porch. "It's going to be hot," she said. "If you guys want, I can do all the loading, except when I need someone for appearances. I really don't mind."

"You think this is funny?" Scott asked.

"It's not that," she said. "It's just a relief. It's been difficult keeping it a secret from you."

Scott thought back over the past month and a half and realized how many clues there had been, how many times he might have figured out what was going on if he hadn't been so lost in his own head.

"Are you all right?" she asked.

"I don't know."

"OK. Take your time. I'm going to grab some more stuff from inside."

"OK." Scott didn't look at her as she went inside.

He looked out at the movers again and wondered why none of the students ever stayed put, why they hadn't all extended their leases back in February. There was always some reason. The apartment was too cold in the winter or too hot in the summer, there was not enough shelf space in the kitchen or in the closets, someone was graduating or there wasn't any parking or the rent hike of forty dollars each seemed too much. Scott thought how much the truck cost, how much time he'd spent packing, how much time it would take to unpack and arrange everything in the new place. Time and money and labor would probably total four hundred or more.

Not for Jack, though. He'd packed in less than a minute. He could have helped Scott pack. He could at least have offered. And all along Charlie had known what he was thinking. He wondered what sort of humiliating things Charlie had been telling the rest of them about him.

Except that was wrong; this had nothing to do with him. That was the point. That was why he'd been feeling that distance, why he'd wanted out of the new lease. Charlie had probably picked that out of his head, and they were trying to make him feel part of the group, which was ridiculous. He didn't have any powers. All he had now was the secret.

"Scott?"

It was Cecilia. She stopped on the sidewalk and smiled, as if she wasn't sure what he would do.

All the words in Scott's mind tripped over one another and fell in a heap, leaving him slack-jawed and silent.

"Hi," she said after a while. "I'm . . . Marshall and I are moving into a place down the block."

"OK." *Marshall.* He sounded like a stockbroker, but Scott had seen him once. He was six-foot-six and his shoulders might require custom door-framing.

"Are you all right?" she asked.

He could tell her about Jack and Charlie and the girls. It might feel good to tell someone. It might make her stay and talk to him, might make her look at him and see something, whatever it was that she used to care about. Scott wasn't sure anymore why he had loved her, he just knew that not being with her hurt.

But telling her wouldn't make any difference. Knowing didn't make him special. Or maybe it was that knowing *did* make him special, but only as long as it was a secret. It was like Cecilia was on one side of a wide river, with Marshall and everyone else in the world. Scott was on the opposite bank with Charlie and Jack and the girls. The idea made him sad and elated at the same time.

"I'm fine," he said.

"That's good." Was he imagining it, or did she sound a little bit disappointed? "Well, I'll see you."

"OK," Scott said. He waved after her, and went back inside.

**J**ack was there almost faster than thought, and Charlie wondered how fast thought was, exactly, and whether there was a delay in transmission like on a satellite interview on a news show. He wondered if by the time he knew Jack was on the scene, running up alongside the stolen car and slowing down—he actually had to *slow down* to match speed with the car, which was somehow more amazing to Charlie than the fact that he could feel the exertion of Jack's muscles, the sweat, the pressure in his lungs, and not just Jack but the shock and fear of the driver and his passenger, just two kids, one of them—Hector—thinking that his dad was going to beat the hell out of him if he got caught doing this, the other—George, but everyone called him Gee, he once put out a smoke on the back of a kid's neck for calling him George—thinking that this fag in the red tights was going down, he's not getting caught, he just needs to make it to Chicago and a bus ride back and he's home free—by the time Charlie sensed Jack slowing down to match speed with the Camry and telling the boys to pull over, was it actually all over? Had the car already stopped, were the boys stepping out of the car, was Jack restraining them for the cops?

No. At least, of the possible scenarios Charlie might have been slow to perceive, this was not the one that happened, because George didn't believe Jack could do anything to him. Or he did believe but wouldn't admit it to himself, because that would mean admitting that he mattered to himself. Teachers and police and shop owners and everyone who ever looked at him and then looked away as if he were dangerous, and thought he didn't care, they all knew he didn't matter, that the world would be better off without him. And he *didn't* care, except that this fag in the red tights wasn't looking away, he wasn't scared, he was talking to him like there were options, and George knew that wasn't true. So he cranked the wheel and tried to sideswipe the guy.

Jack's thoughts overwhelmed Charlie's, a flash-forward of images. Jack saw George cranking the wheel years before the car started to turn, saw the oncoming van weeks before it sounded its horn. He stopped. If he were as strong as Mary Beth, he could stop the collision, but as it was he stood frozen, waiting. Steel shells careened toward each other, about to crumple into a hot embrace, planets whirling toward a collision of dust and sparks and meat.

Except that then he saw it wasn't going to happen. George slammed the accelerator, but the van turned just slightly, and they passed within an inch of each other, the van dopplering away. The man in the van didn't feel drunk, now that the adrenaline was flowing. He drove away.

But the Camry kept moving toward the house on the other side of the street. George couldn't let go of the wheel, his foot was stuck to the floor. The Camry launched up over the curb and came down hard and swerved across the lawn of a darkened house.

Jack was moving again, thinking about how to get George and Hector out of the car. (He didn't know their names were George and Hector.) He felt a bit shaky. He wondered if pulling them out of the car before the impact might actually be more injurious than just letting things take their course. He wondered if their bodies could handle the strain.

All this wondering didn't translate into hesitation, because before the car struck the house Jack made up his mind. He opened the passenger-side door, pulled Hector out, and set him on the lawn next door. He felt nauseated. He dashed to the driver's side and removed George—the seat belt slowed him down—as the car was about to strike the stove. He had just set George next to Hector when he felt the first creeping hint of the explosion and wondered how fast he could really move.

Charlie didn't hear the explosion himself, but he saw it through multiple pairs of eyes, heard it in conscious and subconscious thoughts, felt it in the terrified awakenings of the neighbors.

Their surroundings were more vivid than his own, in that moment. He sat at the kitchen table in the new apartment, his eyes closed, listening to Scott making spaghetti. Scott was so desperate to be involved that he'd finally offered to make Charlie some dinner. Charlie was trying not to worry about Scott. He sat straight as a board because the pieces of his broken rib ground together when he slouched. He wished he could tell Jack about the people upstairs. He was a radio station in reverse, an audience of one to an entire world of talking heads. He was useless.

Jack ran toward the explosion, looking for the stairs. The lower floor was just the living room and kitchen, so if anyone was home they must be upstairs. Flame ballooned out of the stove like a Hubble photograph of some far-off celestial furnace, eternally stoked with gas giants and cold fire. Heat tickled Jack's skin as he found the staircase and climbed.

There were three doors upstairs. The first led to an office, the second to a bathroom. The third was the bedroom. The man and woman there were just waking from dreams about estranged friends and TV stars and falling out of trees.

Jack swept the blankets off the man and lifted him into his arms, cradled him close. The man was sleeping and warm. Jack hunched over him as he ran, shielding him from the bonfire heat of the explosion spreading amoebalike through the kitchen.

Caroline was a half-mile away, thinking that looking for something from the air sounded simple to people who had never done it. At least this time she was needling with a general description of what she was looking for, but she'd rather be flying to Devil's Lake or Door County or even the fucking Dells.

Jack ran through the kitchen once more, breathing cobwebs, the flames so strong that he was sure his costume was burning. They raced him up the stairs, traveling up the wallpaper, sneaking through cracks in the walls to find air. Jack gasped for a lungful of his own.

Charlie yelled at Scott to call 911 from his cell, and Scott knocked the olive oil into the sink with the wooden spoon, looking everywhere for his phone. Jack's thoughts came sharp and immediate. Charlie's heart pounded underneath his sore ribs.

Jack was afraid for himself and for the woman he had just lifted from the bed, cradling her head to his chest. It was the first time since before his powers that he'd felt like he could be hurt by anything. He wished that he could make her move as fast as him, make all of them move as fast as him, snap his fingers and bring the whole world back to full speed, instead of frozen like it was now.

At the top of the staircase he realized he couldn't go out that way. Heat and glow were creeping up, burning insect bites against his skin. He froze. His head spun and his eyes flicked from door to door and he smelled flesh on fire.

He ran for the window at the front end of the upstairs hall, not looking at the woman's skin, trying not to think about how much pain she was going to be in, trying not to think that if he hadn't been so goddamned cocky with those kids in the Camry none of this would be happening and these people who were just sleeping here peacefully wouldn't be about to lose their home and more. His lungs were stuffed with cotton and his legs were made of lead and his knees were held together with toothpicks, but he couldn't stop, he ran through the window and he didn't hear it shatter, he made a nod to gravity and fell forward until his foot met the face of the house. He ran to the ground and kept running toward St. Mary's Hospital with the woman in his arms.

Charlie realized he was lying on the floor, listening to Scott on the phone, the pain in his chest a distant echo of the pain Jack and the woman felt, and Charlie could not process all the pain and he passed out.

**R**ay stomped out his cigarette on the asphalt and helped the prisoner out of the car. The nicotine buzz started to fade immediately. He'd started smoking again. He'd had to.

"If you'd been nice," he said, "we could have left the handcuffs off. But you had to get mean."

The prisoner, a fifty-four-year-old white male named Augustus Jackson, bared his teeth. "You got no right," he said.

"I don't think you ought to start talking about rights, Gus," said Ed as he opened the station house door.

"I got 'em," said Gus. "I got rights, and you got no proof. That was thirteen years ago that happened, and there weren't no witnesses then."

"Thirteen years, was it?" Ray asked, steering Gus inside by his handcuffed wrists. "I don't remember mentioning that. Did you mention that, Ed?"

"Sure didn't, Ray."

"I thought you never heard of Sandy Grusin, Gus. I thought you didn't know what we were talking about."

"I don't," Gus said, but he said it in a much quieter voice.

"Then how'd you know she was killed thirteen years ago?" Ray asked.

"I didn't say nothing about no murder."

"It doesn't matter, Gus. You don't need to say a damn thing. We've got a dossier on you thick as my thumb."

"What's a dossier?"

"Detective Bishop?" Andrea, the lieutenant's assistant, stood in the doorway of the detective's room. "The lieutenant would like to see you as soon as possible."

"Go ahead," Ed said and took hold of Gus Jackson's arm. "I'll explain to Gus here what a dossier is and why we don't give a damn whether he confesses or not. You're going away for a long time, Gus. Hope you got laid this weekend, because it was your last as a free man."

Gus started to squirm, but a uniformed patrolman stepped in, and Ray followed Andrea to the lieutenant's office.

Lieutenant Harvey Bettencourt had been a scruffy patrolman, somehow always having a day or two of stubble on his cheeks, his uniform always wrinkled, his shoes never polished. But since becoming a lieutenant he'd grown a tidy mustache and kept his cheeks smooth, his shirts pressed. His shoes offered up such clear reflections that Harvey could have straightened his tie in them, if his tie ever needed straightening. Ray and Harvey had never gotten along when they were both patrolmen, and less so after Ray had made detective. Now that Harvey outranked him, they were almost friends.

"Have a seat, Ray," Harvey said, and Ray knew something was wrong. Visitors to the lieutenant's office sat: the chief, the DA, well-behaved reporters. Detectives didn't sit. It was a power thing.

"What is it, Lieu?"

"You picked up this Jackson, right?"

"Yeah. He's a reheat." That was what the detectives were calling them, reheats—cold cases reopened by the material provided by the anonymous informer who was helping put all of South Central Wisconsin's hidden rapists and murderers away.

"He cooperative?"

"No. Scared. Doesn't think we can put him away."

"If he's scared, we've got him. Get a confession, though. The D.A.'s complaining that there are too many cases on his dockets."

"The D.A. should be shining our shoes, Lieu. He could run for governor if this keeps up."

"You might be right. You still working the All-Stars case?" Harry didn't quite blurt out the question, but he said it abruptly, and it took Ray a moment to reply.

"I am. There isn't much to go on."

"So no progress?"

*I cracked it wide open. Shut it tight. Case closed.* "Not much, Lieu."

Harvey puffed out his cheeks, making a sound like helium being released from a balloon. "Well, we need to step that up."

"How's that?"

"The bosses are getting a lot of pressure since this debacle on Thursday. This Raymond and his lawyers are trying to hold the city responsible for the All-Stars' negligence."

"That seems like sort of a harsh word."

"Harsh? Ray, a woman is in the hospital with burns over seventy percent of her body. She may be permanently disfigured."

"She's alive," Ray said.

"We wouldn't even be talking about her if the All-Stars hadn't caused that accident. They wouldn't have had to save her life if they hadn't fucked up."

"What about the kids who stole the car? Doesn't anybody think they might be accountable?"

"Don't worry about that, Ray. Worry about finding the All-Stars. It's not just local pressure now. The ACLU is all over this, saying that masked crime fighters are the equivalent of secret police. There are civil liberties suits popping up all over the place. You know it's bullshit and I know it's bullshit and the bosses know it's bullshit, but we can't hold them off anymore.

"I'm assigning Ed to back you up on this, and I'm going to try to pull Murdock off Narcotics to help you out. Get some answers. Lean on that Hatch kid who puts out that conspiracy rag. He just became a witness."

"I doubt he'll give us anything."

"If he doesn't, a night in jail should convince him."

"I think he'd love that, Lieu."

"Then find another way. You're the best detective we've got, Ray, and I need you to come through on this."

Ray's mouth was dry. "I'll do what I can."

"Do better."

**G**ood evening, I'm Dick Datsun. Our top story tonight: the Madison All-Stars have released a statement regarding last week's tragic gas explosion which left area teacher Cheryl Raymond badly burned and homeless along with her husband. The statement was delivered anonymously to this station and others in the area, and reads as follows:

"We whom the media has named the Madison All-Stars deeply regret that our actions escalated a situation and contributed to the injuries suffered by Cheryl Raymond. In the wake of this terrible incident, we plan to take some time to consider our role as crime fighters, and to seek ways to make amends for the hardship our actions have caused."

This statement has fueled speculation that the All-Stars have abandoned their activities as self-appointed guardians of the Madison area, speculation given credence by police reports of increased numbers of assaults and robberies over the past week. An anonymous police source stated that the criminal element has been emboldened by the widespread public outcry against the All-Stars' involvement in last week's tragedy and their apparent disappearance.

Meanwhile, Cheryl Raymond's husband Richard is waging a fight of his own. Prudence Palmeiro has that story. Prudence?

"Dick, Cheryl Raymond teaches at an elementary school here in Madison, and despite the fact that school is out, numerous students and teachers have sent cards and flowers to her here at the hospital. Co-workers say Cheryl is well loved, and her husband Richard would no doubt agree.

"Richard Raymond works in construction, but he hasn't worked since last Thursday. Since that time, he's spent his days at St. Mary's Hospital, where his wife Cheryl is being treated for second- and third-degree burns."

"She's the most important thing in the world to me. Her smile, her laugh . . . I just want to hear her laugh again."

"Richard says he doesn't doubt that the All-Stars acted with the best intentions last Thursday, when their apparent attempt to intercept a stolen vehicle led to the explosion that put his wife in the hospital."

"They saved my life, and Cheryl's. But that explosion wouldn't have happened if they hadn't been there."

"Richard is lobbying local leaders to hold the All-Stars accountable for the accident. So far he's spoken to the mayor and several city council members, and he's hoping to speak to the governor this week. He wants the All-Stars to come forward and take responsibility for what happened."

"I don't hate them, you know, I don't wish anything bad on them.

But they need to take off the masks and—they need to come forward and be accountable. Otherwise they're no better than criminals. To take the law in your own hands like they do isn't right. I know they're trying to help, but they have to let the police do their job."

"Richard says he's grateful that the All-Stars saved his life but doesn't understand why they couldn't have done more for his wife."

"Cheryl . . . sh-she's got burns over sixty-five percent of her body. She's hardly been awake, with the drugs and everything. Sometimes I wish they had left me there, saved her instead."

"Richard says the response from city leaders has been mixed, but he plans to keep lobbying for the All-Stars to be brought in to answer to charges of property damage and negligence. Some good news, though, as tonight Cheryl Raymond's condition has been upgraded from critical to serious. Dick?"

# TUESDAY

 elcome to Shady Meadows Retirement Community. How can I help you?"

"We're here to see Bert O'Brien," Mary Beth said.

"Are you family?" The woman at the reception desk looked them over. The boys wore suits, the girls their most conservative dresses. "We look like a church group," Caroline had said, and Mary Beth had told her that was the idea.

"Mr. O'Brien is expecting us," Charlie said. "We're here to interview him about his experiences in World War II."

The woman raised an eyebrow. "It must be quite an interview, if it requires four of you."

"It's for a video project," Jack said and hefted a large duffel bag. "I'm the cameraman."

The woman nodded. "I'll call Mr. O'Brien's room, to let him know you're here."

"Thank you." Mary Beth rolled her shoulders, trying to loosen up muscles tightened by two hours of driving. They'd had to rent a car to get them all down here, and hardly a word had been spoken among the five of them.

The lobby had no sharp edges, dirt, or feeling of welcome. No one sat on the sectional couch in the corner between the doors and the reception desk, and it looked like no one ever had. There were paintings of violets and daisies above the couch and on the walls. Mary Beth wondered if anyone ever visited here, or if they simply wheeled in relatives of a certain age, signed papers, and then left. They sent checks and Christmas cards and spoke of taking the kids to visit Aunt Gladys, but never made the trip.

"Mr. O'Brien says he's expecting you." The woman held out a clipboard. "Please sign in here. Visiting hours are until six o'clock. Mr. O'Brien is in room 3282. Take a left down the hallway and follow the signs to the Honeysuckle Wing."

Mary Beth signed her name as Kate Nickelby. "Thank you very much."

The rooms that lined the hallway—Craft Rooms 1, 2, and 3— held quite a few older people, quilting, making papier-mâché, working with clay. The place reminded Mary Beth of nothing so much as an elementary school.

"They look like they're having fun," Caroline said.

"Most of them are," said Charlie.

They followed the signs for the Honeysuckle Wing, through a TV lounge where a dozen people in wheelchairs sat watching *Judge Judy*. Some of them wore pajamas and bathrobes. Most stared at Mary Beth and the rest as they passed through. None of them smiled.

"That room was not as happy," Charlie said in a strained voice.

They passed a nurse's station and a small greenhouse and a woman in a nightgown talking to herself as she rocked back and forth in her wheelchair. The walls were yellow above, wainscoting below, and the hall was lined with bulletin boards on the one side, windows on the other. The windows looked out on gardens where residents shuffled along singly or in pairs, some with canes or walkers.

"Did we pass it?" Jack asked.

"No," Caroline said. "It should be around this next bend."

"Feels like we've been walking a long time," Jack said. His skin was still red in spots, but otherwise the burns had almost completely healed.

"If it's been long for us, it must seem like weeks to you," Caroline said.

Room 3282 was around the next bend. Mary Beth knocked on the door.

Harriet answered. "About time you got here," she said.

The room was a pinkish orange color that wasn't exactly offensive but didn't seem entirely soothing either. There wasn't much in the room, just a small sofa, a recliner, a table, and a TV. To the right, an archway led to another room.

Harriet stalked back into the room and stood leaning against the windowsill, her arms crossed. She shrugged in the direction of the man in the recliner but didn't look at him.

The man glared and clicked his remote to shut off the TV. He was a small man, Mary Beth thought, not much larger than herself. He hadn't lost much of his hair, or else he had a really good toupee. Judging by appearances, he spent a lot of time in the recliner; he had a good-size gut on him, and the chair listed to one side as if awaiting the right moment to collapse.

"Come right the fuck in, why don't you?" The man's voice was thick with age and tobacco tar. "Jesus Christ."

Harriet shook her head. "Mr. O'Brien's quite a charmer, as you can see."

"All I said was I didn't know why you sent a Schvarze to tell me you were coming. And she gets all huffy." Bert O'Brien shrugged. "She doesn't like me. No skin off my prick. Shut the door so we can talk."

"Mr. O'Brien," Mary Beth said once Caroline had shut the door, "my name is Mary Beth Layton. This is Charlie Frost, Caroline Bloom, Jack Robinson, and you've already met Harriet Bishop."

"You're the Madison All-Stars," he said. "She tells me you've been all over the news, but I stopped watching the news when Cronkite retired. I don't know the lot of you from Adam, so before you ask any questions I want to know how you found me."

Everyone looked at Mary Beth. "Well, sir, first there were the sightings of an elderly man flying around Milwaukee. I guessed that you might be a veteran, found some mentions of the Yankee Doodle Dandies. After that, a friend helped me cross-reference a database of surviving World War II veterans with residents who moved into assisted living facilities in early 1995."

"Jesus. What are you, a detective?"

"No, sir. I'm just very determined."

"What if I'm not the guy?"

"You are," Charlie said.

O'Brien squinted at him. "What makes you say that, son?"

"I can read minds, Mr. O'Brien. But I'm not getting a thing from you. It's like you're not even here."

Bert O'Brien chuckled. "So how does that tell you anything?"

"It tells me you're different. The only person I've met so far that I can't read."

The old man leaned back in his chair. "Son, I worked with a telepath for eight years. I learned to block her after a while. We all did, except Jacques. He never had the chance. We had to, you know, to keep her—and us—sane. The military folks, though, most of them never learned how. They were all scared of her. They were scared of all of us, but Thea, she had Eisenhower quaking in his boots. Montgomery wouldn't come within a mile of the base when she was there. Not that it kept her out of his head."

"How did you block her?" Charlie asked.

"I don't think I could teach it, son. Hiram was the one came up with it. He read a lot about Zen Buddhism, about keeping an empty head. He sort of adapted it so we could keep the noise down for Thea. She only heard us when we wanted her to. So how did it happen?"

"We don't know," said Jack. "We just all woke up one morning with powers."

O'Brien nodded. "So you got a telepath. One of you a flyer?"

"I am," Caroline said.

"You know, then. What it's like up there. Ain't no one's ever seen the world like we can, when the moon's shining on her, and the stars are bright. I always wanted to take a girl up there. If I were forty years younger, I'd say we ought to take a flight together."

"You can't fly anymore?" Caroline asked.

"I can fly, I just can't get it up anymore. Don't believe in Viagra. Some of these boys around here, they pop that stuff like Geritol and think they're Eddie Albert."

"Who's Eddie Albert?" Mary Beth asked.

"Never mind. Well, sit down. Lots of room on the couch. There's a chair in the bedroom, bring that in here."

Mary Beth sat on the couch. There was a smell in the room like bad broccoli, and she wasn't sure if it was coming from Mr. O'Brien or from his chair. Caroline and Charlie sat beside her on the couch, and Jack dashed into the bedroom and appeared an instant later with a chair.

O'Brien seemed lost in thought. "Well. Sounds familiar. Not that there was anyone else around that changed when I did, but the suddenness, that's how it happened with me. One day I could fly. Couldn't fly the day before. I was at boot camp, is the difference. They had me off in Top Secret land before I could change my shorts."

"What kind of operations did you handle?" Jack asked.

"Impossible ones. Top Secret stuff. Most of it never made the history books."

"Why not?" asked Mary Beth.

O'Brien looked out his window at the traffic. "Hell of a place. Shady Meadows. Doesn't even make sense, does it? No shadows in a meadow. Meadow's grassland. People don't pay attention to words anymore. They don't remember that words are the only things that are real. Without a name things don't exist. No name, no identity.

"Bert O'Brien, he's real enough. Social Security number, driver's license, birth certificate. Stocks and bonds and a safety-deposit box. Even got a grave site, bought and paid for. Names and papers. Numbers. Real things.

"We had other names, back then. Names the papers gave us. The French called us Les Enfants de la Liberté. The British called us the Ultralight Brigade. The Americans called us the Dandies.

The Germans called us lots of names. Most I don't remember. Never did get a good handle on that language.

"Thing was, officially, we didn't exist. Only the top Allied brass and a few technicians knew about us as more than a rumor. We didn't have code names or costumes or anything. The military controlled the press then, you know. Not like today."

"You think it's better now?" Harriet asked.

"Hell, no. It's just not the military that's controlling it now. It's money."

"Did they hurt you?" Charlie asked.

"What?" Bert O'Brien laughed. "No, they didn't hurt us. What, like experiments? You ought to have a little more trust in your government, son."

"It wouldn't be the first time," said Mary Beth. "The Tuskegee experiments, for one. It isn't hard to believe that they'd feel justified trying to figure out how your powers manifested so they could duplicate them."

"We were at war, you know. They took an ocean's worth of my blood over the years, for testing, but they never cut me open."

Mary Beth wanted to be comforted by his words. She wished Charlie could read Bert O'Brien, to tell them whether he was telling the truth or not.

"This isn't what you came here for, is it?" O'Brien asked. "Why'd you come looking for me?"

Mary Beth looked at Charlie and realized that the others were looking at him too. He shrugged.

"Lots of reasons. Because people have been hurt because of us, and some of us are thinking about quitting as a result. Because we don't know where all of this is supposed to take us. Because we don't understand how this happened, and what it means. I guess we were hoping you would say something that makes sense out of what's happening."

"You don't expect much, do you?" O'Brien grimaced. "Meaning isn't something you find on a goddamn quest. It's in you or it's in the people you know, or it's nowhere. You understand? Unless you're a believer, and more power to you if any of you are, there's no point looking for reasons. You changed, somehow, and you've got to live with that. You can dress up in costumes and fight crime or you can walk around wishing you were like everybody else. It's not going to change the world one way or the other. You do what you've got to do, and you don't get too high and mighty about it.

"Thea and Ross called it quits after the war. They wanted a family. They walked away and never looked back, and the War Department let them go. It was the right choice for them. Me, I didn't know where I was headed, so I stayed on awhile. Did some surveillance work in Eastern Europe and the Soviet Union. Got shot at a lot. Hiram worked with MI-5, but he mostly used his brain instead of his powers. He was smarter than the rest of us—smarter than me, anyway. Me and him were still fighting the war, I suppose. But we didn't fault Ross and Thea for quitting. It was their choice."

"What about the other man?" Caroline asked. "Jacques. You made it sound like something happened to him."

"Something did." O'Brien was quiet for a moment. "These powers, they're not always good for a body. Ross and Thea, they both died too soon. I always wondered if the changes wore them out early. Course, I'm still alive, and Hiram. Jacques, though . . . he was fast, Jacques was. Me, I could fly about three miles a minute. Jacques could run a hundred miles in a minute. Thing was—and we didn't realize it until it was too late—he was living fast, too. Aging twenty, thirty times faster than the rest of us. One of the scientists who treated him said it was more like fifty.

"He was a nice guy, Jacques. Didn't speak a lot of English, and didn't talk a lot even in French. He was nineteen when his powers showed up. When he died, about eight months later, the docs figured he was over ninety years old."

"Oh my god." Mary Beth looked at Jack. All the things she had noticed over the past month or so, the thinning hair, the weathering of his skin, his weight loss—things she had attributed to the changes in his metabolism, to his constant running—the true implications of those things were now terribly clear, and she wondered how it was she had not realized it sooner.

"What is it?" Bert O'Brien asked. "What's wrong?"

Jack sat as still as Mary Beth had ever seen him, more still than she had seen him since the morning she had woken up and everything was changed. He seemed incapable of moving. And then she saw that he was shaking, so fast that it was hardly visible, the only evidence the slow wavering of his image as the light traced his form, his body too fast for light, for time.

"Oh, no," said Bert O'Brien. "Oh, god. Oh, no."

# EDITOR'S NOTE

by Marcus Hatch

I hadn't heard of Bert O'Brien or Hiram Crawford or Jacques Claudel or Ross Ingebretsen or Althea Morris Ingebretsen before I started interviewing Charlie Frost. Since then I've searched libraries public and private, government archives, the World Wide Web, and the *Big Book of Conspiracies* for information on those five people and their activities during World War II, and I've found precisely two things: jack and shit. I've been unable to reproduce Mary Beth Layton's research or, as I've said, to discuss any of this with her. Bert O'Brien, as you'll learn, died recently and can no longer confirm or deny any questions I might put to him. Hiram Crawford may be dead as well, although the evasions I encountered from various British agencies lead me to believe that there's some very polite obfuscation going on over there.

So you may be wondering how someone who calls himself a journalist can present such an outlandish story without even a shred of evidence. Here's the thing: I never said Bert O'Brien's story was true. I merely repeated his words as they were told to me by Charlie Frost. Filters, remember?

However, I believe that Bert O'Brien's story *was* true, despite the lack of evidence. Partly I believe it *because* of the lack of evidence. You see, I have a theory, but it involves a digression.

Fact: on December 16, 1998, the UN ordered its weapon inspectors out of Iraq after chief inspector Richard Butler reported that Baghdad was being less than cooperative. The Hussein government suspected that Butler was working for U.S. intelligence, a fact that Butler later admitted.

Fact: in August and September of 2002, an overwhelming number of American media outlets reporting on weapons inspections spoke of Iraq "kicking out" the weapons inspectors.

In other words, the news media rewrote history.

It could be argued that the distinction is minor. Perhaps. But if you think that's the first time something like this has happened, I've got some special Kool-Aid I'd like you to try.

Bert O'Brien spoke of military control over the media during World War II. He believed that the military didn't want the public to know that the "Yankee Doodle Dandies" were on the frontlines, so they kept the story quiet.

"Even assuming he's right," you might say, "the military doesn't control the media now, so that kind of thing couldn't happen today."

The military doesn't control the media now, that much is true. Money controls the media. Corporations that have only our best interests at heart, so long as our best interests are in the best interests of those corporations.

Do you think these people have no stake in controlling information? Do you think they're above portraying their products in a positive light, burying scandals that implicate their advertisers and shading news stories to cast their pet politicians in a favorable light? If so, then you need to put down the rose-colored crack pipe and look around.

I make it a point to bring to light the facts that these people want buried. But what worries me, what keeps me awake at night, is knowing that there are things I'll never be able to find out. I won't even know where to look, because the truth is being concealed. They're hiding the facts. They're rewriting history. And in my darker moments, I fear that there's not a thing we can do about it.

his is the difference between our cultures," Solahuddin said. "Respect for elders is one of the tenets of Islam. My grandparents live in my father's house, and will until their deaths."

They were finished eating. Only their coffee cups sat on the table alongside their separate checks.

"What if they get sick?" Jack thought of his father in the rented hospital bed, tubes coming out of his holes. He wondered if his own death would be gradual, or if his heart would simply seize up.

"We care for them. This can be costly, but we value our elders. They can teach and advise. And as they share wisdom and experience, their own well-being is improved."

"That makes sense." Jack wondered how long he had left. Every second he was dying. Only for him, a second was, what— an hour? He didn't know of an objective way to measure it, and he didn't want one. It would be like counting down to his death.

"Of course. It is this lodging of the elderly in dormitories and waiting for them to die which makes no sense. Do you not agree?"

"I guess." Jack's hair was starting to fall out. He'd lost weight, and his skin had gotten loose. He was having trouble sleeping.

"Your mind is not on our conversation. Are you thinking of this man whom you visited in this elder's prison?"

"Just thinking about something he said." Jack leaned forward. "Sol, what do you think happens when we die?"

Solahuddin folded his hands. "Are you thinking of your father?"

"Yeah." Jack didn't look at Solahuddin while he lied. Solahuddin was a good friend, although Jack hadn't known him very long. Not long in normal time. Years, perhaps, in his own.

"Muslims believe that this world is preparation for the next. There we are sorted according to the lives we have lived. It is much like your Christian afterlife, with Paradise for the just and Hell for the wicked."

"But what is it we need to be prepared for? What's going to happen in Paradise—or Hell—that's so challenging?"

"I do not know, my friend Jack."

"Maybe there isn't anything to be prepared for. Maybe there's nothing."

"I do not believe that, but it is possible."

Jack leaned back. He wasn't ready to die. He wanted to marry and have kids. He wanted long summer days in the fields and warm summer nights under the stars.

He dug his wallet out. "I have to go, Sol."

Solahuddin nodded. "Very well. I have much to do this weekend myself. I cannot believe that school begins on Tuesday. Will I see you tomorrow morning?"

Jack hadn't told his mother about school. Telling her he wasn't going would mean telling her why.

He could do a lot of things in a month. He should get started.

"If I have time," he told Solahuddin.

**H**arriet wouldn't look at him, wouldn't speak. Ray kept talking to fill the silence, saying everything, even the horrible things he'd thought but never intended to say. She just hung her head, and it was ten minutes before he realized she was crying.

Ray looked down at his kitchen table and tried to think when last he had raised his voice to Harriet. He couldn't recall. Being a cop had taught him that shouting never solved anything.

It was Marcus Hatch's fault. Hatch's face was tattooed on Ray's vision—the smug, surprised expression when Ray told him that yes, Harriet was his daughter. Ray knew immediately that there was a history, that Marcus and his daughter were or had been sleeping together. It hadn't made him angry at the time. Sitting there with Ed in Hatch's house, he had been too aware of the things he had to hide. (Hatch had served coffee and sandwiches but refused to say a word about Green Star and politely threatened to bring the ACLU down on their heads, causing Ray to picture ACLU lawyers representing both sides of the case, victims of anonymous superheroes vs. journalist protecting his sources.) The fact that Harriet was sleeping with a boy who believed the government was poisoning the water supply with mind-control drugs was just one more thing he couldn't tell anyone, one more string that could unravel his career and family both.

He wasn't angry anymore, not after having unloaded all of his hurt feelings on Harriet. He was sorry, for losing his temper and making her cry. He *wanted* to feel angry. He wanted to be cold and hurtful until Harriet apologized for lying and screwing up and growing up.

He set his jaw and handed her a box of Kleenex.

She blew her nose and started crying again. "I wanted to tell you."

"Well. You didn't."

"I knew you wouldn't approve."

"I don't. It's unsafe, and illegal, and people have gotten hurt. Do you know how many lawyers have their fingers in this now? They smell money."

"We don't have any money."

"You kids are in the middle. The city, state, police, university, gas company—somebody's going to pay for all this, and you'll be ruined in the process. I know you wouldn't have gotten into this if you didn't think you were helping. But if they get their hands on you, you won't have a future."

Harriet yanked another Kleenex from the box. "I was thinking about quitting," she said as she wiped her eyes. "But I'm changing my mind."

"Goddammit, Harriet—"

"Maybe I should have told you. But I'm not ten anymore. I don't tell you everything. You don't want to know everything.

"I respect your advice. But we can do things no one else can. We've made mistakes. But we've helped a lot of people, too, and I don't see the wrong in that."

"Harriet, I can't let you do this."

"Then you'll have to arrest me."

They were alone. The apartment was clean, everything neatly put away, for probably the only time all semester. Charlie took an air-conditioned breath and dove in.

"I don't think we should see each other anymore."

He read her shock, but there was also relief. She had known this was coming. Charlie already knew the arguments she would raise.

"You made this decision for us?" Mary Beth asked. "Did you read my mind to find out how I'd react? Is it what you expected so far?"

The words didn't hurt much. It was self-defense, and he could feel the remorse behind the anger.

"At first I thought we could just work through things," Charlie said. "But we don't talk anymore. That's my fault, too. But there are things you think sometimes that you never say. You do that because you know that I already know them. You think we don't need to talk about things because I already know what you think. You forget that I don't necessarily agree with you."

"You're holding what I think against me? Why can't you judge me by my actions?"

"I don't want to judge you. That's the problem. You think that because I know your secrets that I'm the arbiter of your worth. As long as we're together, you feel like you've been found worthy of something."

"Please. Don't flatter yourself. You're not that important."

"Exactly. It's not about me. Possibly you think I'm cute, but the reason you're with me is because there's no work involved. You don't have to worry about me finding out anything awful about you, and you don't need to worry about looking inside yourself. Being with me is like confession without the penance."

"I don't know what that means."

"You won't find out if we stay together. I can't make this feel good, Mary Beth. I care about you, but I don't think this is right for either of us, not right now."

"Not right now," she mimicked back at him. "You think after this that we'll ever be together again? You think I . . ." She stopped.

She wouldn't cry until she left the apartment, until she was down the sidewalk out of sight of his window. He heard her thinking this, and he heard her realize that he would know she was crying no matter where she did it, that he knew she was thinking about it right now.

She left without another word.

**S**cott looked around the food court and spotted Caroline sitting by herself. He hesitated—Caroline made him nervous—but finally walked toward her table.

"Do you mind if I sit here?" he asked.

She looked up from a copy of *The Campus Voice*. "Sure."

Scott set his tray down and settled into the chair opposite Caroline.

"I saw you on the news," he said. "I mean, they mentioned you. They said you saved a jumper last night."

"Jesus, say it a little louder, could you?"

He looked at the tables nearby, but it didn't seem like anyone had heard. "Sorry," he whispered. "It's just that I thought you were all taking a break."

"Maybe it wasn't me."

He scooped kung pao chicken over white rice. "Wasn't it? The news said—"

"Do you need to be in on everything I do?"

"I was just wondering if you guys started up again and forgot to tell me. In case you needed help with anything."

She laughed. He tried to ignore it, but he could feel his face burning.

"Are you laughing at me?" he asked.

"Look," she said, "I don't mean to be a bitch, but are we your new girlfriend? I mean, ever since we told you about all this, you want to be in on everything. Jack said you moped for days after we went to Milwaukee without you. It's like you're jealous."

"I'm not jealous. I just want to help. I mean, the Avengers have Rick Jones and Jarvis. The Justice League had Snapper Carr."

"That's great, but my life is not a comic book." She frowned. "You know, I don't think we've ever had a conversation that wasn't about my powers. You never even talked to me before you found out about this."

"That's not true," he said, but he wasn't sure he was right. "We've talked."

"Not actual conversation. Is the fact that I can fly the only thing interesting about me?"

"No."

"What else, then?"

"Well, you're . . ."

"What?"

"You're beautiful." He knew it was the wrong thing to say, but the only thing he could think of to do was keep talking. "Would you maybe want to go out sometime?"

Her face went blank. "You're really creepy sometimes, you know that?"

He looked at the table. "I'm sorry."

She picked up her newspaper. "I have to get across campus for my next class."

After she left he ate alone. He was sure everyone was staring at him. The kung pao tasted awful, and he threw it out before finishing half of it.

**S**he had collected one too many syllabi, and now she couldn't close her backpack. Wednesday was Mary Beth's biggest class day: four lectures, a lab, and Professor Smith's seminar. She'd been on campus for eleven hours now, and she had two worksheets and three hundred pages for tomorrow. And she didn't care about any of it.

She gave up on the zipper, knowing she could force it but knowing that doing so would destroy the zipper and possibly the backpack too. She'd had all summer to adjust to her new strength, but simple things still tripped her up. Shoelaces were a frequent casualty, and Caroline and Harriet wouldn't let her do dishes anymore. She didn't forget as much now, but she still forgot. And whenever she did she saw Charlie lying on her bed, hurt, Charlie telling her he didn't want to see her anymore.

"Miss Layton?" Professor Smith stood near the door in his

tweed jacket and tie. Mary Beth realized she was the last student to leave the room.

"Yes?"

"You were very quiet today. Does Ezra Pound stir nothing in you?"

She stood, mindful that none of her books tumbled out of the half-opened backpack. "I'm sorry. I've got some things on my mind."

"It is not my portion to be concerned with such things. High as my hopes are for you, your voice in discussions will make the difference between a glorious future in this department and a swift departure. Your problems outside of this classroom must remain outside this classroom."

"I can't forget about everything just because you want my attention. Life doesn't work like that."

"On the contrary. Future employers will expect your best performance regardless of any drama occurring outside the workplace. It is the same here. If you cannot meet that requirement, I do not want you in my course."

"You asked me to take this course, and now you want me to quit?"

"I want you to understand my expectations. The fact that I think you are astute earns you no special treatment. If anything, I will expect more from you."

"What if I can't meet your expectations?"

"Then you will fail, and I will become infinitesimally more embittered at my inability to get through to worthy students. So please, for both of our sakes, set whatever it is aside and focus on what you are doing."

Mary Beth left the classroom without saying good-bye. *Set it aside*? Charlie hated her, Jack was dying, and all the good they had done over the summer was falling into nothing.

In the stairwell she lashed out with her fist. She pulverized a fist-sized chunk of the wall, and a large crack appeared. She ran down the steps and out of the building before anyone investigated.

# THURSDAY

D r. McAllister was a wonderful obstetrician and a sweet man, and as telegenic as spoiled ham. He was short, had lost most of his hair, and was forever scratching his nose. But he had been Prudence's doctor from the beginning, and she wasn't about to dump him for someone sexier. Ratings were up since she'd agreed to let the station turn her pregnancy into a miniseries. She'd compromised herself as far as she was comfortable. She wondered if the next time would be easier.

"OK." Tommy killed his light and lowered the camera. "I'm going to try another angle."

Dr. McAllister released the breath he'd been holding. "It's just a camera. Why does it make me so nervous?"

"You're doing great." Prudence touched his arm, both to reassure him and to remind him she was there. Ratings stunt or no, in six weeks she was going to pass a human being, and she didn't need her doctor to be dazzled by the lights.

"Thank you, dear. So are you, in fact. Very healthy, mother and baby both. I was wondering if you had changed your mind about finding out the baby's gender."

"We still don't want to know." She glanced at Gil. She was worried that he felt left out of decisions about the baby, although he'd said more than once that he'd have his say when he carried the child.

He squeezed her hand, and nodded. "It's a terrible strain on my mother. She's bought everything in pink and blue both. But we want to be surprised."

"I understand." Dr. McAllister scratched his nose with his thumb. "It's just that I'm terrible with secrets. I have this urge to blurt it out. Have you thought about names?"

"If it's a girl, Amanda."

"Or Serendipity," said Gil.

Prudence elbowed him. "My husband wants a brood of children named for the virtues."

"We should at least have Truth, Justice, and the American Way."

Dr. McAllister chuckled. "You shouldn't tempt the fates. You'd almost certainly end up with a liar, a criminal, and a traitor."

"I just want *this* baby to be healthy," said Prudence. "We can talk about the brood later."

"As I said, the heartbeat is strong, there's good development, position is optimal. I'd recommend you start taking time off, but I know you too well to expect that."

"Actually, I was thinking about it."

The room went silent. Even Tommy stopped adjusting his tripod and looked shocked. "Really?"

"Don't worry, Tommy. The station will get its updates. But I told Bill earlier today that I'd only be working through next week. It's time for me and this kid to spend some quality time together, let the husband wait on us hand and foot." Gil looked frightened. "That was a joke, honey."

"Which part?"

"Oh, I'm taking the time. A month before the baby comes, and two months after."

"I approve," said Dr. McAllister.

"Thank you, Doctor. Now. You boys ready for another shot? Tommy?"

# FRIDAY

**F**ern sipped coffee and held the phone while Quinn talked. She'd emptied the dishwasher, taken out the garbage, and scoured the sink during the call, but she'd finally had to sit down to wait for Quinn to run out of steam. Fern used to start doing housework during these calls to signal that it was time for her to get off the phone, but Quinn had never gotten the hint. Now it was just habit.

Fern was trying to think of an exit line. She couldn't tell Quinn that she had to run errands, because Quinn would tell Fern she needed to get a cell phone. She couldn't tell Quinn that Grace needed to use the phone, because she'd want to talk to Grace, and Grace wasn't home. She couldn't tell Quinn she was tired, because Quinn would worry, and they were all worrying enough already.

"How's Morty?" Quinn asked.

"I haven't talked to him in about a week. School just started."

"He hasn't been to see you? I asked him to keep an eye on you."

"I don't need watching, Quinn. Grace is here, and I'm quite capable of taking care of myself."

"I know." Quinn didn't sound convinced. "It's— Ursula and I were talking. I wonder if you'd think about moving up here. I know Gracie has another year of school, but once she's gone you'll be by yourself. I don't like to think of you being there all alone."

"You think I should sell the farm."

"Well, what are you going to do? Run it all by yourself?"

"I've thought about it. The Carlsons are doing good work, I could ask them to stay on."

"Mom, I don't know why you'd want to do that. I love the farm, but Randy says—"

"I know what Randy says." Fern had learned to tolerate Randy, but more than once she'd had to leave a room to keep herself from throwing something at him.

"You know, Zeke," he'd said shortly after he and Quinn had announced their engagement, "the time of the family farm has passed. You should think about developing this land. I know some contractors." He'd kept on like that, oblivious to Lloyd's glares and Quinn's poking him in the arm, until Zeke told him how much he'd made off the farm in the past year.

Fern's loss was palpable then, a lack in her arms and her chest. She shut her eyes, squeezing back tears.

"Mom?" Quinn sounded sorry for whatever it was she'd just said. "Are you mad at me?"

"No, honey." To her own ears, Fern's voice sounded husky with emotion. "I'll think about it. I have to go now."

"OK, Mom. I'm going to call Morty right now and—"

"I'll talk to you later, honey." Fern hung up, expecting to burst out crying. But nothing came.

**H**arriet didn't hang out at Café Maximillian, as a rule. It was too expensive, for one thing. Caroline was fascinated with the Café because she'd read that Butch Vig liked to drink there when Garbage recorded in town, but Harriet had "forgotten" to tell her about the show tonight, because she wanted to enjoy it on her own.

Arts editor was a job with many unpleasant duties, but handing out the assignments was not one of them. She'd assigned herself this show, a benefit for the Wil-Mar Community Food Pantry, with three bands on the bill, but Harriet was only interested in one of them. Boba Fettish was a sometime side project of the Ultramaroons, one of her two favorite local bands; the other being the now-defunct Junior High, which had broken up when half its members had moved to Chicago to start the Returnables.

Sometimes Harriet thought that she took more pleasure in knowing the pedigrees of all the local musicians than she did in the music itself. This was not one of those times. She was in front of the stage, grooving along as Boba Fettish covered "Saturday's Child" and forgetting entirely to take pictures for her review, when she saw Xavier Tyler.

He was talking to some girls at a table beside the stage. He wore long black shorts and a red T-shirt that clung to his overdeveloped physique. He wasn't looking at her.

Harriet retreated into the crowd. The music was no longer a welcome diversion from crime fighting and her dad and Jack dying—it was too much, too loud. She weaved among the dancers toward the door and ran directly into him.

He didn't know her. He caught her arms and gently steadied her on her feet. "Sorry," he said, and although the music was loud she heard him perfectly. "I wasn't watching where I was going."

She flinched, and he let go.

"Do you like this band?" He was smiling at her, turning on the charm. Harriet felt sick, and she realized what was wrong. He could see her. It wasn't like the other times. She wasn't invisible.

She tried to brush past him, but it was too late.

"Harriet? Harriet Bishop? Is that you?" His smile widened. "Harriet. It's X. Xavier, Xavier Tyler. From high school?"

Did he really think she didn't know who he was? She wanted a different power, a better one. She wanted Mary Beth's strength. She wanted to beat him so badly that he would never carry a football again. She wanted to knock him off the course he was on, the one that led to money and fame and never having to pay for what he had done.

She couldn't tell anyone now. No one would believe her. "Why did you wait three years?" they would ask. "Why now?" There was no good answer.

Shaking, she turned and walked out of the Café.

# SUNDAY

**H**e was reaching for the Glock when the phone rang. He picked it up and was about to say "Tech Support, this is Bruce" when he remembered he wasn't at work. He should just hang up and get on with what he was doing.

"Will you do something for me, Bruce?" The voice on the phone was familiar. "Will you take the bullets out of that gun?"

"What gun?"

"Bruce, you bought a .357 Glock Thirty-three at that gun show in Green Bay. It's sitting loaded on your bedside table. Should I tell you what else is on that table?"

Bruce looked at the guilty stack of porn magazines. "Are you watching me?"

"Let's not play this game. You know who I am."

"You're that Yellow Star."

"*Gold* Star. But yes. We talked about this once before."

"We *talked*? Your friend tore my gun—my legally purchased and licensed handgun—out of my grasp. The police came and I spent the night in jail. My employers found out, and my seventy-four-year-old mother was questioned by the police. She has Alzheimer's. Six days out of seven she doesn't even remember who I am."

"And you didn't learn a thing."

"I learned not to kill myself in a public place. I was asking to be caught."

"Why do you think that was?"

"You tell me. You're supposed to be able to read my mind."

"I can. And I can tell you this much—there are still things that make you feel like living."

"Like rainbows and puppy dogs, I suppose."

"You're angry."

"Nice observation, Counselor Troi. Next you'll be telling me I'm sarcastic."

"You're angry, but you're enjoying this conversation."

"That's because it's going to be my last." Bruce hung up. His hands were shaking. He listened to his heart beat ba-DUM ba-DUM ba-DUM while he waited for the phone to ring again.

"Leave me alone. I'm not hurting anyone else."

"Not true. There are people who care about you."

"My mother won't even know I'm gone."

"Perhaps. But there are others."

"Name three."

"I don't think I should. I think you should get over yourself and find out on your own."

"I'm over myself," Bruce said. "Believe me."

The phone rang an instant after he hung it up.

"Don't die angry."

"What?"

"The first time we talked you had no anger left. There was hardly a spark. You're more alive now. I think you want to kill yourself just to show everyone that you can, to prove you can accomplish something. But you're not thinking straight."

"Don't tell me why I'm doing this."

"But I *know*, Bruce. Better than you do."

"You have no right!"

He hung up the phone and listened to it ring. He was angry, but he was also powerless. He always fell back into the same patterns. He was a failure.

He unplugged the phone.

Caroline looked to the alley below. Newspaper pages chased back and forth, hiding behind Dumpsters, flattening themselves against brick.

"You aren't planning to jump, are you?"

Joe's white shirt looked transparent in the moonlight, like he was turning invisible. At work he almost was. Caroline had seen him there a few times, but he never looked at her. Not like he was embarrassed, but like he didn't even know her when she wasn't in costume.

"It wouldn't matter if I did," she said. "Survival instinct would kick in before I hit."

"True." Joe looked over the street side. "A man jumped from our town hall when I was a small boy. No one was sure who he was, because his face was a mess. They couldn't figure out how he got up there."

"Maybe he flew."

"What about his survival instinct?"

"I don't know."

"Some of the older women in town were worried his ghost would haunt the square."

"Did it?"

"Not that I ever saw."

Caroline was cold. Lycra wouldn't handle winter in Wisconsin, not alone. She would have to come up with other ideas soon, if costumes were something they would still need.

"I never wanted to be a superhero," she said.

"I did," said Joe. "I used to read American comics. I liked the Punisher because he had guns. I outgrew that, though. Batman is better."

Caroline wondered how old Joe was, exactly. About her age, she thought. Maybe a little older.

"You're thinking about giving it up," he said.

"I guess."

"Is it too hard?"

"No. It is hard, but if that was why, I would have quit in the beginning. It's more . . . do you think we're doing any good?"

"Why would you ask me? Do you think you're doing any good?"

"Some."

"Not enough?"

"We're causing problems, too. People have gotten hurt. And— it's changing things."

"Things always change."

"Yeah, but I don't think people are ready for superheroes. To see movies about them is one thing. But to actually have them living in your town, I think that's too much of an adjustment."

Joe took out his last two cigarettes and threw the pack off the roof to land among the newspapers. He lit both cigarettes and handed one to Caroline.

"It's too late," he said. "You're here, and you have to make the best of it. People will get used to it one way or another. Things always change. Things changed today, and tomorrow they'll change again. But people don't change very much. People die and people lose their jobs and people move, but they stay pretty much the same."

A gust of wind cut through Caroline's costume. She shivered. "Is that a good thing?"

**R**ay heard the ringing long before he understood that it was coming from the phone. He rolled over on the couch and picked up the receiver, blinking at the TV. Something on ESPN was burning.

"Ray?" It was Ed. "Jesus, were you asleep?"

"I worked the four-to-twelve last night."

"Yeah, well, you better turn on the TV."

"It's on." Ray sat up and squinted at the clock. It was about a quarter to nine. He flipped the channel, but the same cloud of smoke was on every channel.

"You see it? Ray, the chief wants everyone here. The FAA just shut down all the airports, and there are more planes missing."

"Planes?"

"Ray, wake up. Are you looking at the TV?"

The building on fire looked like the World Trade Center, and there were things falling from it that looked like people.

"What the fuck is going on?"

Ed didn't answer right away; it sounded like he was talking to someone else. "Jesus Christ," Ray heard him say.

"Ed?"

"Ray, get down here, buddy. A plane just hit the Pentagon."

Ed hung up.

Off in a corner of Caroline's brain that was still rational she thought she should have put on her costume before leaving. But mostly she was thinking about the quiet. She was used to the hum of aircraft around her when she flew. Even when there were no planes near, it was there, like the hum of a refrigerator—you didn't notice it until the power went off. Or when the world went crazy.

It hadn't been even nine o'clock eastern daylight time. Her mom was always late . . . at least, she used to be. Caroline was sure there had been mornings when the two of them weren't getting dressed while eating, searching for keys or homework, snapping at each other for making both of them late. There must have been mornings that weren't like that, but she didn't remember them.

She wouldn't have been there, Caroline was sure of it. She fished the cell phone out of her pocket again. This time she'd answer. Someone would answer.

She'd just crossed the lake, so she knew she was in Michigan. It was almost eight hundred miles from Madison to Manhattan. Sooner or later she'd have to land and get her bearings, but she was afraid to. Up here, with no radio and no TV, she could pretend she was just flying to New York to visit, like a millionaire on a private jet with a craving for deli pastrami on rye.

Voice mail, again. She left another message and tried the

apartment again. No answer, just Arturo's voice on the machine. She'd left four messages there already.

*Please,* she prayed. *Please let her be late.*


The clock radio woke Mary Beth at 10:00. Neal Conan's voice on the NPR station cut through her grogginess. He was saying that the World Trade Center was no longer standing, that a plane had struck the Pentagon. He was saying that all air traffic had been grounded, that more planes were unaccounted for, that the president was on his way to an air force base somewhere.

She wondered if it was April. Last April Fool's Day she had been totally fooled by an NPR report of a new fad of navel removal among California teenagers. This didn't seem like a very funny April Fool's joke, though, and besides, she remembered now that it was September.

She was shaking as she slipped on a robe and eased her bedroom door open. No one else was home. She picked up the television remote and pressed the power button.

Messages scrolled across the bottom of the screen under videotaped images on a loop. People covered in dust running out of a rolling cloud. Crowds of pedestrians crossing a bridge, a tower of smoke standing in the skyline behind them. A firefighter standing on a street corner, the camera whirling and focusing on the World Trade Center in time to see a plane strike the building and dissolve into flame and smoke, glass exploding outward. Smoke flanking the high antenna atop one of the towers, then vertigo as the antenna wobbled and the tower crumpled while people screamed.

Mary Beth delicately set her finger over the power button and pressed it. The TV went black. She walked quickly to her bedroom and slid the switch on the radio to off.

DAVID J. SCHWARTZ

She shook her head. Her breathing was ragged, shallow. She went back to the living room, to sit down. The answering machine blinked at her, and she pressed play.

The first voice was Harriet's mom, asking her to call her. The second was Harriet's dad, asking the same thing. The third was Mary Beth's mom. She sounded like she was crying. The fourth message was Caroline, saying she was on her way to New York, that she wanted someone to call her if her mother called. There was a lot of noise on the line, maybe wind. There were no more messages.

Mary Beth turned on the TV again. There was a graphic showing the projected paths of two planes from Logan Airport in Boston. They traveled west for a short distance, then turned sharply southeast and disappeared.

She shut her eyes and lowered her head. It didn't look real, anyway. It looked like something out of some cheesy disaster flick, something with great effects and no plot.

She didn't realize she was clenching her fists until she heard the remote in her hand crunch and felt the pieces slipping between her fingers.

"I just spoke to the dean's office," said Jake. "They have no plans to cancel classes."

The entire staff of *The Campus Voice* was in the offices, but no one made a move to run off to their 12:05 lectures. Most of them stared at the looping gallery of horrors on the TV.

"Listen up, people," said Darren. "We've still got a paper to put out. We need a front page, and we need local pictures. The campus Red Cross chapter is jammed with people lined up to give blood, and there's going to be a prayer vigil tonight. Harriet, can you cover the vigil? Where's Harriet?"

The TV showed black smoke, white dust, and the malevolent bright blue of the sky. Fire bloomed from the screen in waves of manic orange. *I'm not here*, Harriet thought.

"She was here a little while ago."

"Maybe she's in the bathroom."

"Someone find her, please," said Jake. "Editors' meeting, ten minutes. We need to figure this out."

Harriet sat at her desk and wished she could disappear for real—break up into molecules and drift away. She didn't want this flood of sadness and fear to engulf her. She wanted it all to go away, but she knew it wasn't going to work. Even if she never turned on a television again, the images would stay with her forever.

She didn't like being this kind of reporter. She wanted to write about things that people made, not things that people destroyed. But she wanted to help somehow. Her superpower certainly wouldn't help anyone.

She left the office and walked through the damp eggshell-colored corridor until she found a quiet corner. She willed herself visible and started to walk back toward the office.

Except the colors were still crayon-bold and segregated. She stepped in front of a window and looked for her reflection. Nothing.

She shut her eyes but saw right through her eyelids. She couldn't see her hands. If she couldn't see her hands, did anything she did with them matter? If nothing she did mattered, did she?

She locked her jaw against the terror. She'd turned this on, and she could turn it off. She'd done it hundreds of times. There was nothing to it.

Except it didn't work, and there was nothing to her.

• • •

Caroline's phone said it was 12:24, and she was somewhere over Lake Erie, as near as she could figure. She was calling every half hour now, once her mom's cell, once to her apartment. There was no answer at the apartment, and the cell number kept coming back with a recording saying that the customer was unavailable.

She had never flown for this long before. Cold had gotten into her joints and dried out her eyes. She was thirsty.

At twelve-thirty she dialed her mom's cell phone again, and again she got a recording. She dialed the apartment, and someone picked up the phone.

"Hello? Is calling? *Bella*?"

Caroline's throat hurt when she spoke. "Arturo? Where's my mom?"

"Is you, *Bella*? You are safe?"

"Arturo, it's Caroline. From Madison. Where's my mom?"

"Caroline? No, *mia cara*. No." He was crying.

"Arturo." She wanted to scream at him, but if she started she wouldn't be able to stop. "Do you know where my mother is?"

"I don't know. I don't know." He said something in Italian, sounding angry. "I have to go, if she call. Call later, OK?"

"I'm on my way, OK? Everything's going to be fine, OK?"

"OK, yes. Call later." He hung up.

She tucked the phone away.

From the start flying had been effortless. A thought, and she was airborne. She'd tried to go fast before, but never pushed herself. It was just fun.

*Go faster,* she thought. She squeezed her eyes shut and clenched her fists and tensed until she shook, but when she opened her eyes she couldn't see any difference in her speed.

*Go faster. Dammit.*

"Inebriated," said Charles. He leaned in toward Charlie, a mirror image with perfect hair. "You can't stay here," he said. "Wake up."

"Harsh." Chuck brushed Charles aside. "Listen," he said to Charlie. "You need to maintain, hear me? Deal with the noise in like, a healthy and proactive way. Cool?"

Charlie shook his head, sending his doubles spiraling out of sight. He opened his eyes but couldn't figure out where he was. The shadow patterns on the walls were unfamiliar, and he couldn't think of where he'd seen the tile before. He tried to turn his head to the left but couldn't, so he turned it the other way and realized he was lying under the toilet.

Something was knocking, and not his head, although he was sure he'd finished most of a bottle of Bacardi. It had dulled the torrent of raw emotions that had made his morning unbearable, but it hadn't blocked them out.

He took a deep breath and sat up, holding his ribs. The knocking was Mary Beth, at his door, and her mind opened to him unbidden. She wanted to come in and talk and share and maybe have sex. She knew they were broken up, but she was tense and horny and afraid.

Charlie didn't feel drunk until he dragged himself to his feet and tried to walk to the front door. He couldn't seem to point himself in any one direction, and as he passed through the hall and into the living room he walked into the doorjamb, hitting his ribs. He would have cried out, but the breath abandoned his lungs, and he just stood, waiting for the pain to subside.

The pounding continued, and Charlie wondered why Mary Beth didn't give up and go home. The answer was in her mind; she had called him about forty-five minutes ago. He had talked to her.

He didn't remember it, but the conversation was all there. She had asked if she could come over, and he had told her it was fine. He took the deepest breath he could manage and lurched toward the door.

"Who is it?" he asked.

"Like you don't know? I've been knocking for ten minutes, where have you been?"

"Napping."

"Can I come in?"

Charlie laid his head on the door near the peephole, but didn't look through it for fear that the close focus would make him sick again. He could taste the remnants of his first visit to the toilet.

He reached for the dead bolt but dropped his hand again. "I don't think you should come in," he said.

"Why not?"

"I don't think it's a good idea right now."

"Are you drunk?"

Charlie nodded, his hair scrunching against the compressed wood of the door. "Yes I am."

"Charlie, let me help you."

"I don't need help," Charlie said. "I need a nap."

"Charlie, please. Is it the mindstream? People must be afraid. It has to be hard. Let me in so we can talk about it."

She was near tears. Charlie knew because she was thinking it, thinking she didn't want to cry outside his door, wondering if it would convince him to let her in if she did.

"Won't work," Charlie said.

"What won't work?"

"I want to be alone."

"We talked about this on the phone! I'm afraid too, Charlie. We need to talk about what we're going to do."

"We're not going to do nothing. I'm going to have a couple more drinks and sleep the rest of the week."

"Charlie, please! Caroline's gone, I don't know where Harriet is, and I don't want to be alone. Please."

"Go away."

"Charlie, I can break down this fucking door."

"I know how strong you are, Mary Beth."

"Oh, god. Not . . . Charlie, I don't want to hurt you."

He knew she was telling the truth. She was just afraid, in shock—like most of the country, and much of the world. He heard voices of fear, of rage, of crippling grief. Other voices echoed in his mind, the voices of those who had died, whose last moments he had lived with them, their terror jagged and crippling. Mary Beth was thinking about how many dead there might be. She was thinking about children who'd lost parents, and parents who'd lost children, and about her own parents and her brother, and war, and whether anyone she knew would be drafted and how glad she was that she couldn't be drafted and how guilty she felt about being glad. She could go over there. She could hurt them, and they couldn't hurt her. She was better than a bomb. She could find them and kill them, weed them out. Except she wouldn't know which ones were evil, not for sure, not without being able to read their minds. She never used to believe in evil. Now she wasn't sure. The word carried associations with it, supernatural, religious, political. Like love, it was applied to so many things that it hardly meant anything.

"You don't love me," Charlie said.

"What?"

"Go away." He stepped away from the door, hugging the wall. He made it to his bedroom and shut the door, found the bottle of Bacardi.

Mary Beth kept knocking, but Charlie knew she would give up

soon. He forced down a couple more swallows of rum and pulled the sheets up around his ears.

From the air it looked like Manhattan was burning. The smoke rose hundreds of feet into the air, drifting slowly out to sea, dissipating gradually in the fading light.

Caroline had landed in Pennsylvania to get her bearings. She'd walked into a gas station and studied the map there, ignored the small black-and-white television the attendant had set up on the counter. She'd bought a Gatorade and a package of beef jerky and consumed them in the woods behind the gas station, then launched herself into the sky again.

Just a compass heading and a cell phone to navigate by, and the cell signal had been fading in and out for the last hour. Still, it didn't seem likely she could have missed the smoke, even if she'd been a thousand miles off course.

She tried the line at her mother's apartment again, but it was busy. Was her mother there, trying to call her at home? Or was it Arturo, calling the police and the fire department and the Port Authority?

The towers weren't there. She circled for a few moments, spiraling in toward the wreckage, twisted metal, and heaped rubble trailing floating braids of smoke and dust. She was coughing and shaking. Her phone didn't ring, so she dove for the ruins.

She landed where there were no rescuers, in a barren field of fallen steel. She wondered what floor her mother worked on, and then a cry of raw emotion went through her, painfully scraping through her dry throat. It was an ugly, hopeless sound, and she stopped it as soon as she realized she was making it—but an echo rolled through the terrible canyon and lingered in her ears.

She was too late—if she'd been here a few hours ago, she could have done something. If only she were as fast as Jack. Now she couldn't do a thing—the girders were too large, the rubble too unstable. If only she were as strong as Mary Beth. She didn't even know where to look, had no way of knowing if moving one piece of wreckage would free a survivor or bury one farther. If only she could hear their thoughts like Charlie.

"Hey!" Someone had climbed onto the plain of ruins with her, a firefighter with a rope tied around his waist. "Don't move," he said. "I'll come to you."

She tried to say that it was OK, she would be fine, he shouldn't endanger himself on her account when she could fly to safety with a thought. (If only she could turn invisible, like Harriet.) The words wouldn't come; she was shaky and cold.

She didn't move, just waited, watching her hands tremble and the firefighter pick his way slowly toward her. She looked at her phone, but there was no signal. Above her there was just smoke and the distant sound of fighter jets.

"How did you get up here?" asked the firefighter as he wrapped a blanket around her shoulders.

"My mother works here," Caroline said, and slumped, sobbing, into his arms.

A little before dusk Scott left the Union and walked through Library Mall. The TV lounge had been crowded with students and workers and faculty members, most of them silent, absorbing information more intently than most of them had ever done at a lecture. Still, after more than three hours watching coverage of the attacks, Scott felt like he understood less than ever.

There was a bottleneck of words inside him that he didn't know how to break, and he was grateful when a tall Asian woman in the

Mall asked him if he was there for the vigil. Someone had come through the Union to announce a candlelight vigil, but Scott had forgotten all about it.

"Yes." A bit of tension drained from his shoulders.

"Great." The woman smiled. "Hey, do you mind helping with the candles? Most of the organizers aren't here yet."

"Sure." Scott set his backpack down beside the concrete stage. "I'm Scott."

"I'm Stella." She shook his hand. "How are you?"

He let out a ragged breath. "I'm a little shook up."

"Me, too," she said. "I'm hoping this will help a little. Sometimes just being around people makes me feel better."

Scott couldn't say the same; but he unpacked candles, slid paper rings over them, and handed them to the people who arrived, first in a trickle, then in a steady stream. It felt good to be doing something, small as it was. He didn't even mind the crowd.

After a while they ran out of candles, and only then did Scott realize that night had fallen. Above him the city lights reflected off the night sky, while around him the Mall was illuminated by a few hundred low-orbit stars shining up into worried faces. Stella produced one last candle, and he found himself huddling around it with her and some of the other organizers.

Later, as he was walking home, Scott felt like two connected but separate people whose feet were falling on the same spots on the concrete, but a fraction of a second apart—overlapping, kin to each other, but not the same. The Scott he had been tonight and most of the day was not the Scott he had been for a long time. But he knew that Scott, the one who could interact with people without anxiety, the one who could share something without fear of words. How long had it been since he'd been that person? Since before he'd come to Madison, he was sure of that. There'd been the shock of coming to a place where he knew no one, and then there'd been Cecilia, and somewhere in there he'd become someone he didn't like very much. It was bizarre and disturbing that it should take something like today to remind him of that.

He quickened his steps, hoping to outdistance himself.

**W**hen she walked into the kitchen Fern thought she was seeing a ghost. There was Zeke reading the paper in a flannel shirt and jeans, with the same crew cut he'd had until 1997, when Grace had bet him the Packers would beat the Patriots. She'd always wanted to see her dad with hair, and although the bet was only for two months, Zeke had kept his hair longer from then on, until the chemo made it all fall out.

"Hi, Ma," said the ghost, and she realized it was Morty. "I made coffee."

Fern took down a cup, looked at the coffeepot, then went to the bread box instead and pulled a loaf of wheat bread out. The twister gave her trouble, and she had to concentrate to keep her breathing under control.

When the bread was in the toaster she managed to pour a cup of coffee without splashing it all over herself.

"I've been trying to call you," she said.

"I've been gone. I'm sorry."

"Gone where?"

"All over. Machu Picchu, the Yucatán, the Grand Canyon, Lake Louise, Yellowstone, Rio, Angel Falls, the Amazon, the Great Smoky Mountains—"

"Not in that order, I hope."

Morty smiled. "No."

"Did you have a good time?"

"It was all right. It would have been better if I could have brought someone along."

Fern motioned at the paper. "You know what happened."

He nodded. "I saw a copy of *USA Today* in Buenos Aires."

The toast popped up, and Fern turned. "How are you?" she asked, leaning on the counter for support.

"I found out something, Ma. We went to see a man named Bert O'Brien. He was part of a group in World War II, of people who had powers like us, and he told us something that . . . I should have figured out myself."

"Figured out what?" Fern asked.

"There was a guy like me, Ma. A guy named Jacques, who was fast like me. He . . . something happened with him. He didn't just move fast. His metabolism and everything—the physics of it don't make a lot of sense. But then, I guess nothing does right now."

"Goddammit, Mortimer!" Fern clenched her jaw shut to get back her control. "Please, just tell me what it is."

"Ma. I'm dying. I'm aging something like fifty times faster than everyone else, and I don't know how long I've got left."

Fern gripped the counter. Her legs threatened to give way. She couldn't catch her breath, but Morty kept talking. "I should have told you. I went away—I told myself I wanted to see all those things before I died. But I should be spending the rest of my time here with you—"

Fern's grip failed, and her knees buckled. Of course Morty was there to catch her before she hit the floor, and she couldn't hold back her sobs any longer. She lost all self-awareness, all shame. Snot ran from her nose, and her wails were animal sounds, and she clutched at Morty and flailed at him with her fists and cried.

Harriet slipped into the house when the son—his name was Isaiah; he was eleven; he liked Kid Rock and Randy Moss—opened the door to bring in the newspaper. Everything inside, from the bright white carpeting to the deep mahogany of the staircase banister, was clean and bright, like a model house, or a sitcom set. She followed Isaiah carefully up the stairs.

Nathan Statz was still in bed. He had lost weight since that night in the pizza parlor. It had taken him some time after the shooting to get back his appetite, and since he couldn't drive with one arm, he'd gotten into the habit of walking. He looked good, but there was a wariness about his eyes that hadn't been there before.

His arm was no longer in a sling, but a bandage bulged beneath his T-shirt at the shoulder. He thanked Isaiah and tousled the boy's hair with his good arm.

"Dad?" Isaiah asked.

"Mmm-hmm?"

"Why don't they like America?"

Nathan looked at the picture on the front page, of the twin towers smoldering. "That's not an easy question to answer," he said. "You might say that some of their reasons aren't all wrong. But there's no justification for what they did."

"How many people died?"

"I don't know, Isaiah. Too many. Hey, listen," he said, and put his good hand on Isaiah's shoulder, "you know that you're safe here. Nothing's going to happen to us. Don't worry, OK?"

"OK." Isaiah nodded.

"OK. Do you have more questions?"

"I guess not."

"Then get downstairs and eat your breakfast. The bus'll be here in ten minutes."

"OK, Dad."

After Isaiah left, Nathan sat looking at the paper. Harriet knew that he usually pulled out the sports section and read it first, but today he started with the front page. At one point he whispered something to himself, set the paper down, and put his hands to his face. His breath was ragged. When he moved his hands away his eyes were bright and wet.

"Bye, Dad!" came Isaiah's voice from downstairs, and he slammed the door behind him as he left. Nathan called after him and smiled, then let the smile fade into thoughtfulness.

He had moved on to the local section when his wife—Tamara, age thirty-four, nursing student, church volunteer—came upstairs. She yanked the paper out of Nathan's hands and flung it onto the floor. Then she lay on the bed with her head in his lap.

"I don't know how you can read that," she said.

Nathan ran his fingers through Tamara's long hair. "I want to understand why it happened."

"You never will," she said. "No one can understand fanaticism except fanatics."

"I want to understand the politics," he said. "I want to understand why they're so angry."

"Why?" She sat up abruptly, her back to him. "How's that going to help you? You work in a pizza shop, for Christ's sake. How are you going to make it better?"

Nathan winced and rubbed at his shoulder. There was a long moment of silence, and Harriet's breath sounded thunderous to her own ears. "I'm sorry," Tamara said. "I just can't stand to think about it."

Nathan pressed a hand against his wife's back. "Do you feel better this morning?"

She nodded. "I made an appointment with the doctor already. If that was a panic attack, I never want it to happen again."

"Did you talk to Isaiah?"

"He didn't want to talk about it. I think he was more scared than I was."

"I don't think that's possible."

Harriet pretended she wasn't there, that she was just part of the furniture. If she admitted to herself that she was there watching then she would have to ask herself why, and asking herself would mean acknowledging herself. She wasn't a voyeur. She wasn't here. She wasn't anywhere.

Prudence managed a half hour of alone time in the tape room before Bill found her.

"Go home," he told her.

"I was home," she said. "I was home last night, and I couldn't fall asleep because I couldn't turn the TV off, and when I did fall asleep I had nightmares, and when I woke up I was still having them."

"You need sleep. The baby needs sleep."

"The baby is quite capable of telling me what it needs on its own. I wouldn't have thought up peanut butter and oranges on my own, I can assure you."

"What are you working on?"

"The All-Stars story. Anything to get those damn towers out of my head."

The tape she was viewing held interviews of people who had been saved by the All-Stars throughout their three-month career. There was another tape of people with grievances against the All-Stars, but she was pretending for the moment that the other tape didn't exist.

"Where do you think they are?" Bill asked.

"I don't know," she said. "I don't know if it matters. They couldn't have done much. Superman couldn't have stopped it."

"Maybe not. But it would make me feel better to know they were out there."

Prudence laughed. "Bill, you surprise me! All this time I've been taking you for a cynic."

"A cynic is just a fallen optimist," Bill said.

Prudence shook her head. "Bill, I'm scared. Scared for this baby."

"You're not talking about your health, are you?"

"I'm talking about—there's going to be a war, Bill. And I understand that. It's what happens next that scares me."

"Me too," said Bill. "The question is, are we going to let that fear make us stupid as well?"

"What are you talking about?"

"I'm talking about giving up. You know how easy it is to become jaded on this job. How difficult it is to keep your sense of outrage from becoming dulled. You start to see patterns in how events unfold, and you start to think those patterns will never change, and you'll always be reporting the same depressing things. We're not even supposed to want it to change. We're just supposed to report it.

"Something like this happens, it takes a lot out of the profession. You feel like nothing you do matters. We lose good people that way."

"Are you afraid I'm going to quit?"

"You might," said Bill. "You could take your leave and decide not to come back. You could do voice-over work or go into radio or something more low-key. I wouldn't even blame you. But it would be a shame. You're good at this. You believe in it. Most people don't."

"Do you?"

"On my good days."

"Well, I wasn't thinking about quitting until you brought it up. Now I'll have to seriously consider it."

"Fine," said Bill. "Go home and sleep on it."

"After I finish this edit."

"Leave it on my desk when you go."

It was a fine morning, and it was going to be a hot day. Bert O'Brien stood on the lawn outside Shady Meadows Retirement Home in his sweatpants and a Brewers T-shirt. He wasn't wearing shoes. He wouldn't need them where he was going.

When he was younger and more prone to melodrama he used to imagine what would happen if he kept flying up until he hit the ionosphere. Maybe he wouldn't even make it that far, he wasn't sure. Whatever it was that had given him this gift of flight had equipped him with the resilience to withstand the stresses of flight, but he didn't know how high it would let him go.

"Mr. O'Brien?" One of the orderlies—they called themselves residence coordinators, but they were equal parts nurse, social worker and guard—was standing near the door. "Good morning, Mr. O'Brien."

Bert didn't say anything. He took a deep breath.

"How are you?" The man sauntered toward Bert. "Would you like some breakfast?"

"I don't think so," said Bert and took off into the sky.

He was tired of people asking him how he was, as if old age were a chronic disease. Perhaps it was, but that didn't make everyone who didn't suffer from it any less insufferable.

His eyes started watering almost immediately, and he spent the first two thousand feet blinking them clear. His legs, though, were free of soreness for the first time in months—since the last time he'd flown.

He felt young again until he passed through the clouds and had to fight for breath. He coughed up what air he had managed to gulp down, but willed himself to keep climbing. Up, up and away.

He started to sweat, and his pants started to feel tight. He wondered if his body was starting to swell with altitude, like he'd heard people's feet tended to do on airplanes. Then he realized that he had an erection, something that hadn't happened outside of the early mornings in almost ten years. His coughs turned to laughter, and then his lungs cleared, as if he'd finally become acclimated to the thin air.

This was always how he'd planned to go out. Back during the Cuban Missile Crisis he'd decided that given the choice between this and the bomb, the choice was easy. It would be on his terms, at least. He could fly above the mushroom clouds and the drifting radiation and the retaliatory strikes, and never have to see the earth that was left behind after they'd finished scorching it. Things were going to hell, like he'd always known they would, and he wasn't going to wait to see what happened next.

He wondered if the orderly would have called someone, if there would be fighter jets scrambling to shoot him out of the sky. The idea made him laugh again, but it came out as a thin cackling, and he had to stop to catch his breath. His heart beat in his forehead, but it felt weak, overworked. He was light-headed. He could pass out at any second. Just a little higher, he thought. It's better to burn out than to fade away.

If he could survive the ionosphere, maybe he could make orbit, or even escape velocity. If he could just go a little faster, a little higher.

He should have left those kids a note or something. He hated for them to take this to heart. Just because he'd lost hope didn't mean he wanted to take away theirs. Ah, hell, who was he kidding? He was just an old man. They wouldn't know—they probably hadn't given him a second thought. He felt for those kids. He felt for all the kids.

It was too late for regrets. He was leaving all that behind. If he could just make it a little higher . . .

Caroline didn't know her mother's real hair color. She'd dyed her hair blond until Caroline was twelve, and then they'd both gone through a long period of experimentation. Every couple of months they would color their hair—flax, burgundy, ebony, auburn. For St. Patrick's Day they went green, and for the Fourth of July Caroline went blue and her mother a bright red, with tiaras full of stars.

After coming to Madison Caroline had gradually stopped coloring her hair. She tried making an event of it with girlfriends, but none of them appreciated the ritual significance of it, and it wasn't the same. She'd eventually let it settle into the striking dark color—almost black—that might have been close to her mother's natural color. But Jenna had continued redesigning herself as a platinum blonde, a brunette, a redhead. There were no pictures of her with her natural hair color. There weren't even any pictures of her with her most recent hair color, which Arturo—through his sister—had described as a strawberry blond.

Arturo's family had taken her in. His mother fed her brisket and vinegary salad and hard bread, and although Caroline had no appetite she ate all that was put in front of her.

The family was a spectrum of fluency. The mother's English vocabulary consisted, apparently, of *eat* and *no*, while Arturo's sister Sylvia filled Caroline's silences with monologues in a soothing NPR voice. Arturo was somewhere in the middle, between his older brother, who hardly spoke at all but occasionally came out with grammatically disastrous declarations in a flawless accent, and his niece, Sylvia's daughter, who was six and had picked up enough foul language in the two years since moving to New York to actually embarrass Caroline.

They sat at the kitchen table in the Pinos' small apartment, looking at the pictures Arturo had been able to find. Neither Arturo nor Caroline wanted to stay at the apartment he had shared with her mother. Instead Arturo's younger brother and three friends were staying there, in case Jenna Bloom should emerge, ash covered but otherwise unscathed, from the crater of confusion in the financial district.

They chose a photograph Sylvia had taken of Jenna and Arturo at a Mets game. Jenna's hair was chestnut brown, with honey-colored highlights, and she smiled straight into the camera. Arturo stood behind her, leaning in so the camera could catch him.

Sylvia scanned the photo onto her computer, cropped her brother out of the image, and enlarged it. She and Caroline struggled over the text for a long time. Caroline felt so brittle that she was afraid the least mention of her mother in the past tense would make her crumble. But Sylvia was careful. The headline MISSING, so painful and yet so necessary and true, was the most jarring part of the text. They left out words like "Beloved" or "Adored" or anything else that sounded like a memorial. Caroline suspected that anything beyond Jenna Bloom's vital statistics and the phone numbers was superfluous anyway.

They had lunch at a Chinese restaurant in Brooklyn, and then they fanned out around Manhattan, each with fifty copies of the poster. Caroline and Sylvia went together. Caroline wondered how the rest of the family would manage with their broken English, but Sylvia laughed and said that dogged insistence was something that needed no translation, and all the Pinos had that in excess.

As they wandered, Sylvia alternately carrying her daughter and holding her by the hand, they met others with similar documents. There were grainy black-and-white handwritten flyers and glossy full-color photographs being distributed by women with small children seeking fathers, grown siblings missing mothers, lovers in search of better halves, gray-haired couples lacking sons and daughters. Recognition was in their faces as they met Caroline's eyes, wordless loans of staple guns and tape, but few words. Caroline found that she begrudged these fellow bereaved even the merest wish of good fortune, as if there was not enough hope to go around.

Harriet slipped into the hospital room through the open door just as Richard Raymond hung up the phone and rose from his wife's bed. "Damn it!" he said. "They said they couldn't even guarantee he'd call me back within the week."

"I'm sure the mayor is busy, honey." Cheryl Raymond had elevated the upper half of her adjustable bed. Her husband had told reporters that his wife had been beautiful before the explosion. Her face now was a study in pathos, certain to arouse first disgust and then pity and guilt. The left side was relatively unscathed, but her right cheek was nothing but blisters and scars.

Richard paced, head down. "No one's going to attack Madison," he said. "They're just trying to avoid me."

"Honey," Cheryl said.

"I can't even get through to the deputy mayor. And that city council woman is useless."

"Honey."

"They've got no concept of justice. While you were on TV they wanted to talk to me. Now we'll probably never hear another word from them."

"That's fine with me, Richard."

Richard looked out the window. "I don't know what that's supposed to mean."

"It means that I wish you'd stay off the phone and look at me."

"Honey, this is important. The All-Stars—"

"I don't give a shit about the All-Stars, Richard!" Cheryl's voice broke. "We're going to have to get used to this. I need to know now if you aren't going to be able to handle it."

"Handle what?"

"Richard, look at me. I need for you to start accepting what's happened. Interviews and phone calls and meetings with lawyers don't matter to me."

"Cheryl, the money—"

"Our insurance will cover the bills. I don't need a year in court with maybe a million-dollar payoff and maybe nothing. I need a husband. And if you can't be that, I need you to tell me now."

Richard turned then, and looked at his wife.

The silence was still unbroken when Harriet slipped out of the room.

The sun warmed Charlie's blood and bones and heated the black rubber inner tube in which he sprawled. There wasn't a cloud in the sky—in fact, there was no sky. There was the sun, and the stream, and sometimes there was the shore. Otherwise there was only Charlie and Chuck and Charles and a beer cooler, each with their own inner tube, all four lashed together with twine.

Chuck belched and crushed a beer can against his forehead. "Nice day for it," he said. His gut hung over the waistband of his cutoff jeans. He wore sunscreen on his nose, but the rest of his body was already hot pink.

"One could say." Charles wore a Speedo that fit him perfectly and drank Weisse beer from a tall glass with a lemon wedge.

"This isn't real." Charlie tried to sit up in the tube, but it was slippery.

"You already proved you can't handle reality." Chuck hurled the crushed beer can at a target along the shore. The can struck the painted target and fell into the steel trash bin below it.

"This is your vacation," Charles said. "Not the spot I would have chosen, but I suppose it has the appeal of nostalgia."

"I can't stay here." Charlie tried again to lift himself. He was drowsy from the sunlight, and his arms didn't work.

"I wouldn't do that," said Charles.

"You're really not dealing well," said Chuck. "You go back now and you're going to lose it. Whoa!" He reached out to steady the beer cooler as Charlie's struggles rocked the makeshift raft. "Dude, you're going to flip us."

Charlie shoved at the slick hot rubber, abraded his arm against the air valve, and managed to throw himself out of the tube. He sank under for a moment—*it could happen any second no one knows what aren't they telling us*—and then grasped the side of the tube and dragged himself to the surface.

"You'll drown," said Chuck.

"I can swim," said Charlie.

Charles shook his head. "You can swim in water. In this you were barely staying afloat, and that was before it was stirred up like it is now."

Charlie looked up at the sun. It was shrinking him down. The longer he stayed here, the less likely it was he could ever return.

"Why would you want to go back?" asked Chuck, and slammed another beer.

Charlie let go of the tube. He danced with his arms and kicked, keeping himself afloat. The current carried Chuck and Charlie away. They spoke in low voices but never once looked back.

By the time they were out of sight Charlie's legs were tired, and his arms burned with exertion. There was no shore to swim for now, and no relief from the sun. Steam rose from the water, and bubbles trickled up along his skin, tickling him. He found himself fighting sleep.

*—even the president ran what happens now drop the bomb Nostradamus said the world would end in oil is a religious crusade what if we're—*

He didn't realize he'd gone under until he broke the surface again. The sun was gone, but radiance came from the water itself. He thought he saw a log raft flowing downstream, empty except for a firepot and a lantern hanging from a post, but then it was gone and he was caught up by the sparking, restless water, which stagnated and spun, a vortex that did not drain but rather gathered the waters around it, swirling thoughts together, minds colliding and conflicting, feeding one another's fears, imagination becoming speculation becoming rumor becoming fact growing fingers grasping him pulling him down.

*Afghanistan anthrax draft United 175 Republicans dirty bombs FAA John O'Neill serin sleeper agents American 11 Taliban oil pipeline Wall Street Democrats King Fahd Prince Abdallah Laili Helms United 93 Al Qaeda Timothy McVeigh Karl Rove Thomas Burnett smoke Christina Rocca ash wreckage Saudi Arabia American 77 Carlos Bulgheroni evacuate collapse Mullah Omar Dick Cheney box cutters BCCI Bin Laden George W. Bush fear fire foes*

Ray had slept two hours out of the last forty-eight, and the coffee keeping his body moving was powerless to jump-start his brain. The lieutenant had sent him home to get some sleep.

He shut the front door behind him and stood waiting for his stomach to lose the debate with the rest of him. He was starving but he didn't think he could stay awake long enough to make something. Even the walk to the fridge was daunting.

He trudged to the couch and collapsed without any conscious decision. He heard someone call his name and thought he was already asleep. He snuggled deeper into the couch cushions.

"Dad." Harriet's voice sounded far away, but her poke in the shoulder was immediate enough.

Ray pushed himself up from the cushion. Opening his eyes seemed a greater effort than sitting up, so he rubbed at his face with his hands instead.

"Dad."

"Harriet? I tried calling you, honey. Are you all right? It's been crazy. Bomb threats, security for the peace march, vandalism . . . I know people are afraid, but some of them are fucking idiots."

"Dad."

"Sorry, honey." Ray looked to where Harriet's voice seemed to be coming from, but she wasn't there. "You don't need to hide, Harriet."

"Help me, Dad."

"What's wrong?"

"I can't come back." Harriet's words came in whispers. "I can't turn it off. It's like I'm fading away. You can hear me, right?"

"I can hear you fine," said Ray. "What do you mean, you can't turn it off? How long has it been?"

"Since . . . I don't know. More than twenty-four hours. I was afraid to go to sleep, Daddy." She was sobbing. "I didn't know if I was going to wake up."

"Honey. I don't understand this."

"It's like . . . I think part of me wants to disappear. I was—" Her voice caught. "I was watching people today. I was pretending I wasn't there. It was like I was watching them on television, except they were real and I wasn't. It felt—it felt—"

"Stop it," Ray said. "Harriet. Give me your hand." Ray held out his own hand, and soon felt hers slip into it. He squeezed her fingers hard. "Do you feel that?"

"Yes."

"You're here, honey. Lord knows I don't have the least idea how any of this works, but you're the most real thing in the world to me."

"OK."

"I mean that."

"I know."

"But you're not convinced?"

"Oh, Daddy. There are things you don't know about me. Things I've hidden."

"Are you telling me that I don't know you? I do. Enough to know there are things you've kept hidden from me. Besides this."

"You're not going to like it."

"Maybe not. But I'm still going to like you."

Solahuddin Sutadi felt safe in America. His young cousins were forever e-mailing him statistics, mostly to do with firearms, which made his chances of being shot on the way to class seem equivalent to the chance of precipitation. *High tempers, with a 30 percent chance of drive-bys.*

He always assured them that there was nothing to fear. He kept to himself, mostly, and in any case Madison was not a city filled with danger. If he was honest with himself, he'd been apprehensive when he'd first arrived, and he still scrutinized men in suits for the telltale bulges of shoulder holsters. But the real danger of being a foreigner in America was not bullets but indifference. Solahuddin did not think himself particularly in need of praise and reassurance, but at times he craved it, craved acknowledgment from his professors and classmates, from his co-workers and customers.

This had all changed in the past two days. He felt as if he carried a floating caption that read SOLAHUDDIN SUTADI, MUSLIM. There didn't seem to be room for any more information, to add that he was from Indonesia and not Saudi Arabia, that he was not fanatical, was at times downright lackadaisical about his religion. That this morning, he had almost broken down and wept in his car as he delivered papers with pictures of the black-and-orange fireball striking the second of the twin towers. Almost. It felt in a way disrespectful for him to weep, like a stranger who wailed loudly at a funeral.

Tonight his shift at the Taco Bell had not gone well. The manager had asked him to work in the back for the evening, which he had done amid several lengthy silences between himself and his typically garrulous co-workers. He wondered if things would get better. He wondered if the FBI would want to question him. He wondered if he would be forced to leave the country.

After closing he walked up State Street toward the ramp where his car was parked. He thought he would call his father when he got home. It was early afternoon in Jakarta, and his father might be able to find out something from his friends in the government. Maybe he should just leave now, withdraw from school, pack up his things, and go. But if he did, there would be suspicion. He might never be allowed to come back.

They set upon him as he turned down the alley to take a short-cut to the parking ramp. They seized his arms and shoved him up against cold brick, jarring his skull. *It's the FBI*, he thought. *They're rounding us all up*. But when they spun him around he saw that they were young men like him, students. But not like him. They were white and he was not. They were angry and he was afraid.

"Say it," one of them ordered. He wore a yellow polo shirt, and he was pale and shaky. "Say it!"

"What would you like me to say?" Solahuddin asked.

"The formula. 'There is no god but Allah, and Mohammed is his prophet.' Say that. You're one of them. I've seen you praying."

Solahuddin tried to think when and where this man could have seen him praying. He prayed only twice a day on most days, and very rarely in public.

"He doesn't look Arabic," said a young man with a ball cap. "He looks like a gook."

"I've seen him," said Polo Shirt.

"Where?"

Solahuddin knew, then. "The Islamic Center," he said aloud.

"Shut up and say it," said Polo Shirt. The blood vessels of his eyes stood out like cracks in a windshield.

"Islamic Center?" asked Ball Cap. "You were at the Islamic Center?"

"You prayed with us—" Solahuddin started to say, but Polo Shirt cut him off with a fist in the stomach. Solahuddin clutched his belly, but after the initial cascade of pain, calm entered him. He was afraid, but not as afraid as the boy in the polo shirt. The boy was afraid that his curiosity about Islam had brought him to the fringes of an international society of terror, afraid that he could have done something to prevent the events of the day before.

"You did nothing wrong," Solahuddin said.

Polo Shirt backhanded him across the mouth. "Shut up!"

Solahuddin was stunned by the pain and suddenness of the blow. The inside of his lip was raw and wet.

"Dude, let him go," said Ball Cap.

"He's one of them!" Polo Shirt took hold of Solahuddin's collar and shook him. "Say it!"

Solahuddin spat out blood and straightened. If they would hear the Shahadah, he would give it to them. "*As-salaam aleikum, my friend. There is no god but Allah, and Mohammed is his prophet.*"

They looked at him as if he had changed shape, as if he had revealed himself to be an alien among them. Their fear made Solahuddin angry. This was the worst of the American character: people nestled so deeply in their own comfort zones that they could not even distinguish between unknowns. When they felt helpless and afraid, they saw everything through the filter of their ignorance. Difference was dangerous, in their eyes. Solahuddin was tired of it.

"There is no god but Allah and Mohammed is his prophet," he repeated.

For a moment he thought they might walk away. Then Polo

Shirt kicked him in the genitals, and the others closed in around them.

All he could do was recite the formula to himself, a koan, an incantation, a prayer. "There is no god but Allah and Mohammed is his prophet. There is no god but Allah and Mohammed is his prophet. There is no god but Allah and Mohammed is his prophet. There is no god but Allah . . ."

Mary Beth had walked all over Madison. She'd gotten lost three times but just kept walking until she saw something familiar. It seemed like such a small city until she actually walked the neighborhoods, saw people mowing their lawns and playing with their kids. Then it became overwhelming, every house with its own tragedies, every inhabitant their own heartbreak.

She hadn't slept last night. Every time she approached her apartment something made her start walking again. She walked for most of the night, and when two boys in a Camaro pulled up next to her at 3 A.M. and suggested she get in the car, she tore a concrete bench off its foundations to throw at them. They peeled off too quickly, so she set it back down in its place, fighting the urge to pound it into dust. She was powerful. But what good did her power do her, or anyone? What use was it against bombs, flying or otherwise?

"Screw the hero business," said Wanda Benson. She was as Mary Beth supposed she had appeared at the time of her death— stringy hair, sleep bruises under her eyes, swollen ankles. Aside from her belly, which swelled the hospital gown beyond its limits, she was oddly thin. She shuffled along beside Mary Beth, her legs splayed to support her uneven weight.

"There's money in construction, you know. The one that was probably your dad did that. That'd be great to see you on one of those sites, showing up all those guys that are always whistling at the girls. You could put them all out of work. You could buy a house and a bunch of cars and eat steak every night, and you wouldn't have to wear the spandex you're hiding under your sweats."

"You're not here," Mary Beth said.

"Fuck you, kid. You think because you're older than I ever got to be that you know more than I do? You never lived on the streets. You had it all handed to you. I mean, good for you. But if I'd lived you'd know the real value of cash money. You'd know to get your own shit together before worrying about anybody else's problems."

"I'm sorry you had a hard life." Mary Beth didn't know if she was talking out loud or not. "But I have to use this power the way I think it should be used."

"Spoken like a true white suburban middle-class liberal. You think the people you help are really grateful? Aren't they trying to sue you for that gas explosion thing? And that guy whose collarbone you dislocated pulling him out of a burning car? You better either get out of the racket or start carrying release forms for people to sign."

"Someone has to help."

"Heard of policemen? Firefighters, EMTs? They get paid to do it. What are you getting?"

"Please go away," Mary Beth said. She shut her eyes, and when she opened them Wanda Benson was gone. She was on State Street, beside an alley, and someone was gasping in pain. There were five men stomping and punching someone on the ground.

She had the costume on under her clothes. She liked the feel of it on her skin, but they had agreed not to be seen wearing them until they decided what they were doing. She had promised, and there wasn't time enough in any case.

The muscles in her arms and chest felt like springs, wound to the point of breaking. She ran, and reached out—her hands so small, she thought, too small to contain what was simmering inside her. She grabbed two of the boys by the shoulders and threw them behind her. Too hard. She had to stay in control. She slapped another boy in the chest, and he went down, fighting for breath. She clenched her teeth so tightly that her jaw trembled. She reached for another boy, but the last two were already running. They were all gone except the one she'd struck in the chest, who was gasping for breath, gaping at her.

It wasn't enough to make up for the last two days, the last two weeks, the last four months.

A bloodied Asian man lay on the ground, talking to himself.

"Are you all right?" Mary Beth asked him. "Can you stand?" She leaned close to hear what he was saying.

"There is no god but Allah and Mohammed is his prophet," he said. "There is no god but Allah and Mohammed is his prophet. There is no god—"

Mary Beth dropped her fists to her sides. "I think you should stop saying that." Her breath was shallow, and her throat felt thick. She could call an ambulance from a pay phone. She could go be somewhere far away from people for a while. Almost, she made that choice.

"There is no god but Allah and Mohammed is his prophet."

"Shut up." Hot tears ran down her cheeks, making her angrier. "How can you talk like that now? What is wrong with you?"

"There is no god but Allah and Mohammed is his prophet."

She seized him by his collar and lifted him to his feet, heedless of possible broken bones or internal bleeding. "Don't say that anymore," she said. "Please."

"There is no—"

She didn't hold back when she hit him. It felt good. She hit him and he went quiet and when she could see again she saw that his head lay at an unnatural angle, his eyes half-shut and still, his mouth open.

He was dead. She had broken his neck, and he was dead.

She set the body down so she could turn and throw up. She straightened and met the eyes of the boy who was still catching his breath, and he shook his head, terrified. She put up her hands in surrender, the hands that broke, that shattered, that killed. And then she ran.

# EDITOR'S NOTE

by Marcus Hatch

I've been thinking a lot about change, wondering whether it's possible for one person to change anything. Even five people, even with superpowers. Maybe it takes a paradigm shift, a cultural sea change. And for that, you need for people to believe that change is possible. I don't know how I can expect anyone else to buy into that idea when I'm not sure I do myself.

Sometimes I get lost in all the machinations of power. The people doing things start to blend together until I can hardly distinguish them, until their agency starts to bleed away. It's like the power itself is the only active thing, like somewhere along the way we released an irresistible force that's herding us all over some unavoidable cliff. I guess it's sort of like believing in god, or the devil. I wouldn't know.

I'm getting ahead of myself, though, because this story isn't over.

Read on.

# WEDNESDAY

I n the end it was Stevie Wonder that brought Harriet back.

It wasn't that simple, of course. There was groundwork to lay first. She told her dad about Xavier, but it took some time— she'd hidden it from him for so long that the words wouldn't come.

It would have been bad enough if that was the only thing, but there was the World Trade Center, the Pentagon, and a field outside of Pittsburgh. There was Caroline's mother missing, there was Jack dying, there was Charlie losing his mind, and there was Mary Beth.

It was easier to talk about those things, so that's what she did that first night, and the next, and every night for nearly three weeks. She only left her dad's apartment when she couldn't sleep, to take long walks around the lake. She steered clear of houses, flinched at windows. She dreaded telling her father about the last four months of voyeurism almost as much as she dreaded telling him about Xavier. She'd lost herself in other people's lives so she wouldn't have to deal with her own, but she was done with that, she told herself.

She kept in touch with Caroline and Charlie by phone, though dialing when she couldn't see her fingers was a serious challenge. Caroline was still in New York, though Harriet could tell that she had lost hope of finding her mother. On the phone Caroline's voice drifted in and out, as if contact with Harriet was not enough to connect her to the real world. She told Harriet she hadn't flown since arriving in New York, that she was afraid if she took off she'd just keep on going. Harriet stopped herself from saying she knew the feeling. She didn't feel that she had the right to relate to Caroline.

If Caroline sounded on the verge of being blown away, Charlie sounded like he'd been buried alive—he yawned constantly, as if he couldn't catch his breath, and his voice seemed to come from far away. He spoke to her of conversations they had never had until Harriet realized that he was having trouble distinguishing between things she'd said and things she'd thought.

Charlie had told her Jack was OK but didn't say how he knew. "Did he call you?" she'd asked. "Where is he?" Charlie said Jack had been friends with the Indonesian student that Mary Beth was supposed to have killed. Stunned, Harriet tried to deflect this information with another question, forgetting who she was talking to. "Is Jack still . . ."

"Yes, he's still dying," said Charlie. "Like the rest of us, only a lot faster. And I don't know how long."

Charlie wouldn't say if he knew where Mary Beth was, but Harriet had to believe he did. One night her father had asked to speak to Charlie. Ray Bishop was not in charge of the investigation of Solahuddin Sutadi's death, as the Madison police had not established a definite connection between that case and the All-Stars. But he had obvious interest in finding Mary Beth first. After fifteen minutes, Ray hung up the phone and shook his head.

"I can't tell if he's losing it for real or he just doesn't want to tell me anything."

"Maybe a little of both," said Harriet.

"Harriet?" Ray looked in her direction, his gaze falling somewhere east of her left shoulder. One of the things Harriet missed most was eye contact.

"Yes?"

"You'd tell me if you knew where she was, wouldn't you?"

"Yes."

"Good."

"I'm sure it was an accident, Dad."

"I'm sure it was. But she needs to give a statement to that effect."

"She's still not really used to her power."

"I know, honey."

"You don't really know, though. There's no training for this. One day we were all normal, and the next we can do all these things. It could have happened to any of us. I mean, when I think about all the times I . . ."

"Harriet?"

All those times she'd watched Xavier. In locker rooms, in class, in his apartment. While he slept. She hadn't even known she was thinking it.

"Harriet, you know it scares me when you do that. I can't see you. I don't know if you're all right."

She used to justify not telling her father about Xavier because she was afraid he would kill him. But now she realized that she had been putting herself in situations where she could have killed Xavier without anyone ever knowing. There was no motive, as far as anyone knew, and there would be no witnesses. Only her.

"Dad . . ."

"Harriet, what's wrong?"

"Dad, I'm scaring myself."

She told him all of it, not just Xavier, but all the things she had done since she'd discovered her power. She glossed over some of the details, but even so it took forever to get it all said.

When she was finished he said, "You're a better person than me, Harriet. I'd have killed that kid."

"Dad, don't."

"I won't. But I hope I don't run into him anytime soon, because I'd like to hurt him."

Harriet sobbed. "I'm sorry."

"For what? I mean, the sneaking into people's houses, that's got to stop."

"It has."

"But other than that, which I think I can be persuaded to look the other way on, you haven't actually done anything."

Harriet smiled, even though her father couldn't see it. "Don't you think that sometimes you cut me a little too much slack, Dad?"

"Harriet, you didn't kill anybody."

And maybe that was it. Maybe it was simply that her misdeeds were relatively minor compared to what was going on around them. Whatever it was, he forgave her completely.

And so a couple of days later, on a Wednesday when she should have been in class, when her father was on shift, she put on his old Stevie Wonder albums and danced around the living room without any self-consciousness. No one could see her, and in that moment she remembered how wonderful that feeling used to be, how liberating. She shut her eyes and just moved, and at some point during "Boogie on Reggae Woman" she saw that her fingernails needed clipping. She ran to the bathroom. She needed a haircut and forty feet of dental floss, but she was back.

# FRIDAY

October 5, 2001

Jack almost didn't recognize Caroline. She was pale, and she had pulled her hair back from her face and bound it with a black cloth. He had never seen the clothes she was wearing, and it occurred to him that they might have belonged to her mother.

He waited for the reading to finish, watching the wind animate the priest's comb-over. The flow of traffic in the middle distance was the only ambient noise, and the small crowd of mourners were mostly silent, including Caroline. Jack stood to one side, conscious that his suit hung too large on his frame. He had arrived in time for the church service but found himself unable to go inside. He hadn't been able to force himself to go to Solahuddin's visitation, either—he'd prayed, on his own, but it came out more like "See you soon" than "Good-bye." When he looked at mourners he saw his own family.

He remembered the first time he had seen Caroline. He'd always assumed that they would end up together, even after she slept with Charlie. He'd been so sure of it that he'd never pursued her, trusting that when the time was right things would take their natural course. But the natural course of things had gone out the window, and here he was with a head of gray hair looking at a girl who could have been his granddaughter if his chronological age matched his physical age.

After the casket was lowered into the ground one of the women Caroline was with led her toward the limo. Jack met them there. Caroline seemed dazed, but when she saw him she disengaged from the other woman and put her arms around him. "Jack."

He squeezed her and patted her back, but she did not cry.

"Thank you for coming." She broke the embrace and stepped back. "Jack, this is Sylvia Pino. She would have been my mother's sister-in-law. Sylvia, this is my friend Jack, from Madison."

"Nice to meet you," Jack said.

Sylvia smiled. "There's room in the limo, if you need a ride."

The limo ride was long and uncomfortable. Sylvia's daughter rebelled against the quiet decorum, swinging from hysterical laughter to inconsolable screams all the way back to the church. Arturo, Jenna Bloom's fiancé, sat beside Jack and wept while his mother consoled him in Italian.

"You seem to be holding up pretty well," Jack told Caroline in a low voice.

"I think I'm in shock," she said. "Three days ago she was just missing. Then they called us—do you know what they found? What we just buried? Pieces. Parts of her." She swallowed hard, and breathed through her mouth. "Every time I think about it I want to throw up."

"It's horrible." He wished he had something better to say, but when Caroline heard it she seemed to relax.

"I've been thinking about you a lot lately," she said. "You and your dad. It's not quite the same, but it must hurt about the same."

"It seems like a long time ago now," said Jack. "But it still hurts."

There was to be lunch in the church basement, but once they arrived Caroline asked Jack to take a walk with her. They stopped at a corner shop so Caroline could buy cigarettes and then walked along the tree-lined streets. The haze that Jack had seen when he arrived hung low over the streets, and even this far from the financial district there was a smell of burning.

"I can't stay here," Caroline said. "I want to hurt the people who did this. I'm so fucking angry—I didn't know I could be so angry."

They walked a couple of blocks in silence, Caroline lighting another cigarette from the first, Jack concentrating on taking slow steps. As they waited at a corner for a signal to cross, Caroline spoke again.

"Where did you go?"

"South America, mostly. National parks. Saw the ocean. Saw the mountains. Saw the rain forest."

"How was it?"

"Lonely," he said.

"Yeah."

Sirens filled the air around them, and they waited with a small crowd while a pair of fire trucks passed. Everyone watched the trucks go, speculating to one another about their destination. Jack and Caroline walked a few more blocks before turning back toward the church.

"Has anyone talked to Mary Beth?" she asked.

"I don't think so," he said.

"I'm worried about her."

Jack kept silent. If it was true that Mary Beth had killed Solahuddin, he was angry at her as much as anything.

"How long are you staying?" Caroline asked.

"I don't know."

"Listen, I'm not going to fly back. I'm going to take the train. We could ride together, maybe hang out? I know it'll seem like forever for you—"

"I'd like that."

"Good." Caroline stamped out her cigarette on the sidewalk. "I hope you're hungry. Mrs. Pino has enough food down there to feed the National Guard."

"I'm starving," Jack said.

She started to say something, but her voice came out in a croak, and before her mouth twisted into a grimace of sorrow he had her in his arms. She cried into the shoulder of his suit, and he held on, his heart leaving hers far behind.

**W**hen Professor Smith answered his door Mary Beth saw a look of surprise, fear, or both flicker across his features. But when he spoke it was with his usual professorial cool, which was like gangster cool and hipster cool in its inability to admit to ever seeing anything unexpected.

"Miss Layton," he said. "I don't usually hold office hours at my home, but since I've not seen you in class for nearly a month I suppose I can make an exception." He wore a green cardigan over a white T-shirt and a pair of beige khakis. "Forgive me for being out of costume," he said. "But then I'm not the only one, am I? Please, come in."

Professor Smith's apartment was all wood, leather, and books. Books on wooden shelves, wooden tables, wooden floor. Leather-bound books on brown leather chairs and matching brown leather sofa. Leather paneling on the walls between stained wood bookshelves. The room looked like it ought to smell of brandy, after-shave, and pipe tobacco, but all Mary Beth detected were lemon and ginseng.

"Would you care for tea, or would that not be suited to your sense of drama?"

"What?"

"You've obviously come here with some dramatic gesture in mind. I hope it's not the unmasking, since I've already deduced that you are the costumed vigilante known as Green Star. If I'd known sooner I might have made certain allowances for your behavior."

"Really?"

He shrugged. "It's unlikely. So. Do you come seeking counsel, refuge, or a hostage?"

"I just want to talk."

"Ah. The hero, having strayed from her path, seeks counsel from an elder before making a crucial decision. I suppose I should be flattered that you consider me wise."

"I'm not sure I do. You're close-minded and arrogant and I think you must be pretty lonely. You like the sound of your own voice so much that you probably lecture to yourself when no one's here. You think the answers to everything are in books, but it doesn't seem like you live life enough to know what the questions are. I think the only reason I came here is that I can't go to my friends or my parents, and most of my other professors don't even know my name."

Professor Smith smiled. "Didn't I tell you that you have an amazing eye for subtext? Let's forget the tea. Baileys and coffee, perhaps?"

Mary Beth settled for coffee, which she set down because it was too hot and promptly forgot about.

"So," said Professor Smith, sprawling across one side of his hastily cleared couch, "is it true, what they are saying? Did you kill that boy? The Indonesian student?"

"I did." Mary Beth shut her eyes so she wouldn't have to see the professor's reaction. "I was trying to help him, at first. These guys were hurting him. And I hurt them, but it wasn't enough." She could barely hear herself. "I wanted to hurt him, too."

"Was that because he was a Muslim, or because he was there?"

"Both. I'm not— I don't hate Muslims. But . . ."

"But in that moment you did."

"Yes."

"We've spoken about prejudices before, do you remember? Sometimes they get the better of us."

"But I killed somebody." She forced herself to say his name: "I killed Solahuddin Sutadi. He's dead."

"You can't change that."

Mary Beth tried to imagine what her mother would think of her, her real mother. "I'm a monster, aren't I?"

Professor Smith sipped from his Baileys and coffee. "I can't judge you, Miss Layton. But if forced to answer I would say that depends on what you do now. If you continue to run and hide, eventually you will find yourself in a situation where you may hurt someone again. That is what a sociopath would do, but I don't feel that you are sociopathic."

She almost thanked him. Instead she asked him if she could use his phone. A minute later she was making the only call she could make.

Harvey Bettencourt took a deep cleansing yoga breath and looked at the open door for a moment, as if considering whether or not it should be closed. Then he set his jaw and turned to Ray.

"The Layton girl is booked?"

"Yes."

"She hasn't tried to escape?"

"If she had, I think you'd have heard it."

"Probably you're right." Harvey leaned forward. "You're my best detective, Ray." He let that hang in the close air until Ray felt he should respond.

"Thank you, Lieu."

"You're my best detective, so I couldn't understand why you couldn't figure the All-Stars out. Those kids got sloppy more than once, and I've seen you crack tougher cases plenty of times. So I thought you just needed that one break to put it all together. Sometimes it takes longer, I told myself. He's only human, and he can't break every case. Give him time.

"Finally I tried to light a fire under your ass with that speech about the ACLU and all that. I thought maybe you needed to feel the pressure. But then a month and a half, and nothing. Something about it didn't sit right, but I didn't figure it out until tonight, when I learned that the Layton girl lived with your daughter."

Ray visualized handing over his gun and badge, wondered if he should say something. He wondered if he should become a private detective, like half the fired cops in books or on TV, or get work in security like the other half.

"You're suspended until further notice, Ray. There'll be a hearing. I'm giving you twenty-four hours, but this time tomorrow I want you, your daughter, and her other roommate—Caroline Bloom—I want all three of you down here to answer some questions. I don't have to do this. Hell, I shouldn't. But I'm doing it out of respect for someone who used to be a good cop."

Ray unhooked the holster from his belt and set it on Harvey's desk, took off the lanyard that held his badge and set it next to his department-issued Colt.

"I don't know, Ray. Maybe if she was my daughter I'd have done the same thing."

"You know, Harv, if she wasn't my daughter I would have turned her in a long time ago. But I think I would have been wrong."

"We swore to uphold the law."

"Show me the laws that govern superpowers. How are those kids different from cops? They tried to help people and to stop crime. A couple of times people got hurt, but I'll bet their percentage was better than ours."

"What about Sutadi, Ray? Where's he fall in your percentages?"

"Fuck, Harvey. How many innocent people were shot by cops last year?"

"Don't give me that shit. We're sanctioned, and we're accountable when we fuck up. Those kids have been running around in masks thinking their powers give them the right to do whatever they like. Just because they're stronger or faster doesn't mean the laws don't apply. Now get the fuck out of here before I have you arrested for obstruction."

Ray put up his hands and walked out of Harvey's office. Things were falling out as he had expected they would all along, and now he could start dealing with consequences.

**S**cott had imagined a jailbreak would be exciting. He hadn't taken into account standing around on the sidewalk waiting, or the autumn chill cutting through his T-shirt, or the fact that it was three in the morning and he just wanted to go back to bed.

He decided that staring in the direction of the City County Building would only make him crazy. He looked at the lake, at the Monona Terrace, at Harriet's dad sitting in the passenger seat with his feet on the curb. Mr. Bishop was drunk and hadn't stopped smoking all night.

"Can I have one of those?" Scott asked.

"You shouldn't smoke," said Mr. Bishop, but he handed over his pack of Camels and his lighter. "'S what my mama always told me. 'No smoking, no drinking, and no extramarital relations.'"

Scott took a drag and held it. "What about busting people out of jail?" he asked.

"Mama never really addressed that." Mr. Bishop's words came out in a rush, one running into the next. He'd all but finished off a bottle of Smirnoff before Harriet had thrown it out of the car on their way downtown.

Scott looked toward the City County Building again. It was four blocks away and entirely blocked from his view, but he felt sure they would hear any alarms or sirens that followed the break-out. The break-in. The jailbreak.

"Charlie?" Scott leaned in the back window. Charlie huddled, knees tucked up to his chest, behind the driver's seat. "Charlie, do you know what's going on in there?"

"Sneaking and whispering," Charlie said. "Nice place to raise a family."

"What?" Living with Charlie over the past few weeks had been difficult at best, and unnerving at worst. Some days Charlie was able to make lucid conversation, even walk to the Stop & Shop nearby without breaking down. Other days he didn't leave his bedroom, and when it was quiet Scott could hear him muttering to himself.

Scott felt sorry for Charlie, but he didn't know how to help him. He brought food home and talked to him as if everything was normal. But he couldn't get any studying done at home. Some days he left early and came back late and didn't see Charlie at all. Scott had thought more than once that if Charlie decided to hurt himself, no one would be around to find him until it was too late.

Today Charlie had been all right until Harriet's call an hour and a half ago. "Charlie, are you still with us?"

"Sorry. Try to make up for it. Make them pay. Bomb the fuckers."

"That boy needs help," said Ray Bishop.

He started to say more, but he was drowned out by a train whistle as the 3:10 train rolled into sight next to John Nolen Drive. Scott watched the cars for a moment, and when he turned back toward the City County Building Jack stood in front of him.

"She's not coming," said Jack.

"Why?" Scott asked.

"She says she wants to pay for her mistake." Jack was twitchy. "I have to go. I'll see you at the meeting." He nodded at Scott and then was gone.

Scott dug the keys to Ray Bishop's car from his pocket and walked to the driver's side. Neither Charlie nor Ray spoke as he started the car, and when the rear passenger-side door opened and shut on its own, none of them looked. Scott eased the car into drive and pulled out onto West Wilson Street.

"What happens now?" Scott asked.

"We're meeting in an hour at our place," Harriet said from the backseat. She was visible again. "Caroline's really upset. I don't know what we're going to do."

"About Mary Beth?"

"About anything."

Charlie was whispering something, but Scott ignored him. "If they find out about Charlie and Jack, will they want to talk to me?"

"Yes," Ray Bishop said.

"I need a snack or something," Scott said. He turned into an all-night Amoco. Except for Charlie's whispering, no one made a sound.

Scott pulled up outside the convenience store and put the car in park. "Anyone else want anything?" he asked. He looked in the rearview mirror and found Charlie staring at him. He realized what Charlie was whispering.

"Help me," he was saying. "Help me. Help me."

"I don't need anything," Harriet said, "but get a bottle of water for Dad, will you?"

"Help me," Charlie said.

"I will," Scott said, and stepped out of the car.

Four pairs of socks, two white, two black. Two pairs of black nylons. Six pairs of underwear, various colors. Three good bras. One pair of jeans, two pairs of black pants, and two skirts, one black, one camel brown. Three white blouses, two white T-shirts, and two tank tops. One pair of sandals and one pair of black flats. That, and the clothes she was wearing: jeans, a blue sweatshirt, chunky-heeled boots, and a black leather jacket.

"What about the clothes you made?" Jack asked.

Caroline shook her head. Her closet was filled with dresses she had designed and sewn herself, with one-of-a-kind blouses and tops, even a suede coat. "The idea is not to stand out," she said. "I can always make more."

One hairbrush, one bottle of shampoo, and one of conditioner. One stick of deodorant, one electric razor with five replacement blades, and one can of shaving gel. One nail clipper. A box of tampons and a bottle of Midol. Toothpaste, toothbrush, floss, and a bottle of Scope.

"I could do this much faster," Jack said.

"Yes, but then it would be done," she said. "Just relax."

A copy of *The Wind in the Willows* her mother had given her for her first communion. Two cassette tapes: one of Jeff Buckley's *Grace*, which she and her mother were obsessed with while she was in high school, and a mix tape that her first boyfriend Tony Ditaglia had given her when she was thirteen. A sketchbook of her designs. Pictures: her and her mother, her and Harriet and Mary

Beth, her and Harriet with their mothers, taken when they had visited in August.

"I don't have any pictures of you," she said.

"I could run home and get some," Jack said.

"No. Stay here."

"I'd like to say the same to you."

"Don't."

"Where will you go?"

"Canada, first. After that, I don't know." She hefted her backpack, amazed that her life fit inside it. "I wish you were coming along."

"I wish I could."

"We could meet somewhere. In a month, maybe?"

"I don't know. A month might be too long."

"Oh." It had all happened so fast. On the train, she had talked until she lost her voice, and then she had listened, and then they had just sat together. She lay her head on his chest and heard his heart racing, so fast that it sounded like one continuous hum. She had wondered how long the train ride was, for him. She already felt like she'd known him forever.

"Have you tried just . . . slowing down?"

"It doesn't work like that," Jack said. "I can stand here and talk to you pretty normally, but it takes an effort. Like the way Mary Beth has to be careful. . . ." He didn't finish the thought. "I just get more and more wound up. I have to burn this energy somehow. I guess I'm sort of a speed addict."

"Don't joke."

"Sorry," he said.

"In two weeks?" she asked.

"Where?"

"Niagara Falls, maybe? The Canadian side."

"It's a date."

Caroline slung the backpack over her shoulder. "They're waiting."

Fog hung over Madison, spreading from the lakes and blocking the rising sun. Caroline wondered where Joe was now, if he was still smoking on Christos's roof. She didn't suppose she would ever see him again.

Harriet and her father sat on the porch, Ray drinking Gatorade, Harriet twirling the car keys. She stood when she saw Caroline.

"I'm driving," Harriet said.

They walked to the car. Caroline took Jack's hand and held it, felt the hum of his pulse.

"I can't believe I'm going on the run," said Ray Bishop. "Your mother is never going to forgive me for this."

"No, she isn't," said Harriet. "We'll come back sometime, won't we?"

Ray finished his Gatorade before answering. "Maybe."

Harriet hugged Jack. "We'll take the car as far as Superior," Harriet said. "We'll get in touch with you when we can."

"What if they just want to ask questions?" Jack was looking at Caroline when he spoke. "What can they charge you with?"

"They may not bother to charge us," Harriet said. "They may just decide to hold us. Marcus says it's happening all over the country. I'm not taking that chance."

Jack nodded. "All right."

"Take care of Charlie," Harriet said, and got in the car.

Ray shook Jack's hand. "Good luck, son."

"Good luck to you, sir."

Caroline wrapped her arms around Jack and kissed him. She thought about taking off with him in her arms, flying somewhere

where things made sense. But when she opened her eyes her feet were still on the ground.

"October twenty-second," she said.

"Niagara Falls." He nodded.

She got in the car, and left everything behind.

Charlie tensed as Scott parked outside the Administration building of the Mendota Mental Health Institute. The Institute sprawled over a space the size of several football fields, with dormitories, recreation halls and support buildings, but much of the campus was shrouded in fog, making it appear that nothing existed beyond.

"I don't think you're crazy," Scott said. "You just have everybody else's thoughts drowning out your own. If you go in there, you're going to get a headful of people who really are sick."

"That's why I need to be here," Charlie said.

"You need to be in an asylum because you're not crazy?"

"I need to learn to separate my own thoughts from the rest of the mindstream. I'm hoping that here I can get a better sense of how my own head works. In the long term that'll help me keep it together."

"Are you sure they let people do this voluntarily?" Charlie saw Scott's worries. He was afraid Charlie would fail a Rorschach test, be put in a straitjacket, and given shock therapy.

"It doesn't work like that," Charlie said. "I mean, yes, I can do it voluntarily, after an evaluation, and check out when I'm ready."

"You seem fine right now. Maybe you don't need to go in there."

"Scott, if you could hear what I hear right now, you'd understand. I'm working hard to keep it together." Charlie didn't dare think about the others, about what had happened, or it would all slip away again. "When this all started, I had to be as close as you and I in order for it to work, but every day it's more. I don't know what to do with a planet full of voices. I need to be ready."

Charlie pushed back tears with a deep breath. "I have to do this," he said. "In there I can have bad days and not risk being put away *in*voluntarily."

"Do you want—"

"I'll call my parents once the evaluation is through." Charlie ran his hands through his hair, which was getting shaggy again. "But there is one thing you can do for me. On my desk in the apartment there's an envelope addressed to the Madison police. Use gloves when you touch it. Take it to a mailbox out of town and mail it."

"You're not going to—"

"No, I'm not confessing to anything." He reached out, looking for one voice among millions. "It's just some unfinished business. One last batch of criminals to turn in." He put a hand to his rib cage and winced. "The guys who were there the night Mary Beth . . . the guys that started that. Their names. They share the blame."

He couldn't feel her. Maybe she didn't want to be found.

"I'll do it." Scott opened the door. "I'll come in with you, too."

It was like a band that had been constricting Charlie's chest suddenly loosened. He nodded. "Thank you."

**H**appy Birthday, baby."

Paris Palmeiro looked up at his mother with wide brown eyes, yawned, and made a cranky noise.

"Perfectly healthy, Dr. McAllister says." Gil sat on the bed beside Prudence and slipped his index finger into his newborn son's grasp. Paris took hold of the finger and squeezed, and Gil grimaced. "He's strong," he said. "Ow!"

"Three hours old and already tougher than his father," Prudence said.

"Bet I can take him in a footrace," Gil retorted.

"Smart-ass," Prudence said. "I love you, you know."

"You'd better." He kissed her on the forehead. "I have more people to call, and they still won't let me use my cell phone in here. Be back in fifteen minutes."

"Five."

"Say ten." He extricated his finger from Paris's tiny fist and blew kisses as he left.

Prudence touched fingertips with the baby, amazed at his smallness. She should be sleeping—in two hours she was supposed to do a live feed about the birth for the five o'clock news, and she felt like a train had passed through her—but all she could do was stare at Paris, counting his fingers and toes and watching him struggle to keep his eyes open.

He grasped at nothing a couple of times before he managed to latch onto her pinky. He yanked at it so hard that Prudence thought it was broken.

"Ow!" She reclaimed her finger while he was yawning and flexed it. "Baby doesn't know his own strength," she said, and tickled him under the chin.

"Happy Birthday, baby."

"Mom! I'm not a baby." Grace folded her arms as Fern pulled her into a hug.

"You sure act like one sometimes," Fern said.

"Mom!"

"For pity's sake, honey, I'm kidding." Fern squeezed her youngest daughter until she squeezed back.

"I wish Daddy was here," Grace said.

"Me too, honey."

"I wish Jack wasn't sick."

"Me, too."

"I don't really feel like celebrating today, Mom."

Fern kissed Grace on the forehead, thinking that the hardest thing about being a parent was reassurance. Telling your kids that things would get easier, that everything would be OK, was sometimes a necessary lie, but harder to do when you couldn't bring yourself to believe it even a little bit.

So she told the truth. "I know, Gracie. But everyone's coming, and I think we all need this. We can't sit around being sorry all the time." She sighed. "Life has to go on."

"It's not fair," Gracie said in a tone that said she knew it never would be.

"No," said Fern. "It's not." And that was true, too.

# EDITOR'S NOTE

by Marcus Hatch

Mortimer "Jack" Robinson died on October 20, 2001; he did not make his scheduled rendezvous with Caroline Bloom. He's buried in the same cemetery as his father, or at least that's what I've been told. I've also been told there was no autopsy, although the cause of death is listed as "brain hemorrhage." How do they know that's what caused his death, if no autopsy was performed? Call me cynical—everyone else has—but I doubt that Jack Robinson is buried in Jack Robinson's grave.

Jack's mother, Fern, sold the family farm to the Carlson twins in July of 2002 and moved to Appleton, Wisconsin. Her daughter Grace was headed to Eau Claire for college. They both refused to be interviewed for this book, so any episodes concerning them were reconstructed with the help of Charlie Frost.

I interviewed Charlie Frost extensively while he underwent treatment at the Mendota Mental Health Institute. What he hadn't personally witnessed he was able to describe for me based on the accounts of the other All-Stars and the images and thoughts he had gathered from his teammates and the others who played a role in these events.

It took Charlie nearly a year to feel well enough to leave Mendota. I visited him three or four times a week, usually at lunch. Charlie was medicated, and often when I first arrived he was sluggish and found it difficult to concentrate. Once he had some food in him, he became livelier. Our conversations often went far afield of the topic of the All-Stars, and I consider Charlie Frost a friend. He told me once that talking about what had happened was helping him with his therapy.

The day after Charlie left Mendota, he disappeared. I hope that he joined Caroline Bloom and Ray and Harriet Bishop in their self-imposed exile. There have been occasional reports of possible All-Star activity in places as far apart as Portugal and Singapore, but none of them have been substantiated. For the most part, people seem to have forgotten that the All-Stars ever existed.

Harriet, if you're reading this—I hope you're all right, and I'm sorry.

On the surface of it, Bert O'Brien's theory is too far out even for me—that someone is out there actively rewriting history, editing out facts and episodes that are inconvenient or damaging. But I've begun to wonder if he might not be right. I don't know who would profit from hiding the existence of superpowered individuals, but I wish I did, because then I might be able to find out who had Jack and Charlie's roommate Scott Silverstone killed. He died in a hit-and-run accident in March of 2002, shortly after agreeing to speak with me about these events.

Then there's the matter of Mary Beth Layton. I tried to interview her for this book, but Madison Correctional had no record of her. There was no record of her arrest or of where she was being held, and her case never went to trial. In fact, there are no records of her existence—no driver's license on file, no record of her enrollment at the university, nothing. Her family moved to California and won't return my calls.

I dug deeper and found there was no record of Solahuddin Sutadi either—no immigration records, no student transcripts, no tax or payroll records. All the articles on his death have disappeared, from print and Web sites both. All the journalists who covered it and the All-Stars have left Madison or retired from journalism altogether, and none of them would respond to my requests for interviews—not even Prudence Palmeiro, who works behind the scenes now, as a segment producer on a UPN affiliate in Florida.

I don't know if all these people have been threatened, or paid off, or what. But what it comes down to is that I'm the only one who will talk about what happened, and as far as anyone is concerned I'm a crackpot with an agenda. When I bring up the All-Stars most people laugh—they remember them as goofballs in silly outfits. Fools in tights.

That's why I wrote this book. At first I just wanted to get the story before anyone else, but when I realized that no one else was going after it, I wanted to prove that I wasn't crazy.

So that's the end, or at least it's as much of the story as I know. Maybe they'll show up again someday, with their five-pointed stars across their chests. It was nice having heroes for a while, even for a cynic like me. But in the end I guess we have to get by without heroes. Even the best of them is as human as the rest of us, and the only thing you can count on with humans is that they'll let you down eventually. You, for instance. You'll forget this story eventually, and it'll be like it didn't happen. Maybe you don't believe in superpowers or conspiracies or . . . hell, some days I don't know if I believe it.

No. I believe it. I just don't know if it matters, in the end.

# ACKNOWLEDGMENTS

Thanks are due to many, but in particular to Jeanne Cavelos and the Odyssey Fantasy Writing Workshop, Keith Demanche, Troy Ehlers, Derek Hill, Lynda Rucker, Susan Winston, Marianne Westphal, Meghan McCarron, Haddayr Copley-Woods, Gavin Grant, Kelly Link, John Trey, Lois Tilton, the East Side Chicago group, the Semi-Omniscients, the Supersonics, the Sycamore Hill Workshop, Super-agent Shana Cohen, Jason Pinter, Will Francis, Beth Coates, Lindsey Moore, and Carrie Thornton.

I'd also like to acknowledge the Mifflin Street Animal Shelter, the Remedial House gang, the Rathskeller crew, the staff at Mancini's, and John, Elaine, Gretchen, Stephen, and Mary Schwartz.

Finally, this book wouldn't have happened without comic books, especially the works of Stan Lee, Jack Kirby, Steve Ditko, Chris Claremont, Peter David, Keith Giffen, J. M. DeMatteis, Kevin Maguire, Bill Sienkiewicz, Walt Simonson, Alan Moore, Dave Gibbons, Frank Miller, Fabian Nicieza, Mark Bagley, and everyone who ever worked on an issue of *The Defenders*. Remember: they're all mailed flat!

ACKNOWLEDGMENTS